ABOUT THE BOOK

It's estimated that the combined blast force of USA and USSR stockpiles of nuclear warheads is equivalent to 6,667 World War II's. It's also estimated that such a force is sufficient to destroy the world 100 times over. Meanwhile, virtually nothing is being done to assure mankind's survival. . .that is, nothing until now. From a small, fictional, rural Minnesota town called Taylorsville, in the novel, *The Krasnodar Affair*, comes the opportunity for lasting world peace and disarmament.

The story begins with an American wheat sale to the USSR. The first shipment is loaded on the Soviet ocean bulk freighter Krasnodar at Duluth, Minnesota, USA. Unfortunately, tragedy strikes the Krasnodar, and almost immediately afterwards the Kremlin and White House get caught in an international crisis threatening worldwide nuclear warfare.

Military and civil defense forces in both nations are alerted and thrust into full scale mobilization, while tensions mount to a feverish pitch. Just when chances of war avoidance seem least likely, an amazingly clever and simple strategy for world peace emerges.

While an international love affair between an American man and a Soviet woman blossoms and develops, world leaders decide to shun the hostility producing litigation of the world's adversarial legal systems. Instead, they trust their instincts and choose a nonviolent dispute settlement alternative.

The Krasnodar Affair is a novel with an urgent message for every man, woman, and child concerned about the growing threat of nuclear doomsday and what might be done to prevent it.

To Gary,

With best wishes &
For peace,

D.E. Montgomery

THE KRASNODAR AFFAIR

A STORY OF CRISIS, WORLD PEACE, AND DISARMAMENT

by

D. E. Montgomery

St. Johns
PUBLISHING, INC.

Published by

St. John's Publishing, Inc.
6824 Oaklawn Avenue
Edina, Minnesota 55435

ISBN 0-938577-01-8

First Printing: January, 1988

Cover design: Tim Montgomery

DEDICATION

To people working for world peace, friendship, and disarmament.

ACKNOWLEDGEMENTS

The author gratefully acknowledges Alan T. Johnson, Director of International Marketing for the Seaway Port Authority in Duluth, Minnesota; Sam L. Browman, Manager of Port Trade Development; and Bill Cortes, Director of Port Public Affairs. These three individuals helped the author with information about grain movements and Great Lakes shipping.

A debt of gratitude is equally owed Sven Hubner, President, Guthrie-Hubner, Inc., vessel agent and cargo broker in Duluth, Minnesota. On a late Friday afternoon, ex cargo ship captain Sven Hubner patiently instructed the earthbound author about shipping in general, the vessel agent's role in particular, and various shipping hazards.

The author's wife, Donna, and son, Tim, are acknowledged for their helpful editorial assistance. A debt of gratitude is also owed Tim for his outstanding cover design.

Although assistance of various individuals is gratefully acknowledged, the author alone is responsible for the contents and apologizes in advance if anyone is offended. No offense is intended. World peace and friendship are the hoped for future realities this book attempts to reflect.

PROPHECY

They shall beat their swords into plowshares,
And their spears into pruning hooks:
Nation shall not lift up sword against nation,
Neither shall they learn war any more.

Isaiah 2:4

CONTENTS

PART I. AGREEMENT

1

H. B. EXPORTS, INC.

Harry Brown paced back and forth in the intense heat of his small town grain brokerage office. Sweat dripped from his forehead as midmorning sunlight flooded through east facing windows, turning his small room into a solar heated sauna. How odd it seemed under these circumstances that he'd neglect so obvious a remedy as turning on an air conditioner or opening a window. What unearthly calamity could so preoccupy him, prompting him to indulge in such fitful behavior? It seemed unlikely any earthly concerns could bother him. He lived in a happy, peaceful, friendly little farm town called Taylorsville, Minnesota, USA.

Relentlessly, Brown's six-foot-two, hundred-ninety-five pound frame kept struggling with some difficult inner problem or group of problems. Shuffling back and forth behind an antique tilt chair and matching desk of varnished oak, he behaved like a lion in a zoo, rounding his cage in search of escape.

Brown was wearing an open-collared, red plaid shirt beneath a blue denim vest. He also wore denim jeans, a two-inch wide black belt, and black leather boots. Although Brown's red plaid shirt seemed newer, his denim jacket and jeans were stonewashed to a somewhat bleached out light blue. Likewise, Brown's boots showed wear, but reflected a respectable shine, even though they squeaked in time to his nerve-racking, back and forth movements.

Brown's head was bent forward slightly, forehead all furrowed in a frown. At first he grabbed the back of his neck with his right hand and rotated his head toward the ceiling. Next, he folded his hands together in a nervously prayerful clasp, only to unclasp them again and momentarily press them to his temples. He released them afterward in a gesture of desperation, thrusting them downward, palms up in a pleading manner.

At times the midmorning sunrays flooding through Brown's office windows appeared to set him aglow, giving him a somewhat angelic look. At other times, Brown looked like he'd just died and gone to hell, where eternal flames were about to consume him. In the dazzling illumination of his corner office, however, it was difficult to tell from moment to moment whether it was sunshine or hellfire shooting from the top of Brown's head.

A closer look revealed Brown's brushed back head of faded black hair. It was definitely thinning on top, graying at the temples, and receding from his forehead. His face had a pained look, relieved only by his deep blue eyes. Also, his ruggedly handsome features combined with his tough, suntanned skin to indicate anything but an easy life. Rather, they suggested the weather-beaten look of an outdoorsman or fieldhand undergoing some kind of mental anguish.

Eyes downcast in depression, body somewhat bent, Harry Brown kept up his caged lion routine, ignoring the opening of his office door and the entry of his trusted partner, Bert Jackson. After a moment or two, however, Brown hesitated, raised his head, then glanced inquiringly at the intruder. Bert Jackson, taking the cue, began speaking.

3

"Good morning, Harry. Didn't want to disturb you. Here's the contract on the Min-Dak Co-op wheat deal. Say, you look like you held a press conference and nobody came. What's the matter?"

Jackson, always full of smiles, usually tried to cure grim situations with a humorous touch. Brown, however, didn't laugh. Instead, he came to a full stop, faced Jackson squarely, and began looking intensely into Jackson's eyes. For a few brief moments, Brown gazed worriedly at his young General Manager, as if wondering how to break some bad news. Then Brown began studying Jackson's conscientious business attire, perhaps looking for some kind of relief in the semblance of order he saw.

Jackson wore a dark brown suit over a clean white shirt. He also sported a dark brown tie with white stripes. His entire clothing ensemble accented his striking combination of thick, reddish-gold hair, dark brown eyes, and smooth shaven, fair-skinned complexion. Bertram Jackson was visibly much younger than Harry Brown, his partner and boss. Also, Bert, as everybody called him, presented such a picture of competency and efficiency, Brown appeared even more desperate by comparison.

Finally, having held his breath a few moments, Brown let it all out with a long, heavy sigh, punctuated by a few agonized moans. At the conclusion of this display of frustration, Brown walked around to the rear of his desk and attempted an answer to Bert.

"It's extremely bad news I'm struggling with right now, Bert. You may as well know it, we're at the end of our finances. Our grain brokerage business is drying up. The bank just phoned to say we're overdrawn. I'm afraid it's over for us; we're coming apart. Our situation is tragic, unbelievably so."

"Harry, don't let it get to you like this," Bert replied. "Did somebody die? Come on, pull yourself together. Sit down here awhile. We'll work things out and shake those blues."

Bert quickly moved around the desk to where Harry was standing. Putting his arm around Harry's shoulders, he eased him into the swivel chair. When Harry was comfortably seated, Bert sat down in one of the two guest chairs in front of Brown's desk.

"Let's talk this thing out, Harry," Bert continued, "maybe I can help you. Don't say anything to Maxie just yet. We three have been partners for so long, there must be some way out of all this. Let's get a handle on our difficulties and find a way to save our business. Let's not rush into any unhappy endings.

"The first thing we do is open some windows in here and cool this place down. How can you stand such heat, Harry?"

Bert got up, walked to the windows, and opened them. Turning to face his business partner and boss, he continued the conversation. "Maybe our timing is off, Harry. Think back to our beginnings. What can you recall?"

A cooling breeze entered the room through the newly opened windows, coaxing Harry to relax a bit and start reminiscing. He recalled his military service in the Korean War, his years at the university on the GI bill, his wife Josie and their four children, meeting Bert and Maxie at the high school where the three of them taught, their years of financial struggle together as school teachers, and their entrepreneurial venture into the business world as grain brokers.

"Ah, but so what? Who cares? It's all over for us," Harry complained. "Look what's happening now!"

Pausing a moment, Harry suddenly changed his attitude. "I'm sorry, Bert. I guess I got carried away. You and Maxie made me president of this business, even insisted on naming it after me, then I let you both down. How could I have known such powerful grain merchants

5

as Julius Fiske would deliberately undercut our prices, squeeze us dry, and knock us down? Guess I'm a simpleton to expect honesty when dealing in the business world."

"Harry, we can fight Julius Fiske in court along with the other greedy grain lords." Bert suggested. "We can sue every one of them for antitrust violations and conspiracy in restraint of free trade."

"Warfare in courtrooms isn't the answer, Bert," Harry shot back. "In their obsession to win, lawyers make black look white and white look black, deceiving judges and juries alike. When it get's down to competing for a favorable verdict, there's no honor among lawyers. Also, win or lose, lawyers seem to always get paid. Where will we get the money?"

"That's true," Bert conceded. "Still, it seems we ought to be able to get back at the crooked grain merchants by going after them in court."

"Our situation is frustrating," Harry concluded. "We can't go to war and we can't go to court. Either way, nobody wins. Everybody loses, especially small guys like us. If we don't have any money to survive now, how can we afford a lawsuit? Even if we borrowed to do it, we'd lose out to the rich merchants like Julius Fiske, with their fast-talking, slippery tongued, big-fee lawyers. There's just no future for us, Bert. We can't go to court and we won't deal dirty. What a society! To survive, it seems we have to be ruthless like everyone else. The problem is, I just can't bring myself around to doing it."

"But you're an experienced combat veteran, Harry," Bert cut in. "You've been able to beat the best."

Harry turned his memory back 35 years and silently recounted his endless weeks of basic combat infantry training, advanced training, and leadership school. How proud he was then, when he graduated among the army's best. However, now that he was older, he'd come to view his army training in a different light. The U. S.

6

Army, he realized, had given him only three courses of study: beginning, intermediate, and advanced killing — all useless in civilized society. Unfortunately, they only instilled in him an overly aggressive manner with which he instinctively approached potential conflicts. As a result, he acquired a genuine fear of argumentative human encounters, a fear he constantly forced himself to suppress, because he didn't want to hurt anybody.

Too often in the past, Harry had expressed his anger in a sudden explosion of emotional reactions and outbursts, but he always managed to stop short of the physical violence his killer training prepared him to unleash. He fully realized that when his temper erupted, it could be intense. To compensate for this regrettable tendency, Harry strained at establishing and maintaining amicable relationships, sometimes to the point of appearing awkward.

Bert and Maxie were acutely aware of Harry's difficult problem, but never having been trained to be killers, perhaps they didn't entirely understand it. Why, they asked, did Harry occasionally doubt his role as head of their partnership? The reason, of course, was Harry's fear of himself, that his decisions were too conservative, or that his leadership was weak. For example, had he made the wrong choices? He couldn't bear the thought of causing Bert or Maxie any hardships. The thought of bringing unemployment or financial ruin to his partners devastated Harry.

"You worry too much," Bert scolded. "You need to clear your mind of worrisome clutter and start thinking pleasant thoughts. Our partnership isn't ended yet. We've all kinds of options. I'll talk to Maxie. I'm sure she and I can help you cover the bounced checks. Maybe we can even loan our company a little extra. We've saved nearly a third of our earnings for just such an emergency. We figured with your large family and heavy expenses you'd have a tough time coming up with

7

additional cash in a pinch like this. So don't upset yourself worrying about money, Harry. Not yet, anyway.

"And, Harry, don't worry about your standing with Maxie or me. It's because of your honesty and fair dealing that we respect you. It's the reason we went into business with you in the first place, and made you head of this company. After all, the grain brokerage idea was yours, and you're even a decent fellow sometimes. The fact that you're over fifty has nothing to do with our making you top dog. Maxie and I would never discriminate against you on the basis of your old age."

Bert paused for a hearty laugh while Harry, smiling for the first time, got up and moved out from behind his desk, making faces and playfully shaking his fist.

"Why you...,that's insubordination!" Harry protested. "Ah, but you and Maxie are too good for me."

"Get off it, Harry," Bert shot back. "What we need now are sales, S-A-L-E-S, period. We can get them if we just keep at it. Sooner than you think, our run of bad luck will break and good times will come. Is there anything you haven't tried yet?"

By now Harry was behind his desk again, comfortably leaning back in his swivel chair, resting. He seemed soothed by Bert's encouraging comments and the good news of Bert and Maxie's prospective loan of money. Relaxing even more and closing his eyes, he reminisced.

"You know, Bert, I've tried a lot of careers in my life, from teaching to owning my own business. Seems the only thing I haven't tried is preaching. You ever think of becoming a preacher, Bert?"

Bert said he thought about becoming a priest when he was a young boy. His mother and father died in an auto accident, so, at the age of seven, he was placed in an orphanage.

"The priest there was so kind," Bert recalled, "I wanted to be just like him."

However, when Bert got older, he found out that priests can't marry, so he abandoned any idea of becoming one. He knew he'd want a wife and family someday. When Harry asked if he had anybody in mind, Bert said he hadn't found the right woman yet. However, he was still looking.

This rare, Harry and Bert office hours chitchat came to an abrupt end with the ringing of a telephone. It was answered by a charming female voice.

"H. B. Exports, Maxine Gadsden speaking, may I help you?"

Maxine's desk was just outside Harry Brown's office. "Maxie", as everyone called her, was the grain brokerage's third partner. She held the position of Office Administrator.

Maxie was an attractive, black American woman, dressed in a charcoal and white herringbone suit. Under her suit jacket she wore a white, open-collared blouse, and around her neck was a string of assorted semiprecious stones, brightly polished. Her low-heeled shoes were glossy black and cut from good quality leather. From head to toe, her tall figure was youthfully slender and neatly groomed. Also, her curly black hair was carefully styled in a fashionable French cut, and her lipstick and eye makeup were expertly done, too. At 28 years, Maxine Gadsden wasn't taking any chances. She wanted to be sure she was ready for the right man whenever she happened to meet him.

"Just a moment, please," Maxie said. Pressing "Hold" and "Intercom" buttons on a control panel, she called out, "Harry, there's a woman on the phone with a Russian accent. Her name is Helga Baranovna. She says her boss, Nikolai Novikov, Director of Soviet Grain Sales, wants to talk to you."

Like an exploding blockbuster bomb, Harry Brown boomed to life with such a shock wave, that Bert Jackson scurried out. Brown jumped up from his chair, and in a manner mindful of an eagle pouncing on its prey, ignored his intercom and shouted, "Got it, Maxie!" Then he grabbed his telephone.

Both Bert and Maxie were somewhat amused by Harry's bizarre behavior, and began observing the ensuing scene from his doorway.

"Harry Brown here! Nikky, is that really you?" Brown's voice began burning up with enthusiasm. Immediately he started talking in Russian.

"Dear Nikky, Hello! How are you? How good to hear your voice after so many years. Tell me what you're up to, Nikky!" He paused a moment, then, in mock shock and disbelief, he asked in English, "Here in Taylorsville, Minnesota?" After pausing again he reverted to Russian, "Remarkable!" Switching back to English, Brown asked, "Buying Hard Red Spring Wheat, you say? Have I got any for sale? Aha! Just a minute, Nikky!" Holding the phone outward for Nikky's benefit, Brown yelled, "Maxie! Bert! Have we got any HRS Wheat today?"

Bert and Maxie enthusiastically shouted their affirmations, and Harry answered, half seriously, "It's possible, Nikky. What do you have in mind?....Good idea! Who have you got with you and when can we meet?....Tonight? Agreed! We'll meet you for dinner tonight at 6:30, Taylorsville Hotel Restaurant and Dance Lounge....Do I know where it is? Nikky, I live here, remember? Taylorsville is my hometown. I was born and bred in this place. See you at six thirty. I'll tell the others. We'll have fun tonight, you old Bolshevik. Buying wheat are you? You knock me down! See you at six-thirty!"

Brown put the phone down and called Bert and Maxie in, sitting them in the guest chairs at the front of his desk. Then, positioning himself in a forward-leaning stance behind his swivel chair, hands on the backrest, he began briefing them in earnest. This was it, the deal of their lifetime, the deal they'd all been praying for. They each knew the Soviet Union had another bad harvest, its sixth, successive, bad crop year. It was difficult enough for the Soviets to cope with a short growing season, but then came the long drought. Add to that the USSR's shortage of such modern farming aids as hybrid seeds, soil-enhancing fertilizers, selective herbicides, crop protecting insecticides, widespread irrigation, and extensive mechanization. Without doubt, they had a disaster to cope with. Some parts of the Soviet Union were still trying to progress beyond a horse and buggy agriculture.

"They're making tremendous progress," Brown conceded, "but not quite fast enough. We already know the USSR's grain shortfall is in the neighborhood of 50 to 55 million metric tons. Our U. S. analysts estimate the Soviets must buy at least 20 million more metric tons this year to partially offset their serious crop failures. They'll mostly be buying feed grains to build up beef, pork, and poultry stocks, so their people can have more meat in their diets. Feed grains bought from the U. S. will be shipped out of New Orleans and Gulf port elevators by Julius Fiske and other merchants. However, as you both know, when it comes to bread wheat, we've got the good stuff right here in Taylorsville, Minnesota."

H. B. leaned forward and thumped his fist on the desk as he made that last point. Then he continued emphatically, "14% protein, Hard Red Spring Wheat! Good old HRS Number One! Bread wheat from Western Minnesota and the Dakotas! That's us; that's what we've got; that's what we're going to sell the Soviets."

After pausing for some spontaneous applause from Bert and Maxie, Harry began describing the scenario for their 6:30 meeting that night with the Soviet delegation. Bert, Maxie, and Harry were invited by the Soviets to dine at the Taylorsville Hotel, and Nikolai wanted to meet Harry's wife, Josie, so she was invited, too. All this, of course, was somewhat awkward for Harry, who was troubled at the thought of a potential customer taking him out to dinner. On the other hand, Brown rationalized, Nikolai Novikov was an old friend in a buying mood, so why not let him buy?

Maxie, smiling, leaned forward and asked, "Harry, how did you just happen to know Novikov? And you speak Russian! You're full of surprises, Harry. You never told us about any Russian study, not even when we were teachers together. Why don't you tell us about it?"

Harry overcame his embarrassment and reluctantly accepted Maxie's invitation to explain the matter. As he did so, he began moving back and forth behind his desk like some determined general talking to his troops. Briskly, in a matter-of-fact manner, he started briefing his wide-eyed partners.

Harry Brown first met Nikolai Novikov over 20 years ago in the Soviet Union. Harry was in a student tour group, and Nikolai was a young Soviet tour guide. The two soon became fast friends, even cutups.

"Lucky, for us we weren't arrested and sent to Siberia!" Brown exclaimed.

The students were completing a U. S.-sponsored Russian Language program intended to train Americans to become teachers of Russian. Harry Brown had been teaching English in the USA for two years, but had an interest in learning Russian. He felt the U. S. was culturally ignorant of the Soviet Union. Also, he believed the U. S. desperately needed to improve its understanding and cross-cultural communication with that major world power. True to his convictions, Brown started studying Russian on his own for two years, and was eventually able to pass a written test in Russian, though his speaking was bad. When the U. S. Government established a special program to develop

12

Russian Language teachers, Brown volunteered, passed a qualifying test, and got accepted.

The Soviet Sputnik achievement had shocked America. When Sputnik, the first orbiting space satellite, was launched, people in the U. S. worried that the Soviets were ahead scientifically. Their worries inspired their federal government to establish a Russian Language program to train American teachers to teach Russian.

"Russian-speaking Americans were as rare then as taxicabs in Taylorsville," Brown observed, "and in the ensuing years, there has been little or no improvement."

When Brown finally learned Russian and was certified to teach it, he couldn't find a job. Most schools in the U. S. didn't want anyone learning Russian. One school superintendent, who interviewed Brown for a teaching job, labeled him a Communist for even having an interest in Russian. Brown, a decorated veteran of the Korean War, was outraged at such imbecility on the part of education system administrators. As a result, he decided he'd eventually quit the teaching profession altogether and never look back. Nor did he ever tell anyone he studied Russian. It was all a bad memory.

Without remorse, Brown said he was relieved when he finally did quit teaching, admitting that another compelling reason was financial. He bitterly recalled how his wife Josie used to lay awake at night crying, because she didn't have any food to put on the kitchen table the next day. They'd bought a house with a seemingly endless number of hidden expenses. Then, when their family began growing, their expenses increased twice as fast as Brown's income.

"Teachers had no health benefits in those days," Brown recalled. "Josie worked as a receptionist for her baby doctor just to pay his fee and earn enough to pay her hospital bills."

The lack of a living wage was Brown's greatest frustration with teaching. He knew he'd have to throw in the towel someday and find something with a better income. Now he may have finally found it, he enthused. The opportunity for their partnership had at last arrived. Brown was certain it could be the deal of their lifetime. All they had to do was plan their moves carefully.

At this point, Bert leaned forward and asked, "Harry, who's coming tonight besides Novikov?"

"There are two other Soviet citizens traveling with Nikolai," Brown answered. "Helga Baranova is Nikolai's administrator. She's the woman you talked to, Maxie. Then there's Nadezhda Konya, Novikov's Deputy Director. I don't know anything more about either of them, though Nikky told me Nadezhda is a knockout, and quite useful to him for spying. Bert, this is your lucky day. You get to sit with Nadezhda this evening and keep her entertained, but remember, she's a spy."

Bert replied, smiling, "Do I get combat pay for this, Harry?"

Eyes twinkling, face grinning, Harry retorted, "Bert, don't knock it, this may well be that one in a billion females you're looking for."

Bert blushed and snuck an embarrassed glance at Maxie, who rolled her eyes playfully. Then Brown turned to Maxie and spoke.

"Maxie, fate has smiled on you today, also. By virtue of the authority and power vested in me as your duly elected boss, I hereby assign you to: (1) Sit next to Novikov; (2) Dance with him in the unlikely event we two stop talking, or in the less likely event Josie forces me onto the dance floor; and (3) Save us all from making fools of ourselves, should we be having too much fun."

"Oh wow, Harry, thanks!" Maxie commented. "But you forgot Helga. Who gets Helga?"

Harry frowned thoughtfully, stroked his chin, then brightened and said, "I'll sit next to her. Josie won't mind. If Helga turns out to be beautiful, then that's fate

14

for you. I'll just have to talk fast, so I can handle both Josie and Helga.

"Meanwhile, Bert, we need you to contact the Min-Dak Farmers Co-op on our other deal. Here are the papers. Get the co-op to agree to our standard Goldstrike Formula price. Also, find out the total wheat inventory in its elevators, especially the eight and eleven million bushel elevators in Duluth. Determine how much we can shave off our Goldstrike bushel rate, if we buy volume quantities of five, ten, or twenty million bushels

"We've got to make all the money we can on this deal, but beat the wealthy merchant's prices. You can be sure Julius Fiske and the others will be orbiting like hungry vultures to gobble us up. We'll simply have to outflank them, and to do this, we've got my old friend Novikov. I'm sure he'll throw us a bone to keep us alive. We'll never get it all, or even half, but if we do our homework and sell at the right price, we could close a deal tomorrow and wind up with lots of money.

"Three factors give me confidence: (1) Competition from Argentina, Australia, and Canada is way down this year, due to bad droughts and resultant low-yield conditions. Thank heavens we don't have to worry about being undercut by those countries!

"(2) The big grain merchants have too high an overhead to be able to shake us off. Our recycled desks and small town offices keep our overhead down to almost nothing. Also, we don't have expensive fleets of ships, hundreds of costly railroad hopper cars, or thousands of employees. That's why we'll beat the big guys. They're fat and overextended.

"Finally, (3), as I said, we've got the inside track: Novikov and I are old buddies."

Brown suggested Bert and Maxie brainstorm with him a few moments about how to handle their prospective wheat deal. Bert, who was half up and out, settled back down, and the three began discussing their

15

evening dinner meeting. Brown wondered who was playing at the hotel dance lounge that night, and whether the entertainment was any good.

"Lonny Steele and his Red River Gang are there this week," Maxie responded. "Sheila Song-Maker is Lonny's singer. She's Lonny's recent discovery, and has an exciting style you'll enjoy very much. Bert and I heard her Monday night when we hosted the Min-Dak Co-op group. She gave her audience three encores with a new song called, 'Running Brave.' I'll bet she'll put the Soviets in orbit, eh, Bert?" Maxie got up, rolled her big eyes flirtaciously at Bert, then danced around him as though she were Sheila Song-Maker. Bert, blushing, enthusiastically agreed with Maxie's assessment.

"You've got no worries with Sheila or the rest of Lonny's gang," Bert affirmed. "They're lots of fun."

Brown was visibly pleased and smiled his approval. He asked Maxie to phone the lounge and let the management know what was happening. He especially wanted Maxie to inform Lonny and Sheila that the Soviets were in Taylorsville and would be in the audience that night.

"Also, Maxie," Brown added, "see if Sheila's got some feathered thing she can put on Novikov's head after one of her songs. Maybe she can make him an honorary Ogalala chief or some such. Have her put some beaded jewelry on the Soviet girls, too, and don't forget something for yourself and Josie. I want a fun gift for everyone in our party. Tell Sheila and Lonny we'll be happy to pay them for helping us out, and how about asking them to play a special song like 'Red Cavalry March?' Glenn Miller's orchestra did a great job on that number for the Soviets in World War II.

"Seems a long time since World War II when we were closely allied with the USSR. Through the United Nations, however, we should regard the USSR as still allied with us. The Soviets don't always vote with us, but at least we sit in the same room together.

"The USA and USSR ought to become friends again. Maybe if both countries paid closer attention to the U. N. Charter and followed its peacemaking advice, they'd be on better terms. There wouldn't be a ridiculous, expensive, and wasteful arms race, either. Maybe we can at least give a few Soviets a good feeling about us tonight.

"Let's do a Russian song first, then we'll have an American song, something Sheila and Lonny can choose."

"Leave it to me, Harry" Maxie insisted. "I know what to do and I'll devote the rest of today getting it done. What about grain sale negotiations tomorrow, want the hotel?"

After some hesitation, Brown reacted. "That's a fall back, last resort. What do you think, Bert? Seems we should get the Soviets away from that hotel awhile."

Bert lit up with an idea. "Harry, you're a member of the Veterans of Foreign Wars. How about using the VFW's meeting room for a day. We ought to be able to get a U-shaped table arrangement there."

"Good thinking, Bert!" Brown complimented. "That's perfect! See if we can reserve it for the day. As a past commander of that post I ought to get some red carpet treatment. Also, order fresh flowers for the table, plus coffee and tea, fresh Danish, the usual good stuff. Find us a Soviet flag, too, if you can, and put it up near our flag. Let's show the Soviets we really value their friendship. Nikky's my old friend. He treated me well in the Soviet Union. It's my turn to be a good host to him now."

Harry Brown continued giving instructions as Bert and Maxie took note. A flipchart stand was needed for some visual aids they'd be using. Also, they decided to construct a sample contract. Bert suggested reworking some figures from an Indonesian deal they'd done a year ago, and this was agreeable to Harry and Maxie, except for chartered shipping. Harry felt the Soviets had plenty of their own ships, which they'd undoubtedly insist on using. Although this would be a setback to U. S. shipping, there'd still be plenty of American labor involvement in railroad transport of the grain, ship loading, port movements, and Great Lakes and St. Lawrence Seaway pilotage.

Another matter of concern was Soviet vessel capacity. If Soviet vessels could carry more than what the occasionally shallow seaway depths could accommodate, then Maxie suggested that Soviet cargo holds could be topped off at Port Sorel. There, where the Richelieu River flows into the St. Lawrence, the USSR's freighters could take on all the added tonnage they're able to carry on their journey through deeper ocean waters.

The only problem remaining was selling price. At this point in the deliberations, Maxie hurried out to her desk. She grabbed a clipboard hanging on a nearby wall nail, and quickly returned to H. B.'s office. Standing in front of Bert and Harry, she began reading.

"The market's 14% protein HRS price increased slightly last month from its $3.28 per bushel winter low, following last year's $3.98 high. It finally settled at $3.58, which is close to the $3.55 average bushel price. However, a large supply at Duluth-Superior could have some downward pressure on this year's pricing, due to a bumper crop forecast. European Common Market Countries are expected to have price depressing surpluses also, but they'll be offset by decreased production in Argentina, Australia, and Canada. The probability is that we can expect the world's grain need to exceed its supply by 8-10 million tons."

"Thanks, Maxie." Brown acknowledged. "Now let's work up our Goldstrike Formula to determine a target price. The United States Department of

Agriculture anticipates no significant change in last year's average, so we can begin at the interpolation segment of our equation."

Brown took out his pocket calculator. "Let's see, $3.98 high, less $3.28 low, gives us a 70 cents per bushel spread. Dividing by our factor of three and adding the answer to last year's low, we get $3.51 per bushel as our Goldstrike high-side price.

"You can be certain the Soviets will push for a discount from the average $3.55 bushel price. Also, powerful grain merchants like Julius Fiske are betting we'll shave the average by a mere one or two cents, so they think they'll deal with the Soviets in huge volumes for three cents under, or $3.52 per bushel. Our Goldstrike maximum, however, calculates to $3.51. Since that price probably undercuts Julius Fiske and the others by a penny a bushel, we should be able to bring home the gold.

"Let's assume grain merchants like Julius Fiske need at least a 15% return to cover their heavy overhead. This means they'll have to buy from the farmer for, let's see...," Brown calculates, "$3.52, less 15%, less costs, plus the various government export and other subsidies...,why, they'll offer farmers only $3.44 per bushel, I'll bet. We'll offer the Min-Dak Co-op $3.46 per bushel and blow the big guys away.

"Subtract our low base cost from $3.51, add government subsidies, get 34 cents per bushel spread. Divide 34 cents by $3.51. That's a 9.7% return! Painfully small for the biggies, but a fortune for us.

"Nine point seven...,I like those numbers. If we sell 100,000 tons of grain at $3.51 per bushel, what's our return on that?"

Bert and Maxie punched their calculators in a race for the answer. Maxie vocalized her calculations, stating that 36.7 bushels per ton, times 100,000 tons, equaled 3,670,000 bushels. Multiplying the number of bushels times a $3.51 price yielded a total order value of

$12,881,700. At 9.7% of that total, Bert, Maxie, and Harry would split $1,249,525. Since this was an unprecedented sum for their small partnership, the thought of that much money made them ecstatic, especially when they realized they'd be giving the farmers a better price than the other merchants. The Soviets would get the best buy, too. These were quite pleasing prospects, indeed.

Harry, however, cautioned Bert and Maxie to forget the money and concentrate their efforts on putting the deal together.

"One more point," Harry urged, "let's get our usual clauses and payment terms in the Soviet contract proposal. Let's be especially sure we insert our Reconciliation Clause for settling disputes. We don't want any more lawsuits. We've all had enough of them. Our whole nation has had it with lawsuits."

After pausing a few moments for questions, Harry gave his partners a final instruction. "It's 11:38 a.m. We only have seven hours to finish our work, so let's get going. I'll see you both in the Taylorsville Hotel Lounge at 6:30."

After Bert and Maxie left the room, Harry turned on a radio behind his desk. He was eager to hear the latest market forecast being broadcast at that moment. The announcer's voice, blaring from the speaker, enthusiastically reported:

> ....Cattlemen are hoping feeder cattle numbers will decline and demand will shoot up to the low $80's by midsummer. The average for choice steers, Omaha, is now running in the $62-66 range.
>
> Here's your radio station KJXL report on hogs. Hogs are in a holding situation while producers wait for prices to reach the $58-60 range. Current prices are up $6 a head at Nebraska Terminals, due to

rising market demands and falling numbers.

USDA officials just announced the estimate of this year's wheat crop. Looks like a 1.97 billion bushel total, close to last year's near record 2 billion 6. Yields are slightly higher this year at 40.8 bushels an acre, compared with 40.1 last year. According to the USDA, farm pricing for Hard Red Spring Wheat this coming year is anticipated to average $3.55 per bushel. Current HRS pricing at $3.58 is hovering around the average.

Our KJKL corn report is up next, after this brief message from your local farm implement dealer....

Harry turned off the radio, smiling confidently. He knew he was onto something big: a U. S. bumper crop, worried farmers ready to sell for a reasonable return above the government loan rate, and hungry Soviets eager to buy at almost any price. Soon Harry's smiling turned to happy whistling. The tune was one of his childhood favorites, "Turkey in the Straw".

Entertaining himself in this manner, Harry began shuffling various papers on his desk. His characteristic self-confidence returned as his anxieties about money matters faded into a dim memory. He realized the rest of the day would be busy for Bert, Maxie, and himself, but the prospect of selling wheat to the Soviets was rare indeed, and a truly once in a lifetime opportunity. Much preparation was needed, however, and, fortunately, Brown loved preparations. He never forgot what he learned in the Army's Leadership School at Fort Riley, Kansas: "A battle is won the day before."

2

THE BROWNS

Harry Brown drove his four-year-old station wagon into the driveway of his modest, three-bedroom, split-level residence at 127 East Second Street. It was half past five. He only had an hour to change clothes, freshen up, and get to the evening dinner meeting at the Taylorsville Hotel.

Walking to the front door, Harry couldn't help thinking how long he'd lived at that address and how worn his house appeared. White wood trim needed repainting. Faded, cracked stucco needed repairs and redashing. The storm door needed a new screen. The roofing was twenty-five years old and Harry was sick and tired of patching it every summer against the severe Minnesota winter coming. He'd postponed re-roofing the place several years too many. Then there was a broken garage window one of the kids hit with a basketball. Also, the lawn needed raking, mowing, weeding, bare-spot seeding, even edging, but Harry suddenly pushed his concerns aside. Soon he could afford to have all these things done for him, now that his grain brokerage business was on the verge of prospering. In fact, if the Soviet deal succeeded, there'd be no limit to what Harry would be able to do. His mind ran away with the prospect. He'd even build a brand new home for Josie and the kids, and hire a full time gardener, too.

"Josie!" Harry shouted as he entered the doorway. "I'm home! We have a dinner appointment at 6:30. That leaves us only forty-five minutes to get ready, and fifteen minutes to get to the Taylorsville Hotel. This is it. We pull off this one and we're rich."

Into the room hurried a somewhat harried looking, middle-aged mother of four, who was also surrogate mother to one additional overgrown kid named Henry Cornelius Brown. Nobody at home dare use those names, of course, nor were they ever used in public or private. When Harry left teaching, he left behind the "Henry Cornelius" to become plain old "Harry". One time he almost slugged an army sergeant who mockingly shouted "Henry Cornelius Brown" during a roll call.

"Harry, I'm glad you're home!" Josie enthused. "Can you watch the kids a few moments? I just finished feeding them supper. Won't take me five minutes to get ready."

Josie took off her white and blue striped apron, revealing a burgundy colored dress. She was about to put the apron in the closet, but Harry suddenly swept her off her feet and kissed her. The shock of this rare gesture caused Josie to giggle and kick off her shoes, so Harry eased her down on the sofa, then sat in a stuffed chair nearby. He began looking right at her, and his expression grew serious, as though he had some grave secret to tell.

Noticing Harry's mood change, Josie stopped giggling and adopted an attentive look to show him she was listening. She was a slightly heavy set, strong-armed woman, kept so by lots of housework, including tedious years of changing, washing, and folding diapers. Yet, for all her housework, Josephine Anne Brown managed to keep her youthful looking beauty and shapely female form well into middle age. Though she was only a few years younger than Harry, her hair still reflected its

23

natural brunette color, and her smooth, unblemished skin was without any wrinkles. Perhaps Josie's faithful, twenty-two year love affair with Harry kept her young looking. Maybe having four children helped, too.

Harry loved looking at Josie. He admired her and was grateful for her. He apologized that he didn't take time to tell her everything when he phoned her from his office. The prospect of a Soviet wheat sale had overly excited him. It was worth over a million dollars of commission, he estimated. Plus, it meant a touch of prosperity for hard pressed farmers in Minnesota, North and South Dakota, Nebraska, and elsewhere, depending on how much wheat the Soviets bought. In view of such an important opportunity for their business, Harry advised Josie they really had to please their Soviet hosts. The fact that Novikov was Harry's old friend would help, of course, but Harry said Josie could be a big help, too, by keeping the conversation lively and dancing with Novikov.

Josie playfully scolded Harry by emphatically telling him she wasn't one of his students, nor was she stupid. She said she was completely capable of civility, and it was really Harry who needed the advice. She told him not to talk too much, and warned him not to have more than two drinks, because she'd be counting. She reminded him he never could hold much liquor and didn't know when to stop. She concluded by telling him how fortunate he was to have such a loving wife who could save him from himself. Harry stood dumbfounded, his mouth wide open, while Josie kissed him on the cheek, winked playfully, and scurried off to the bedroom.

After Harry recovered his senses moments later, his youngest daughter Jeanie came running up to him, sobbing. He picked her up and held her in his arms. She was only four years old and a pretty brunette like her mother. She was sensitive, too. She complained that her older brother Johnny tried to steal her dessert, then called her "a fat hog." Harry comforted her, stroked her hair, wiped her tears, and hugged her. He assured her he'd have a talk with Johnny and get an apology. Then, in a loud voice, he ordered Johnny to come out of the kitchen.

Johnny, Harry and Josie's second youngest child, ran up to his dad, laughing and skipping. He was all of seven years old, glowing with mischief. He looked somewhat like his father, if it's at all realistic to determine strong resemblances at such a young age. His hair was jet black, cheeks plump and healthy looking, body stocky, eyes dark brown. He asked his dad what he wanted, and Harry asked him to apologize to his younger sister, then kiss her in friendship. Johnny protested, but after some stern coaxing, timidly told his sister Jeanie he was sorry. Harry kissed them both, and Suzie and Jack came out of the kitchen to greet their father.

Jack, firstborn of Harry and Josie, was seventeen and a senior in high school. Suzie, second oldest, was a ninth grader, just turned fourteen. After Suzie was born, Josie had two miscarriages, so there was a seven-year gap between Suzie and her younger brother Johnny. Both Jack and Suzie were holding dishtowels. Harry greeted them excitedly.

"Jack! Suzie! You're my lucky stars. I've got tremendous news. Some Soviet officials are here in Taylorsville, hopefully to buy wheat from us. They're from 'Exportkhleb.' Did you know that 'Khleb' is the Russian word for 'bread?' Think of it as the Soviets coming here to buy bread from us. I can tell you all about it later, but right now I've got to get ready for a 6:30 reception at the Taylorsville Hotel, because the Soviets invited your Mom and me to dinner.

"Jack, you're in charge tonight," Harry instructed. "Suzie, I want you to help, too. Johnny and Jeanie, I know you'll both be good and go to bed when you're told. Also, I'm sure Jack and Suzie have homework for school tomorrow, so they'll need a quiet house. You're all such good children and so helpful! If my company is

25

successful in selling wheat to the Soviets, I'll take you on a vacation to Duluth to see the big ships."

Brown's two younger children began jumping and clapping when they heard about the Duluth vacation. Jack and Suzie were delighted, too. Jack hoped they'd all take a boat trip, and Suzie looked forward to seeing Lake Superior. Impressed with his children's happy reactions, Harry's heart melted, prompting him to say they'd take the Duluth vacation for sure, even if he didn't succeed with the Soviets. Then he excused himself to prepare for the Taylorsville Hotel dinner party.

3

TAYLORSVILLE HOTEL DINNER PARTY

Harry and Josie Brown arrived at the Taylorsville Hotel Restaurant and Lounge just after 6:25 p.m. The maitre d' led them to a slightly elevated, partially enclosed corner section near the dance floor. It was somewhat removed from the central dining area, and far enough away from the bandstand to enable the dinner guests to converse without shouting, once the band began playing.

The Taylorsville Hotel, as might be expected, was a central building in town. Over the years, it became a popular meeting and entertainment spot for the greater rural population beyond its locale. Its management was conservative, accommodating, and efficient, and its cuisine surprisingly good.

A pioneer family founded the business, and a succession of heirs kept it thriving through several generations. Recently an extensive search had been made to find an accomplished chef who could add a touch of culinary elegance to the otherwise routine fare. Such a chef was found, too, so now the restaurant had a dining standard that matched the hotel's reputation for high quality hospitality.

Eight months previously, the restaurant was

remodeled to provide an expanded seating capacity for the increasing crowds. Even the red brick building exterior had been sandblasted to complement the interior's renovations. Inside, the same oak tables and chairs, though refinished, retained their suggestion of old world charm. Also, wagon wheel chandeliers hung from vaulted wood ceilings, and, combined with plush, rich, deep brown carpeting and a rich looking, cream-dyed wall covering of rough burlap, there was a hint of frontier opulence to the place.

"What a perfect setting for the evening!" Harry exclaimed to Nikolai, who smiled as he got up and extended his hands in welcome. Moving out from behind a large, linen-covered table, Nikolai greeted and hugged Harry like some long lost member of the family.

"My dear friend Harry!"

Harry enthusiastically responded, "Nikky! Nikky!"

"And this must be Josie!" Novikov majestically and admiringly announced.

Josie's yellow dress with elbow length sleeves and dark brown belt and trim was captivating. Her long brunette hair was pulled back into a French braid, and topped with a yellow ribbon that matched her bright dress. She wore a necklace and earrings of radiant topaz.

"What a magnificent woman!" Nikolai exclaimed. "Harry, she's too good to have all to yourself. You must share her with me. Let her sit next to me tonight. My own dear wife Anna is home with our children in Moscow. I haven't seen her or our children for three weeks, because of all this grain buying. I need to find out all I can about your Josie, so I can tell my Anna what an extraordinary woman you married."

Nikolai Novikov was wearing a charcoal colored, stylishly vested suit with white shirt and maroon tie. He presented a strikingly formal, dignified, even official appearance in contrast to Brown's less formal, rural, more relaxed look. Both Brown and Novikov were similarly middle-aged, well built, and ruggedly handsome men, but there the similarities ended. Novikov's hopelessly thinning, but carefully trimmed and neatly combed gray hair combined with his light, delicately colored, unweathered skin to suggest a man who spent long hours working indoors. Under his vested suit, Novikov still had the remnants of a once powerful and muscular torso, which reminded everyone he was a man who'd done his share of physical labor. Brown by contrast was more the outdoorsman, sporting a tan corduroy sport coat over an open-collared, red plaid shirt and new, dark brown corduroy slacks. Both Brown and Novikov had an alert manner and ready smile.

"Permit me to present my deputy, Nadezhda Konya," Novikov continued. "We call her Naddy for short. Also, please meet my associate, Helga Baranovna."

The various introductions culminated in handshaking and individual greetings, after which Harry Brown's partners arrived and the process began all over again.

"Here's Maxine Gadsden, our Office Administrator," Harry said. "We call her Maxie. This is Bertram Jackson, our General Manager and secret spy. We call him Bert."

After the introductions and acknowledgments were done, Novikov invited everybody to sit down, but he personally arranged the seating. Josie was seated on his right, and Harry to the right of Josie. Then Bert and Naddy were seated together, and Helga was assigned to Bert's right. Maxie completed the circle, sitting at Nikolai's left. Nikolai, still standing, continued his playful banter from behind his chair.

"Do you know, Josie, that Harry tells me everything? Sometimes he tells me things I don't want to know or shouldn't know. Usually, however, he tells me what I don't care to hear, like the outrageously high price for wheat he's going to quote me tomorrow." Nikolai smirked at Harry when he said this, and Harry feigned a cringe, displaying a pretense of pain on his face. Nikolai continued.

"But, Maxie, I'm especially pleased I met you and Bert and Josie. I really don't think Harry could survive on his own. I'm sure he'd never survive at home, either, without the genius of his Josie." Harry riled in mock shock at this rapid succession of jibes from Nikolai, and was about to respond when Nikolai smilingly shot his hands forward and waved his palms outward in a restraining gesture. Then, turning to the others, he continued.

"Now, good friends, I've ordered the very best champagne, so we can toast each other before our salad is served. No need to order, it's ready when we are. I already arranged to have the chef delight you with a special recipe of Russian dressing. They say Comrade Lenin's mother prepared it for him just before the Revolution."

"Is that what caused it?" Harry wisecracked.

"Now, now, Harry!" Nikolai scolded. Then, changing the subject, "While the waiter is pouring champagne, I'll tell you more. After our salad, we'll enjoy some hearty borscht, accompanied by an exquisite chablis, then some fresh-baked, whole grain people's bread. I'm so delighted you have a People's Bakery in Taylorsville. It makes me feel there might be hope for you Americans after all. Finally, the *piece de resistance*...ladies and gentlemen, permit me to announce, good old down yonder corn fed Nebraska beefsteak, New York cut, hurray!"

Everybody laughing, Harry Brown chided, "Why, tricky Nikky, you old fake! You haven't changed a bit,

30

except you now know something about beefsteak. Bet you didn't learn it in Moscow!"

"Attention! Attention!" Novikov commanded. Then, sitting down with the others, "Friends, let's raise our glasses in a toast." All complied as Novikov continued. "To each other and the friendship of our two countries."

After everyone sipped some champagne, Novikov raised his glass again. "To Harry, that he accepts our generous offer tomorrow of $3.45 for 14% protein, Hard Red Spring Wheat."

Harry earnestly interrupted, "I can't drink to that, Nikky. Our farmers are getting an average of $3.55 a bushel right now. Some even sold out last year at $4.25, and the current market price is $3.58. You've got to raise your offer a bit, Nikky."

"To $3.45 tomorrow!" Novikov repeated, even more enthusiastically, as if enjoying himself.

"$3.45 plus 6!" Brown bellowed back.

"Truce!" declared Bert. "Let's sleep on the pricing and toast each other!"

"Hear! Hear!" Brown agreed. "I'll drink to that!"

"Good!" smiled Novikov. "To us!"

When they finished their toasting, salad was served, and Novikov opened the conversation again by asking Josie a question. "Josie," he said, "who is this Taylor of Taylorsville?"

Josie politely replied that Taylorsville was named after her great grandfather, Colonel Edward Taylor, who was the first commander of an old Army fort once located there. Before the turn of the century, the town was called Fort Taylor, after Josie's ancestor, but the old log fortress burned down, and the Army decided not to rebuild it, because the fort wasn't needed anymore. Shortly afterwards, with the fort gone, the settlers voted to

31

rename their town Taylorsville, after Colonel Taylor's family, which was the very first family to settle there.

Earlier, in 1874, Colonel Taylor signed a treaty with the native tribe, headed by Chief Iron Bow. Chief Iron Bow's name came from a 30-caliber Springfield rifle he received in a trade of buffalo hides to an Easterner. The story was that when Chief Iron Bow first saw the rifle, he called it an "iron bow," then purchased it, and a case of ammunition, in trade for ten buffalo hides. Soon ten of his best braves each had Springfield rifles and cases of ammunition, which they, too, bought with buffalo hides. They must have traded at least a hundred buffalo hides altogether. Unfortunately, when Iron Bow's tribe ran out of ammunition, there was a minor uprising.

Chief Iron Bow and his braves tried taking Colonel Taylor's fort at night by stealth, but were defeated when alert guards gave the alarm. Afterwards, Colonel Taylor negotiated a major treaty with Chief Iron Bow's tribe. In return for three hundred thousand acres ceded to the U.S., Chief Iron Bow's braves got guarantees of food and clothing, plus ammunition for their Springfield rifles, and a promise they could stay on the remainder of their tribal lands "as long as the grass grows and the wind blows."

Soon after, however, the U. S. Government encouraged increasing numbers of settlers to keep taking more land, so Chief Iron Bow's tribe eventually lost most of the territory it had once been granted by sacred treaty.

"It seems Chief Iron Bow's heirs got the last laugh, however," Josie said. "The U. S. Supreme Court recently ruled that Colonel Taylor's treaty with Chief Iron Bow was a valid contract, and the U. S. Congress just passed a law to pay Chief Iron Bow's heirs a hundred million dollars compensation for their lost lands. The tribal council will get $20 million of the settlement, all of it to be spent on social services for the tribal members. Also, since it was determined that there are 2,556 legal heirs left of Iron Bow's tribe, each heir will get close to $30,000 from the remainder of the settlement. As of right now, the tribe, for its part, says it doesn't want any money. It wants its native lands, which it regards as sacred."

Josie added that if it were up to her, she'd "grab the money and run, before the government changes its mind." On the other hand, she reflected that if the tribal members accepted the money, the U. S. Internal Revenue Service would probably declare it to be taxable income and insist that taxes be paid, so Chief Iron Bow's tribe would get shafted all over again.

"I'm sure the IRS would think up a capital gains tax or some such other way to confiscate the money." Josie argued. "What any government gives with one hand, it usually takes back with the other."

Nikolai complimented Josie on her interesting conclusion, and proceeded to offer one of his own. "It seems to me, Chief Iron Bow's tribal heirs would be wise to take the money, instead of insisting on the return of the land. In the Soviet Union, land belongs to no individual person. It's the property of all workers represented by the state. If the U. S. Government is crazy enough to offer the tribal heirs so much money, better they take it now, before a lot of lawyers get into the act and grab huge chunks of it. As for the IRS, the settlement money should be tax free. Maybe Chief Iron Bow's tribe could even declare a substantial loss for tax purposes, and get some additional money in the form of a refund. We Soviets aren't dumb. We know what goes on in the USA with the IRS. You've got to be very clever, or the IRS will take everything you have. Thank you for your intriguing story, Josie, now it's your turn to ask a question."

Josie reflected a moment, then, in a serious tone,

asked Mr. Novikov what was happening in his country that it had to buy wheat elsewhere?

"Ah, Josie, that's a good question!" Nikolai acknowledged. "I'm going to let Helga, our agricultural expert, answer that. Helga..."

"Thank you, Comrade Nikolai," Helga replied. "It's a privilege to be of service. Your question, Mrs. Brown, is excellent." Shifting herself slightly, and adjusting the skirt of her bright blue dress to avoid wrinkling it, blond haired, stocky built, pink cheeked Helga began again in earnest.

"Our leader, Chairman Vasil Golgolev recently instructed us on that very subject. As General Secretary of the Communist Party and Chairman of the Supreme Soviet Presidium, he announced last week that our crop harvest this year will be one-fifth lower than targeted. We tried hard to grow the 250 million tons of wheat needed to feed our huge population. Now we're struggling desperately to reach 200 million tons, an amount that's 20% short of our needs."

Helga's face flushed, as though she were embarrassed to admit such a failure. She seemed ready to cry. After a brief pause, however, she continued her explanation.

"Bad weather is our major problem. For several years we've made giant advances in our farming methods and in our increased use of fertilizers. We've made many other improvements, too, but bad weather on top of an already short growing season prevented us from reaching our grain harvest goals. Perhaps if such problems of Mother Nature eventually leave us and frustrate your country, we can sell grain to you instead of buying."

Helga began smiling as she continued. "Now, however, until we solve our problems, we must buy our additional grain from you, West Europe, Canada,

34

Argentina, Australia, or any other country with surplus grain to sell us at a competitive price.

"It wasn't always so, this buying of grain by us. For many centuries, wheat and oats out of our Port of Odessa on the Black Sea, fed countries all over Europe and the Mediterranean. Around the year 1800, we even helped feed far away England. It's also a fact that in 1845, one-third of our huge grain crop rotted in the fields for lack of workers to harvest it, while thousands died of starvation in Ireland when potato blight destroyed its 1844 crop. Now, more than ever, it's important we help each other, so we may all live. If you help us today, tomorrow we'll be able to help you. You could even be desperate for our help tomorrow.

"The heroic people of our many Soviet Socialist Republics have been struggling only a few decades, yet, already we've achieved success. From a nation of impoverished, exploited serfs under a czar, we've become a major world power. Comrades, our revolution has achieved in a few short years what it took the U. S. over 200 years to develop. Today, because of our military and industrial might, we stand shoulder to shoulder with America. Our powerful weapons make it possible for the world to enjoy lasting peace, growing friendship, and mutually beneficial trade."

At this conclusion of Helga's response to Josie's question, Harry Brown jumped the conversation with a quick comment: "I sure hope we don't blow each other up before we get the chance to enjoy the peace, friendship, and mutually beneficial trade."

Novikov quickly regained control of the conversation by giving Helga some appropriate recognition. Enthusiastically he said, "Congratulations, Helga! What an appropriate conclusion! Harry's observation was appropriate, too. You see, we're all friends. Helga is a dedicated worker for our people, and an esteemed member of the Communist Party. Before she came to us, she was a teacher like Harry and me. What a wonderful background she has in agriculture, and how gifted she is in other subjects."

Helga blushed. Then, recovering, she turned to the others and said, "Comrade Novikov is too kind, but I thank him anyway, and now it's my turn for a question. Maxie, can you tell us about H. B. Exports, Inc? I know we're supposed to have fun tonight, but the entertainment and dancing hasn't started yet, and some of my American friends tell me the IRS demands you talk business before you can...how do they say...write it off?"

At this, Harry and Bert laughed out loud. Then Bert supplied an explanation. "It's true about a write-off, Helga, but only if you're the one paying the bill. A meeting must have a business purpose before you can deduct its cost from your income and expect to pay less tax. Also, it's essential you talk business at the meeting, and under tax reform legislation, only a reduced percentage of such expenses are deductible."

"Aha!" said Helga. "That's why you Americans are always buying lunches and dinners for each other. I understand now."

"But this night is on us, Helga," Novikov reminded her, "The USSR is paying the bill. Now go ahead, Maxie, Helga has a good question. Let's hear about Harry."

As continuing courses of dinner were served, Maxie graciously responded. She was the picture of elegance in her light beige, smooth silk dress. When she began, she said she was happy to answer Helga's question. She explained that H. B. Exports, Inc., called 'HBE' after Harry Brown, was a Minnesota company that Harry, Bert and she had started three years ago. Their primary business purpose was to make money by helping farmers get the best prices for their grain during slow selling times.

"Harry, as you know, used to be a high school teacher," Maxie confided. "So were Bert and I. Seems we have a majority of ex teachers here tonight. Are you an ex teacher, too, Naddy?"

"No, Maxie," Naddy half laughingly replied. "Nikolai says I'm a spy, but then Mr. Brown also says that about Bert. Really, though, I'm not a spy. I think Comrade Nikolai likes to tell people I'm a spy to keep them from bothering me. Or, maybe he says I'm a spy because he knows your CIA would be unhappy if there were no spies in our group for its agents to follow around and write reports about. What I studied at the Odessa Technological Institute was human organizational and social behavior, cybernetics, computer science, productivity, subjects like that. But continue, Maxie, I want to know all about H. B. Exports."

Bert kept looking at Nadezhda as she talked. He was completely captivated. Her sleek black hair accented her delicate white skin, creating an effect that set her apart from other women. She had a youthful, innocent looking face and the suggestion of purity about her. Also, her dark eyes were compelling, casting hypnotic spells on her unwary male admirers. Perhaps Nadezhda looked like some kind of goddess to Bert, dressed as she was in a dark-red velvet suit with snow-white trim. Such an attire was quite extraordinary in Taylorsville, and even Minneapolis or St. Paul, Bert thought. To top it off, her artfully sculpted and symmetrical facial features fit in just right with everything else. "She's perfect!" Bert mentally noted as he forced himself to pull his eyes away from her and focus his attention on Maxie.

Naddy, for her part, was not unaware of Bert. She frequently glanced at him and was attracted to his handsome features and sincere manner. Fate, if not Nikolai Novikov, had thrown these two highly eligible young people together.

"Harry, Bert, and I started our company three years ago," Maxie continued, "at which time Bert and I elected Harry president. We also named the company 'H. B. Exports' in honor of Harry Brown, because it was mostly Harry's idea. His Goldstrike Concept of grain merchandising caught on and spread quickly. Originally a regional business, H. B. Exports has grown to where it's now capable of doing business nationwide, even internationally. Who could have anticipated such success three years ago? Who would have believed then that our Goldstrike Concept could become so universally popular?

"The idea is simple enough: give grain growers the best price and quickest outlet. Other brokerages pay farmers on the basis of a 'spot price' quoted at grain exchanges. There's give and take, of course. A seller might quote $3.58 a bushel for HRS 14%. Then, if a buyer offers $3.57, the deal might close at $3.57-1/2. Harry does it differently.

"Harry's formula calculates the difference between last year's high-low price range and next year's anticipated high-low range. Next, it calculates the median selling price. To that is applied our secret factor, which achieves an estimated median price farmers can live with, since it's always well above the U. S. Department of Agriculture's loan guarantee price.

"An additional advantage of HBE's Goldstrike approach is that it gives farmers a quick outlet for their harvest. Powerful merchants like Julius Fiske pay farmers much less, then charge customers much more, and create numerous shipment bottlenecks that slow down the movements of a farmer's harvest.

"Back in the 1960's, 70's, and 80's, movement of a farmer's harvest posed serious problems. Grain storage facilities were scarce; railroads couldn't handle the many movement demands; and railroad hopper cars were in short supply, due to insufficient quantities of new cars. Trackage was down, too, because railroads canceled unprofitable runs, and removed many deteriorated rail, which they sold for scrap and didn't replace.

"The situation is changed now. Movement of grain is no longer the problem it used to be, at least not for our company. However, it can still pose serious problems for some companies.

"In brief, HBE's concept is to buy grain from farmers on a contracted, stable, price guarantee and consignment basis, such that payment is due at the time grain is resold and paid for by resale buyers. After consigned grain for export is moved to various seaport loading points for shipment to Algeria, Japan, Indonesia, and other cash customers, farmers get immediate bills of sale they can use for accounts receivable financing at local banks, plus they get a good price in return for their hard work. We're pleased, too, because we've accomplished our company's business purpose of providing the best service to farmers."

Novikov complimented Maxie on her thoroughness and called an intermission in their round of table talks. The band was ready to play, and the evening's entertainment was about to begin.

"Feel free to leave the table any time to dance or do whatever you like," Novikov urged. "We'll have no formalities, please. Let's all enjoy ourselves tonight."

On the bandstand at the other side of the dance floor, country western singer and Red River Gang bandleader Lonny Steele directed his musicians in a rousing opening number. The pickin' and grinnin' and good old country music put everyone in a relaxed mood, so that couples got up to dance in increasing numbers. There were a brave few at first, then more, soon filling the dance floor to capacity.

Bert and Naddy danced. Nikolai and Josie danced.

Finally, Harry and Helga decided to dance, but as they were about to leave the table, a tall, distinguished looking, middle-aged black man approached and introduced himself with a smooth southern accent.

"Name is James Baston; Jamie for short. I'm a special reporter for the Southern States Newswire Service. Here's my card. I'm on my way North to do an investigative feature on the recent Canadian pipeline explosion and the tragic deaths of the work crew. Now I'm told there's a Soviet delegation here tonight and a possible news story. Forgive my intrusion, but could you help me? I really don't know anything about this place."

Maxie introduced herself and the others to Mr. Baston. Helga smiled, nodding slightly from her waist towards Baston when Maxie mentioned her name. Likewise, Harry, after somewhat admiringly scanning Baston's expensive looking, black and gray tweed sports coat, smiled and shook Baston's hand saying, "Nice to know you, Jamie. Welcome to Taylorsville. It could be there's a story someplace here in town. Maybe if you stick around awhile you'll get it."

"I'll sure give it a try," Baston affirmed. Then, turning to Maxie, he asked, "Could I begin with this dance, Maxie?"

Maxie agreed, and both couples went out on the dance floor. Nobody ever heard of Baston's Southern States Newswire Service, but it sounded convincing. Baston was so polite and sincere, almost anything he said was believable. The truth was, James Baston worked for Julius Fiske and was there on Fiske's orders, nosing around Taylorsville to find out about any Soviet grain deals. Julius Fiske, Baston's employer and owner of a multi-billion dollar, multinational grain sales company headquartered in Texas, got word the Soviets were headed for Taylorsville, so he lost no time dispatching

Baston with orders to "Get on up there, Jamie! Find out what they're up to!"

Baston didn't like spying or telling lies, but he decided to oblige his boss, Julius Fiske, who paid him well. Baston had worked several years for his employer, and earned a generous salary. That's why Baston didn't dare upset Fiske or jeopardize a paycheck by arguing. Baston simply flew up to Taylorsville in Fiske's private jet, arrived at the airport by dinnertime, then got a ride to the hotel and tipped the maitre d' twenty dollars to learn about everyone in Novikov's party. When he spotted Maxie and noticed she didn't have a dancing partner, he figured he'd maneuver himself into the group as soon as the dancing started.

"So you're Maxie," Baston said admiringly, cooing out his honeyed words with his charming Southern accent. "You sure are a mighty fine looking woman! Are you one of the Soviet officials everyone in Taylorsville is talking about?"

"Why, no, Mr. Baston, don't be ridiculous," replied Maxie. "Several others in our party are from the USSR, but I live right here in good old Taylorsville, Minnesota, USA."

"Please call me Jamie, and tell me what you do here, Maxie. Also, what is this Soviet business all about?" Baston acted as if he didn't know.

"That's not for me to say," replied Maxie. "Perhaps my business partner, Harry Brown, the man you just met, and the Soviet man, Nikolai Novikov, can help you. Are you with the CIA or something?"

"Heavens! No!" laughed Baston. "I'm just a typically curious newsman."

When the dance ended, nearly every couple remained on the dance floor, waiting for the next song to begin. Lonny Steele announced he'd sing one of his favorites, "It's Hard to be Humble." As Lonny's Red

River Gang began playing, the dancing started again, but stopped moments after it started. Lonny was so funny, it was difficult for anyone to concentrate on dancing. Most couples were just standing around and laughing or singing along with Lonny. Baston and Maxie, however, continued talking with each other in earnest, presumably about themselves, since they appeared to be getting quite absorbed in each other. Eventually, Lonny's next selection began. It was "The Tennessee Waltz," which got everyone back to serious dancing.

By this time, Bert and Naddy were well acquainted and becoming quite friendly. Perhaps it was a matter of love at first sight for both of them. Naddy seemed struck by Bert's golden hair, good looks, and gentle manner; Bert seemed infatuated with Naddy's honesty and beauty. They were both completely enchanted and helplessly transported, and becoming increasingly joined together at each turn of the waltz. Finally, Bert whispered into Naddy's ear, "Naddy, I simply must see you again."

Naddy replied, "I want to see you, too, Bert, but I don't know when we'll find time. Our plane leaves tomorrow afternoon at 5:00."

"How about early tomorrow afternoon," Bert suggested, "right after our wheat negotiations are ended? Maybe we'll have something to celebrate and can meet in the Taylorsville Park. I'll wait for you there at 2:30. You'll be able to find me: I'll be sitting on a bench behind the pavillion. It's a good place, because there's nobody around there at that time of day. We'll have the whole park to ourselves. We can talk all we want."

"I don't know, Bert. I could only stay for an hour," Naddy whispered in his ear.

"That's perfect!" Bert smiled happily, hugging Naddy in a momentary squeeze to affirm their agreement. An hour on such short notice was as good as a whole day, he reasoned with himself.

Bert and Naddy knew it would be hard waiting for 2:30 p.m. the next day. Their heartbeats quickened at the mere thought of their secret meeting in the empty Taylorsville Park. Yet, for all their excitement with each other at that moment, they could do no more than dance. It was one of those rare situations where the right man and woman meet for the first time, are soon infatuated, then can't escape the exciting, overpowering, mysterious force that attracts, holds, and binds them together.

Nobody else noticed anything particularly unusual between Bert and Naddy. Everybody was too busy having a good time. Harry kept chattering away as he danced with Helga. Nikolai kept questioning Josie for every tidbit of gossip about Harry and their four children. Josie asked Nikolai questions about his wife, Anna, and their three children. Maxie and Jamie kept talking, too, until Lonny Steele came to the big moment of the evening, the performance of his featured songstress. Waiting until after the dance crowd dispersed and everyone was seated, Lonny finally began his introduction.

"Ladies and gentlemen, here's the red hot gal we're all so proud of," Lonny enthused. "She's a real live Ogalala, Nebraska, Lakota Sioux maiden with a message of love for us. Sheila says 'Lakota' means 'alliance of nations.' It's a 40,000-year-old coalition of Native American tribes. How grateful we are to the Lakota for Sheila. Ladies and gentlemen, Sheila Song-Maker!"

Lonny's Red River Gang instrumentally awakened with a combination of lively Native American rhythms and ceremonial music. Soon Sheila Song-Maker started dancing out onto the bandstand from a side entrance. She moved all around to the exciting sounds and drumbeats. What a spectacle she was, dressed in her leather skirt and top, which were both decorated with variously colored and beaded designs. She also wore a

43

petite headband with a tall feather at the back, and around her neck were several strings of shiny red, white, and blue beads.

After a few turns around the stage, Sheila grabbed the microphone and began singing a song called "Running Brave." At the conclusion of her opening number, the crowd went wild with applause. It was no nursery school rhyme or music appreciation song Sheila had sung. Her fun-loving turns and churns, and body "yumpf's" and "humpf's," put everyone in a high stomping, hoot and hollering mood. It was a combination Grand Ol Opry hoedown, bluegrass breakdown, Smoky Mountain banjo duel, and Lakota Sioux celebration dance, all blended into one. Everybody had a good time.

Sheila smiled appreciatively with the applause, then performed a few more body "yumpf's" and humpf's," accentuated by a drummer and two guitarists. Afterwards, she politely bowed several times, until the applause died down and she was able to announce her next number.

"Ladies and gentlemen," Sheila began, "You're all so very kind. What a wonderful audience! For those of you who haven't heard the exciting news, we have important visitors with us tonight. They're officials who came here to Taylorsville, all the way from the Soviet Union."

An audible note of surprise was heard from the audience as heads followed a spotlight to the corner booth. "Ladies and gentlemen," Sheila repeated, "let's give a big welcome tonight to our Soviet visitors."

The audience applauded, and Sheila spoke again. "In honor of our Soviet guests, Lonny Steele's gang and I are going to do a special number, 'The Red Cavalry March.'"

Immediately the band began playing, and after a

quick run-through of the song, the band continued playing the melody in the background while Sheila pointed towards Novikov's party and said, "Put a spotlight on that corner booth and get a microphone over there. Let's hear how this song sounds in Russian."

Nikolai coaxed Harry to get up with him, Naddy, and Helga, then the four of them sang 'The Red Cavalry March' in Russian. Afterwards, the spotlight shined on Sheila again, and with a swinging gesture of her hand, she directed Lonny and the band to keep playing in the background as she spoke.

"You're all so good," Sheila complimented, "let's do it again. This time, while you're singing the Russian, Lonny Steele, The Red River Gang, and I will sing the English. Here we go. Ready? Now don't be bashful. C'mon! One, two, and...."

So they sang again. At the conclusion, everyone enthusiastically applauded, and Sheila, with Lonny's assistance, put variously colored, handmade bead necklaces on Helga, Naddy, Maxie, and Josie. An honorary Lakota Sioux Chief's headpiece was placed on Nikolai, and peacepipes were presented to both Nikolai and Harry. Bert got a beaded leather wampum pouch. As a conclusion to the frolic, Sheila sang a stirring American song, then declared an intermission "so everyone can get to eating, drinking, and being friends." Smiling and waving at the applauding audience, Sheila then walked off the stage arm in arm with Lonny Steele.

Nikolai Novikov and Harry Brown turned to each other at their corner table and Harry remarked, "Nikolai, in that last song, when we came to the last line about the Russian army heroes, I couldn't help wondering where all the world's heroes have gone."

"That's an important question, Harry," Nikolai replied, "but what do you mean by 'heroes?' We have many heroes in the Soviet Union. It would take me

45

more time than I have here to name even a small percentage of them, since there are so many. In fact, you might say the masses of people in the Soviet Union are all heroes. They're making great personal and financial sacrifices to build our glorious new society. Here's to the masses, heroes all!" With that toast, he raised his glass and was joined by Helga and Naddy, who both said "True!" and "Of course!" in Russian. The rest politely raised their glasses, too, though half-heartedly, and drank.

Harry frowned and looked down, as if thoughtfully reflecting. Then, looking up, he said, "I'd define a hero as someone who voluntarily does something hazardous for others and who serves the common good, even to the point of suffering deprivation and ridicule.

"For example, George Washington and his army endured great suffering at Valley Forge in the cause of our American Revolution. They didn't do it for money; there wasn't any money to speak of. They didn't even do it for themselves; they'd be crazy to suffer through a bitter winter in primitive circumstances just for themselves. They could have returned home to warm clothing, decent beds, and plenty of food, but they didn't. They were volunteers who hung on for the common good, which is the good of their loved ones: wives, children, parents, relatives, neighbors, friends; the good of the freedom revolution; the good of humanity's future. Likewise, others who served in like manner on the world's battlefields are heroes.

"Also, I believe a true hero shuns publicity. Those who publicize their own deeds aren't heroes; they're self-serving. There's too much self-serving publicity in our press release world of today. Self-proclaimed heroes are really anti-heroes who put themselves in front of others, rather than serving others first."

"I agree, Harry," Helga remarked. "Those who put

themselves ahead of their society are enemies of the people. I believe when all is said and done, it's society, the people, who determine our heroes."

"But Helga," Bert cut in, "what about those heroes society ignores or even ridicules? Copernicus was ridiculed because he proved our earth is a sphere, not flat, and that it's not the center of our solar system."

"True," Helga replied, "but society eventually determined Copernicus to be right, and Church Inquisition officials wrong. Subsequent generations gave Copernicus the respect he deserved. Too bad he didn't get a better reception in his own lifetime."

"Maybe our problem is the press," suggested Josie. "Newspapers ought to quit writing so much about playboys and criminals. Reporters should start telling us who our heroes are, why they're our heroes, what they do, how they do it, and where they do it. Only once in a rare while will you read about someone who jumps into icy water to save a drowning person. Newspapers write mostly about crime."

"You're right, Josie," Harry agreed. "Newspapers need to write more about heroes and less about criminals, so we can praise and reward bravery as much as we expose and punish corruption. Also, newspapers shouldn't suppress honest dissent by inappropriately taking sides on issues, or prejudicing readers by making dissenters look like criminals. Newspapers should strive to honestly present both sides of an argument. They should display respect for dissenters, they shouldn't be propaganda machines for a particular viewpoint."

As Brown made his last point, he looked at Novikov, who immediately responded: "Aha, Harry, that's all well and good, but your U. S. newspapers, magazines, radio, and television would never bite the hands that feed them, the advertisers. Have you ever heard criticism of an advertiser?"

47

"Just like your Soviet reporters wouldn't criticize your elite and all-powerful Communist Party," Harry retorted. "Rather, your newspapers and other media, which are controlled by the Communist Party, seek to propagandize for the Party's viewpoint, even to the extent of rationalizing such irrational positions as your country's presence in Afghanistan."

"Truce!" declared Maxie. "Thank goodness we all agree heroes should get more press coverage! Heroes *need* the press. David's encounter with Goliath is known to us because a reporter wrote about it. Hercules, Achilles, and Ulysses are all famous because Homer or someone else *wrote* about them. Or how about King Arthur, Robin Hood, even the Lone Ranger and Tonto? Without writers, reporters, and storytellers, such heroes wouldn't exist for us at all."

"Too many of today's so-called heroes," Josie added with a frown, "are manufactured by the communications media. Rarely are they truly heroes. They're usually some publicity agent's dream. Whoever controls our communications media determines our heroes, or, more likely, our lack of heroes."

Maxie picked up again, "It's true, the news media today tell us more about the dirty side of life than the good. Bad news about murderers, kidnappers, hijackers, and terrorists fills newspaper front pages and prime time newscasts the world over; rarely does good news about our heroes ever get there. Maybe we have no heroes and there's mostly bad news today, because news people play up non-heroes and bad news so much. Also, since such non-heroes as criminals, terrorists, and skyjackers seem to be getting most of the publicity, news people may be guilty of breeding more of them."

"Whoa, Maxie!" said Jamie Baston, who, after their several dances together, was invited by Maxie to take a nearby seat. "In other words," Baston argued, "are you

48

saying we don't have any real heroes today, because news people prefer not to tell us about them? Therefore, without any real heroes, we're headed for disaster and most news people are the crooks who're paid to take us there?"

"No, Jamie, I'm not saying that," Maxie protested. "Those who control news want sensation in the form of rape, robbery, and rebellion, the three R's of today's news people. That's not to say all news people are bad. Of course, there are good ones, as I'm sure you are, Jamie. The question is, how are we going to change the three R's? Maybe the Soviets have a good idea: they award hero medals to super-achievers in their society, even though those super-achievers often serve some useful propaganda purpose more than they're heroes in the true sense."

"Now, my dear comrades, listen to me a moment," Nikolai cut in. "I have a few words to tell you about our Soviet heroes. We don't have false heroes in the USSR, nor do we dwell on crime in our newspapers. Our Soviet news people don't worship rape, robbery, or other dirt. We praise productivity. Our heroes exceed production goals to advance the common good of our people. We also praise revolutionaries everywhere who rise up against the exploiters of the working masses.

"Friends, I submit to you that the lack of heroes in America is because America forgot its real heroes. I mean those heroes who freed you from an imperial, colonial, and exploitive monarchy. Your real heroes are your revolutionaries of 1776. We haven't forgotten such heroes in our country. Maybe you have.

"Who are these heroes today? Consider Fidel Castro and his comrades, who threw off the yoke of a corrupt regime in Cuba to establish a people's republic there. Consider Ho Chi Minh, who gave his life to his people, that his people could have a better life, free from the yoke of colonial imperialism and exploitation. Consider..."

"Nikky!" Brown cut in. "We haven't forgotten our own nation's heroes. We even have national holidays to honor a few of them, including our war veterans who risked their lives for their country. Among our heroes today, as yesterday, I also include our free citizens who labor to advance the common good and protect our hard won freedoms from tyranny.

"True, we need to change the negative emphasis of some of our news media. We need to concentrate more on publishing stories about our heroes, rather than dwell on the Dillingers and Al Capones among us. We realize we have a problem, and we're seeking a remedy. It's not just a problem with us, however. It's universal. The whole world needs to focus on its true heroes.

"Nikky, you say you have no false heroes in the Soviet Union. Isn't it just a little bit possible you have a few contrived heroes, such as publicized workers whose achievement of work goals is arranged in an effort to prod your people into greater production? Whether yours or ours, I think heroes in both our societies are too often created to serve some useful propaganda purpose, or promote some special cause.

"You and I, Nikolai, your country and mine, can be friends. We can like each other, because we may be more alike than we dare think or admit. Wouldn't you agree?"

"Harry, we're old friends," Novikov reminded him. "Let's live together in peace and friendship. Although you and I, and all of us here tonight, can talk on and on about heroes, of one point we can be certain. Even though we can learn to agree with each other, your heroes won't always be ours, and our heroes won't always be yours. The real heroes in both our countries may well be our citizens. Why? Because they have to put up with corrupt parasites, grafters, and opportunists.

I mean those criminals and enemies of the people who put their personal and special interests above the common good of the workers. They're our real enemies. The question is, how do we get rid of them? Maybe when we learn more about ourselves, we can help each other solve that problem, since it's a problem of the common good."

Everyone voiced their approval of Nikolai's conclusion, then Harry stood up and spoke. "Nikolai, Helga, Naddy, the rest of us are indebted to you for the excellent dinner and evening. Also, Bert, Maxie, and I look forward to our meeting tomorrow morning at 10:00 in the Commander's Room at the Taylorsville VFW building down the street. We decided we'd get you out of the hotel, so you can see some more of our town. Maxie will meet you at 9:30 to escort you, and Bert and I will be waiting at the VFW. We'll buy your breakfast and lunch, too.

"We're each thankful for this memorable evening and dinner. You and your associates are gracious hosts. Are you sure I can't share the expense? Taylorsville is my town, you know."

"No, Harry," Nikolai replied. "You, Josie, Maxie, and Bert are my guests. I invited you and you're most welcome. We'll meet tomorrow as arranged. Good night to each of you, and let's plan to deal tomorrow at $3.45 per bushel!"

Novikov smiled and politely bowed to his guests, who then laughingly said their goodbyes and dispersed. Harry and Josie went home to bed, Harry determined to deal at $3.51.

51

4

WHEAT SALE NEGOTIATIONS

Harry Brown arranged a few flipcharts on a stand in the Commander's Room at the Colonel Taylor VFW Post. Nearby were two large bouquets of freshly cut, red and white carnations. They were displayed attractively in blue ceramic vases on tall pedestals, and the pedestals stood at each side of the front of the room, where a large speaker's stand had been placed in the opening of a U-shaped table arrangement. Slightly to the rear of the speaker's stand, and off to each side next to the flowers, were flags of the USA, USSR, Minnesota, and the VFW, mounted on poles anchored in heavy cast iron bases. Bert Jackson had the Soviet flag flown in from an embassy in Chicago the night before.

In the back of the room near the entrance, there was a long table covered with a white linen tablecloth. On the table was a continental breakfast assortment of Danish pastries, fresh fruit juices, several insulated pitchers of regular and decaffeinated coffee, cups, saucers, silverware, napkins, and other service items. A matronly waitress was standing next to the table, finishing her attractive arrangement of food items. She was wearing a black uniform with snow white trim and white apron, and on her head was a white, crown-shaped headpiece.

The U-shaped table arrangement in the room's center consisted of heavy, varnished oak tables placed end to end, three per side. There were two padded chairs behind each table, for a total of six chairs, all of which were facing the empty center area and speaker's stand. On the table in front of each chair was a place setting, consisting of a glass of ice water, writing tablet, pen, silverware, neatly folded white linen napkin, and small name card of white posterboard. The name cards were shaped like an inverted "V," and measured about 3 x 10 inches. The center-facing panel of each name card displayed, in sharp black lettering, the name of one of the six meeting participants.

"Bert, you and Maxie set everything up just fine," Harry complimented as Bert walked in.

"They're here," Bert said. "Maxie is bringing them into the building now."

"That's great!" Harry acknowledged, glancing up at the large electric clock on the back wall of the room. "It's almost 10:00. Our goal is to successfully conclude a wheat sale by noon today, then celebrate the deal at lunch."

While Harry made a final check of preparations, Maxie ushered in Novikov and the others. "Good morning, Nikolai!" Harry exclaimed.

"Good morning, Harry!" Nikolai replied, smiling. "Are you ready for $3.45 a bushel?"

Harry laughingly remarked, "We'll see! We already sharpened our pencils to get $3.51." Then, turning to the others, he greeted them and invited them to help themselves to the coffee and Danish. He also asked them to bring their plates to their assigned places at the conference table, so the meeting could get started while they were eating.

When Harry concluded, the guests approached the breakfast table at the back of the room. As they lined up for the buffet, they began talking with one another. Bert and Naddy said little at first. They simply gazed longingly into each other's eyes. Bert's voice was lower and somewhat hushed when he at last greeted Naddy. He told her how happy he was to see her and how splendid she looked.

Naddy was every bit as attractive in the daylight as Bert had remembered her from the previous night. Today she wore a plain, dark gray suit, which was quite appropriate for their business meeting. Nevertheless, on Naddy, it seemed as stunning to Bert as the red velvet suit she had worn the night before. Perhaps Bert was dazzled by the blazing morning sunlight which was flooding the room and illuminating Naddy with a kind of incandescent glow. Or, maybe Bert was still fascinated by the contrast of Naddy's dark hair, dark eyes, and light complexion. Whatever the reason for his infatuation, Bert had to struggle to keep his mind on the meeting. He could scarcely take his eyes off Naddy. He knew he'd been deeply affected by her. The mere sight of her created a powerful magnetic force within him that seemed to draw him towards her, forcing him to mentally struggle with himself to keep his mind on the day's important business.

Naddy, likewise, spoke in low tones to Bert. She was genuinely afraid of paying abnormal attention to him, though she felt even more attracted to him when she saw the sunlight shining on his crown of golden hair. "What a remarkable man!" she thought to herself. "I hope he remembers our afternoon meeting in the park."

When everybody was seated at the conference table and enjoying breakfast, Harry Brown, who'd already eaten earlier at home, rose to speak. Positioning himself behind the speaker's stand, he said, "Let's begin! To save time, you can finish your breakfast while I discuss the agenda I've prepared. First, on behalf of the mayor and everyone else in town, I extend an official welcome to each of you. Our meeting purpose this morning is to negotiate a wheat sale contract. You want to buy wheat;

we have wheat to sell, so let's get it done; the quicker, the better. As I see it, our meeting can be logically divided into several segments."

At this point, Harry picked up a long wooden pointer and referred to his flipchart. "First, Nikolai, we need to have some input from you as to what you're planning to buy and in what volumes." Referring to the chart again, Brown continued, "We also need to know from you, Nikolai, what delivery dates you require, your mode of shipping, and whatever method of payment you propose. As soon as you give us these particulars, we'll be able to estimate a firm, bottom-line price, and draw up a mutually beneficial contract. The rest of our meeting will be based on your initial inputs.

Harry proceeded to outline five segments of his meeting plan:

1. Details of Buy - N. Novikov.
2. Selling Price Determination - M. Gadsden.
3. Contract Terms - H. Brown
4. Shipment Movements - B. Jackson
5. Agreement Signing - Everybody

He then turned the meeting over to Nikolai, who approved the meeting plan and promised to be brief.

"As I told you all yesterday," Nikolai recollected, "we're here to buy wheat from you, the 14% protein, Hard Red Spring variety. On later trips, assuming you give us the best price and all goes well, we'll be buying corn, soybeans, and other commodities, also. As for volume, we're prepared to buy 1,500,000 tons of 14% HRS today, maybe more later. That's 55,050,000 bushels."

At this announcement, Harry, Bert, and Maxie went into momentary shock. Nikolai noticed their surprised reaction and remarked, "Is something wrong? Is our quantity too low?"

"No! No!" Harry nervously assured. "It's just that

we already calculated our $3.51 bushel price on a different quantity basis. We'll simply have to recalculate, that's all. I'm sorry, Nikolai, I didn't mean to interrupt you. Continue!"

"Think in terms of $3.45, Harry. Now, then, your delivery dates should start three weeks from today when our first ocean bulk freighter, the Krasnodar, will be able to reach your Great Lakes inland seaport at Duluth. At this moment, the Krasnodar is approaching from across the North Atlantic. With a mere radio message, I can have it heading for the St. Lawrence Seaway and your Duluth harbor whenever we reach an agreement. We'll soon have 50 large freighters like the Krasnodar on their way to you. Most of them will be from our Port of Odessa on the Black Sea. These giant vessels will handle your shipments at semiweekly intervals, so you can ship us all 1,500,000 tons of our wheat purchase in less than six and a half months.

"As for payment, we'll pay you cash based on our agreed bushel price. Payment will be made to you within 30 days of each freighter loading date. In other words, we'll pay you cash each time you get one of our ships loaded, and we'll pay you within 30 days, as soon as proper verification documents and executed export manifests are received by us from our appointed vessel agent in Duluth.

"The only other matter is price. As I told you last night, my government authorized me to pay you a generous $3.45 per bushel. Your $3.51 is a penny more than the maximum $3.50 price I'm allowed to pay, but I need to buy at the $3.45 price because of added shipping expenses our ships must pay for St. Lawrence Seaway tolls, and because I must show my supervisor what a good negotiator and friend of the people I am. You can appreciate all this, can't you? Think of it: 1-1/2 million tons of wheat! This is your big chance, Harry. I sincerely want you and your partners to get the sale, because you're my good friends."

Harry expressed his appreciation to Nikolai for the wheat sale opportunity, but sidestepped any discussion of price at that moment. Rather, using the pointer to refer to his flipchart, Harry introduced the next subject on the meeting agenda, Selling Price Determination, which was presented by Maxie.

Maxie walked over to the flipchart, picked up the pointer, and flipped over Harry's agenda sheet. Looking back at the others, she said she'd show how their firm calculated the $3.51 bushel price, and why it was needed.

Referring to the new sheet on the flipchart, she pointed to the top line, which showed last year's $3.98, high end bushel price for 14% protein HRS. Below it, she pointed to last winter's $3.28 bushel low. Finally, she identified $3.58 as the present bushel market price, which was listed third on the chart. The $3.58 current price also happened to be close to last year's $3.55 price average, which Maxie defined as the average a person would pay if he or she kept buying 14% HRS all year long. However, since the Soviets wanted to buy wheat that day, they'd have to pay that day's market price of $3.58 per bushel. Maxie explained that if the Soviets went down to the grain exchange in Minneapolis to buy wheat, $3.58 is the price they'd most likely be quoted that day.

"Fortunately for you, you came to us!" Maxie exclaimed. "We're able to give you the lowest price of all for the best quality wheat in the world. Here's why: our overhead is rock bottom. We don't own any expensive, high rise, multi-office complexes. We don't own a skyscraper full of costly computers, either, nor do we employ an army of overpaid paper shufflers, like the major grain merchants do. Also, we don't charge you for maintaining fleets of hopper cars, company-owned railroads, or oceangoing freighters, because we don't own any. What we do is simply give you the best quality wheat at the least possible cost. Also, with no internal bureaucracies to wade through, we give you the fastest delivery."

Maxie continued her discussion of selling price by reviewing the mechanics of Brown's Goldstrike formula. Calculating the spread from a $3.28 bushel price low to a $3.98 high, which is 70 cents, Maxie divided by the Goldstrike factor of 3, added the 23 and 1/3 cents result to the $3.28 low, and got $3.51 and 1/3 cents per bushel. Dropping the 1/3 cents as a further concession to the Soviets, she declared $3.51 per bushel to be the Goldstrike price.

"Since our competitors like Julius Fiske will offer you wheat at or near the current market price of $3.58 per bushel," Maxie disclosed, "our $3.51 Goldstrike price saves you over six cents on each bushel you buy from us. On your initial quantity of 55,050,000 bushels, for example, that means a savings to you of $3,303,000. If we saved you seven cents a bushel, your total savings would approach $4,000,000. Any questions?"

Helga had one. She noted that Maxie's revelations were impressive, but she wondered how it was possible anyone could sell any wheat that way. "What magic has you buy for more, then sell for less and still stay in business?"

"Aha, Helga, you asked a key question," Maxie acknowleged with a big smile. "The answer is a closely guarded company secret. We don't like publicizing it, because it might become a source of irritation to those who don't fully understand the delicate nature of grain sales. Since we're here in this room, however, meeting privately, I can speak freely. The reason for our ability to sell wheat at a lower price is government subsidies. As you probably know, U. S. government subsidies enable us to buy from farmers at better than low-ball prices.

"Actually, as long as we pay farmers an acceptably higher price than the U. S. Department of Agriculture's loan guarantee of $3.30 per bushel, we'll make money. For example, if we buy from the farmer at $3.55 per bushel, then sell to you at $3.51, or four cents less than we pay the farmer, we're still able to make money, because of the government subsidies we get. In reality, U. S. taxpayers pay us to sell you wheat. The reason for this seemingly crazy circumstance is that various costs to the government of acquiring and storing national grain surpluses amounts to many billions of dollars. Therefore, it's cheaper for the U. S. to subsidize and sell, than to acquire and hold, and have to pay enormous storage charges."

Maxie went into greater detail, describing what happens when the U. S. acquires grain for storage purposes. For example, it has to pay transportation expenses to ship the grain to storage depots. Then it has expenses for storage building construction, operation, and maintenance; plus, it has to compensate an army of bureaucrats to administer the whole program.

"Oh! I almost forgot to tell you," Maxie elaborated, "there are so-called 'dockage' expenses, too, for lost grain, spoiled grain, stolen grain, and so on. Once you understand the horrendous costs of grain storage, U. S. subsidies for foreign grain sales are understandable. Any other questions?"

Maxie paused for a moment, but heard none. The group was apparently satisfied with her explanations, so she turned the meeting back to Harry, and, before sitting down, flipped the charts back to Harry's meeting agenda chart.

Picking up the pointer, Harry thanked Maxie for the good job she did. Referring again to his meeting agenda chart, he identified the next topic as Contract Terms. While Bert distributed copies of the proposed wheat sale contract, Harry urged everyone to look it over carefully, commenting they'd probably seen most of the terms and conditions before, because they were fairly standard. He indicated they were already operating under several identical contracts, including one with Poland, which the Soviets were, no doubt, aware of, having some considerable dealings with that country themselves. So, other than a couple questions about contract terms, Harry felt the group ought to be able to move quickly to the last two segments of the meeting, Shipment Movements and Agreement Signing. He pointed out that the blank space on the proposed contract was for writing in a bushel price whenever they reached a price agreement.

"Shall we reach that agreement right now?" Harry asked. "If you prefer, Nikolai, we can take a short break, and Bert, Maxie, and I can leave the room, so you can confer with your associates."

Nikolai said he appreciated Harry's suggestion, but wouldn't need to confer with anyone at that point. He felt it would be better to complete the presentations on Contract Terms and Shipment Movements. They could then break afterwards and discuss a specific price. Harry agreed to that arrangement and asked if anyone had any further questions regarding contract terms and conditions.

"Mr. Brown!" Naddy exclaimed. "I don't understand the part of your agreement requiring various pilots on our freighters. We would object to your military people coming on board our ships."

Brown replied that he'd also object to military people coming on board the Soviet ships, but assured everyone it would be highly unlikely. He said Bert would make the pilot requirement clearer to her in his discussion of shipment movements along the St. Lawrence Seaway. However, he emphasized that the pilots referred to in the proposed agreement were nonmilitary specialists who were trained and experienced in navigating the hazardous canals, locks, and stretches of sea-lanes assigned to them. Soviet helmsmen would not be at all familiar with those dangerous areas. They'd have great difficulty navigating them, and are accustomed to having special pilots aboard for that purpose.

"St. Lawrence Seaway pilots are a necessary requirement for all seaway shipping," Harry affirmed. "You'll find them to be unusual individuals who have studied, passed tests, acquired experience, and become licensed and certified. Your own country must also require such pilots to guide ships through the hazardous sectors of your own harbors and waterways. I'm sure Bert's presentation will help you understand this point better, Nadezhda. Any other questions or comments?"

"Harry, you say 'shipment payments are due at loading.' I mentioned our payment terms earlier in this meeting," Novikov commented. "We pay within 30 days of ship's loading, and after receiving appropriate export manifests and other documentation."

Harry conceded Nikolai was correct and instructed him to simply cross out the words, "at loading," and write the words, "within 30 days of loading" in the blank margin space. "We'll make sure each agreement copy contains that wording before we sign it," Harry promised. "Also, we can both inital each change. Please keep in mind that when we prepared this sample agreement, we didn't know what your terms were going to be. Are there any other concerns?"

"I don't have any objections to the usual terms and conditions, Harry," Nikolai commented, "but what is this Reconciliation Clause? You talk of using Reconciliation in the event of any disputes. I don't know what you mean by Reconciliation, but are you suggesting we're going to have difficulties?"

Harry didn't expect any difficulties whatsoever. However, he explained that political relations between their countries being what they were, it was desirable to have some provision for the peaceful settlement of disputes. He argued it was not at all unusual for a contract to talk about solving problems, resolving discrepancies, or eliminating conflicts. He admitted he wasn't an attorney, but he remarked that most contracts he'd seen had some kind of clause on that subject. For example, Brown mentioned that some contracts required certified mail notification between contracting persons, whenever problems needed solving. This gives each person a chance to correct a potential conflict situation before someone starts a lawsuit over it, or takes other drastic action.

"Many business contracts now specify arbitration as an alternative to expensive and frustrating lawsuits." Brown observed. "However, I can tell you from personal experience that lawsuits and arbitration, are generally both bad. They're bad because they're adversarial. Rather than make friends out of enemies, they either make enemies out of friends or intensify hostilities between those who already hate each other. Lawsuits and arbitration are also bad because they're too costly, creating economic hardships that result in financial ruin for hardpressed individuals and families. Another reason lawsuits are bad is because they're not geared to solving people's problems or promoting their friendly relationship. Unfortunately, courtroom litigation and adversarial arbitration proceedings too often create more destructive difficulties than those they pretend to eliminate.

"Most existing legal systems in the world today produce either winners or losers. Highly paid lawyers fight viciously for a winner-take-all result, usually without regard to equity, honesty, truth, justice or ethics. With such an adversarial approach to settling disputes, there are usually only losers, and few, if any, winners among opposing parties. Lawyers and judges are the real winners, because win or lose, they usually get paid.

"The Reconciliation Clause I'm proposing will (1) make sure we shut out lawyers and judges if we ever have a problem or dispute between us; (2) eliminate the possibility of either of us becoming losers; and (3) make sure both of us are winners to preserve our good relationship. The last thing we want to do in a dispute is pay an army of expensive lawyers to go to some adversarial courtroom and fight a disastrous legal battle. If we let that happen, we'll both be in trouble.

"Look at it another way, Nikolai. The whole truth rarely gets told in a courtroom. When it does, it's usually an accident. Elaborate legal procedures force witnesses to tell only certain fragments of a story allowed by the tunnel–visioned lawyers and judges. Witnesses can tell only what lawyers want judges and juries to hear, nothing more. In such a system, truth is obscured and outcomes rarely reflect justice.

"Lawyers must win their cases. That's what they're being paid to do. Therefore, human as they are, they'll often twist reality, distort facts, take matters out of context, coach witnesses, and even falsify or otherwise abuse the truth. At the end of this outrageous process, guess who gets paid? Lawyers and judges, of course. They're the real winners.

"The losers are you and I, Nikolai, if we're the unfortunate one's to become locked in a legal battle. At the hands of unscrupulous, money-mad lawyers, plus misguided, unjust judges and misled juries, we'd both be doomed. What would happen is that like us, our two countries would become intolerably bitter towards one another. Social unrest and upheavals would intensify. Eventually, there'd be nuclear war and the death of the earth.

"It's the old story about the loss of a nail that caused the loss of a horseshoe. The lost horseshoe caused a horse to be lost, and the loss of a horse resulted in one less warrior on the battlefield, causing a battle to be lost, and resulting in the loss of the war. Sooner or later, with the presently primitive and adversarial mentality of our world's legal systems, we'll murder one another, eliminate all life, and destroy the entire earth. It doesn't take a great thinker to understand the simple truth that our existing legal processes are leading to the death of the earth. Don't you see, Nikolai, I don't want adversarial minded lawyers, judges, and arbitrators to ever come between you and me or any of us, or between your nation and my nation or any nation.

"Adversarial systems of dispute settlement are definitely not working. Courts and hearing rooms everywhere are keeping us on a personal-interpersonal, national-international, suicide brinkmanship. With 50,000 nuclear warhead missiles aimed at each other, it's a miracle we haven't already annihilated ourselves. You can readily understand, therefore, why there's considerable urgency to get a practical Reconciliation process going. It can be accomplished by means of a simple Reconciliation Clause inserted in every agreement. Inserting such a clause in our wheat sale agreement is merely the beginning of our cooperation. The more we urge others to use such a clause, too, the safer our world will become."

"You're right, Harry," Nikolai agreed. "You've done us a good service to put a Reconciliation Clause into our agreement. I know the word, 'reconciliation,' means 'to make friendly again,' and that's a good idea in today's world. I know only too well how futile and frustrating legal systems can be, especially the USA's. That's why I was thinking of inserting some kind of dispute settlement clause, if you didn't.

"It's a shameful fact that the USA has most of the world's lawyers, but only 5% of the population. The U. S. doesn't train its citizens in scientific problem solving or friendly settlement of disputes. Instead, it keeps graduating more and more lawyers who only know how to sue. The more lawyers there are each year, the more lawsuits are filed. The entire USA seems afflicted with sue-mania.

"Did you know that in Washington, D. C. alone, there's one lawyer for every 23 men, women, and children? Did you also know that over half of the members of the U. S. Senate and House of Representatives are lawyers? I don't think your nation's founding fathers ever intended there to be such an unrepresentative, undemocratic government. No wonder your own people are so frustrated. Your legalistic government is bleeding them to death with taxes to feed an evergrowing system of adversarial courts, lawyers, and lawsuits. Your multi-billion dollar congress alone passes over 400 lengthy new laws every year, and more lawyers and more courts have to be paid to interpret them, because so many are so vague. Poor old Moses would die of shock to see what the USA has done to the Ten Commandments. No wonder my nation can't seem to get along with yours.

"Harry, the USSR isn't the only nation frustrated with the U. S. legal system. Others are fed up, too. For example, I remember when Nicaragua complained to the World Court that the U. S. mined its harbors. Incredibly, your government reacted by sending a delegation of eighteen lawyers. This army of lawyers used manipulative legalisms to evade World Court jurisdiction. Yet, your government, some thirty years earlier on August 2, 1946, entered an agreement to abide by the World Court in such matters. How can we ever expect to achieve world peace when the USA uses armies of lawyers to intimidate the rest of the world? Such dealings are adversarial and unscientific. They fail to solve any problems. Rather, they create even more problems."

"Now hold on, Nikolai!" Harry protested. "You're in trouble on that one. Truth is, at the outset of Nicaragua's revolution, the U. S. gave more economic aid to the Sandinista Government than anyone. What was the result? The Sandinista betrayed the U. S. and the entire world by pouring military shipments into peaceful El Salvador, then training rebels and terrorists to destroy the peace. You talk about us, Nikolai, but don't tell the whole story."

Calming himself down somewhat, Harry raised his eyebrows at Nikolai and asked, "Need I remind you that your USSR makes a national prison out of every nation it controls? Also, you talk about U. S. manipulation of the World Court as though your USSR had never done it. Yet, in 1959, when one of your military aircraft shot down one of our B29's over Japan, we went to the World Court for help and your government denied the jurisdiction of that court, even though your USSR signed the same August 2, 1946, agreement we did, which was to abide by the World Court in such matters."

"Slow down, Harry!" Novikov retorted. "You twist reality and smokescreen the truth. You ignore the USA's bad record. Mining Nicaragua's harbors was against World Law and violated your nation's pledge to support the U. N. Charter. You slander the Sandinistas of Nicaragua with a tale about El Salvador, but keep silent about your nation's own acts of war against the Sandinistas. I'm talking about the enormous interventions in nearby Honduras, where your U. S. military built roads and military airfields, then poured in war weapons and sent military advisors to teach Contras how to kill Sandinistas. Why does your peace-talking country continue to commit such international crimes in violation of peace? Also, lest we fail to mention a few other instances, how can you explain away your CIA's 1961 Bay of Pigs intervention in Cuba? And what about your President Reagan's violation of the sovereignty of Granada with his invasion there, or your nation's foolish meddling in Lebanon?

"Don't forget your U. S. Government's biggest

disaster of all, Harry, its massive invasion of Vietnam, where it spent billions of dollars, waged its longest war in history, and sacrificed the lives of 50,000 soldiers, so it could murder hundreds of thousands of Vietnamese. Your U. S. Government is a colossal warmonger, Harry. It continues to violate the United Nations Charter and defy the World Court by making bombing raids on such small countries as Libya, killing innocent men and women, even infants. Your government is corrupt."

"Nikolai," Harry angrily responded, "you keep jumping to hasty conclusions about history, and seem to enjoy your distortions about the USA. You know the U. S. was in Vietnam honoring a defense treaty. The U. S. fought there to save peace-loving South Vietnamese citizens from the treacheries of your nation's warmongering North Vietnamese allies. Just as your USSR's Communist puppet regime of North Korea violated the sovereignty of peaceful South Korea in 1950 by warring on it, so did your nation's puppet North Vietnam violate South Vietnam by starting a war there. The United Nations forces held their ground in Korea, but, without U. N. support in Vietnam, we, unfortunately, had to pull out. As soon as we left, all Vietnam became a vast national prison, and the Communist Government began waging war on Laos, Cambodia, and Thailand. Communist Vietnam has emerged as a major imperialist and warmongering power in Southeast Asia.

"And don't ignore the enormous stockpile of Soviet-made weapons and ammunition discovered by our army in Granada. Also, don't ignore the Cuban Communist military prisoners captured there, who were violating Granada's sovereignty and using it as a base for revolutionary warfare and terrorism elsewhere. Fortunately, the U. S. saved many thousands of lives by preventing your nation's Cuban Communist puppets from using Granada to war on numerous other South American countries.

"Our raids on Libya were self-defensive, intended to counteract a rash of terrorist acts that were killing many innocent victims and destroying much property. Certainly you must know these facts, Nikolai, but let's put them aside a moment, so I can ask you a fundamental question.

"How can you have the boldness to distort the USA's role in Korea, Vietnam, Granada, or anywhere else, when your Soviet armies made a protracted battleground of Afghanistan? I'm shocked and saddened to recall the USSR's mass murder of men, women, and children, and its monstrous destroying of villages, crops, hospitals, everything. Your nation even used chemical warfare against the Afghans. What kind of...."

"Stop it!" screamed Maxie, suddenly jumping up and throwing her hands outward. "You're both caught in the time-worn trap men have been using on each other since the dawn of history. If you keep at it, you'll end up destroying each other and any friendships we're trying to develop. Don't you know what you're doing? Trouble is, you men keep ignoring us women and continue to make a shambles of our world. Down through the ages, always, you primitive men keep fighting each other, and it's always the women and children who suffer.

"Helga! Nadezhda! Help me! We can't let them do it. We must stop this stupidity, this foolish bickering about who has the worst government. It's not productive. It's not constructive. Can't you see where it's leading? It's leading to mutual destruction.

"Harry! Go ahead and cut me out of our partnership, if I'm embarrassing you. In fact, I'll quit right now and walk right out the door, if it's come to that. Otherwise, why don't you and Nikolai just stop your verbal warfare, shake hands, and get on with the meeting. You're wasting everyone's time."

Helga stood up and earnestly supported Maxie. "Maxie's right! We women must speak up. We've kept silent too long. But please, we don't accuse you, Comrade Novikov, or you, Mr. Brown. We love you both. It's just that we women have something to say. You're both good men. You're both good friends, old friends. You didn't want to hurt one another ever. Yet you slipped into an argument. It grew worse. Now we women have to take action to stop it, or you'll destroy us all, and we don't want that to happen."

Naddy was next to join Maxie and Helga, saying, "We're such good friends after last night. Let's stay that way. We women stand together on this."

Bert, who'd been sitting quietly all this time and carefully avoiding any controversy, finally decided to speak. Walking over to the women and smiling at everyone, he said, "Friends, we've come to an important climax in our meeting. We've just proved to ourselves why a Reconciliation Clause in our contract is essential. There's no need to feel ashamed of what happened. We each learned a valuable lesson. Let's acknowledge the futility of disputes by agreeing to the Reconciliation Clause right now, and getting on with the rest of the meeting."

Harry and Nikolai were becoming increasingly embarrassed and ashamed of their rash behavior. Finally, they both got up and approached each other. Harry spoke first, saying, "I'm sorry, Nikolai. I apologize to you and everyone."

Then Nikolai hugged Harry and said, "Harry, I apologize to you and the others, too."

Repeating their apologies to the others, Harry and Nikolai hugged each of the girls. Bert lost no time hugging the girls, too, thanking them for being so courageous. He was especially happy to hug Naddy.

Finally, when everyone was seated again, Nikolai looked up and said, "Harry, I want to hear more about this Reconciliation concept of yours. What is it, how does it work?"

Harry remained sitting. Somewhat embarrassed, he replied. "Since my own big mouth destroyed any credibility I had on the subject of Reconciliation, I don't feel competent enough to talk about it. Instead, Bert or Maxie should explain it."

"No! No!" pleaded Nikolai. "Don't blame yourself, Harry. I'm to blame for offending you first with the remarks I made about your government. You simply defended against what I said and hit me back. I'm the one who provoked you, so I'm to blame."

"Forget any blame!" Maxie advised. "Don't be so hard on yourselves! You both reacted as people usually do. It takes two to tango, as the saying goes. Forget the past! Don't look back! We're all better now."

"You win!" Harry conceded. "I'll try not to make a mess of things again. Funny how sometimes we become our own worst enemies. Josie always warned me my big mouth would get me in trouble. It's finally dawning on me what she meant. You might even say my idea of Reconciliation is designed to protect me from my own big mouth." Harry began smiling and his face brightened as he contemplated developing that line of thought further.

"The Reconciliation process protects each of us from our own big mouths. Nikky, sometimes you have a big mouth. Perhaps Reconcilation can help you. Maxie, Helga, Naddy, Bert...sometimes each of you have big mouths, too, so Reconciliation can help all of you."

At this sudden change in Harry and the humorous thrust of his conversation, everyone began smiling again and relaxing. Meanwhile, Harry continued his explanation, defining Reconciliation as "a scientific, problem solving process of peacemaking, whereby individuals or groups cooperate amicably to reach a mutually satisfactory settlement of their disputes." For example, Harry pointed out that one such settlement of disputes might be an agreement to accept them. Another might be to eliminate disputes by finding a better way of doing something.

Harry emphasized that the words "mutually satisfactory" describe a basic requirement of Reconciliation, since any settlement must promote peace and friendship among those being reconciled. According to Harry, the specific steps or methods used in this process are extremely important and difficult to master. They require a knowledge of the scientific process of problem solving and skill in its disciplines, as well as a deep understanding and mastery of communications, negotiations, behavioral modification and other processes.

In describing Reconciliation, Harry presented what he regarded as three, key characteristics: (1) *cooperation;* (2) *mutual need satisfaction;* and (3) *scientific problem solving.* "First," he said, "it must be understood that Reconciliation is a *cooperative* process."

The underlying idea of Reconciliation implies *cooperation,* not competition. At no time must Reconciliation be allowed to become bitterly competitive, as in the present, adversarial, and intolerable systems of court litigation and arbitration. Specifically, the Reconciliation process must avoid such current abuses as enforcing inequitable, one-sided settlements; forcing participants to pay administrative costs of proceedings; extorting additional administrative assessments based on a percentage of claims; or employing untrained, poorly trained, or otherwise incompetent persons to administer the process.

A second characteristic of Reconciliation is that, in addition to being *cooperative* and noncompetitive, it's also *mutually need satisfying.* Unlike traditional, adversarial court processes, including arbitration, which

71

frequently enforce unfair judgments or unwanted compromises, the Reconciliation process aims at *mutual need satisfaction* and all participants winning; none losing.

That's not to say a particular Reconciliation settlement can't, in fact, be a compromise. If a particular compromise satisfies everybody's legitimate needs, and is mutually acceptable, it can readily serve as a Reconciliation settlement. Also, if individuals or groups being reconciled are unable to reach a mutually satisfying settlement within a specified time, it's appropriate for Reconciliation session facilitators to assist in such a settlement.

Harry spoke in terms of "individuals or groups being reconciled," rather than "opposing individuals " or "conflicting parties." The reason he gave is that word usage is important, since it's divisive to talk of "opposing" or "conflicting" sides in a process that's intended, above all, to be *cooperative*. It's never appropriate in a Reconciliation session to talk negatively or reinforce any idea of competition or contention. Labeling individuals as "opposing" one another or "conflicting" with one another implies they really are, when the truth might be they're trapped in a misunderstanding or have an inadequate view of the facts. The basic idea of Reconciliation is not to cast blame, but to emphasize *cooperation* and *mutual need satisfaction*.

Before discussing the third characteristic of Reconciliation, it's *scientific* approach to *problem solving*, Harry wanted to make sure the others realized why *mutual need satisfaction* was essential. Failure of a settlement to be mutually satisfactory suggests that it's one-sided. Such settlements are dangerous, and unacceptable. One-sided settlements lead to trouble. They waste time and effort. They tend to multiply problems. For example, what kind of settlement would it be if one person were allowed to own a car or plane, but couldn't get fuel for it? Not very practical. It's important, therefore, that Reconciliation settlements satisfy the indispensable needs of those being reconciled. Unfortunately, *mutual need satisfaction* is difficult to achieve, which is why the third characteristic of Reconciliation, it's *scientific* approach to *problem solving*, is required.

Before a mutually satisfying dispute settlement can be achieved, individuals must employ all the skills of good listening, thinking, investigating, discussing, and systematic problem solving. Systematic problem solving should be a scientific effort, requiring Reconciliation participants to first locate and define the specific problem they're trying to solve.

"Sounds too basic, perhaps," Harry remarked, "but I'm reminded of a story about a professor who wrote '2 and 2' on the blackboard, then, pointing to it, said to his class, 'What's that?' One student said, '4.' Another said, '5.' A third said, '1.' After many such attempts, the professor said, 'How can you possibly give a solution when you haven't even defined the problem?'

"We too often behave like the professor's students by offering solutions without first locating and defining the problem we're trying to solve. That's unscientific and wasteful of money, energy, and time. What we should do instead is first identify the precise problem in a crisis situation, before we attempt any solutions. One way we can do this is by asking questions, such as, 'We didn't always have this crisis; therefore, what was done or is being done that's different?' We must look at the various differences and seek to understand them.

"After we've fully analyzed the individual differences that created a problem, we'll be better prepared to define it. Such effort requires us to study the problem, break it up into its component parts, analyze it, reconstruct it, and comprehend it in every possible way.

73

Afterwards, we can consider all the possible solutions, evaluate them, choose the best, test it, evaluate our test, and keep the process going until we reach some kind of mutually satisfying settlement. It could take many years, but if we keep working at it, maybe we'll avoid killing each other.

"On the other hand, many historic settlements were achieved quickly. For example, at the invitation of former U. S. President Jimmy Carter, Anwar Sadat of Egypt met with Menahem Begin of Israel, and, in less than a day, reached the historic Camp David Accords. This proves quick settlements are possible.

"Finally, a *scientific* approach to *problem solving* implies skillful questioning. Individuals in a Reconciliation session should ask open-ended questions of each other and of experts to discover unknown needs and wants, correct facts and circumstances, and appropriate settlement goals and requirements. No attempt should be made to force anyone to do anything."

"Thank you, Harry," Nikolai acknowledged. "Your concept is impressive, but how do we get it done? Who will there be to do it?"

Harry responded by explaining that the entire process would be guided by trained Reconciliation facilitators. These facilitators would act as catalysts in enabling participating individuals or groups to create their own settlements. Such facilitators should be the best trained, most respected, honored, cooperative, and scientific problem solvers the world can offer. Their ranks might include Nobel Peace Prize winners and other distinguished problem solvers, including women as well as men, and all races and all creeds.

"Facilitators shouldn't be salaried for their services," Harry continued. "Rather, they should be reimbursed for necessary travel and other expenses, including any reasonable loss of income while serving in a session. Also, no facilitator should serve unless approved by the individuals or groups to be reconciled. Emphasis in a Reconciliation session is on individuals cooperating to create their own settlements, rather than on outsiders like a judge, arbitrator, referee, or umpire enforcing acceptance of unwanted settlements.

"In some particularly difficult situations, of course, facilitators who assist in a Reconciliation session may help create a settlement that eventually gets accepted. *Acceptance* of a settlement by those being reconciled, however, is the test of whether a Reconciliation session has been successful. Failure of those being reconciled to freely and voluntarily accept a proposed settlement means there's really no settlement at all. Therefore, the Reconciliation process must continue until there is one.

"But I'm afraid we're getting too far afield here. It's the school teacher in me," Harry confided. "We need to conclude this sketchy, impromptu presentation by a quick review of the basic points. Just keep in mind that *Reconciliation is a scientific, problem-solving process of peacemaking, whereby individuals or groups cooperate amicably to achieve a mutually satisfactory settlement of their disputes.* Some key characteristics of Reconciliation are that it's a *cooperative, mutually need satisfying, and scientific system of problem solving.*

"In order for a settlement to be successful, it must be mutually satisfying. This requires that the settlement be freely and voluntarily accepted by those being reconciled. The world's existing adversarial legal systems are intensifying hostilities and animosities by fanning the fires of anger and hate, causing enemies to become even more alienated and aggressive towards one another. Adversarial systems waste time, money, and human lives. Worse yet, they're going to cause the death of the earth. There has to be a better way. I believe it's Reconciliation.

"Hope I've answered your questions, Nikolai, and that I've clarified the matter for the rest of you. And by the way, my criticism of the world's adversarial legal systems wasn't intended to reflect unfavorably on any particular individuals or legal practitioners. Rather, it's the systems that are bad and so desperately in need of change. It's the competitive, win or lose, conflict reinforcing, friendship destroying, adversarial legal systems that are dangerous to world peace.

"Please be assured, many judges and lawyers feel trapped and victimized by the present system. They're the first ones who will tell you that replacement with a better designed system is needed. In my opinion, the best system for peacemaking is Reconciliation, and we need that system right now, since worldwide nuclear annihilation is where our existing adversarial systems are speedily taking us. Reconciliation is nonadversarial. It's a peacemaking, problem solving, and scientific kind of dispute settlement system."

As Harry sat down, the group applauded and Nikolai began speaking. "Harry, I believe your Reconciliation concept has the core elements of greatness. I must confess I, too, was thinking of solving our future problems scientifically, but your idea seems much more developed. You're to be commended for your insights and your action to get the Reconciliation concept into our agreement. However, could you please tell us what you mean by your reference to a 'Reconciliation Alliance International?'"

Without getting up, Harry quickly responded. He envisioned "Reconciliation Alliance International" to be a group of representatives from the world's various Reconciliation organizations, which would be established in every nation. A representative elected by each national organization would be sent to Reconciliation Alliance International. Each representative would be elected on the basis of extraordinary wisdom, outstanding problem solving abilities, an openly cooperative nature, and other exceptional characteristics, including unusually good character, honesty, and reputation.

"As I see it," Harry suggested, "the specific charter objective of Reconciliation Alliance International is to assure the amicable, mutually satisfactory settlement of disputes among individuals, nations, or groups of nations, whenever local, regional, and world peace are endangered. National, regional, and local Reconciliation organizations would then have corresponding dispute settlement objectives in their respective charters. The idea is to promote peace and friendship worldwide."

"Excellent, Harry," Nikolai affirmed. "There are no longer any doubts in my mind that you truly have something worth putting into our agreement. It's much more thorough than what I'd have proposed. I freely admit your Reconciliation Alliance International mechanism goes beyond what I envisioned. However, it's a logical enlargement of my own version of a scientific approach to settling disputes, so I'm pleased to accept it."

"I like what you're both doing," Maxie volunteered. "Perhaps if this Reconciliation idea catches on elsewhere, we'll eventually achieve the climate we need for world peace and disarmament."

"That day can't come soon enough, Maxie," Bert added. "I remember 1979 was the year when worldwide spending on death-dealing weapons grew to more than a billion U. S. dollars per day. It's far beyond that now. At this late date, the creation of Reconciliation Alliance International may be the only real hope we have left."

"I agree with Bert," said Naddy. "We're running out of time on this planet. Either we work together now or we'll all die too soon."

Helga expressed her views, also. "Dear friends, let's work together for world friendship and cooperation."

"I'm overwhelmed," Harry gratefully acknowledged, as he rose to refer to his flipchart. "Your reactions are most reassuring and appreciated. Without any further need to discuss that subject at this time, we're now ready for the next item of our meeting agenda, Shipment Movements. Bert Jackson, I'm sure, is ready to present this briefing. Bert...."

Harry sat down, and Bert got up to begin his presentation. He complimented Harry for what he was trying to do, and indicated they all supported him 100%. Then, walking to the flipchart stand, Bert flipped over one of Maxie's charts to reveal a sketch. Using Brown's long wooden pointer, Bert referred to the chart, saying it was an overview of the St. Lawrence Seaway System, which is the international, transoceanic shipping access to the Great Lakes and inland seaport of Duluth, Minnesota.

"The Great Lakes border both Canada and the United States." Bert commented, "however, the entrance to the seaway is from the gulf of the St. Lawrence River in the Atlantic Ocean, which is entirely in Canada. The Soviet freighters, the first of which I think Mr. Novikov states is named the Krasnodar, will be entering the seaway at that point.

"Also, since the question of pilots was raised by Nadezhda," Bert smiled at her, "I can state right here your freighter captains are well familiar with the need for pilots in canals, seaways, and ports elsewhere in the world. To navigate the difficult St. Lawrence Seaway channels, your vessels need a certified pilot from one or more of various seaway pilotage authorities. It's a mandatory safety requirement to protect each of your ships throughout the 2,342-mile run from the Atlantic Ocean to Duluth. Certified pilot sources include the Laurentian Pilotage Authority in Montreal, Quebec, Canada; the Great Lakes Pilotage Staff in Cleveland, Ohio, USA; the Department of Transport, Nautical and Pilotage Division, Ottawa, Canada; and the Upper Great Lakes Pilot Association, Duluth, Minnesota, USA. Your freighter captains will be fully informed of these particulars, and every assistance will be provided them along the way by their vessel agent representatives."

Bert began tracing on the map the anticipated Soviet shipping movements. He explained that freighters first proceed inland a thousand miles from the Atlantic Ocean to reach Montreal, Canada, where the Seaway begins. The first pilot would come aboard at Escoumains, Canada, and guide the ships along the St. Lawrence River segment of the seaway to Quebec. At that point a second pilot would take over and guide the ships to Montreal. A third pilot would guide the ships from St. Lambert through the 190 miles of seven St. Lawrence Seaway System locks to Lake Ontario.

After a 160-mile Lake Ontario crossing, vessels arrive at the 28-mile Welland Canal System of eight locks connecting Lakes Ontario and Erie. There a fourth pilot would be required to help ships navigate the Welland system to Lake Erie. From there it's a 236-mile run across the lake. Then comes a 77-mile run along the Detroit River, across Lake St. Clair, and up the St. Clair River to Lake Huron. Finally, after a 233-mile run across Lake Huron to Sault Ste. Marie, there's a 70-mile passage through the Soo Locks before freighters reach Lake Superior for their final, 383-mile run to Duluth, Minnesota.

The total trip distance from the Atlantic Ocean to Duluth is 2,342 miles. By the time ships cross Lake Superior and reach Duluth, the series of sixteen locks they've navigated will have raised them 602 feet above the Atlantic Ocean. "That's the approximate height of a 60-story building," Bert remarked.

Referring to another flipchart, Bert showed a view representing the depths of the five Great Lakes and their various sea level elevations. "Notice how much deeper Lake Superior is than the other lakes, and how high above sea level it sits. The deepest point in Lake Superior is about 1,400 feet from the surface, and the surface is 602 feet above the Atlantic."

According to Bert's calculations, total trip distance for each ship, measuring from the Port of Odessa on the Black Sea to Duluth, Minnesota, is 6,834 miles. Traveling that distance takes nineteen days at average 15 knots. Higher vessel speed averages would shorten the trips.

Another matter Bert discussed concerned maximum ship dimensions allowable for navigating the seaway system. A ship's length must not exceed 730 feet. Width is restricted to 76 feet. Maximum draft or penetration below the water line is 26 feet; any lower it might scrape bottom in one or more shallow spots along the way. Also, numerous vehicle and railroad bridges cross the St. Lawrence Seaway. To keep a ship's foremast and aftermast from striking any overpasses, vertical height above the waterline cannot exceed 117 feet.

"These are important restrictions on the size of your freighters," Bert observed, "but I'm confident your Krasnodar will be well within the seaway's allowable dimensions."

Bert continued his briefing on shipping by noting some interesting history of the Seaway. The 190-mile St. Lawrence Seaway opened in 1959 and became one of the greatest engineering marvels in history, a greater engineering achievement than either the shorter Suez or Panama Canals. The project took five years; required the dredging of over 360 million tons of rock; arranged the resettlement of thousands of people, even entire towns; raised the Jacques Cartier Bridge at Montreal by 50 feet to provide a 120-foot ship clearance; and added numerous other bridges, as well as locks, dams, and the world's largest, bi-national, joint power facility. Also, the shortest stretch of channel, which is between the Lower and Upper Beauharnois locks, had to be blasted foot by foot and yard by yard out of hard Potsdam sandstone. It cost $50 million to channel this short, one mile length, but today, several times as much money would be needed to do the job.

Volume of shipping in the first 25 years of the seaway's operation exceeded one billion tons, hauled by 142,577 vessels. Of that tonnage, 39% was major grains, 28% iron ore, 7% manufactured iron and steel products, and 26% assorted cargoes.

With the opening of the St. Lawrence Seaway, over 40 deep draft seaports were created inland. These huge inland ports now serve the heartland of North America with world commerce. Ships of half a hundred nations use these inland ports each year. "It's reassuring," Bert added, "that Soviet ships are now among them, and we hope even more of your ships will be coming to Duluth."

Another information point Bert offered concerned the cost savings benefit to those who use the St. Lawrence Seaway for moving their cargoes. Energy savings, for example, are highly significant, since shipping can move a ton of freight over 500 miles on only one gallon of fuel. Railroads require twice as much. It made good sense, therefore, for the Soviets to buy wheat from H. B. Exports and move it out of Duluth along the St. Lawrence System. They get a better price, plus they keep their grain fresh via a fast ocean trip with no expensive load transfers.

The final topics Bert covered were movement of wheat from the interior and the loading of ships at Duluth. Wheat moves by rail from elevators located in various inland farming areas, such as the Red River Valley. Giant, sanitary hopper cars 40 feet long, carry 100 tons of wheat each. They keep wheat clean and fresh, because they have no doors and are sealed when loaded. Elevator chutes load hopper cars through top hatches, then, at Duluth, the cars are gravity emptied via the flow of wheat out of the car bottom into a pit at one of the dockside elevators.

"Right now, we have two fully stocked elevators in

Duluth ready to load your Krasnodar," Bert announced. "One has eight million bushels of 14% Protein, HRS wheat; the other, eleven million. Total bushel inventory is nineteen million, which is more than enough to load a dozen and a half Krasnodar-size vessels. We'll move the wheat from our elevators into the holds of your ship by high speed conveyor, and it'll take less than three days to do it. Also, at the same time we're loading your ship, more hopper cars will be arriving from inland and unloading, so we'll be prepared to load all your ships just as soon as they arrive. This will eliminate any lost time waiting at anchor. There's no other port in the world where your ships get such fast service. This is another way we save you money. We keep your ships moving.

"However, we won't be completely filling your freighters in Duluth," Bert noted. "We don't want them riding too low in the water where they could ram rocks or sustain other hull damage by scraping the bottom of shallow channels. Instead, we'll only fill them about four-fifths full. The load remainder we'll add later, after your freighters complete their return trip through the seaway and reach deeper water. We'll top off their loads at Port Sorel, where the Richelieu River flows into the St. Lawrence. We have an arrangement with an elevator there to provide you additional quantities of 14% HRS wheat for completely filling the holds of your ships. This will enable them to make complete use of their full capacity during their deep-water, transoceanic run to Odessa. Any questions?"

Bert waited a moment, but there were no questions, so he sat down and Harry got up to speak. "There's one more concern I should mention before we wrap up Bert's portion of the meeting," Harry began. "It's the matter of obtaining U. S. Government approval for the sale. Any grain purchase over 100,000 tons requires government approval. Our agreement must reflect that."

"No problem, Harry," Nikolai responded. "Since

my country and yours already transacted a long-term grain sale agreement, I took the initiative of obtaining a certificate of approval from your government two weeks ago. Ms. Konya brought an extra copy with her to this meeting. Naddy....."

"Here you are, Mr. Brown," Naddy replied, handing a copy of the government approval document to Harry.

"This sure is good news," Brown reacted, accepting the document. "It saves us valuable time. You and your associates are amazingly efficient, Nikolai. The only matter left now is our agreement on a bushel price.

"Since H. B. Exports has set its price at $3.51, and you've already offered us $3.45 against your maximum spending authorization of $3.50, we ought to be able to work something out. Our $3.51 price is only a penny more than your government spending authorization, and represents a total order savings of $3,303,000 off the current $3.58 bushel price. When you inform your people about that, they'll be impressed with your clever buying ability and the multi-millions of dollars you're saving off the much higher price the other merchants are demanding. Now that you have the advantage, Nikolai, let's deal at $3.51."

"Harry, you make good points, but you forget our added shipping costs. We'll have vessel agent fees, St. Lawrence Seaway joint tariff tolls, pilotage expenses, tugboat costs for docking, plus miscellaneous other expenses dealing with you out of Duluth, rather than with Julius Fiske on the Gulf Coast. St. Lawrence Seaway expenses alone will run us an additional $100,000 per ship, at least. I'm sure the actual figure will be more like $130,000 per ship. Multiply that by the fifty ships we need to haul your wheat, and our total additional expenses exceed $5 million. Harry, the absolute best I can do for you is $3.45, and even that price doesn't give me enough savings, due to the $5 million seaway expenses. I'll end up with a mere half million dollars savings on the $3.55

average bushel price, but I'll exceed my $3.50 government spending maximum by more than four cents per bushel. Do I have to go to New Orleans for a deal? You know I'll save a bundle down there, Harry."

"Nice try, Nikolai. But you know you won't get 14% protein HRS in New Orleans. We've got the good, hard, high protein, spoilage-resistant wheat right here, and you know it. Buy wheat on the Gulf and you'll get low protein, easy spoilage, soft stuff. Besides, if you tried buying our northern wheat out of New Orleans or Galveston, you'd pay added rail expense, plus you'd have vessel agent fees, tolls, and other expenses down there. There's no doubt you'd end up paying much more than up here.

"Tell you what, Nikolai, lets compromise. Because we're old friends, I'll deal with you at $3.48 and that's final, take it or leave it. It's a savings to you in excess of 5-1/2 million dollars on the current $3.58 price. Then, too, it's over $1,100,000 in savings on your government spending authorization. You'll be a new hero in the Soviet Union for saving so much. Take it while I'm still offering it, Nikolai, because there's no way I can go lower. It's either $3.48 or no deal."

"Write it up, Harry, if that's really the best you can do," Novikov graciously conceded, "but will you be happy with $3.48?"

"Nikky, since I'm dealing with you, I'm completely happy. Anyone else, I'd be redfaced. Just indicate your acceptance on this document, and we'll get your wheat moving fast." Brown wrote down the price on the agreement copies and handed them to Nikolai. After Nikolai signed them, Harry signed, too, and asked Naddy, Helga, Maxie, and Bert to sign as witnesses. "We're all in this together," Harry concluded.

After everyone had signed, Harry presented Nikolai with two copies, then gave Maxie the other two for H. B.

Exports, Inc. files. Turning back to Nikolai, he said, "Congratulations, you've got yourself some wheat!"

Harry and Nikolai shook hands, as Nikolai congratulated Harry and his partners for getting the biggest order of their career, an order worth two hundred million dollars. Harry agreed, and, grinning happily, said that in view of such a large order, he'd buy lunch. When everybody was through shaking hands and congratulating each other, Harry suggested some champagne to celebrate the occasion. Walking over to the door, he motioned the waitress to come in, then took a chilled bottle from a cooler on the cart she'd brought. Ceremoniously he opened it, poured the golden fluid into some fragile crystal glasses on the cart, and soon everyone was enjoying the bubbly drink and impromptu party.

When the waitress left the room shortly afterwards to get the luncheon cart, Brown refilled the small, delicate champagne glasses several times. Then Nikolai asked Helga to contact the Krasnodar as soon as possible after lunch, and confirm its Duluth destination. Also, he requested her to get Captain Grigor Rezhnikov's estimated Duluth arrival time, and suggested she phone it to Harry, so he'd know it too. Helga agreed to do it, and Nikolai thanked her.

Turning to the others, Nikolai said he had important scheduling matters to attend to early that afternoon, but that Helga and Naddy were to meet him back at the hotel at 4 p.m. and be ready to leave at that time. Their plane was scheduled to take off at 5:00.

"By the way," Harry remarked, as he filled Nikolai's glass a final time, "I plan on bringing my family to Duluth for a few days. I hear it's a wonderful place for vacationing. Also, I want to inspect the loading of your ship, the Krasnodar, and make sure everything is satisfactory. Any chance you, Helga, and Naddy could be our guests? Duluth is a pleasant, scenic place; quite friendly, too."

"Thank you for your invitation, Harry, but maybe another time. I've been on the road too long. Helga and I both have to get back to Moscow. Perhaps Nadezhda can meet you in Duluth and report back to me on the first loading. She can make sure everything runs smoothly. Is that agreeable to you, Nadezhda?"

"Of course, Comrade Nikolai," Naddy replied. "I'll be happy to go to Duluth for you." Then she stole a quick look at Bert Jackson, who caught her glance and smiled.

"Fine, then, that's settled," Novikov concluded.

"Lunch is ready!" Harry announced, as the waitress rolled in a buffet cart. "Let's get it while it's hot!"

5

LAST MINUTE ARRANGEMENTS

Harry Brown hollered enthusiastically out of his office door, "Come in here, Maxie, Bert, this is our lucky day!" As the two scurried in, Brown thanked them for their help with the Soviet wheat sale. He also told Maxie he was indebted to her for saving Nikolai and him from their battle of harsh words.

"I don't know why we ever stooped to arguing," Harry wondered aloud. "The whole world has this verbal sickness. Somehow it's got to stop. I've got to stop. I've got to learn to keep my big mouth shut, as Josie always warned me. Seems I spent the first third of my life learning how to open my mouth, and the second third learning how to keep it shut. Maybe in the last third I'll be able to open and close it at the right times.

"Maxie, you saved Nikolai and me from destroying ourselves and everyone with us. Bert, you were helpful, too, and I'm grateful. You're both magnificent. Just think, we scored a remarkable $3.48 per bushel. How much do you suppose we'll make at $3.48?"

Maxie volunteered to run out an answer on her calculator. Since they'd be getting wheat from the Min-Dak Co-op for $3.46, their gross margin with government subsidy amounted to 8 cents per bushel. Multiplying that times 55,050,000 bushels, produced an answer of 4.4 million dollars. Finally, subtracting their low expense factor, Maxie looked at the answer and exclaimed, "WE'RE RICH!"

"Not quite!" Harry cautioned. "We'll have to use a third of the money to stabilize and expand our operations. The next third we'll need to invest as a backstop for lean times. However, the final third can go to us."

"Hold on!" Bert cautioned. "Let's not spend our wealth before we get it. We haven't even collected a dollar yet. The Soviet sale is all blue sky until we get it in the bank."

"You're right, Bert," Harry conceded. "We've got to get back down to earth and get to work. Maxie, we need to have our wheat procurement documentation firmed up and transacted. You're the one who can do it, and the time is now. It's 1:25, so we have the rest of the afternoon to pull the loose ends of this sale together. Bert, we need you to contact the Min-Dak Co-op about their stored wheat in Duluth. Tell them we'll take it all for $3.46 a bushel, the price we negotiated earlier, not a penny more, and we require that price for the rest of the wheat we'll need to fill the Soviet order. Make sure you have it all in writing, then get it signed, witnessed, notarized, duplicated, and done. When you bring it back here later this afternoon, we'll countersign it.

"Let's move fast! The Krasnodar arrives at Duluth a week from Tuesday, and there'll be other freighters stacked up behind the Krasnodar. Soviet ships will be popping into port at the rate of two per week. We'll have a nerve-racking ordeal just making sure the wheat's all there on time. We'll have to work closely with the Min-Dak Co-op and railroad people. It's important we review their scheduling of trains, so we get our full order of wheat from inland elevators. Let's determine right now how many hopper cars and trains we'll need."

Harry and his partners began punching their calculators. One and a half million tons of wheat, less 517,711 tons in Duluth, left about a million tons to be moved from inland elevators for filling the balance of the Soviet order. Since each hopper car carried 100 tons, 10,000 hopper cars were needed.

"If we pull a hundred hopper cars per train," Harry speculated, "we'll need a hundred trains, and we've less than six months. That's a one-hundred car train every day of the week for twenty weeks. Can we do it?"

"We'll have to, Harry," Maxie urged.

"We'll do it!" Bert assured. "As soon as Maxie has the paperwork ready, I'll bring it to the co-op, get them to sign it, then have it back here late this afternoon. I'm confident we'll get our purchase documents countersigned by 4:30 and our wheat sale finalized before 5."

"Good, Bert! See you at 4:30," Harry affirmed.

"I'm gone, too," Maxie said.

"Right," concluded Harry. "Let's run!"

6

BIG JULIE FISKE

A huge balloon of a balding, gray-haired, fat-faced, beady eyed, sunburned man routinely pressed a button on his speaker phone and leaned back in his oversized, leather-upholstered, tilt-back chair. Julius Fiske was his name, but most acquaintances called him "Big Julie," because of his unusually large size. Fiske loved that name, "Big Julie." It had a way of keeping everybody's attention focused on him, giving him the recognition he so desperately craved.

Big Julie Fiske was an enormous, fat-bellied, multi-billion dollar dealer in the grain business. It was his personal practice, if not full time hobby, to keep tabs on every grain deal going and everybody dealing. The reason was simple: Big Julie had to have it all. His six-foot, two-inch, three-hundred-fifty pound frame was so intimidating no one dared challenge him. Not even an official as powerful as Nikolai Novikov would chance a "no" on a grain buy from Big Julie.

Nobody but nobody said "no" to Big Julie. The reason wasn't any kind of secret. Not only was he physically big, but he just happened to control a substantial portion of the world's surplus grain. A "no," therefore, to such a powerful man, was lunacy. Where else could anyone go to buy 12 million tons of grain on a moment's notice? Also, how much more would a person have to pay? Big volume grain buyers like Nikolai Novikov knew that nobody undersold Big Julie Fiske. That's why Novikov bought from him in the first place.

Yes, even Novikov made it a point to do his buying from Fiske before calling on his old friend Harry Brown. After all, Novikov didn't want to hurt Fiske's feelings, and, most certainly, if Novikov had gone to Brown first, Fiske would certainly have heard about it. Novikov knew Big Julie's hobby was finding out about grain deals, so Novikov went to him first, even though it was widely known that Brown had the best quality wheat.

Harry Brown sold 14% protein, Hard Red Spring Wheat, the northern climate's best variety of wheat. Fiske's southern climate soft wheat was low in protein, didn't keep long, and wasn't as good quality as Brown's. In cold northern climates, Brown's Red River Valley wheat grew lean and hard with plenty of protein. Also, being harder, it resisted spoilage much longer. The cold, rugged, low humidity climate of northern growing areas helped make 14% HRS wheat the best in the world.

Fiske's wheat strain, on the other hand, was quite different. Hot, humid, southern areas caused it to grow soft and fat with much less protein. Novikov needed the high–protein, superior quality wheat he bought from Brown, but made it a point to buy something from Fiske first. Novikov bought and bought from Fiske, a total of fifteen million tons of grain, mostly corn. The 1-1/2 million tons of HRS wheat from Brown was a mere tenth of Novikov's purchases from Fiske, so Fiske grew richer and richer, while others languished.

Yet, rather than celebrate his $2 billion sale to Novikov, Fiske kept brooding about the prospect of the Brown deal. He knew Novikov had gone to Brown to buy wheat. That's why he ordered his assistant, James

Baston, to snoop around Taylorsville. Now, at last, Baston had some news to report and was phoning his boss.

Big Julie sat in his air conditioned Gulf Coast office, one hand twiddling with the lapel of his pastel pink and white seersucker sport coat, while the other hand kept playing with the volume knob on the desktop speaker phone.

"Hello, Jamie, that you?" Fisked asked. "I've been wonderin' what's goin' on up there. Let's hear what you've got to say. Uh! Oh! There, Jamie, I'm hearing you better now," Fiske acknowledged, after adjusting the speaker volume. "Go ahead!"

"Mr. Fiske," came Baston's voice from out of the speaker phone, "I got up here as you ordered, then went right over to the Taylorsville Hotel. Good thing I did, too! The Soviets were dining there with Harry Brown and his partners. What a setup! I couldn't have arranged it better myself. With four women and three men, their group was a man short, so when the dancing began, I managed to join them, get acquainted, and dance with Brown's Office Administrator, Maxine Gadsden. She's a black beauty, Big Julie. I like her very much."

Big Julie roared out in laughter, his gloom suddenly transformed into glee. "Why, Jamie Baston, haw! You black devil, you! Gonna invite me to the weddin'?"

"I showed everybody my fake business card, Big Julie, and told them I was a reporter for the 'Southern States Newswire Service.' Eventually I was introduced to the others and we got along just fine. I found out they all met this morning to negotiate some kind of wheat deal. I'll keep right on it, Big Julie.

"By the way, I found out Nikolai Novikov and Harry Brown are old friends. Did you know Brown speaks Russian? Years ago, he toured the Soviet Union with a group of American students who were studying Russian."

92

"Well slap my sides and call me a pork belly!" Fiske reacted, astonished. "I do declare, Jamie boy, I never knew about that. Now listen hard! You've got to stop Brown's wheat deal real quick, you hear? I don't know how you're goin' to do it, but I've got great faith in you. I know you can get it done, if you set your mind to it. Why, just offer Novikov the same stuff for less. Tell him we'll sell for three-fifty-one a bushel if Brown wants three-fifty-two. If you can't deal with Novikov, find out where Brown gets his stuff, and buy it out before Brown does. If you can't do that, Jamie, then get on up to where Brown's stuff goes, prob'ly Duluth, and see if you can screw it up real good. Jamie, I'm relying on you to get the job done. And don't worry about money! Just tell the folks what you want, then send the bill down here to me, I'll pay it. Now then, I'm wiring you another $10,000 this afternoon. Holler, if you need more. You understand, Jamie? I want this Brown deal stopped."

"I don't like doing that kind of thing, Big Julie," Baston protested. "It only leads to trouble. Can't we work things out some other way? They're good people up here, Big Julie."

"Jamie, you do what I tell you," Fiske bellowed. "Y'all hear me now?"

"As you say, Big Julie," Baston replied. "I'll get going on it right away. I don't like it, but I'll get it done somehow."

"That's fine, fine, Jamie boy! You can call me any time and let me know what's happening. I just won't be able to sleep, thinkin' about this Brown feller getting my sale. Bye, Jamie!"

"Goodbye, Big Julie! I'll need the ten grand."

7

BASTON'S BRIBERY AND DECEIT

James Baston phoned Maxie from his hotel room at 2:10 in the afternoon. He knew a Brown-Novikov wheat agreement may have already been concluded that morning, and wanted very much to meet with Maxie. He needed information quickly, especially in view of Big Julie's instructions.

"Maxie, that you? James Baston here. I'm calling from the Taylorsville Hotel. Any chance we could get together a few moments before I leave town? I can't bear to leave you without saying goodbye. How about coffee?"

"Oh, Jamie! Nice to hear from you! We had such a good time last night. Tell you what, I have to go over to our accountant's office for some paperwork. On the way there, I could stop by for coffee. Don't leave; I'll see you in a few minutes."

"That's wonderful, Maxie!" Baston gushed. "I'll be in a booth near the hotel entrance."

Baston hung up the phone and left his room for the hotel lobby. When he got there, he noticed Nikolai Novikov at the front desk. Seizing the opportunity of the moment to underbid Brown's wheat price, Baston politely said, "Good afternoon, Mr. Novikov! How are you today?"

"In a hurry!" Novikov briskly replied. "Get your pipeline story yet?"

"Matter of fact, I'm just leaving now to get it. Had some things to do here, first. Got a call from a Julius Fiske down our way. Don't know him, but he's one of the owners of the newswire service I work for, and my editor put him on the phone. Fiske said he wanted me to do him a favor by finding you and informing you about an important matter. Do you know Julius Fiske, Mr. Novikov?"

"Why, yes indeed!" Novikov replied, looking somewhat surprised. "Is something wrong?"

"Not really," Baston replied. "Seems Mr. Fiske located a surplus supply of 14% protein, HRS wheat. Several million tons, he says. He wants to make a deal with you...cheap...$3.52 the bushel price, for openers. Also, he has a special bonus for you personally, Mr. Novikov, if you'll deal now.

"Mr. Fiske says to tell you he'll deposit in advance, in your own private Swiss bank account, a 1-1/2 cents per bushel bonus, all your own. He also says you can use any name you choose on your Swiss account, so you can preserve your privacy and safety. Just give Mr. Fiske your account number and he'll deposit the money.

"Mr. Novikov, Mr. Fiske says if you buy three million tons of wheat from him right now, your bonus will exceed 1-1/2 million dollars. If I had that much money, Mr. Novikov, I'd live like a king for the rest of my life. What do you want me to tell Mr. Fiske?"

Novikov reflected for a moment, then asked Baston to inform Fiske that the offer to sell the Soviets so much wheat was interesting. However, no "bonus" arrangement of any kind was either necessary or acceptable. "In fact, in the USSR," Novikov pointed out, "such a kickback 'bonus,' or 'baksheesh' is regarded as a bribe, and a very serious crime against the people.

"I could be executed for such a crime," Novikov

warned, "and so could you, Mr. Baston. Bribes, kickback bonuses, or 'baksheesh' might be standard operating procedure in the USA, as well as in other capitalistic and exploitive countries, but in the USSR, and in other socialist communist, democratic people's republics, bribery is a serious crime against the people. Please, Mr. Baston, stress these points politely to Mr. Fiske. Tell Mr. Fiske we Soviets demand that his so-called 'bonus' amounts be deducted from his already quoted prices on our other contracts, and that we shall insist on this arrangement in the future.

"Also, I'm not looking for any 14% protein HRS at this time, but please tell Mr. Fiske I'll certainly keep him in mind, should there be a need for it in the future. As of the present time, however, we already have purchased sufficient stocks of that wheat.

"In conclusion, Mr. Baston, please advise Mr. Fiske that our government is looking forward to prompt deliveries from him on our current order. In fact, my superiors in Moscow want Mr. Fiske to give them an update right away on our order status. Ask Mr. Fiske to wire me a reply as soon as possible. I'll be in my Moscow office day after tomorrow."

"Yes, indeed, Mr. Novikov," Baston responded. "I jotted down all your instructions, and I'll relay them to Mr. Fiske. Mr. Novikov, it has been a pleasure meeting you and your associates. If you don't mind, I'll ask my editor if I can do a feature on you and your delegation, including, perhaps, some info on the current Fiske deal and any other deals you've negotiated."

"I'm sorry, Mr. Baston," Novikov replied. "Under other circumstances, I might be able to oblige you, but I must be going. Maybe Mr. Fiske can help you. He's the person you should contact anyway. I myself am not an appropriate person to talk to. Also, in view of my official status, my government wouldn't authorize me to talk to you at anytime about my deals.

"Really, Mr. Baston," Novikov continued, "there isn't any newsworthy story here anyway. You already know, or should know, that our government and your government concluded a long-term grain sales agreement quite some time ago. This agreement has been very well publicized worldwide. I think your reading public is probably bored with it by now. Thank you for your initiative anyway, and good luck to you, Mr. Baston."

"Best wishes to you, also, sir," Baston replied. "Have a good trip home!"

On that conclusion, Novikov hurried away and Baston walked into the restaurant. He managed to get a booth as Maxie arrived. "Maxie! How nice you look!" Baston greeted her. "I'm so glad I met you last night."

When Maxie and Jamie were seated, the waitress came for their order, and Maxie said, "Coffee black for me."

"Have a caramel roll, too," Baston urged. "I hear they're delicious. Or how about some strawberry pie? It's a specialty here, I'm told."

"Oh, Jamie, I couldn't have that," Maxie protested. "I need to watch my figure."

"No, you don't, Maxie!" Baston playfully chided. "You go right ahead and have the pie; let me watch your figure."

"You win," Maxie gave in, somewhat embarrassed by Baston's remark. Then, to the waitress, "I'll have the strawberry pie this afternoon."

"Ditto here," Baston instructed the waitress, who took the order and quickly left. "Now, then, Maxie, tell me all about yourself. We really didn't get much time with each other last night."

"There isn't a whole lot to tell, Jamie," Maxie began. "I grew up in a small town, attended school, became a teacher. Now I'm a partner with Harry Brown and Bert Jackson. Also, I was once married when I was very young, and have an eleven-year-old daughter named Sara. My ex husband never saw her. He left me when he found out I was pregnant. He said he didn't want any children and wouldn't support any. Truth is, he wouldn't even support me at the time. He simply refused to get a job. After he abandoned me, I never heard from him again. Several years later, I decided to go to college, get a degree, and become a teacher. I was absolutely sure life would be better for me if I did something about it."

"How courageous of you, Maxie," Baston reacted. "I admire your honesty, your ambition, and your accomplishment. You're a very unusual, very special person. I'm glad I met you."

"What about yourself, Jamie?" Maxie asked. "Have you been a reporter long?"

"Only a couple of years. I grew up in Atlanta and became a reporter after two other jobs, one as a cost accountant, the other as an accounting supervisor. I got sick of numbers, decided I needed people and excitement, so now I'm a reporter. Also, I've never been married. Guess I was a bachelor so long, I became afraid of settling down, but now I often wish I had a family to fuss over."

After the waitress brought their order, Maxie and Jamie continued their conversation. "I suppose you're on the road all the time," Maxie remarked, frowning. "Where will you go next, after the pipeline story?"

"Don't quite know yet," Baston replied. "My editor wants me back at the main office in Galveston as soon as I get my pipeline assignment done. However, I remember him saying something about doing a story in Duluth, week after next."

"Why, Jamie!" Maxie squealed delightedly. "I can't believe this. Do you know I'll be in Duluth the week after next? We sold a big order of wheat to the Soviets this morning, so I have to go to Duluth and arrange the export paperwork for the various shipments. Duluth is a marvelous place to visit. It's scenic, charming, and fun."

"Let's enjoy Duluth together, Maxie," Baston suggested. "I'll meet you there week after next. Bring your daughter Sara. I'd like to meet her, too. I'll phone you from Galveston next week to find out where you're staying, then I'll arrange a room at the same hotel."

"You mean it, Jamie?" Maxie asked, raising her eyebrows and opening her eyes wide. Baston nodded, smiling, as Maxie spoke again. "It would be wonderful to see you up there, and we'd have plenty of time to visit. I'll make my reservations tomorrow. Call me Tuesday, and I'll tell you the name of the hotel."

"Good! Agreed!" Jamie enthused, reaching across the table to shake Maxie's hand. Baston decided not to ask Maxie any more questions. Besides, he'd gotten enough information. He could ask a vessel agent in Duluth for the name and location of any Soviet freighter docking there. Baston knew he could get that information in less than ten minutes. However, he still had to figure out how he'd screw up Brown's wheat shipment and make Big Julie happy. He certainly didn't want to do it in a way that would hurt Brown or his partners, especially Maxie. He didn't want to get into trouble, either. What could he do?"

"What are you thinking, Jamie?" Maxie asked as she finished her pie.

"I'm thinking about you, Maxie, wishing I'd met you sooner," Baston oozed. "Never met such a good person as you, or a woman so beautiful. Never met many girls in fact. Seems I was always too busy or too shy."

"Why Jamie, that's the biggest line I've heard yet," laughed Maxie. "Bet you say that to all the girls you meet."

"Oh, no, Maxie," Baston responded, acting

somewhat hurt. "How could you think I'd make up something like that?"

"You win, Jamie. I guess I liked what you said so much, I was worried it might not be true. A girl like me has to be very careful, you know. There are so many traveling men these days. They'll tell a girl anything to get her attention. I'm glad you're not like that, Jamie."

"Maxie, my word is my bond," Baston pledged. "Guess I'm old-fashioned, but that's the way it is for me."

Maxie thought Baston was sincere. He had aimed his big eyes and innocent look at her, and she soaked up every word he said. "How remarkable, Jamie! How wonderful!" Maxie sighed, gazing into Baston's handsome face.

Suddenly, remembering what time it was, Maxie exclaimed, "Oh! Good heavens! I have to get to the accountant's office. I've got to get going, Jamie. Call me Tuesday and I'll tell you where I'll be staying in Duluth. I enjoyed the pie and coffee."

Jamie got up with Maxie, then, looking into her eyes again, said, "Maxie, thank you for coming here on such short notice. I wanted so much to see you. Now I can't wait to see you again."

After paying the bill and tipping the waitress, Baston took Maxie by the hand and walked her a short distance beyond the restaurant door to a coat check room, where he took her in his arms and kissed her lips. When he relaxed his hold on her, Maxie kissed him back. Finally, moving slowly away while looking into his big dark eyes, she reluctantly waved goodbye. Baston waved back and kept looking at her until she was gone.

8

BERT AND NADDY

Bert Jackson waited on a cement bench in the center of the Taylorsville Park, just behind the bandstand. There was no one else around until he saw Nadezhda Konya. He rose to greet her as she approached. "Hello, Naddy, I'm so glad you're here!"

Naddy, blushing, said, "I wasn't sure I'd find you."

Bert slipped his arms around her. For the first time they kissed. As they held each other close, Naddy lovingly touched Bert's golden hair, and Bert stroked Naddy's sweetly scented, shiny black hair. Stepping back slightly to admire each other and look into each other's eyes, they hesitated momentarily, then came together again in another embrace. At one point, Bert held Naddy's face between his hands and gazed longingly into her eyes. At another point he passed his fingertips over her smooth cheeks and neck, then they kissed again for a much longer time. When they finally stopped to catch their breath, Naddy whispered, "We'd better sit down."

Bert thanked Naddy for keeping their appointment under such awkward circumstances. He said he simply had to be alone with her to tell her he loved her. Yet he felt foolish. They hardly knew each other. It seemed as though some powerful magnetic force had drawn them together. Never before in their lives had either of them been so attracted to anyone.

Naddy said she felt a strong attraction to Bert the first moment she saw him. Never had she met anyone like him. Never had she experienced such love for anyone as the love she felt for him. Up to then, her entire youth and adult life had been dedicated to building a new society. She never had time for such love, nor such a person to love as Bert.

Bert and Naddy kissed each other again and again until they had to stop themselves before losing all control. After a lengthy silence, Bert impulsively looked into Naddy's dark eyes and asked how she ever started building a new society as a child.

Naddy told Bert that when she was only a baby her father had died. He'd been severly wounded by the Nazis in World War II, and, eventually, died of his wounds. Naddy was told when she was older that her father had a piece of shrapnel near his heart, and another at the base of his spinal cord. The doctors said neither could be removed by surgery because of the danger. It was merely a matter of time until one of the sharp metal objects would kill him.

Naddy's mother died soon after her father. A stroke-producing clot developed from an injury her mother got from an accident at the factory where she worked. An automatic punch press cycled suddenly and mangled her left hand and arm. Naddy looked as if she were about to cry when she was describing the tragedy, but Bert reassuringly hugged her and she continued. She said she had become an orphan and ward of the state at the age of eight. There were no relatives to care for her. They had all been killed in World War II and were among the twenty millions of Soviet casualties.

In answer to Bert's question as to how she started building a new society as a child, Naddy said she entered an orphanage when she was only eight years old. While there, she began learning about the Communist Party and its building of a new Soviet society. She was recruited to participate and was enrolled in the Young Octobrists, an organization of elementary school children who tend monuments, march in parades, and receive instruction in socialist values. The organization is named after the month that the Bolshevik Revolution started. Later, Naddy joined the Young Pioneers, a junior high school age organization where members receive further instruction in the ideals of the socialist collective state and preparation in the military defense of their nation. Then came the Senior Komsomols, a senior-high age organization which trains members to be model citizens of the Soviet state. After concluding her brief biographical sketch, Naddy wanted to hear all about Bert and the story of his life.

Bert kissed Naddy again after hearing her story. Then he began telling her what had happened to him. By some weird coincidence, he, too, had grown up in an orphanage. Nobody else wanted him, he insisted, and at this, Naddy's dark eyes opened wide and glistened over. Then she tenderly touched Bert's face and said she loved him and wanted him.

Bert reacted by expressing his love for Naddy and confessing that he really shouldn't have said nobody wanted him. He did get adopted eventually, when he was twelve years old. Also, he said the orphanage wanted him before that, and he was quite happy there. His real mother and father died in an automobile accident when he was two years old.

At the conclusion of Bert's comments, he and Naddy regarded each other with a new understanding that bound them together deeply and beckoned their lips to a final, impassioned kiss. It ended abruptly when Naddy recalled her four o'clock rendezvous with Nikolai and Helga at the hotel, and their need to be on time for their airplane.

Bert reluctantly bid Naddy goodbye, but arranged to meet her again in Duluth. He said he'd contact the Soviet's vessel agent in Duluth and inform him where he, Maxie, and Harry would be staying. Naddy could then make her reservations for the same hotel. On that point of agreement, Bert and Naddy kissed each other once more, then Naddy broke away and hurried off, turning once for a quick wave to Bert who looked longingly after her as he waved back.

9

DULUTH, MINNESOTA, USA

Harry and Josie Brown sat in the front seat of their four-year-old station wagon, headed for Duluth. Their children sat in back.

"How much farther do we have to go, Daddy," asked seven-year-old Johnny. "I'm tired of riding."

"Won't be long now," Harry answered. "We're close to the Lake Superior bluffs. Say, why don't we hold a quick election? Jack, here's an auto club travel folder. Read what it says about the major attractions in Duluth, and we'll vote on each one, whether or not to go."

"All right," Jack agreed. At 17 years old, Jack was the oldest of Harry and Josie's children, and Harry often put him in charge of the other children. "First I'll read what the folder says," Jack instructed, "then everyone can vote 'yay' or 'nay.' Here goes!

"Harbor Cruise: See America's..."

"Yay! Yay! Yay!" The chorus of two younger children cried, attempting to out-yell each other.

"Hold it! You didn't let me finish," Jack scolded. "Wait 'til I'm through telling you what it is, first."

Jack began reading again. "See America's greatest inland port. A two-hour harbor cruise gives you close-up views of foreign ships and lake freighters. These ships are loading or unloading cargo at the world's largest coal and iron ore docks, or at the world's tallest grain elevators....See also the famous Aerial Lift Bridge, Arrowhead Bridge and more."

"Do they got any popthikles? Hmm?" asked four-year-old Jeanie, who had a missing front tooth.

"Let's see," Jack answered. "It says here...'Snack bar and souvenirs.' I bet the Snack bar has them. Now, how about the Harbor Cruise? Do we all want to take it?"

"Yay! Yay! Yay!" The children yelled, followed by Josie and Harry who yelled last. Then Harry, smiling and stealing a look at Josie, said, "This is fun! Let's try another one, Jack."

Jack read from the travel folder again. "Lake Superior Marine Museum....The Canal Park Marine Museum operated by the U. S. Army Corps of Engineers is Duluth's most popular waterfront attraction. There are displays and relics....The Edmund Fitzgerald shipwreck display includes the story, photos, and model of the shipwreck....Tour full size cabins, a pilothouse, and see a two-story steam engine. Other shipwrecks and cargoes are also featured....See films, shows, model ships, plus, you'll like this, Dad, it's free."

"Yay! Yay! Yay!" The children roared.

"I vote 'yay,' also," Harry added. "I remember the wreck of the Edmund Fitzgerald, too. There's even a song about it. It was a huge lake freighter loaded with ore. It sank in a sudden storm in the middle of Lake Superior. The whole crew went down with it. Not a single survivor. Not even any distress signals. Experts think the heavily loaded ship, which was riding down low in the water, was moving at full speed and got swamped by giant storm waves. It kept taking on water until it dove under a huge wave and propelled itself to the lake bottom. It all happened so fast, not a single crew member had a chance to escape. We'll have to be sure to see the Edmund Fitzgerald display."

"Here's another attraction," Jack continued. "The Duluth Zoo has more than 500 animals representing over 100 species. Founded in 1923, the zoo covers 12 landscaped acres. The Children's Zoo houses a nursery for baby animals, including petting areas for children...."

"Yay! Yay! Yay!" The two younger children screamed.

"Only one 'yay' apiece," Josie advised. "Musn't stuff the ballot box! The zoo sounds fun. I'd like to go. I vote 'yay!'"

"Count one big 'yay' for me, too," voted 14-year-old Suzie.

"Here's another one," Jack began again. "Glensheen Mansion...completed in 1908...built along the shore of Lake Superior at a cost of nearly a million dollars. Today, almost a century later, the estate is priceless. It includes the 39-room mansion, carriage house, boat house, formal gardens, clay tennis court, and bowling green."

"Wait a minute!" Josie exclaimed. "I don't think you want to go to that one. Somebody got murdered there a few years back."

"Yay! Yay! Yay! Yay!" All four children shouted.

"Let's go see that one, Daddy," little Jeanie pleaded enthusiastically.

"How about this one," Jack suggested. "Skyline Drive...runs 600 feet above the city and Lake Superior. This exciting drive is 30 miles long with scenic pull-overs to enjoy historic landmarks, plus spectacular views of Duluth, Lake Superior, Great Lakes shipping, and other interesting scenes."

"Yay! Yay! Yay! Yay!"

"Looks like we'll take time to enjoy all the attractions," Harry concluded.

As the car approached the Lake Superior bluffs, Harry pointed to Spirit Mountain, commenting that it was a famous recreation area and popular place for winter skiing. When they drove over the top of the bluffs, they were astonished at the spectacular scene below. Sunshine, blue sky, and cotton candy clouds joined a vast expanse of water at the horizon.

Looking down towards Lake Superior's shoreline they saw the cities of Duluth, Minnesota, and Superior, Wisconsin, plus a whole panorama of individual sights, including huge grain elevators, ocean freighters, tugboats, landing docks, and other harbor objects. On the right, spread out from the foot of Spirit Mountain, was the St. Louis River, Spirit Lake, and a multitude of other splendid landscapes.

On the left was the long, picturesque approach to downtown Duluth, displaying such scenes as the Aerial Lift Bridge, the old Arrowhead Bridge, and the newer Blatnik Bridge, plus various harbor areas, and myriads of buildings and residences climbing huge bluffs from the lakeshore. There were intricate ribbons of concrete and blacktop highways, and miles upon miles of city streets running in every direction. It was an indescribably fascinating view, with nothing to match it in the entire Northwest.

10

HAGGARSON'S
HEADQUARTERS

The large oceanic bulk freighter Krasnodar had docked in Duluth several days early, and was still tightly secured to its mooring in the vicinity of the giant, Min-Dak Co-op elevators. Crew members scurried about the deck while large loading chutes spewed tonnages of wheat into the ship's holds.

The Krasnodar was named for a major Soviet city located in the Greater Western Caucasian Mountain Region, on the right bank of the Kuban River, just east of where it flows into the Sea of Azov, but with accesses also to the Black Sea. How ironical that a ship picking up wheat in the USA should be named for a major Soviet wheat processing center and one time wheat exporter to the world! What a silent testimony of the reversal of circumstances leading to the ship's mission!

Nearby the docked Krasnodar, Harry, Bert, and Maxie were entering a small, red brick building belonging to the vessel agent hired by the Soviets to administer the comings and goings of its freighters. The three grain brokerage partners had met each other earlier that morning in downtown Duluth, and were now visiting the vessel agent.

"Mr. Hjalmar Haggarson, my name is Harry

Brown." Brown introduced himself to the Krasnodar's vessel agent. "I represent H. B. Exports, Inc., of Taylorsville, Minnesota. This is Mrs. Maxine Gadsden, our Office Administrator, and Bert Jackson, our General Manager."

"Mrs. Gadsden, Mr. Brown, Mr. Jackson, I'm very pleased to meet you," Haggarson responded, vigorously shaking their hands.

Vessel Agent Hjalmar Haggarson was a most unusual gentleman and an ex ship captain. His gray, well-trimmed, close-cropped beard and modest moustache distinguished him from other men. His rugged Nordic features, blue eyes, tanned skin, and well-proportioned physique combined to give him a decidedly striking look that was accented by his authoritative attire. He was dressed in a navy blue blazer with bright brass buttons and matching blue trousers. He also wore a white, crisp-collared shirt with navy blue tie. From head to toe, his appearance was neat, impeccable, and tidy.

"We've been expecting each of you." Haggarson acknowledged. "Ms. Nadezhda Konya of the USSR, whom you've already met, is here, too. She's in the back office talking on our VHF Marine Radio to an officer on board the Krasnodar. The ship's Captain is with her, checking the status of the loading.

"The Krasnodar docked several days early, and we began loading it shortly afterwards. We anticipate it'll soon be underway later today. I know the Captain and crew are anxious to get back through the St. Lawrence Seaway. They've had quite a trying time of it, as I'm sure the Captain will tell you. Please be seated in my office, I'll be back in a moment."

Brown and the others entered Haggarson's office and sat down as Haggarson left. "Quite an impressive office," Brown remarked.

"Vessel agents must make a heck of a lot of money,"

Maxie commented, after she, like the others, eyed Haggarson's comfortable furnishings, which included elegantly framed photographs of various freighters, plus painstakingly constructed model ships, and an assortment of seafaring relics. Most of the furniture, including a ship captain's heavy mahogany dining table, seemed to have come from several different vessels.

"Look at all this," Bert respectfully observed. "What do you suppose a vessel agent earns to afford such an office?"

"Yeah," agreed Brown, "I'm wondering, too. When we drove into the parking lot, did you notice the Mercedes 560 SEC parked in the front slot next to the building? Probably Haggarson's. And this office looks like a museum of rare nautical antiques. They have to be worth a fortune."

"Here we are," said Haggarson, approaching his office door and gesturing for Nadezhda and the Krasnodar's Captain to enter.

"Good morning, Nadezhda," Harry exclaimed, rising with Maxie and Bert to greet Naddy. "Good to see you again!"

Naddy greeted Harry and the others, then introduced them to the Captain of the Krasnodar, Grigor Garoldovich Rezhnikov. She announced that the Captain was eager to meet the others and air some problems he encountered on his voyage to Duluth. After Naddy's brief introduction, therefore, Captain Rezhnikov spoke.

"Thank you, Comrade Konya. What a pleasure it is meeting friendly persons in this crazy country! Forgive me if I seem forward, but in truth, I'm worried and upset. All the way here from the Atlantic my ship and crew were threatened by terrible hazards, so I'm completely pessimistic and fearful about our safe return.

"Various seaway pilots brought us within inches of major damage, disaster, and death. They did this by

111

narrowly missing massive steel lock gates, reinforced concrete canal markers, submerged bridge abutments, jagged stone harbor breakers, and channel bottom hull obstacles. Never have I sailed down such a seaway. Several times our ship was nearly punctured. I agonize to think what'll happen when we're almost fully loaded, low in the water, and hellbent for home. This just isn't my kind of trip, mates. Forgive me for being so frank."

Grigor Rezhnikov was a no-nonsense captain who commanded a considerable ship and crew. He looked every bit the part, too, dressed as he was in his seagoing uniform, complete with red-star insignia, longtime service hash marks, and other trappings of high rank. His austere features, swarthy skin, and solid, erect stance suggested a natural leader concerned about the welfare of his crewmen. Harry Brown and the others sympathized with Captain Rezhnikov's seaway concerns and wanted to somehow relieve his anxieties.

"Captain Rezhnikov," Brown began. "It's unfortunate your trip down the St. Lawrence Seaway was so stressful. I realize how frustrating it must have been for you and your crew to navigate this relatively new wonder of the world. Your ship is so big, I'm sorry you didn't have the advantage of some extended briefing before you began your seaway trip. What do you think of the pilots? Were they helpful?"

"Certainly they were cordial and capable, Mr. Brown," Captain Rezhnikov acknowledged, "but I alone am responsible for the Krasnodar. Therefore, how can I completely turn over my control to foreigners? Consider that if the Krasnodar is damaged, it is I who will be blamed by my countrymen. Nevertheless, I had to allow the various required pilots to assist me, but without control of the helm I felt I had died many times throughout the voyage. My crew suffered, too. We are all on edge.

"Perhaps, as you say, Mr. Brown, some thorough

112

briefing at Baie Comeau or even Escoumains, Canada, would have prepared us for our frenzied, 2,342-mile seaway run from the Atlantic. We had very little briefing, however. Only the pilots told us a few things. We argued again and again about the close calls my ship was subjected to. It was a terrible experience. Perhaps if we'd been in contact with Americans who spoke the Russian Language, or if Russian–speaking officials could have thoroughly briefed us at the other end, we'd have had a better understanding of seaway navigation requirements. As it turned out, however, we had very little understanding."

"Truly we regret your difficulties, Captain Rezhnikov," Haggarson sympathetically responded. "Please remain with us awhile, so we can benefit some more from your thoughts. We'll also help you all we can, so you'll enjoy your return voyage. You have an outstanding ship in the Krasnodar, and your responsibility is tremendous for both ship and crew, and now your new cargo of fresh wheat. We, therefore, share your concerns and appreciate your need for additional briefing on the Atlantic side of the seaway. I assure you, I'll personally look into the matter."

"I agree with Mr. Haggarson," Naddy added. "Communications about seaway navigation can be improved. Captain Rezhnikov's experience was regrettable. In the future, I hope our other vessels can avoid such experiences."

Naddy continued her remarks, referring to the Krasnodar's early arrival from its home Port of Odessa on the Black Sea. She also noted that the sailors had enjoyed some brief shore leave, enabling them to relax after their long, difficult ordeal. At that moment, she noted, wheat was still pouring into the Krasnodar's huge cargo holds, as it had been the past two days, but the vessel was nearly loaded now, and would be underway shortly.

Vessel Agent Haggarson said he'd first brief the

group on the loading, then answer their questions. Afterwards, they'd go out and get a quick look at the ship before it began its return voyage. Also, Captain Rezhnikov was invited to assist in the briefing, now that he, too, had successfully made the seaway trip. However, before any discussion began, Haggarson announced he'd taken the liberty of arranging a selection of coffee and other beverages for his guests, plus a tempting assortment of freshly baked Danish pastry.

While Haggarson was pouring some lemon-lime soda for Naddy and Maxie, he began his briefing by referring to a wall-mounted photograph of a typical "saltie," or ocean bulk freighter. The Krasnodar was just such a ship, and a very large one, much larger than the usual "laker" vessel. The Krasnodar, in fact, was just about the biggest oceangoing ship to ever enter the Duluth harbor, since it was just inside the maximum dimensions allowable for a ship navigating the St. Lawrence Seaway System. Haggarson indicated this was probably the major reason why Captain Rezhnikov and his crew had such a harrowing journey. Even experienced pilots would have had a worrisome trip with so large a ship to maneuver in so small a space.

Through with serving refreshments, Haggarson picked up a telescoping pointer from a receptacle on top of his desk. He pulled the pointer open to its full length, then handed it to Captain Rezhnikov, asking him if he'd use it to tell the group about his ship's dimensions in terms of the maximums allowable on the St. Lawrence Seaway.

Captain Rezhnikov agreed to discuss his ship with the group, and began referring to the large, wall-mounted photograph of an ocean bulk freighter. Moving the pointer from ship's bow to stern, he pointed out that the Krasnodar measured 222 meters or 728 feet in length, versus the 730 feet maximum allowable, bow-to-stern length through the seaway. Since the Krasnodar was a mere two feet inside that limit, it was a very tight fit.

The Krasnodar measured 22 meters or 72 feet from port side to starboard side, versus the 76 feet maximum allowable St. Lawrence Seaway width. With only four feet to spare, the ship's sideways movement was extremely limited.

Unloaded, the Krasnodar measured 32 meters or 105 feet from the water line to the top of the aftermast, which was the highest-reaching structure on the ship. Maximum height for clearing overhead bridges on the Great Lakes sea lanes is 117 feet above the water, or just 12 feet above the Krasnodar's full height. Captain Rezhnikov expected no difficulty on the return trip with this dimension, since his ship would be heavily loaded and riding much lower in the water. It was the below water dimension that presented the greatest danger on the return trip.

The Krasnodar drew a full seven meters or 23 feet beneath the water surface when fully loaded. Maximum ship depth for the seaway is 26 feet down from the top of the water. This depth limitation is due to several shallow channels and locks in the seaway. The Krasnodar rode a mere three feet inside the 26-foot depth limit, dangerously increasing the possibility of underwater damage to its hull.

It was clearly understandable to the group from Captain Rezhnikov's comments about ship dimensions and seaway limits, that the Krasnodar was an enormous ship for the seaway. Also, with its wheat capacity of approximately 30,000 tons or 1,101,000 bushels after load topping, the Krasnodar was one of the heaviest cargo ships to ever navigate the St. Lawrence system. Average capacity of ships using the system runs between 17 and 20,000 tons, which is considerably less than the Krasnodar's tonnage.

Referring to the wall photograph again, Captain Rezhnikov pointed out various identifying characteristics of an ocean bulk freighter. He seemed to relish the use of the pointer and the instructional role he was playing. As a result, he became much more relaxed. His earlier frustrations with the seaway trip soon faded. He even acquired a hint of pride he'd made it.

As Captain of such a large ship as the Krasnodar, he was thoroughly experienced in the operation of many smaller kinds of vessels. He was familiar, too, with naval architecture and other nautical subjects, making him exceptionally well schooled in the ways of the sea.

Rezhnikov explained that the Krasnodar had six large-capacity holds like those of the vessel shown in the wall-mounted photograph. Each hold carried 5,000 tons of wheat, and was loaded or unloaded through an elaborate arrangement of deck hatches, hydraulically removable by a system of deck-mounted lifts.

The pilothouse was mounted on top of the superstructure at the aft end of the ship. Cabins for the officers were located just below the pilothouse, and quarters for remaining crew members were at deck level. The aft superstructure also contained the galley and dining areas.

At the extreme rear, below the after-end stern of the ship, was the rudder, which is the mechanism used for the vessel's directional control. Huge twin propeller wheels or screws were mounted forward of the rudder and turned by giant engines to give the ship its thrust.

The engine smokestacks were located just behind the after-mast, and the ship's fuel bunker was just forward of the smokestack.

"Any questions about the ship?" Rezhnikov concluded, hesitant at this point about getting too technical for his guests.

"Yes, Captain," Maxie responded. "What about the crew of the Krasnodar. How many seamen are there, and what do they do?"

"Good question, Mrs. Gadsden," Rezhnikov

complimented. "Our Krasnodar has 40 hands aboard. There's the skipper, that's my job, and the chief officer, and the second and third officers. Also, we have three radio operators, a chief engineer, and three additional engineers. There's a chief cook and three additional cooks in the galley, six oilers in the engine room, 15 deckhands, and four politicals."

"Politicals?" Maxie asked, sounding puzzled.

"Every Soviet ship has a few politicals," Rezhnikov explained. "On the Krasnodar, one of them is a commissar, and the others help the commissar. They're all Communist Party members who provide instruction on political subjects, and help keep crew members informed about world news events and social developments. Also, politicals supplement their training duties by providing assistance in security matters. Can you add anything to that, Ms. Konya?"

"That's a good response to Maxie's question, Comrade Captain," Naddy answered. "I can't add much to what you've said."

"What about docking and loading the Krasnodar, how are they accomplished?" Bert asked.

"Since Mr. Haggarson is knowledgeable about this harbor and I'm not," Rezhnikov replied, "let's have him tell us about docking and loading. Mr. Haggarson?"

"Very well," Haggarson acknowledged. "We're using two tugboats, the Lakota and Ashinabe, which are named after Native American tribes, as all tugs around here are. These two tugs assisted the Krasnodar in docking. As you might suspect with such a large vessel, tugs are required, because it could take up to a mile for the Krasnodar to stop at slow speed, due to its forward momentum and immense weight. It's like gliding on ice and trying to stop. You need tugs to help you.

"Our two tugboats picked up the Krasnodar in the bay area, then assisted in guiding the vessel to the Min-Dak Co-op's elevator dock. Each tug is an 80-footer,

117

with two, 1,200-horsepower engines, and a crew of four. Working together, pushing and pulling, the two tugs were able to get the Krasnodar docking job done.

"Once docked, the vessel rolled back its hydraulically operated hatch covers and soon began taking wheat into its holds. The hatch covers, I'm told by Captain Rezhnikov, have been malfunctioning lately, operating somewhat strangely. The unpredictable units opened by themselves several times when the ship was at sea, but Captain Rezhnikov assures me that the entire hydraulic system is due to be overhauled as soon as the Krasnodar gets back to Odessa.

"The Min-Dak Co-op elevators have been loading wheat through drop chutes into the Krasnodar's holds at the rate of 1,000 tons per hour, so the ship is just about loaded. Now is an appropriate time for us to see it. Do you approve, Captain Rezhnikov?"

"Of course, Mr. Haggarson," Rezhnikov replied. "Let's go now, it's time."

"We appreciate your helpful briefing, Captain Rezhnikov. Yours, too, Mr. Haggarson," Brown finally spoke. "Thank you both."

"On our way to the ship, Mr. Haggarson," Maxie inquired, "could you please tell us something about your role as vessel agent?"

"Yours is a frequent and welcome question, Mrs. Gadsden," Haggarson replied. "Let's start walking to the Krasnodar and I'll explain my job to you on the way." Haggarson continued his briefing as the group exited the building and walked to the docks.

"In a word, we vessel agents are a ship's mother away from home, taking care of practically every need imaginable. First of all, consider that a $15 million cargo ship isn't making money sitting empty at anchor. Planes make money when they're flying, and cargo ships make money when they're moving cargo. Vessel agents keep cargo ships on the move, helping ship owners keep expenses to a minimum. That's why ship owners hire agents like us. We act in part as purchasing agents, saving ship owners money on many of their expenses."

"What are some of those expenses?" asked Bert.

"Major expenses are for tugboats, line handlers, St. Lawrence Seaway pilots, and fuel," Haggarson continued. "We arrange all these, plus we assist in getting food supplies on board, as well as lining up stevedors to load and unload the ship.

"Other vessel agent duties include arranging National Cargo Bureau ship inspections, or securing customs clearance and visas for crew members. Sometimes we even get out of bed in the middle of the night to take a sick crewman to the hospital. Also, remember that mail is extremely important to a seaman, who may be away from home for many months at a time. We often track down lost letters and help seamen handle emergency situations.

"Since time is money, an essential part of a vessel agent's job is getting ships loaded or unloaded quickly. To do this, we keep in close radio contact with ships when they're as far away as Montreal, Canada. Then we follow them all the way through the St. Lawrence Seaway and across the Great Lakes to Duluth. We keep shippers advised of their shipment movements, too, making sure each ship, upon arrival, gets right into the dock to unload or load its cargoes. Ship owners are especially anxious that their ships don't sit at anchor for days on end waiting for dock space. Such waiting is terribly costly. Did you know there are some overseas ports where ships have been known to wait several months at anchor for their turn to get to a dock? In Duluth, we won't let that happen. We get a ship in and out fast.

"When a ship is fully loaded, receipts and bills of lading have to be signed, and much other paperwork is necessary. I'm talking about export declarations, weight certificates, grade certificates, certificates of origin, and other documents. We vessel agents get very little time to do all the work that has to be done, and there's not much room for error. We have to get our jobs done right and always be on time. Otherwise, we can't expect to get paid and stay in business."

"How are you paid, Mr. Haggarson?" asked Maxie.

"How we're paid is based on a schedule of fees for the different services we perform," Haggarson replied. "For example, our fee is $2,000 for a full cargo loading, as in the case of the Krasnodar. If we handle all arrangements for both discharging a load and loading another cargo, our fee would be $3,000 for a load in excess of 20,000 tons.

"When we act as brokers to load an empty ship for a return trip, as we often do, or, if we arrange to have a cargo delivered somewhere else, in addition to the one being picked up, we get a commission of 1-1/4%. Whether we find ships for loads or loads for ships, our commission, which is a standard vessel agent percentage, is almost always the same."

"Excuse me, Mr. Haggarson, I don't mean to interrupt," Bert cut in, "but why are those hopper cars over there getting red flags put on them?"

"Red flags on hopper cars are a danger sign," Haggarson advised. "They warn us of fumigation with a toxic gas that destroys any insects found in the grain. We have to be very careful unloading those cars with red flags, because the poisonous gases in them are quite harmful. They can be dangerously explosive, too, since fumigant gases are combustible and easily ignited by a spark or flame. No smoking is allowed anywhere near red-flagged cars."

"If red flags mean fumigation, why don't I see it being done?" Harry questioned. "All I see is a man running around, sticking red flags on our hopper cars. Shouldn't we be seeing someone with fumigation

120

equipment working on one of the cars before it's red-flagged?"

"Frankly, I don't know," Haggarson reflected. "It does seem a bit strange. Why...."

"It's James Baston!" Maxie exclaimed, shocked.

"Get him over here! Find out what he's up to!" Brown demanded.

At this, Haggarson took a bosun's whistle out of his pocket and blew it, gesturing to Baston to come over. Baston, realizing he was recognized, threw down the remaining flags he carried and, looking quite embarrassed, walked up to where Haggarson and the others stood.

Harry Brown, frowning, spoke sternly. "Baston, this is incredible! We thought you were a news reporter. Now we find you're red-flagging cars carrying our wheat. Surely you must have some kind of explanation for this."

Baston lowered his head dejectedly. He was caught in an illegal act and was too scared to respond.

"Well, James Baston, what have you got to say for yourself?" Maxie lashed out. "What are you doing here? Why are you red-flagging our wheat cars?"

"Sorry, Maxie," Baston quietly replied, ashamed of himself. "Sorry, Mr. Brown, Bert, Nadezhda and you, sirs," nodding to Haggarson and Rezhnikov. "It was terribly foolish of me. I was trying to satisfy Julius Fiske. He ordered me to do everything possible, Mr. Brown, to block your wheat deal with Novikov, but I'm no saboteur. I'm just trying to humor Big Julie. I thought those red flags might create a little confusion, possibly hold up your shipment loading, maybe even raise some Soviet suspicions."

"How could you even think of doing such a thing to us?" Maxie angrily and bitterly complained.

"It was a stupid idea," Baston confessed. "I admit the whole thing is crazy and completely wrong. I apologize and assure you I meant no harm. Please forgive me. I'm going to tell Big Julie I refused to sabotage your wheat deal. If he blows up at me, I'll resign. In fact, I intend quitting anyway. I resent Big Julie ordering me to block your wheat sale. I don't want to break any laws. I prefer to quit my job, rather than wrong anybody. I'm very sorry about this; please forgive me."

"Baston, you violated our trust," Brown replied sternly. "Your tampering with our wheat shipment was dangerous. You're lucky you didn't damage it. You say you didn't intend to do any damage either, and you've certainly been completely honest about the matter. I'll let you go this time, but I want you to tell Big Julie about the favor. He owes me plenty for this kind of dirty dealing. Tell him to leave my business alone from now on, or I'll go after him with the evidence of what you did right here, in front of all these witnesses. Now go get those red flags off our hopper cars and get out of here fast."

"Yes, sir, Mr. Brown. I'm sure sorry about this," Baston admitted, retreating quickly to carry out Brown's orders.

When Baston left to retrieve the red flags he'd placed on the hopper cars, Brown asked the others to overlook the incident and forget it ever happened. However, Naddy said she'd have to inform her boss, Nikolai Novikov, about the matter, since they had some contracts with Fiske. "Do you mind, Mr. Brown?" she asked.

"Of course not, Naddy," Brown replied. "I'd tell Nikolai myself, if he were here. Tell him the incident proves Fiske isn't very trustworthy. As for the red flagging, Baston didn't know it, and I didn't want him to, but we already unloaded those hopper cars, so they're completely empty. If we hadn't caught Baston, he wouldn't have harmed us anyway. He and Big Julie have only harmed themselves. Baston showed us he has a conscience, but I wouldn't bet on Big Julie."

"Comrades, there's our Krasnodar," Captain

Rezhnikov remarked proudly. "Looks like the loading is done and the tugs will be coming to move our ship away from the dock. I'm told we'll have 25,000 tons aboard here and we'll be picking up another 5,000 tons from an elevator in Port Sorel."

The group approached the Krasnodar as several inspectors were preparing to leave the ship, accompanied by Haggarson's representatives who were carrying their completed paperwork. The gigantic freighter was an impressive sight, dwarfing the small delegation of spectators who walked in quiet astonishment from one end of the ship to the other with Captain Rezhnikov, who pointed out its unusual features. When they reached the end of their long walk, Bert commented to Harry that shipment number one to the USSR was almost underway.

Next, Maxie began speaking. "Congratulations, Harry," she managed to say softly, still recovering from Baston's treachery and struggling to conceal her bitter disappointment. Then, perking up, she remarked, "This is a significant moment in the history of H. B. Exports."

"Indeed it is," Brown observed. "And I say thank you everyone for your help. Naddy, it's good you're here, too, and we're indebted to you and your associates for giving us the order. We're grateful to you, too, Hjalmar, and to you, Captain Rezhnikov, for your splendid hospitality and briefing."

Captain Rezhnikov replied that he was glad to have had the chance to meet and talk with them. Then both he and Haggarson excused themselves. The Captain had to prepare his ship for departure and Haggarson needed to get to his representatives to make sure the paperwork was completed properly on this first shipment. After they said their goodbyes, Brown indicated he had to leave also, since he had an appointment for lunch with his wife Josie and the kids. They planned to go sight-seeing in Duluth afterwards. Maxie left, too, because she had to get a shipment form signed at the Min-Dak Co-op elevator office. Only Bert and Naddy remained. They were alone together at last under the warm soft rays of the late morning sun. Bert spoke first.

"Naddy, wasn't it a shock to discover that Baston was a phony news reporter?"

"Maybe it was for you, Bert, but I knew all along Baston worked for Fiske. Our security people checked him out, right after our Taylorsville Hotel dinner. They informed me later Baston worked for Fiske. How could you Americans believe Baston without verifying his credentials?"

"We're a trusting people, Naddy," Bert responded. "We assume others are telling the truth until we catch them in a lie. After that, we aren't so ready to trust them any more. I suppose you had secret police check me out, too."

"Oh, Bert, don't be sarcastic. Of course our people checked you out, but I didn't ask them to. They did it anyway. It's their job. They told me all about you, shortly after we met in the Taylorsville Park. Almost everything they told me I already knew from what you had said, so I'm glad I put my trust in you. There aren't many people you can trust anymore. That's why security is needed. It's better to check people out first, than suffer later for the consequences of a lie."

Bert smiled at Naddy and gently took her by the hand. He led her to a bench by the wharf, where they sat and watched the Krasnodar's departure. Soon they began hugging each other to keep warm, while bad weather began brewing out on the lake. Whitecapped waves were beginning to form, and the air blowing in from the cold lake had a chilling effect.

While the two lovers clung to each other's warmth on the wharf bench, they exchanged comments about their innermost feelings. They had both looked forward to that day, and it seemed to take so long to come. Naddy felt bad she had to fly back to Moscow later in the afternoon, but Nikolai said he wanted her to hurry back. Unfortunately, she and Bert only had a little time left to be together.

Bert was grateful for what time they had, and said he cherished each moment. Naddy responded with her body, as their lips tenderly touched. The two remained wrapped in each other's embrace for a long time. They seemed to have removed themselves from their surroundings until they were only conscious of each other.

Suddenly a succession of whistle blasts from the Krasnodar roused the happy couple from their raptures. One long, one short; one long, one short! That was the signal to the Aerial Lift Bridge to raise itself high, while the Krasnodar slowly powered ahead through the high winds and whitecapped water, until it reached the open lake. The two tugboats that had helped the big ship ease itself away from its Min-Dak Co-op docking were now chugging back to their own inner harbor moorings.

Bert and Naddy got up from the bench and drew themselves together in a final embrace. Moments later, the two walked slowly away. At first they held each other tightly while trying to walk. Then, laughing, they began holding hands. Soon they broke into a brisk jog, which quickly changed to a fast run. They appeared to be racing each other. Their youth and fresh love must have lightened their hearts that they could run so. Or was it the threat of a coming storm that moved them?

PART II. HOSTILITIES

11

HAGGARSON'S RADIO ROOM

In a back room at Vessel Agent Hjalmar Haggarson's headquarters, there was a clustered array of marine radio equipment. Scratchy squawks, screechy howls, and other staccato sounds of heavy static alternated with Haggarson's persistent vocal attempts at contacting the USSR's freighter, the Krasnodar.

"West Lake Radio to Soviet ship Krasnodar — come in, please!

"West Lake Radio, this is West Lake Radio, calling Soviet ship Krasnodar — come in, please!

"West Lake Radio to Soviet ship Krasnodar — come in! Come in!"

"Krasnodar....West Lake....hard....hear....sudden storm, 1860 hours....Mayday!.... fifty-foot waves....hatch hydraulics....gone....shaking....shuddering....breaking up! We're breaking up!....Help!....Anybody!....Water in here!....Can't hold!....Going down....Mayday! Mayday! May...."

"West Lake Radio to Krasnodar — come in! Come in! Come in!

"West Lake Radio, this is West Lake Radio, calling Soviet ship Krasnodar — come in, please! Come in! Come in!

"Krasnodar, come in, please!"

Haggarson threw three switches, turned a knob, then started transmitting again.

"West Lake 15 to U. S. Coast Guard 22A — Mayday! Mayday! Come in, please! Mayday! Mayday!"

"U. S. Coast Guard 22A to West Lake 15 — you're on!"

"Duluth Vessel Agent Hjalmar Haggarson here. Urgent! Am reporting probable midlake ship disaster, 1943 hours. The Soviet ship Krasnodar, an ocean bulk freighter underway from Duluth to Sault Sainte Marie with 25,000 tons of wheat, got caught in sudden storm violence midlake. Made last radio contact three minutes ago. Ship's radioman reported 'fifty-foot waves,' 'hatch hydraulics gone,' 'shaking,' 'shuddering,' 'breaking up.' The radioman yelled 'Mayday!' repeatedly. Looks like they've gone down, over."

"Roger! We'll notify Air Sea Rescue at once. We'll have our cutter Holcomb work that area immediately. Have you got a reading? Over."

"Roger, CG22A. The Soviet ship Krasnodar left the Duluth Aerial Lift Bridge at 1259 hours, headed for open lake along the southern route to Sault Sainte Marie. Speed was maximum 15 knots. Last contact was 1943 hours, so looks like 6.91, or nearly 7 full hours out from the lift bridge. Over."

"Roger, West Lake. Nice work! We'll get a good plot on that, over."

"West Lake, here. I'll contact ship's owners and shippers immediately. Over and out."

Turning quickly to his telephone, Haggarson contacted the operator and requested the Soviet Embassy in Washington, D. C. While waiting for the connection, he nervously tapped the desk top with his fingers a few moments, then said, "Soviet Embassy? This is an emergency! Please let me talk to your Maritime Affairs Attache."

128

Haggarson waited a few more moments, nervously tapping the desk top again. When someone answered, Haggarson quickly asked, "Are you the Maritime Affairs Attache? Thank God I reached you at this late hour. I've terrible news to report. Your ocean bulk freighter Krasnodar has broken up in the middle of Lake Superior, approximately 1943 hours. I fear it's lost."

After Hjalmar Haggarson identified himself as the ship's agent in Duluth, he was quickly informed that the embassy had already monitored the Krasnodar's last message. Haggarson was astonished at this news, and indicated he wasn't aware the Soviets had any such radio contact with their shipping. Lake Superior is so far inland from the Atlantic and so far away from Washington, D. C., he said it never occurred to him there'd be such contact. The Soviet Embassy official commented further that he suspected foul play and intended to take drastic action.

Haggarson pleaded with the embassy official to reconsider. The U. S. Coast Guard was presently patrolling the Krasnodar's location, Haggarson noted, so the Soviets should wait and see what the U. S. can do first, rather than attempt anything rash. Haggarson pointed out that he reported the tragedy to the U. S. Coast Guard a few minutes previously and Air Sea Rescue was launching its search mode at that very moment. Moreover, the U. S. Coast Guard cutter Holcomb was assigned to work the Krasnodar's distress area, and for any further news on the matter, the Soviet Embassy official should get in touch with the U. S. Coast Guard directly. Haggarson even gave the official the phone number for the 9th District Headquarters in Cleveland, Ohio, instructing him to identify himself and request the Coast Guard to keep him informed about its search efforts.

After the call was ended, Haggarson slowly hung up the phone, got up from his chair, took out his handkerchief, and patted the sweat off his brow. He wiped under his eyes, too, and pressed the handkerchief to his nose, mouth, and neck. After performing these somewhat soothing actions, he put his handkerchief away and paced around the room a few times, displaying a pained look on his face. Eventually he sat down. Then, picking up the phone again, he moved his finger around quickly to push the buttons for a local number he read from a slip of paper he'd taken from his shirt pocket.

"Mr. Brown, is that you? Haggarson here. Thank God you left me your hotel room phone number! I didn't think I'd ever need it, but now a most tragic situation has developed. I'm afraid the Krasnodar has sunk.

"Yes, that's right. You heard me correctly, Mr. Brown. I happened to be on duty at our marine radio transmitter this evening while our office crew attended its bowling league's championship dinner. I kept trying to contact the Krasnodar for several minutes to check its location. When the ship's radioman finally responded, it was very hard to understand him, because of all the radio static, storm sounds, and background noise on the ship. However, I did manage to pick up a message of sorts.

"The Krasnodar radioman shouted that his ship got caught in a 'sudden storm' with 'fifty-foot waves.' Then I remember him yelling, 'hatch hydraulics gone,' and that the ship was 'shaking' and 'shuddering.' Next I could make out the words, 'breaking up! We're breaking up!' He shouted for help from anybody, and his last words were, 'Water in here!....Can't hold!....Going down....Mayday! Mayday! May....' His radio cut out, right in the middle of the word 'Mayday!'

"Yes, Mr. Brown, he repeated twice, 'breaking up! We're breaking up!'

"Please be assured, Mr. Brown, I'm doing all I can. I immediately notified the U. S. Coast Guard, and Air Sea

Rescue efforts are underway. The Coast Guard has dispatched its cutter Holcomb to the scene. I'm keeping on top of this situation all the way."

Haggarson told Brown everything else that had been done, including the phone call to the Soviet Embassy's Maritime Affairs Attache in Washington, D.C., and the suggestion that the Soviets keep close contact with the U. S. Coast Guard. Then Haggarson extended his condolences to Brown and regret that there was nothing more they could do. He advised Brown to continue vacationing with his family in Duluth. Haggarson concluded by observing that such tragedies can and do happen. He promised to phone Brown immediately about any new developments, but was certain that Brown would be getting plenty of additional information from the newspapers, radio, and TV. Brown thanked Haggarson, then Haggerson said he was glad to be of help, and on that comment the conversation ended.

After hanging up the phone, Haggarson impulsively got up and walked over to his office window, which he quickly opened. Peering out into the stormy night, he saw a vast armada of giant waves smashing their whitecaps along the rock strewn shoreline. His ears were overwhelmed by the roaring sounds these exploding monsters made as they slammed into the harbor entrance breakers beyond the lift bridge.

Late into the stormy night, Vessel Agent Haggarson stood looking out his office window while maintaining his marine radio vigil. He seemed mesmerized by the sight of Lake Superior's water shooting skyward in a violent spectacle of exploding waves and foaming spray, all of which was illuminated by harbor area beacon lights. Also, he kept wondering whether the storm would ever end.

At one point during the night, when experiencing his moment of greatest anguish, he seemed certain he saw the ghostly spirits of the Krasnodar's drowned

131

crewmen. They appeared to be soaring skyward towards some distant galaxy. Perhaps they were in a hurry to leave the scene of their recent suffering, so they could get to some bright new world beyond the stars.

At last, as the storm subsided, an exhausted Haggarson closed the window as impulsively as he'd opened it. He wanted to turn away from the frenzied lake and leave his wild imaginings behind him. In the inner calm of his quiet office, he bowed his head in silent prayer for the drowned Krasnodar crew. Their terrible tragedy had become his longest night.

12

NOVIKOV'S REPORT

Pacing behind the desk of his Moscow Exportkhleb office, a troubled, disappointed, and frustrated Nikolai Novikov began advising his two key employees. "Comrades Baranovna and Konya, the tragic Krasnodar sinking must not catch us off our guard," he warned. "We must not fail for one second to function in our jobs, less we put our glorious Union of Soviet Socialist Republics in danger of destruction. At trying times like these, citizens should voluntarily join together, renew their determination, and render superior service.

"When our embassy contact in Washington, D. C., informed me about the destruction of the Krasnodar, he reported 'foul play' by the Americans, and indicated that our country would take drastic action. How agonizing it is to face the reality that the U. S. betrayed us and sank our splendid ship.

"Forty good crewmen drowned. Our Krasnodar destroyed. Comrades, let's move swiftly. Let's aid our threatened nation during these dangerous times by dedicating ourselves to action."

"Nikolai," cried Naddy, "I'm so ashamed. I fully trusted and loved the Americans. I confess I fell in love with Bert Jackson. I thought he loved me, too, but how stupid I am! What a simpleton to let myself be duped by those smooth-talking Americans! We even caught one of them, that Julius Fiske agent, James Baston, trying to sabotage our wheat during the loading of the Krasnodar. Maybe Baston caused our Krasnodar to sink. Baston could be part of another U. S. plot to destroy us. I offer my resignation to you, Nikolai. I'm unworthy to serve our people, because I've been such a trusting fool."

"Now, now, Naddy," Novikov took heart, "no need to blame yourself. You forget I have an old friend named Harry Brown. I just can't believe he's involved in this. Nor is Bert Jackson or Maxine Gadsden behind it. I tell you, there's more to this than we know. Let's not close our minds or blame ourselves.

"If you say you're a fool, Naddy, then I'm the fool of fools. Remember who introduced you to the Americans? Who led you into all this? If you're a fool, then it is I who am the Czar of Fools! No, let's not blame ourselves or Harry, Bert, or Maxie. Rather, let's blame the U. S. Government for its treachery, and move swiftly to pick up the pieces. We must make our citizens proud that we're their representatives. Remember, we're all representatives of the people."

"Agreed," Helga Baranovna affirmed. "I, like you, still trust Harry Brown and Bert and Maxie. I think the U. S. Government is behind the Krasnodar sinking, because the U. S. Government is full of CIA saboteurs, terrorists, and warmongers. I stand with you, Nikolai, to do my best for our people. Please tell me, what should I do right now?"

"We'll work together on this and move quickly," said Nikolai. "First thing let's do is list the demands we'll have to make of the Americans to compensate us for our losses. I'd appreciate you both working on this, while I contact Chairman Vasil Golgolev. I must inform him of our actions."

When Novikov concluded his instructions, Helga and Naddy began making a list of demands. Meanwhile,

Novikov picked up his phone, pressed one of the buttons, and said, "Chairman Golgolev, please. Urgent!" Then he rearranged some papers on his desk as he waited for a reply. When it came, he stiffened his body into a position of attention and began speaking.

"Comrade Chairman, Nikolai Novikov here. I presume you've heard about the sinking of the Krasnodar by the Americans?" There was a brief pause as Novikov listened, after which he again spoke.

"Yes, Comrade Chairman, we have the same information as you. Our Ambassador to the U. S. says it's foul play. We're preparing a list of losses and demands right now. Deputy Director Nadezhda Konya and my assistant, Helga Baranovna, are working on it. We'll have it ready for you very soon." Novikov paused momentarily to listen to Golgolev, then said, "Yes, Comrade Chairman, I'll be at your office with the demand list by the time Marshal Plekhanov arrives. Goodbye, Comrade Chairman and thank you for your support in this."

After hanging up the phone, Nikolai told Helga and Naddy they'd meet with Chairman Golgolev and Marshal Plekhanov as soon as the demand list was completed. Naddy said they could leave right away and finish the list in handwritten form while they were driving to Chairman Golgolev's office. Novikov was satisfied with that approach, so they all left.

13

CHAIRMAN GOLGOLEV'S DEMANDS

Marshal Gavril Plekhanov, the highest-ranking military official in the Soviet Union, arrived at Chairman Vasil Golgolev's Kremlin office. Earlier in the morning he had traveled to the outskirts of Moscow to attend a retirement breakfast for a senior officer and close friend. Unfortunately, the weather that day was rainy and the road was quite slippery under the Marshal's fast limousine, so he was relieved to have reached the end of his trip safely.

"Marshal Plekhanov, it was good of you to come this quickly," Chairman Golgolev commented.

Golgolev was a man of medium height and stocky build, who made an authoritative impression on his many rivals. Maybe it was due in part to the fact that he stood behind an immense, highly lacquered, mahogany stained desk, and had a large Soviet flag draped across the wall behind him. Or, perhaps, it was his graying and balding appearance, augmented by a solemn manner. His bushy, untrimmed, dark brows were accented by dark eyes that seemed to look right through a person. Big, hairy-backed hands opened in welcome or clenched into determined fists. This time his arms were extended outwards and his hands opened in friendship.

"Comrade Nikolai Novikov of Exportkhleb is on his way here right now," Golgolev announced. "He's bringing something important for us to review. Have you heard the news that the Americans destroyed our freighter, the Krasnodar?"

"Yes, I heard it earlier this morning, Comrade Chairman," Plekhanov responded. "Our intelligence agents in North America immediately notified me, so I could activate Plan Overlook out of our base at Sakharovka, near Chuguyevka. Plan Overlook is now in effect."

As head of the Soviet Military General Staff, Marshal Gavril Plekhanov was almost as powerful a man as Golgolev. With his erect military bearing and uniformed appearance, the Marshal seemed an even more commanding person than his boss. Wiry haired and weathered, Plekhanov looked like he'd led the rugged, disciplined life of a soldier. He stood comfortably, though somewhat rigidly, while continuing his comments.

"As you may recall from my earlier briefings, Comrade Chairman, our Plan Overlook consists of continuous patrols by our 'Product 84's.' These are our new, MiG 25 series aircraft. These ultramodern, ultrafast, ultrapowerful airborne systems are capable of being flown anywhere in the world by our thoroughly trained pilots. We have several 84's in the air right now, scanning American borders, probing American defenses, and determining the magnitude of America's war preparations against us. As of this moment, we're not sure of the nature of the U. S. threat. We've detected some military movements, but we're presently analyzing them to determine the thrust of any grand plan."

"Good, Comrade Gavril," Golgolev complimented. "Keep moving fast! We can't allow ourselves to be caught unprepared. In fact, I'm ordering you to activate Plan 7-21, our full scale emergency alert and mobilization. We simply can't take any chances. I, for one, refuse to assume any optimistic view of the U. S. Government. It's too risky. After the U. S. violated the U. N. Charter by its military attack on Granada, its wild-eyed raid on Libya, and its reckless incursions into Nicaragua, who's to say that now, with its destruction of our Krasnodar, the Americans aren't planning some kind of preemptive, first-strike nuclear attack against us? When you get Plan 7-21 operational, please come back here for a videoscreen report to our Politburo. We need to inform them of your readiness."

There was a momentary interruption at this point as Golgolev's assistant, Tatyana Borshak, announced over the intercom that Nikolai, Nadezhda, and Helga had arrived. Golgolev told Tatyana to show them in. When Tatyana opened the door to the outer office, various voices could be heard shouting in the background. The barely audible voices were coming from a gathering of angry citizens just outside the Kremlin walls. They were an assemblage of workers, bureaucrats, peasants, even some military, and included men, women, and children. They were standing in the lightly falling rain, angry, frustrated, and grimly determined that their demands be heard.

"My only son went down on the Krasnodar and I'm a widow, what can I do?"

"The American saboteurs must pay. Tell Golgolev!"

"Our father was murdered by the American assassins."

"We're lost, too, unless Chairman Vasil does something. Help us!"

"Down with the terrorist Americans!"

"Don't let the American warmongers get away with this! They've killed our people!"

"They've murdered my husband!"

"Make them pay, Comrade Chairman! Make them pay!"

"Don't forget the crew of the Krasnodar! Don't betray the shipmates!"

"Get the American butchers for this! Avenge our dead comrades!"

Soon Novikov and his assistants were inside Golgolev's office and the door was closed behind them, so that the shouts from outside the Kremlin walls could no longer be heard. However, Golgolev asked Tatyana to send a spokesman out to the crowd and thank them for their concerns. He also wanted to inform them he'd heard their demands, was in the process of acting on them, and would report all progress to the news media. He then turned to greet Novikov and the others, after which Novikov spoke.

"Comrade Chairman, we prepared a list of losses and demands resulting from the American act of treachery to our Krasnodar and the drowning of its crew of forty. This list was written by my two assistants, who are witnesses with me to all our dealings with the U. S. We can answer any questions you or Comrade Marshal Plekhanov may have."

"Good! Thank you, Comrade Nikolai," Golgolev approvingly acknowledged. Then, after quickly scanning the demand list, he put it on his desk, pressed a button on his office intercom, and asked Comrade Borshak to bring in the Swiss Ambassador who'd been summoned to the Kremlin earlier that day.

"I'll send for him now, Comrade Chairman," Tatyana Borshak replied through the intercom. "The officer of the guard notified me that Ambassador Clayborn is at the front entrance talking with the angry crowd. He'll be here in a few moments."

Taking his finger off the desk intercom button, Golgolev stood erect and faced his visitors. He suggested that while they waited for the Swiss Ambassador, it was a good time for him to ask a few questions. He began by asking Naddy about her impression of the Americans and what she thought of them.

"Comrade Chairman," Naddy began, "some of them are good people, but others are smooth saboteurs and tricksters. For example, one of them we met posed as a news reporter and charmed everyone into trusting him. These Americans will betray you when you least expect it. You must be on your guard at all times with them. They're very tricky."

"I assure you, Comrade Konya, the U. S. Government won't catch us asleep," Golgolev promised. Turning to Helga, he asked for her opinion of the Americans.

"I agree with Comrade Konya, " Helga replied. "The capitalistic American warmongers talk softly to get you to come in close, then they hit you with a big stick. We met a few good Americans, but we also met too many of the other kind: crazy capitalist gangsters, drunk with wealth and power. They engage in wild speculations, indulge in unconscionable depravities, and are reckless with the lives of others."

"You mean they think to bring us all down?" Golgolev questioned.

"I'm not so sure of that," Helga answered. "I'm just suspicious of a nation of rowdies who would deliberately sink a harmless ship like our Krasnodar, drowning its innocent crew of forty comrades. I fear for what such a murderous nation might do next."

"Please be assured," Golgolev concluded, "we shall guard against the possibility of any future treachery. Marshal Plekhanov, do you have any questions?"

"Yes, Chairman Vasil. I wish to ask Director Novikov about any American military buildup or unusual armaments activity he may have observed."

"In my travels across the United States," Novikov reflected, "I must admit I haven't seen any unusual military activity other than those your intelligence forces already reported. However, it seems strange there'd be no military activity, if the Americans were preparing to attack us. Perhaps the Krasnodar sinking was the work of a gang of saboteurs or terrorists. Whatever the provocation, I agree we can't take any chances and that we should let time tell us the true story."

"Your observations are appreciated," Golgolev acknowledged. "Here comes Swiss Ambassador Manfred Clayborn."

As the door opened for Clayborn, more shouting could be heard coming into the outer office from the outside walls beyond.

"Let Chairman Golgolev come down here! We'll tell him what to do!"

"Make the warmonger Americans pay! Make the warmonger Americans pay!"

"Nuke the USA! Make them pay!"

This last remark led the angry voices to chant in unison, "USA must pay! USA must pay! USA must pay! USA...."

Then the office door closed and the crowd's chanting became inaudible again. At this point, Chairman Golgolev began speaking. He introduced Ambassador Manfred Clayborn to Marshal Gavril Plekhanov, Exportkhleb Director Nikolai Novikov, Deputy Exportkhleb Director Nadezhda Konya, and Exportkhleb Administrator, Helga Baranovna.

"Pleased to make your acquaintance," Clayborn replied politely in Russian, one of several languages he spoke fluently.

Ambassador Clayborn was a tall, slender, youthful looking man about fifty years old. He wore a dark charcoal suit, white shirt, and striking, red-orange tie with white stripes, similar to the colors of the Swiss flag. It contrasted sharply with his dark suit, and gave him a rather distinguished appearance. Dark haired and

141

handsome for his age, he also had light skin and deep blue eyes. These combined with his soft, courteous, well-educated manner to make a persuasive impression. It was easy to see why his countrymen appointed him an ambassador.

"I'd very much like to be of service to you," Clayborn added.

"Good!" Golgolev exclaimed. "That's precisely why we called you here. Thank you for being so prompt!" Clayborn nodded in acknowledgment, and Golgolev reached to his desk for the demand list he'd received from Novikov. Holding the list in his hand, Golgolev spoke again.

"You were already briefed earlier by my representative, so you're aware of the Krasnodar's sinking by the American warmongers. Subsequent to your earlier briefing about this latest U. S. provocation, I've ordered, in the name of our Soviet people, the expulsion of the U. S. Ambassador. I've already recalled our own Ambassador from Washington, D. C.

"Now, then, Ambassador Clayborn, since you're from neutral Switzerland and have agreed to be our representative to the Americans, I have an important assignment for you. You've heard the angry shouts outside of concerned relatives and friends of the dead Krasnodar crew. Here's a list of our losses and demands. I'm asking you to present this to the U. S. President, John Morrison. The Americans must satisfy our demands quickly, if our two countries are to continue living in peace."

At this point, Golgolev began reading aloud from the list:

1. The USSR demands full compensation for the loss of its ocean bulk freighter

Krasnodar. The amount to be paid is $25,000,000.

2. The USSR demands full compensation to surviving families and heirs of the forty dead Krasnodar crew. The amount to be paid is $1,000,000 per each lost crew member.

3. The USSR demands full satisfaction of all its grain contracts with the Americans. All conditions of these contracts must be met on schedule."

Golgolev stopped reading, looked at Clayborn, and remarked that these were just the first three demands. The Ambassador could read the rest of them later, on his way to Washington, D. C. Then Golgolev added a somber note, vowing that if there were any more treachery, the full force and nuclear warhead power of the USSR would be unleashed on the USA.

"I'm talking about twenty thousand nuclear missiles and bombs," Golgolev warned. "Also, tell the U.S. President our demands must be quickly met."

"I'll tell President Morrison exactly what you said, Chairman Golgolev," Clayborn promised. "I'm truly grateful for the opportunity to render this service to your country. I realize it's a life and death matter for the whole world that the Krasnodar affair be resolved by peaceful means. I plead with you, therefore, don't do anything rash or provoke any kind of armed conflict over the sinking of the Krasnodar. Let's resolve this whole matter peacefully. Surely there must be some rational explanation for this tragedy. The Americans wouldn't intentionally sink anyone's cargo ship, especially one that was carrying wheat."

"Aha!" cut in Golgolev. "Don't be too sure on that point, Mr. Clayborn. To the Americans wheat means nothing. Don't you know? They pay farmers for *not* growing wheat. In a hungry world, they plow crops under, then dump their surpluses on world markets at below cost. The U. S. Government actually pays American farmers to sell grain below cost. The U. S. calls these payments 'subsidies.'

"I tell you, Ambassador Clayborn, these Americans probably caused our Krasnodar to sink so they could get rid of even more surplus wheat. Why, the U. S. Government is so deeply in debt and dangerously near bankruptcy, it probably doesn't have enough money to pay any more subsidies, and that's another good reason the U. S. wants a war with us. It wants to get its citizens to stop thinking about their enormous national debt and rapidly expanding taxes. The simplistic strategy of the U.S. Government is to get its citizens to forget their economic woes by exciting them with talk of war. Americans love to go to war, and they'll do anything to win it, because they hate losing. Americans can't stand to lose."

"Nevertheless, Chairman Golgolev," Clayborn urged, "I beg you to allow sufficient time for the matter to be resolved peacefully. I'm confident, if you give them the chance, you'll find Americans to be your trustworthy friends, maybe even best friends."

"Very well, Ambassador Clayborn," Golgolev acknowledged. "We'll watch and wait, but we'll mobilize, too. Even now our technological eyes are probing the remotest regions of the earth for evidence of America's newest deceit and treachery. Nevertheless, we'll patiently await President Morrison's reply and swift satisfaction of our demands. But we'll not be asleep while we wait. Good luck to you, Ambassador Clayborn. We appreciate your assistance in this dangerous Krasnodar affair."

"Chairman Golgolev, the whole world appreciates your willingness to wait," Clayborn complimented, shaking Golgolev's hand in farewell.

144

14

PRESIDENT MORRISON'S RESPONSE

Several days elapsed during Ambassador Clayborn's journey to Washington, D. C., and call on President John Morrison at the White House. Meanwhile, news of the Krasnodar affair filled the world with fear and anxiety, especially the U. S., where military intelligence gatherers and leaders were becoming increasingly aware of the Soviet Union's massive mobilization. Particularly noticeable were the drastic increases in Soviet armed patrols and the many daring probes of U. S. radar defenses. What had initially been a routine American concern was now becoming an agonizing alarm that spread over an entire continent and escalated into a media crescendo that finally reached the White House. For these and other reasons, President Morrison was eager to receive Ambassador Clayborn the very moment he arrived.

"You say, Ambassador, the Soviets actually believe we sabotaged their ship and we're about to attack them? It's insanity!" Morrison protested. "Why, the evidence our people have suggests the Krasnodar sank in Lake Superior during a violent storm. It's rumored that the ship's hydraulic hatch-closing mechanism failed.

"I read in our newspapers that lake water from

fifty-foot high waves flooded the ship's holds and got into the hatch hydraulic mechanism. Water shorted the electrical circuits, the hatches opened, and the holds filled with lake water from fifty-foot waves that swamped the ship. Maybe the 25,000 tons of water-soaked wheat rapidly swelled, causing the ship to break up and sink. The U. S. had nothing to do with any of that. It was entirely accidental, a tragic quirk of circumstance.

"However, since it happened deep in the midwest, some 2,000 miles inside our own territorial waters, I can readily understand why the Soviets suspect us," President Morrison thought aloud, slowly pacing back and forth behind his oval desk in the White House. "Still, it's insanity. Why would we want to sink a Soviet cargo ship and start a nuclear war? Somebody isn't telling me something."

Elected President of the U. S. in a landslide victory, President Morrison was truly a man of the people. During the election campaign, his simple honesty was apparent in the unusual respect and kindness he showed his opponent. It was no surprise, therefore, that Morrison would look for possible justification of the USSR's warlike actions.

"Mr. President," Clayborn responded in English, a second foreign language he'd learned, "Chairman Golgolev is willing to settle the matter peacefully. He agreed to patiently await your reply and quick satisfaction of his compensation demands. However, he assured me his country will continue mobilizing for all-out nuclear war to protect themselves against an American surprise attack and any further U. S. aggression.

President Morrison thanked Ambassador Clayborn for his frankness, then excused himself to press a button on his desk intercom. He asked his secretary to get ready to admit General Daniels. Releasing the intercom button, Morrison spoke again to his guest.

"Ambassador Clayborn, I'm going to ask a special

favor of you. I want you to stay here at the White House, until I get a better handle on what's happening. We can't reply to Golgolev's demands until we're more fully informed about the circumstances surrounding the sinking of the Krasnodar. Is that acceptable to you?"

Clayborn agreed to remain in the White House and wait for a reply. Then President Morrison thanked him, acknowledging the importance of his help. Next, Morrison pushed the button on his intercom and asked his secretary to send in General Daniels and see to it that Clayborn was assigned a comfortable White House room for an overnight stay. As President Morrison walked with Clayborn to the front door of the Oval Office, General Daniels entered, so the President introduced him to Clayborn. Clayborn and Daniels both expressed their pleasure at meeting each other, then Clayborn left the room.

General David Daniels was a modestly muscular, trim-looking General, whose alert stance and military bearing signified a man of power and authority. Though his skin had a somewhat roughened appearance, and his brownish gray hair had receded at the forehead and thinned with age, nevertheless, his uniform was new, and his many campaign ribbons, medals, and battle stars looked fresh and distinctive. Also, his bright brown eyes and quick movements suggested a man who was physically fit.

The President liked Daniels, because he was always friendly and wore an honest smile. Over the years, the many men and women who were the General's military contemporaries acquired a high regard for him, also. For these reasons, the President usually called Daniels by his first name.

"Now, then, David," Morrison began, putting his hand on the General's shoulder and walking him to a chair near the Presidential desk, "we've got some serious business with this Krasnodar affair." Going behind the desk, the President continued his comments to Daniels. "Here's what has happened so far: USSR Chairman Vasil Golgolev presented a list of demands to Swiss Ambassador Clayborn, who just gave it to me."

Morrison handed the list to Daniels, then waited for the General to scan it. Several moments later, the President spoke again.

"I'm sure you've already heard that the Soviets expelled our Ambassador and recalled theirs from Washington, D. C. Now I'm told they're mobilizing for all-out war. What's your assessment, David?"

"Mr. President, Sir," General Daniels replied. "As Chairman of the Joint Chiefs of Staff, I've been informed of these developments from the very beginning. Our intelligence sources are very close to the situation, and I think the Soviets are over-reacting by mobilizing. It's costly. It's tragic. It's too dangerous a development resulting from a single ship loss, especially one that we had nothing whatsoever to do with. Therefore, we must get this matter settled quickly, before it gets any further out of hand.

"Unfortunately, we must also mobilize ourselves to defend against the nervous Soviets in the event some screwball over there starts firing nuclear missiles at us. That's my assessment of the situation, Mr. President."

Morrison expressed his appreciation and said he agreed with Daniels. Then he formally gave the General that dreaded order to mobilize U. S. armed forces and prepare them for the possibility of a Soviet attack. Civil Defense was also put on an alert status, so the entire U. S. population could be protected.

After implementing the President's orders, Daniels was instructed to return to the Oval Office and give a thorough report of progress. Morrison placed his videoscreen equipment at the General's disposal, so the two of them together could evaluate their nation's readiness. Before leaving, Daniels saluted the President in acknowledgment of the mobilization order, and Morrison, as Commander in Chief, returned his General's salute.

15

BROWN'S INITIATIVE

After Maxie, Bert, and Harry had returned to Taylorsville from Duluth, the increasing volume of news about the Krasnodar affair created an anxiety in them that bordered on chaos. Their enormous wheat sale to the Soviets was now in limbo. Pressures from the Min-Dak Co-op were mounting daily, because farmers wanted to be paid for their 25,000 tons of wheat, never mind that it went down with the Krasnodar. Government officials, special agents, and news reporters were scurrying around everywhere, asking questions, construing answers, and generally making it difficult for the partners at H. B. Exports, Inc., to get any kind of work done.

At least Brown's wife, Josie, and four children were able to enjoy their brief Duluth vacation. Harry managed to keep the Krasnodar news from them as long as he could, so that it wouldn't spoil their fun. They enjoyed all the attractions, saw all the sights, and bought some enticing souvenirs, clothes, and toys in a liberal sampling of Duluth's extraordinary shops. Harry paid for everything with bank cards. So what if he didn't have any money at that moment. He and Josie decided to simply borrow against their future income, preferring to take a vacation with their children right away, rather than risk the possibility of not having one later.

Harry had immediately communicated the Krasnodar news to his two partners while they were still in Duluth. Both of them were disheartened to hear it. They were especially shocked and saddened at the loss of Captain Grigor Rezhnikov and his crew. Also, their high income hopes were dashed; their futures insecure; their routines shaken. It seemed they had just about lost all their *esprit de corps*, until back in their Taylorsville offices, during their morning coffee break in their company conference room, Harry reminded them they still had a valid contract for the biggest wheat sale of their career. The sinking of a single cargo ship didn't mean their world had ended and their lives were over. What they had to do now was keep themselves calm, pick up the pieces, and get their huge sale going again. It was high time they got control of their lives, too, Harry noted. Nearly a week had gone by since the tragedy, and they hadn't yet talked to Novikov about the matter.

Outside the conference room a telephone rang and Bert volunteered to step out and catch the call, since he was closest to the door. "H. B. Exports," he announced, after pressing a button on a desk speaker phone.

"Mr. Harry Brown please," came a soft voice from the handset.

"Just a moment, I'll...Naddy, is that you?"

"Yes!" Naddy replied. "I'm trying to reach Harry Brown for Nikolai Novikov. Nikolai wants to talk to Brown and...oh, Bert! Why did your country do it? Why would your people sabotage and sink our Krasnodar, murdering its crew?"

"No, Naddy, that's wrong! We had nothing to do with the sinking of the Krasnodar. There was no sabotage. Please don't even think it of us. We're as shocked and saddened at this tragic affair as you are. The Krasnodar disaster was a dreadful accident, a fluke of

151

nature.   Remember how stormy the weather was becoming during the Krasnodar's departure? We both saw the huge whitecap waves coming in from the Lake.

"Naddy, our Coast Guard is investigating the possibility that giant storm waves swamped the open holds of the Krasnodar, causing it to sink. Just before it went down, the radioman said the Krasnodar's hatch hydraulics were gone. Perhaps the flooded cargo holds caused the wheat to swell and break up the ship. Ex ship Captain Hjalmar Haggarson says too much water in the Krasnodar's holds could cause the 25,000 tons of wheat to rapidly expand and break up the ship. Wheat swells swiftly in water, Naddy. Ask Helga, she'll confirm what I'm saying."

Bert continued his conversation with Naddy, reminding her what they both heard in Haggarson's office concerning the Krasnodar's hatches, and how they had occasionally malfunctioned and opened on the high seas.   Captain Rezhnikov told them in Duluth the Krasnodar's hatch hydraulic system was due to be overhauled back in Odessa at the end of its trip.

Another point Bert made is that over the years there have been a number of odd, freakish shipwrecks in Lake Superior. For example, in the mid 1970's, a heavily loaded ore freighter named the Edmund Fitzgerald sank in Lake Superior during similarly stormy circumstances. Knowledgable seamen say it propelled itself right to the bottom, taking its entire crew with it.

Naddy was impressed by Bert's remarks and admitted she believed him. She said she was relieved to contemplate the possibility that the Americans had nothing to do with the Krasnodar disaster, and she promised she'd review the whole affair more closely.

"The Krasnodar sinking was a dreadful accident, a fluke of nature," Bert earnestly repeated. "We're not at war with you; we're at peace and I love you. Oh, Naddy, if you only knew how much I love you!"

Naddy confessed she loved Bert, too, and that she looked forward to seeing him again soon. She wanted to keep talking with him, but Nikolai was anxious to get Harry on the phone, so Bert and Naddy said their tender goodbyes. Then Bert pushed a "Hold" button and yelled excitedly, "Harry! It's a phone call from Moscow. Nikolai Novikov wants to talk to you."

"I've got it, Bert!" Harry yelled back, pressing two buttons on his speaker phone. "Harry Brown here! Nikolai? Oh, Nikky, I'm so glad you called. We're all shocked and saddened at the loss of Captain Grigor Rezhnikov and his crew. Also, we're distressed at the loss of your Krasnodar. You have our deepest sympathy. Please, tell us what we can do; we want to help you all we can."

"Harry, I can't begin to tell you how much pressure we're getting from our people here," Novikov complained. "Our government doesn't want to pay for your 25,000 tons of wheat. Instead, we're demanding your country pay us 25 million dollars for our lost ship, plus 40 million dollars for the families of the drowned crewmen. Also, there are other demands. Our people think you deliberately started a war with us. I was half believing it myself, until I recalled our discussion in Haggarson's office about the Krasnodar's malfunctioning hatch mechanism. I specifically remember Captain Rezhnikov telling us it was scheduled to be overhauled in Odessa. I now realize this Krasnodar affair has gotten completely out of control. It's becoming extremely dangerous to all of us.

"Do you know my government is mobilizing our nation this very minute to defend itself against your nation? Do you know your U. S. President Morrison is ordering an all-out nuclear war mobilization, too?"

"No, Nikolai, I wasn't aware of anything like that,"

Harry reacted. "I find it hard to believe. How could our world be endangered so quickly and so easily? We can't let it happen! We have to stop it!

"Nikolai, remember the Reconciliation Clause in our contract? Let's get to our leaders right away and tell them about it. If we don't act immediately, our contract words may become empty and useless. Nikky, you and I may be the two most important people in the world right now, because we could have the means to prevent nuclear destruction. Governments are people, and without people, there's no government. As individual people, therefore, we can influence other people, government people, even heads of state. Let's try to do it now, so we can prevent any rash military action."

Nikolai agreed he and Harry shouldn't sit on the sidelines and complain. Like Harry, Nikolai insisted he, too, was a man of action who cherished world peace. As a representative of his people, he had his own mission of service, and he wasn't one to leave any of his assigned work or initiative to others. Nikolai realized, too, as did Harry, that they were both important links in a chain and formed an extremely valuable connection between their two nations.

"I'm also not one who believes bureaucracies are too big to change," Nikolai asserted. "As you say, Harry, the Soviet government, like your government, consists of people. If it's necessary to change the government, then it's necessary to change our people. But I don't have to change our people to make them want peace. We've always wanted peace. Just as you want peace, I want peace also. My people are as weary of war as I am. Therefore, I assure you, I'll act at once and go to our Chairman Vasil Golgolev. I'll show him the Reconciliation Clause in our contract and plead with him to honor it. If you'll go to your President Morrison and get some sanity into him on this, maybe we can peacefully settle the matter.

"Meanwhile, we lost a freighter and crew of 40,

Harry. Do you know what kind of task I have now? I have to get our people to accept Reconciliation when they're absolutely convinced some American government saboteurs and terrorists destroyed our Krasnodar and murdered its crew. Forty of our brave comrades have gone to a watery Lake Superior grave. Must I now tell their families to think of peace and friendship?"

Harry admitted Nikolai's task wouldn't be easy. Nevertheless, they both agreed they had a tremendous opportunity, as well as responsibility, to assure the world's survival. Tomorrow could be doomsday. Tomorrow would be too late. World peace might very well depend on the success of their immediate actions at that moment.

The known facts regarding the Krasnodar's sinking had to be considered amid the agitation, frenzy, and hysteria over its loss. A malfunctioning hydraulic hatch system and its scheduled overhaul at Odessa, for example, were more relevant at this point, than endless arguing about conflicting political ideologies. It was a matter of deep conviction for both Harry and Nikolai, as well as their contractual agreement, that the Reconciliation process would peacefully settle what 50,000 nuclear missiles and bombs couldn't.

With their mutual commitment and determination thus renewed, the two quickly acted to bring about a more realistic assessment of the matter by their respective leaders. Nikolai was already in Moscow and close to Chairman Golgolev's Kremlin office. Harry, on the other hand, had to make use of long distance telephone calls and high speed jet aircraft to get to President Morrison's office in Washington, D. C. Eventually, however, the two would be able to reveal their high priority message to their national leaders.

Unfortunately, what was happening in the interim raised a serious question of timeliness. Would Harry and

Nikolai be too late? Once committed to military mobilization and action, could USA and USSR war plans be reversed? How about the likelihood that some lower echelon officer or enlisted person might misinterpret the situation and push a death dealing button in error? What if somebody somewhere became so irrational as to spontaneously push such a button? These questions were too frightening for Harry and Nikolai to comtemplate. They couldn't even spare any time to think about such questions. All their energies now were focused on their mission. Their desperate hope was that there'd still be time.

16

MARSHAL PLEKHANOV'S ALERT

A full week had passed since the sinking of the Krasnodar. At the very moment Nikolai and Harry were making long distance telephone contact with each other via a satellite communications system, the scene in Chairman Golgolev's office was becoming deadly serious. Marshal Gavril Plekhanov had long since activated Plan Overlook to scan the earth, oceans, and skies for evidence of U. S. military preparations and related actions. Product 84's, the sleek Soviet MiG 25 series of aircraft, were methodically patrolling and probing U. S. defenses worldwide. Meanwhile, Marshal Plekhanov had returned to Golgolev's office and was just starting to report his implementation of the Chairman's earlier order to activate Plan 7-21, the USSR's full scale nuclear warfare mobilization.

"By looking at this screen as I report to you, Comrade Chairman, you'll be able to see that our Strategic Rocket Forces, as well as our Army, Navy, and Air Force, are completely prepared for all-out victory over the Americans."

Plekhanov gestured, pointer in hand, towards a giant, wall mounted videoscreen in Chairman Golgolev's office. Punching buttons and pointing at the screen, Plekhanov continued his report. He described the Soviet strategic defense force of powerful SS-20 missile installations, which were arranged in a nuclear warhead encirclement of Western Europe. Plekhanov explained that each of over 500 SS-20's carried three nuclear warheads, for a total delivery capability in excess of 1,500 warheads.

Next, an enormous SS-18 missile was viewed. This single missile had a full megaton of explosive power in each of ten warheads. There was a total inventory of over 2,500 of these SS-18 warheads. Plekhanov noted that one megaton meant that a single warhead had the equivalent destructive blast force of one million tons of TNT, and one thousand warheads would yield a blast force equal to one billion tons of TNT. He said the entire allied firepower in World War II totaled only three megatons. The SS-18's alone, therefore, provided the equivalent firepower of 834 World War II's. The total of over 20,000 Soviet nuclear warheads of all kinds had a combined firepower greater than five thousand World War II's.

In another videoscreen display, Plekhanov revealed an installation of SS-19 missiles, three-fourths of which were carrying six warheads per missile. The USSR had a total inventory of over 2,000 of these warheads, with a destructive force of approximately five megatons each. Their entire stockpile of SS-19 missiles yielded a blast equivalent of ten billion tons of TNT, or more than several thousand World War II's.

Plekhanov followed up his report of the SS-19's by showing Golgolev the installations of SS-26 intercontinental ballistic missiles at Plesetsk, beyond the Arctic Circle near Archangel. He displayed many older missiles in the Soviet arsenal, also, assuring Golgolev they were ready to be launched at the Americans via a simple push of a button.

"You can appreciate by all this, Comrade

Chairman," Plekhanov briefly concluded, "that our Strategic Rocket Forces are thoroughly prepared. Also, I might point out, we have an overwhelming, 3:1 advantage over the U. S. with respect to our ICBM's, yet ICBM's are only one third of our strategic forces' nuclear warhead delivery capability. Consider that we also have a vastly superior number of bombers and submarines in addition to our missiles, and all of them will deliver nuclear warheads to U. S. targets."

"Excuse me, Comrade Marshal," Golgolev interrupted. "I meant to inform you earlier that we have others receiving your report by means of a ceiling mounted camera. You may want to look at it occasionally, since members of the Politburo, as well as your own General Staff officers, are using it to view us. Please excuse my interruption, Comrade Gavril."

"Your comments are most welcome. Now then, Comrade Chairman and respected comrades of the Politburo and General Staff, we have a report from our Intelligence Chief, General Mikhael Sakrov. I'm calling him up on the screen right now. General Sakrov, come in, please, and report."

At this command, General Sakrov's face began appearing on the screen, and he began speaking. "General Sakrov here, Comrade Marshal. Our intelligence units report that the Americans are moving swiftly to place their surface ships and submarines in dispersed areas. However, we know their exact locations and are ready at your command to destroy them.

"By contrast to the Americans, as you can see me trace our movements on our warroom map, we're concentrating our submarine movements from both our northern bases westward, toward the Norwegian Sea, and eastward out from Kamchatka. From these areas within our own boundaries, and without ever leaving our own boundaries, our subs will easily destroy all their American targets."

"Excellent, General Sakrov," Plekhanov acknowledged, dissolving Sakrov's image on the screen. Then the Marshal announced the next portion of his report.

"Consider now, comrades, what we have in nuclear submarines. I'm calling up Admiral Yaroslav Belyaev to brief us. Can you come in, Admiral?"

The Admiral appeared on the screen. "I hear you, Marshal. What are your orders?"

"Admiral Belyaev, please review for us your state of readiness."

The Admiral acknowledged the Marshal's request and began confirming the readiness of his command. There were 20 nuclear powered, ballistic missile submarines (SSBN's) equipped for launching the big SS-N-18 missiles, which, like the land based SS-18 missiles, had ten nuclear warheads each. Three subs were designated as Typhoon models, having 20 missile tubes each for SS-N-20 and SS-N-23 missiles.

There was a total of 340 ICBM launch tubes in immediate readiness on the various, Soviet, nuclear powered submarines. Also, there were 25 ballistic missile submarines with a combined total of 325 tubes for launching the smaller SS-N-8 missiles. Tube for tube, the Soviets had 665 to 470 for the Americans. In other words, according to Belyaev, the Soviets had a 3:2 superiority over the Americans, with respect to submarine launched nuclear missiles.

Admiral Belyaev showed examples of the other Soviet, nuclear powered, ballistic missile submarines. In addition to the Typhoon model, there was a total of 36 Deltas, 25 Yankees, 5 Hotels, and of all other classes, including nuclear powered, hunter–killer attack submarines and non-nuclear, ballistic missle or attack submarines, there were in excess of 300. Total number of Soviet submarines was over 400, while the Americans had a mere 100.

"Very good report, Admiral Belyaev," Plekhanov complimented. "At this time, General Alexei Vashnev will review our Air Force preparedness. General Vashnev."

"Our long–range bomber fleet is alert and ready, Comrade Marshal. Our bomber fleet gives us a third delivery capability for nuclear warheads. Currently, as shown on the screen, we have 100 Bears, 43 Bisons, and 200 Backfires. We have a total of 343 long–range bombers. Adding to that total the rest of our bombers, gives us a capability of delivering over 1,000 nuclear warheads to U.S. targets. These warheads are in addition to the several thousand ICBM's of our Strategic Rocket Forces and submarines."

"Well stated, General Vashnev. Thank you!" Plekhanov acknowledged, as Vashnev's image faded from the screen.

"There you have our three major nuclear warhead missile systems," Plekhanov continued, "(1) land-based intercontinental ballistic missiles, or ICBM's; (2) nuclear powered, missile–launching submarines; and (3) long range strategic bombers. Yet, there's a fourth advantage we Soviets have over the inferior American weaponry. It's our enormous, well-equipped Army. General Olov Kamenov will report on this."

Marshal Plekhanov manipulated the videoscreen controls and called in Kamenov's image. After exchanging greetings, Marshal Plekhanov requested General Kamenov to report.

"Chairman Golgolev, Marshal Plekhanov, other comrades," Kamenov replied through the videoscreen, "In the event of any U. S. or Western European nation aggression, troops of our Soviet Third Shock Army are ready right now to move out of their present positions near Magdeburg, East Germany." As Kamenov said this, he tapped the end of a pointer on various map locations, which were immediately magnified on the videoscreen as he talked. "Our troops will proceed west, passing right through our own mine fields, via prearranged safe lanes. At the same time, our other armies will be striking up and down a north-south line.

"Each of our 47 armies will send out an Operations Maneuver Group, called an 'OMG.' These groups are prepared to move at high speed, bypassing cities and large troop concentrations of the U. S. allied, North Atlantic Treaty Organization nations, or NATO. Each of our OMG's consists of a tank regiment and individual battalions of mechanized infantry, artillery, and antiaircraft, plus a company of engineers.

"Our OMG's are trained to penetrate far behind enemy lines, using multiple airstrikes to give them cover. They'll undermine NATO defenses and capture every airfield and missile-launching installation. Western Europe will be captured before it has a chance to retaliate. We'll outnumber, outgun, and outflank the enemy forces before they ever get mobilized. By leapfrogging NATO defenses, we'll be able to surprise its armies and win the day.

"Comrades, NATO commanders have said they need a full 48 hours to become completely mobilized. Our OMG's are trained to win the war in just 24 hours, which is one-half the NATO mobilization time. NATO simply cannot strike at our fast-moving OMG's within West Germany, for example, so we'll surely win!"

"Excellent, General Kamenov," Plekhanov approvingly commented. Then, turning from the videoscreen to Golgolev, he began concluding his report.

"I'm confident, Comrade Chairman, we're well armed and well able to win any kind of war with the Americans. In brief, our General Staff is prepared right now to win an all-out war, if necessary. The reason for our assured success is that we've taken pains to arrange the use of nuclear weapons by all our armed forces. Our basic strategy is to wage war by a massive, preemptive,

162

first strike nuclear rocket attack on European NATO forces, and simultaneously on the U. S. itself, as well as on various U. S. targets throughout the world. Such a strategy will destroy any U. S. ability to retaliate. I must restate and emphasize, however, that we must be the first to use nuclear missiles to destroy the Americans, before the Americans and their allies get a chance to use their missiles to destroy us. A massive, preemptive nuclear first strike by us is the key to our victory.

"We're prepared to destroy all major U. S. communications centers, including the White House, Pentagon, satellite relay stations, missile command centers, air bases, naval bases, and other strategic targets. Also, we're prepared to destroy all of America, before America can destroy even a small portion of us. But we must launch a surprise nuclear first strike against the U.S. Being the first to launch a massive nuclear strike is our key to defeating the Americans, as well as our only means of saving the USSR. Let's strike now, therefore, and let's strike with all we have, so the Americans can't strike us back. Our future depends on it."

Marshal Plekhanov sat down in a chair by Golgolev's desk, and Chairman Golgolev got up to speak.

"Comrade Plekhanov, as usual, you've been efficiently thorough. However, I fear your General Staff hasn't thought the matter through to all its consequences, especially some adverse ones. Consider, for example, that your first strike will merely attempt to destroy the various targets you suggest. Unfortunately, the reality of such a mission is that, inevitably, there will be some percentages of U. S. retaliatory targets you'll not be successful in destroying. You'll not be successful, because you'll experience a certain number of equipment malfunctions and breakdowns, plus you'll have navigational errors and other unexpected, adverse circumstances. The single most adverse consequence of all, of course, is that the aroused Americans and their allies will desperately retaliate.

"Do you know what will happen if just 10% of U. S. ICBM's get through, or a mere 10% of U. S. nuclear powered submarines survive our attack, or only 10% of the U. S. long range bombers get through? I tremble to tell you what will happen. For example, I've been informed that just a single American submarine of the Trident class will launch enough nuclear warhead missiles at us to destroy as many as 200 of our big cities. I said 200 big cities, Comrades. We don't even have that many big cities!

"What if only 15 American submarines out of 100 survive our attack? Assuming 24 missiles per sub, and 8 warheads each, the surviving 15 U. S. submarines will hurl 3,000 nuclear warhead missiles at us. Such a disaster would be the end of our people, the end of our country, the end of our social revolution, and the end of our civilization. There's no way we'll survive 3,000 submarine launched, nuclear warhead missiles, each dozens of times more destructive than the U. S. atom bomb dropped on Hiroshima. Just think for a moment that one new American Trident submarine contains eight times the firepower expended in all of World War II. That's 24 megatons or 24 million tons of TNT from only one U. S. submarine. Eight World War II's! Think about that for awhile! Remember, too, there are other countries with nuclear weapons besides the U. S. For example, consider the United Kingdom, many Western European countries, and numerous other countries throughout the world. You'll have to destroy all of them, and at the same time, too, or they'll most certainly join the Americans in retaliating against us.

"Consider, moreover, that many, surviving, land launched ICBM's will be hurled against us by the U. S. In addition, a few U. S. bombers will inevitably escape our massive, first-strike attack, and drop hundreds of hydrogen bombs on us, or launch even more nuclear warhead missiles at us. There's no way anyone can win in such an exchange. Any unexpected, preemptive, first strike attack on the U. S. by us, therefore, will be what the world refers to as M-A-D, Mutual Assured Destruction. We cannot venture into any such disaster. In any nuclear warhead exchange, please understand there can be no winners. It's suicide for anyone to launch such an attack.

"Marshal Plekhanov, you and your staff members have specified various U. S. targets for destruction, such as the White House, as well as all other command and control centers. Who, then, may I ask, will there be left alive to surrender to us, or who of us will be left alive to accept a U. S. surrender, if such is the case?

"In our powerful Union of Soviet Socialist Republics, Civil Defense is a fifth arm of our military. Because of that, I know you've said many times we'll survive better than the Americans, who have no real civil defense against nuclear attack. Yet, how will we survive 5,000 hydrogen bombs and missiles? How will we even survive 500? Marshal Plekhanov, I don't believe we can be so suicidal as to ever attempt a nuclear first strike against the Americans or anyone else.

"Permit me, please, Comrade Marshal, to offer you and the others another view of our situation. My assistant, Tatyana Borshak, has been doing some research for me on the effects of a nuclear exchange. Although Tatyana hasn't yet completed her assignment, let's hear what she thinks. Comrade Tatyana...."

Tatyana got up from her chair near the door and walked to the center of the room where she could easily be seen and heard by Golgolev and Plekhanov, as well as by members of the Politburo and Military General Staff. She walked slowly, yet deliberately, as if she carried the weight of the world on her shoulders. Her figure was middle-aged and somewhat stocky. Also, she was of medium height, and her hair was a graying blond. She wore a navy blue dress that matched her blue eyes and accented her clear, smooth, light complexion, giving her an attractive appearance that made a highly favorable impression. When she spoke, however, it was with such authority and in such a captivating manner, that everyone's attention soon focused on what she had to say, rather than how she looked.

"Chairman Golgolev, Marshal Plekhanov, respected comrades of the Politburo and Military General Staff, it's with a deep sense of responsibility and humility that I respond at this time. Our respected Chairman and leader asked me to review with you for a few moments, the effects and consequences of a nuclear warhead exchange between our country and the U. S. Also, it's appropriate for us at this time to consider this serious and basic question.

"The reason is clear: at the present moment, throughout the world, there are 50,000 nuclear warhead weapons in place, ready for use at any moment. This number is about equally divided between our country and the U. S. Unfortunately, the combined destructive power of such an enormous number of nuclear warhead weapons is well over a million and a half times greater than the force of the Hiroshima atomic bomb. It's doubtful, therefore, that any life on earth could survive such a force.

"To give you an idea of the devastation that would result from present day nuclear warfare, let's first review the effects of the Hiroshima atomic bomb; second, let's reflect on the effects of a nuclear warhead missile exchange; and third, let's consider the consequences of such an exchange for future generations. First, let's look at the effects of the atomic bomb dropped on the City of Hiroshima.

"On August 6, 1945, 8:50 a.m., a U. S. B-29 Bomber aircraft named the 'Enola Gay' dropped the 'Little Boy' atomic bomb on Hiroshima, Japan's seventh largest city at that time. The 'Little Boy' bomb exploded 1,000 feet above the ground, with the result that ninety-eight percent of the buildings below were instantly and completely destroyed, and more than 130,000 people were killed or are still missing and presumed to have been killed. Many additional thousands of victims died slowly of severe, agonizingly painful radiation burns and other injuries, so that the total bomb related deaths numbered over 200,000 in just five years.

"A total area of 12.2 square kilometers was destroyed by the bomb blast. As far as 1.6 kilometers away from ground zero, people were instantly killed by the searing heat of the enormous fireball. As far as 2.4 kilometers away from ground zero, paper, wood, vegetation and other burnables were scorched by severe heat radiation from the fireball. Within a full 1-1/2 kilometers radius away from ground zero, a firestorm created by the millions of degrees of heat emanating from the explosion center totally burned everything. Also, a killing hurricane wind resulted from the firestorm, creating a vacuum in its wake that caused a reversal of the wind's direction in a kind of seesaw hurricane effect.

"Radiation from the bomb in the form of neutron and gamma rays instantly killed all life up to a full kilometer away from the blast center. Beyond a full kilometer, radiation sickness occurred in varying degrees, depending on the extent of exposure.

"Effects elsewhere of nuclear fallout radiation from earthen debris sucked up into the Hiroshima bomb cloud is difficult, if not impossible, to measure. Extent depends on the precise distance of the blast from the earth, and the exact volume of radiating fragments sucked up into the enormous mushroom cloud. Many radioactive fragments stayed in the troposphere and stratosphere for prolonged periods of time, some for many years, so that they were dropped in varying amounts on the entire earth's surface. It's generally known that a large number of leukemia and other cancer related deaths, some occurring many years later, were directly caused by the Hiroshima bomb. Similar deaths in other parts of the world are also suspected of being caused by the Hiroshima bomb, since fallout was eventually carried to nearly every part of the world.

"My observations, comrades, are but a quick sketch of the 1945 'Little Boy' Hiroshima bomb effects. These effects, shocking as they are, become insignificant when compared to the awesome destructiveness of today's incredibly more powerful missiles and bombs. Consider that the Hiroshima bomb was equivalent to a mere 12-1/2 kilotons of TNT. By comparison, just one of our many SS-18 missile warheads has the explosive force of a full megaton, which is a million tons of TNT. This means that just one of our many SS-18 missile warheads is eighty times more powerful than the 'Little Boy' bomb.

"After having reviewed the incredible destructiveness of the Hiroshima bomb, it's alarming to contemplate the devastating effects of an exchange of our present day, Intercontinental Ballistic Missile warheads. In such an exchange, we have to talk of hundreds of millions of instant deaths, rather than the mere 130,000 from the Hiroshima bomb. Eventually, too, the painfully slow deaths resulting from today's missiles would total over a billion, rather than the 200,000 deaths from the Hiroshima bomb.

"By way of introduction to my second discussion, reflecting on the effects of a present day nuclear warhead missile exchange, consider what some scientists say. The Swedish Royal Academy of Science, for example, asked 13 international experts to predict what would happen if 15,000 nuclear warheads were exploded in the northern hemisphere within the span of a few days. Comrades, the answers were unanimous. No one could survive such an inferno.

"It's generally considered by scientific minds that a brief nuclear war between the USA and our country would be destructive of all mankind, leaving the earth totally uninhabitable. Here are some reasons why:

(1) There will be 300 million instant dead. As many as 600 million to a billion or more will be severly injured, most of whom will eventually die from lack of adequate medical care.

(2) Deadly radioactive fallout will cover all the earth, destroying animal and plant life, and contaminating most of man's food and water sources.

(3) Nitrogen oxide particles will destroy the earth's atmospheric ozone layer, drastically increasing the sun's ultraviolet radiation reaching the earth. This will kill many different kinds of life, thus upsetting nature's ecological balance, causing even further disasters.

(4) Increased water vapor and clouds of radioactive dust, soot, and other debris sucked up into the earth's atmosphere will block out the heat radiation from the sun, lowering the earth's temperature and triggering an instant ice age. Such an ice age or nuclear winter will be destructive of whatever remaining life, if any, has survived to that point. The threat of nuclear winter has become a growing concern of scientists throughout the world.

(5) Nuclear blasts from thousands of warheads, each as powerful as a megaton of TNT, will send shock waves around the world. These shock waves will flatten all structures within a radius of 10 to 25 kilometers from each blast center.

(6) Intense heat from each and every one of the 15,000 estimated nuclear explosions will be hotter than the temperatures in the center of the sun. This searing heat will vaporize virtually everything within a ten kilometer radius away from each blast center. Also, there'll be thousands of violent firestorms, so hot they'll completely melt automobiles up to fifty kilometers away and kill all life up to and beyond eight kilometers away.

(7) Instant and deadly radiation will saturate an extremely wide area up to 7,000 kilometers away from each nuclear warhead blast center. If some persons survive the deadly radiation, their resulting infections, cancers, and slow healing condition, coupled with the lack of any intensive medical care facilities, would soon kill them. However, the agonizing pain of their injuries would most likely kill all of them right away or force them to commit suicide.

(8) For each of millions of victims exposed to deadly radiation, massive medical resources would be required for bone marrow transplants, blood transfusions, frequent antibiotics injections, and so on. However, since medical facilities will be destroyed by the blasts, only minimal, if any, medical care will be available. As a result, hundreds of millions more will die agonizingly slow and painful deaths.

"Comrades, these are but a few expected effects of a present day nuclear warhead exchange. I won't impose on any more of your time to discuss such additional problems as the complete breakdown of all national economies and essential government services; the problems of evacuating and relocating surviving humans, should there be any; the complete destruction of food and water resources; or the difficulties of disease control, crime control, and other such problems. Instead, let's briefly discuss our third and final topic, nuclear missile exchange consequences for future generations.

"One obvious line of scientific thinking is that there couldn't be any consequences, because there won't be any future generations. Absolutely nobody, nor life of any kind, will be able to survive a modern era nuclear exchange, so say some of the experts.

"However, if by some quirk of fate there are a few survivors, their severe sterility will considerably limit the prospects of any future generations being born. Those few who are born will most certainly have genetic aberrations, deformities, and other serious problems, including social, as well as physiological, and psychological. Added to these consequences are the numerous expected disease plagues, food poisonings, and lack of essential sanitation and other services.

"Please, I must stop here. The many horrors of a nuclear warhead missile exchange are too repugnant to contemplate further. I only hope what I've said is sufficient to instill in each of you some alternative thinking. I, for one, cannot believe we'll be building an ideal socialist world, if we pursue a course of action designed to make that world uninhabitable.

"If we can't find ways to keep the peace, then we'll cause the death of the earth. Think of it! The death of the earth will be the direct consequences of our failure to keep peace with one another. Comrades, we mustn't be responsible for the death of the earth. We cannot allow others to be either. Even our supreme revolutionary leader, Vladimir Illyich Lenin, wrote a statement on this before his death. In an article entitled, 'No Compromises?' Lenin said, 'To carry on a war...is not this ridiculous in the extreme?'"

The room was deathly still when Tatyana finished. As slowly and deliberately as she rose to speak, she returned to her chair near the door, the burdens of her knowledge not lessened by her sharing. After several moments of silence, Golgolev at last spoke slowly and with deep respect.

"You're to be commended, Comrade Borshak, for your most illuminating report. You've rendered an important service to our people with your assessment of nuclear warfare effects. In fact, your report has convinced me of the course we must take. We must prevent any kind of nuclear warfare whatsoever. To accomplish this, we must use any and every possible means we can.

"One good way of preventing a nuclear exchange is to promote peaceful relations between all the nations of the world. At the same time, we must also strive to develop peaceful alternatives to war for settling disputes and avoiding armed conflicts. Nobody can win a war. The truly great advances of Socialist Communism can and should come from agitating and propagandizing for peaceful, bloodless revolutions. Progress cannot come from waging wars of annihilation.

"Let's proceed, therefore, on the basis of promoting a peaceful competition among nations and adjusting to all new circumstances by peaceful means. This will enable us to refine our modern socialist system, so that it ultimately succeeds, as capitalism and other archaic systems fail. Above all, we must never initiate or allow any kind of nuclear warhead exchange to happen. Therefore, let's devote our energies to finding peaceful pathways to progress in our competition with capitalist and other obsolete societies. In this way, we'll affirm the correctness of our socialist hypothesis."

Everyone who heard Chairman Golgolev's remarks reacted favorably to his sensible solution to the world's dilemma. In many minds, peace at any price was the approach to take. When Golgolev spoke again, therefore, it was with a renewed self-assurance that he gave orders.

"Comrade Marshal Plekhanov, your strict orders are to maintain our alert status only until after the Americans have satisfactorily replied to our demands. Under no circumstances are you to initiate any kind of nuclear or other attack. As terrible as the Krasnodar affair may seem to our people now, it's but another tragic incident in the history of human affairs. It's like the unfortunate destruction of a South Korean commercial jetliner that wandered off course into our Asian territory some years ago, ignoring the landing instructions from our fighter pilot. Comrades, I'm confident there's more to the Krasnodar affair than we know about at this time. Let's not make the mistake of destroying the earth because of a sunken ship."

17

GENERAL DANIELS' ALERT

While Harry Brown was making his way to Washington, D. C., with his urgent message for President Morrison, General David Daniels was supervising the Joint Chiefs of Staff in a frenzy of nuclear warfare preparations. Due to the high priority of Daniels assignment, he was given immediate access to the President, so the status of the nation's mobilization effort could be fully reported.

Meanwhile, Brown's appointment to see the President was regarded with little, if any, priority by those in charge of White House security, who delayed him. When Brown's appointment was later verified, instead of being admitted, he was led to a front entrance lobby, where he was forced to wait until an appropriate moment when the President would send for him. Up to that point, it had been little more than seven days since the loss of the Krasnodar. Yet, the whole world was in a turmoil over the matter, and the President at that moment was determined to hear about the defensive capabilities of the nation's armed forces. In his Oval Office, he urgently began speaking to his immediate military subordinate.

"General Daniels, the clear and present danger to

our country's leadership makes it necessary for my cabinet to meet via our videoscreen communications system. As you know, we dare not meet together in greater numbers than two, because if we did, a determined enemy could eliminate our entire leadership with just one, well-placed blow. My cabinet, therefore, is carefully dispersed, but they're watching us right now through the eyes of a remote-controlled video camera suspended from the ceiling." President Morrison pointed to the ceiling-mounted camera.

"Very well, Mr. President, and distinguished members of the cabinet," General Daniels acknowledged, "I'll keep the camera in mind while I'm reporting to you.

"Our Strategic Command and Control System has been functioning for many years now, since February 3, 1961." General Daniels paused momentarily to extend a telescoping pointer he'd removed from the slim portfolio he carried.

"Looking at this videoscreen," the General continued, "you can see an EC-135 aircraft taking off right now from Offutt Air Force Base in Omaha, Nebraska."

The General pressed various buttons on the videoscreen call-up panel, then gestured towards the screen with his pointer while he kept talking.

"This EC-135 is a jumbo jet carrying an Air Force General and his complete staff of officers, all of whom are immediately ready to do battle with the Soviet Union. Let's make radio contact right now with the commanding general of this mission, so he can report to us directly. General Richard Edwards, seven-zero-one-five-three, this is Daniels, come in, please."

"Edwards here, sir, standing by, over."

"General Edwards, I'm requesting a briefing on your mission for our Commander in Chief and his cabinet. Go ahead, over."

"Roger on that one, sir," General Edwards replied via the videoscreen. "Mr. President, respected members of the cabinet, General Daniels, this mission our men are on is code named 'Looking Glass.' As this airborne EC-135 battle command jet begins its eight hour, top secret flight pattern, another EC-135 jumbo jet battle command, flying a different pattern, is landing somewhere else, at any of our 46 Strategic Air Command or 'SAC' bases throughout the U. S., perhaps at Ellsworth Air Force Base in South Dakota.

"Our constantly changing flight patterns make it virtually impossible for any enemy to destroy this airborne, battle command headquarters. Therefore, our EC-135 command system can and will survive any surprise attack. Night and day throughout the year, we'll always have an airborne, battle command post patrolling our skies. It's a command post the enemy is unable to destroy.

"Right now I'm the on-duty, airborne, battle command General. I'm called 'The Doomsday Officer,' because I'm the one who gives our missile and bomber forces the fatal doomsday order to completely annihilate the Soviet Union and all our other enemies."

"Just a moment, General Edwards," General Daniels cut in, "I think the President wants to ask me a question. Stand by, please." Daniels pressed a button on the control panel, then turned to face the President.

"General Daniels," President Morrison began, "am I to understand the lives of millions upon millions of people at this very moment depend on the sanity or insanity of some general in an EC-135 airplane?"

"Mr. President," Daniels replied, "I'm sorry I didn't point out to you that first place battle command authority goes to the EC-135, if, and only if, our Colorado Strategic Air Command Headquarters is destroyed. In other words, Mr. President, the EC-135 is our fail-safe, last ditch backup to a destructive first strike by Soviet enemy missile forces. Let's call back General Edwards and let him brief you further on this."

176

Turning to the videoscreen control panel, General Daniels pressed two buttons and brought back the image of General Edwards. "General Edwards, come in again, please. The President is interested in how you process an emergency order."

"Very well, sir," Edwards acknowledged. "Our EC-135 Looking Glass operation builds, processes, and disseminates an emergency action order as soon as we receive it. We have all the necessary authentication codes required to do that. Here's what happens when we get an action order."

Edwards pushed several buttons on a control panel aboard the EC-135, then began his explanation.

"There are four missile–launching modes for our EC-135 Looking Glass command. In the first mode we immediately transmit a code word to 100 underground missile launching units. This code word launches various nuclear warhead missiles at their predetermined Soviet targets. You should be able to see some examples of these missile–launching units on your videoscreen." As Edwards said this, a succession of launch site views appeared on the screen. Then, continuing his briefing, Edwards began showing other scenes.

"A second missile-launching mode is initiated by other aircraft. Our Strategic Air Command has numerous airborne EC-135 planes, plus other aircraft with missile–launching capabilities. All our airborne planes serve as backup to various underground control centers. In the event these underground centers are destroyed or can't give their missile-launching order, our airborne EC-135 aircraft are ordered to fire the missiles. Such a second chance, missile–launching, command mode, using airborne aircraft, increases our retaliatory, fail-safe condition.

"A third mode of missile–launching control is possible with the airborne EC-135 I'm presently flying in. This Looking Glass EC-135, if necessary, can fire all the missiles of all our centers simultaneously. It can do this by transmitting a single, ultrahigh frequency or UHF radio signal to a special UHF antenna next to each intercontinental ballistic missile silo.

"For our fourth and final missile-launching mode, we have an Emergency Rocket Communications System or 'ERCS.' My airborne EC-135 Command Post can activate the ERCS with a simple UHF radio signal. This signal fires rockets, which, in turn, travel all over the country transmitting UHF signals that launch all our defensive missiles against their preprogrammed enemy targets. The ERCS rockets are fired from Whitman Air Force Base."

General Edwards manipulated some nearby controls on the aircraft in which he was flying and began describing the displays as they appeared on the President's videoscreen. "Each ERCS rocket contains a nosecone UHF radio transmitter, instead of a nuclear warhead. Each nosecone transmitter sends a coded signal for 30 minutes as the rocket traverses its assigned, suborbital trajectory."

General Edwards' image reappeared on President Morrison's videoscreen momentarily, so the General could conclude his remarks. "Every missile site receiving the special UHF signal from an ERCS rocket will immediately launch its intercontinental ballistic missiles. These nuclear warhead missiles will hit their designated targets in the Soviet Union, and every single Soviet target will be thoroughly destroyed in a matter of minutes after our missiles have been launched."

"Excuse me, General Edwards," Daniels cut in. "Your briefing has been received and is all we need at the moment. Thank you for assisting us."

Punching two control panel buttons to clear the videoscreen, Daniels turned to the President and spoke.

"Now, then, Mr. President, getting back to your very important question, please be assured that our retaliatory capability will never depend on only one man. We employ a minimum, 'two man rule' and other safeguards. Let me explain for a moment how our 'two man rule' and other safeguards operate.

"There are two separate staff teams on each EC-135 command flight. These teams must cooperate with each other before any missiles can be launched. An individual commanding general is incapable of transmitting a missile-launching order by himself. One important reason for this is that he wouldn't know the secret coding for such a message until he received it from another source. This shared-command approach also applies to our submarine forces, which we'll be reviewing in a moment. Staff teams on a submarine must cooperate and share their knowledge of a secret-code message, before a commander can issue a nuclear-missile firing order. In like manner, two Strategic Air Force officers in each missile silo control room must cooperate and agree to an incoming radio-signal order before their missiles can be fired."

"General Daniels," President Morrison interrupted, "all this Looking Glass talk sounds like a hypothetical, last ditch defense. What do we have up front to protect us?"

"Thank you, Mr. President, for asking about that," General Daniels replied. "As you previously ordered, all our military forces, including our National Guard units and our entire Civil Defense, have been called into an immediate alert status to defend against the Soviet mobilization that our military intelligence informed us about earlier. In response to the Soviet plan, we've activated our own plan called 'Zephyr,' which will deploy our forces for immediate action.

"Sir, our entire system is ready for your 'Commence Fire' order. Within moments of your order, we'll destroy all our Soviet military targets, as well as the other, strategic, non-military targets we've planned to destroy.

"Our mobile, MX, 'Peacekeeper' missiles are ready for launching, also. Each of these MX missiles has a 6,000 mile range and carries ten nuclear warheads, every one of which is independently targeted. Mr. President, our MX warheads are highly accurate to within 400 feet of a target. Each warhead is eighty times more powerful than the 'Little Boy' atomic bomb we dropped on Hiroshima nearly half a century ago."

"Hold on, General," President Morrison demanded. "Do you mean to say the 1,000 warheads carried by our 100 MX missiles will each explode in the Soviet Union with a force equal to 80 Hiroshima bombs? General Daniels, that's 80,000 atomic bombs! If my memory hasn't failed me, the original 'Little Boy' bomb dropped on Hiroshima August 6, 1945, killed over 130,000 human beings instantly, not to mention the tens of thousands who died later of burns, diseases, cancers, and bomb related injuries. Now, if you multiply 130,000 killed, times 80,000 MX missile 'A-bombs,' you'll kill 10-1/2 billion people instantly. That's more than the entire human population on this earth! Are you aware of that, General?"

"Yes, Mr. President, the death figures are grim, but then not all our warheads will explode. Those that do will destroy Soviet missile–launching silos and other military targets. Only several hundred, perhaps as many as a thousand missiles or bombs, will affect large population centers."

"Well, General, how many warheads are needed to destroy the major Soviet cities?" President Morrison asked, irritated.

"Mr. President, we'd need fewer than 200 nuclear warheads to wipe out the major Soviet cities. We can easily do that with the firepower of just one of our many, nuclear powered, Trident missile submarines. If the Soviets destroy as many as 24 of our 25 Trident subs, which is unlikely, we'll still be able to fire enough missiles from the one remaining sub to completely destroy the Soviets. However, it's highly unlikely the Soviets would be able to destroy so many of our Trident subs.

"You see, Mr. President, we have an 'ASW,' antisubmarine warfare strategy that protects our subs from the Soviets and increases our nuclear missile retaliatory capabilities."

Daniels showed an image on the videoscreen of a general purpose, hunter–killer attack submarine. He described it as five times larger than the largest World War II sub, and pointed out that its nuclear powered engine made it much faster and more maneuverable.

"Right now," Daniels noted, "we've ordered 80 of our 90 attack submarines to go on submerged patrol. Each of these subs will detect, identify, attack, and destroy any Soviet surface ship it encounters, but its primary mission is to destroy any and all Soviet nuclear missile submarines."

"All right, General Daniels," President Morrison responded, "but what happens if the Soviet subs detect our subs first?"

"Aha, Mr. President, good question," Daniels commented. "Let's contact Admiral Wendell Phillips to tell us about that. Admiral Phillips, come in, please, and brief the Commander in Chief on our defenses against Soviet subs."

"Aye, sir," Phillips responded as his image appeared on the videoscreen. "We're trained to anticipate Soviet strategy. We send our subs where the Soviet subs are, then order our surface ships away from those areas. To avoid detection, our sub commanders operate quietly and independently. To track Soviet subs, they use the best sound detection technology available, with computers as backup.

"Both the Soviets and we know that the most terrifying of all weapons is the nuclear powered submarine equipped with intercontinental, nuclear warhead missiles." Admiral Phillips displayed a film sequence showing one of these subs in action. "Our primary mission is to destroy all such subs the Soviets have. To do this, we use conventional, non-nuclear weapons, because all we need to do is puncture a Soviet sub's pressurized hull to destroy it. A small hole will do, only a foot or two wide, for example. It will cause tons of seawater to pour into the sub and sink it quickly.

"Each of our subs, as its primary target, is assigned to destroy a specific Soviet sub," the Admiral continued. "Secondary targets are surface ships equipped with ICBM's, plus land-based, missile-firing installations."

As he spoke, the Admiral pointed out the distinctive profiles of several classifications of Soviet battleships which he displayed on the videoscreen for all to view. These were followed by a map of primary land based missile installations and flipchart diagrams of other primary targets.

"Through our combined intelligence services," the Admiral noted, "we're able to keep our sub commanders informed of all enemy ship locations, movements, and other data. For example, we know every Soviet ship's status, whether it's in drydock for repairs, or taking on fuel and supplies, or at sea on a mission. Also, we track all Soviet surface ships by satellite."

To provide his audience with a better understanding of U. S. capabilities for Soviet sub detection, the Admiral displayed a warroom map table. Outlined on the map was a worldwide system of computer controlled grid sonar. The Admiral explained that the grid sonar system consisted essentially of microphones mounted on the ocean bottom for detecting Soviet submarines.

"However, I must warn you," the Admiral cautioned, "our Sound Surveillance System, called 'SOSUS,' isn't able to cover all of the world's ocean bottom areas. Our SOSUS system is only good for those areas we've covered with our sonar transponder grid. In other words, there are vast ocean-bottom areas that aren't covered. Soviet nuclear missile subs could be hidden in these non-SOSUS controlled areas, creating serious problems for us.

"Once our system has detected a Soviet sub, we must use a sonar-fitted helicopter to keep the sub's location identified at all times."

At this point the Admiral displayed a film sequence on the videoscreen, showing one of the special, sonar equipped helicopters, and the ASW, antisubmarine warfare ship on which it was based. He explained that the sonar helicopter must pinpoint a Soviet sub location first, before an ASW ship can destroy the sub. As an example of this process, he showed a sonar being lowered into the water from a helicopter to determine a reading, then the sonar being lifted and carried to a new position, and the process repeated over and over again, until a Soviet sub was detected and targeted for destruction.

"We also keep patrol aircraft in a Soviet sub area," Admiral Phillips added, "to maintain contact and surveillance of the sub at all times, so information about the sub's movement can be kept accurate and current. Even if we gave an order right now to destroy a particular Soviet sub we're tracking, it's unlikely we'd be very successful. By the time we get a reading, fire a missile, and the missile reaches its destination, the Soviet sub will have slipped away to a different location. Therefore, accuracy in hitting what we shoot at is an enormous, extremely complex problem.

"One consolation is that the Soviets have the same problem. Another consolation is that all our missiles have laser-controlled aiming mechanisms to assure they hit their targets. Finally, to further support our success in the event of a Soviet attack, we'll be launching all our missiles simultaneously from our aircraft, our ground installations, and our subs.

"Sir," the Admiral concluded, "all our weapons have been thoroughly tested before their release for service. I can certify for you now that they're ready!"

"Thank you, Admiral Phillips," General Daniels acknowledged. "Your readiness is essential to our survival."

"Roger and out," Phillips replied.

Working the videoscreen controls again, Daniels began summarizing his report by showing a numerical listing of America's nuclear submarine capabilities. Using his pointer, the General referred to each item and read it aloud.

"Our primary, ocean-based, missile-launching weapon systems are the nuclear powered, ballistic missile submarines, or SSBN's. These consist of the following:

   31   Lafayette class
    6   Ohio's
    3   Ethan Allen's
    2   George Washington's

"Of the above 42 SSBN's, 25 are Trident missile launching subs, each with 24 launching tubes. Nine of the above are each equipped with 144 Poseidon tubes.

"There are, in addition to the SSBN's, a substantial number of nuclear powered attack submarines, or SSN's. These consist of the following:

   25   Los Angeles
    1   Glenard P. Lipscomb
    1   Narwhal
   39   Sturgeon
    1   Tillibee
   13   Permit

5 Skipjack
4 Skate
1 Seawolf

Finally, we have a small number of conventional submarines, or SS's. They consist of:

3 Bonfel
1 Darter
1 Grayback

"Of the hunter-killer, SSN type subs, 80 are first rate. The rest are somewhat less than first rate in comparable effectiveness, but still functional and deadly.

"There's another area of our preparedness, Mr. President. It's our top secret chemical warfare capability. For example, there's a 'GB' or 'Sarin' nerve gas capability we can create when we combine two chemicals inside a 155 millimeter artillery shell. This gas is odorless, colorless, and extremely effective. Just one-fiftieth of a drop will kill a Soviet victim in minutes. It causes shallow and difficult breathing, forcing the victim to gasp for air, convulse, and start vomiting. Death comes fairly quickly.

"Also, there's VX, which is formed in a bomb and absorbed through the skin. Just 4/10 of a milligram paralyzes the nervous system in a minute.

"Then there's phosgene gas, which chokes people to death, and Tabun, which causes all the muscles to contract, so the whole body contorts itself to death. I know all this sounds grotesque, Mr. President, but it's better than being burned alive. We have 40,000 tons of chemical warfare weaponry ready for your command, sir.

"Our ground forces...."

President Morrison ordered General Daniels to stop, it was enough. The President apologized for his interruption, but said he just couldn't accept the idea that the U. S. was prepared for any kind of nuclear warfare. He referred to a Department of Defense bulletin entitled, *Defense Against Ballistic Missiles*, then opened his desk drawer and took out the book. Holding it up and waving it, he said that the Foreword to the bulletin was written by a former Secretary of Defense. When the President first read it, he recalled that he got an uncomfortable feeling about it, making him very suspicious of America's defense preparedness and concerned about the future safety of the nation. General Daniels videoscreen presentation had confirmed the President's suspicions.

"Both the Defense Secretary's bulletin and your presentation, David," the President reflected, "have failed to mention the only real defense option we really have. Think of it! Over the years, American taxpayers have paid billions of dollars for defense, but not a single dollar of it has gone for the most important defense option, and, perhaps, the only one. General Daniels, distinguished members of the Cabinet, the most important defense option we've got right now, and the only realistic one, is *the option to prevent all the other options from happening*. All the Department of Defense talks about in its bulletin, and everything your presentation reflects, General Daniels, are options that mean the destruction of the earth."

Pointing to the "hot line" telephone on his desk, the President explained that it was a direct line to Soviet Chairman Vasil Golgolev, and the one instrument that could postpone doomsday.

"It's unfortunate," the President pointed out, "that the so-called defense options of the U. S. would bring about the end of the world and the death of everyone in it. Who wants to commit suicide?" Morrison asked, pleading with Daniels to think the matter through. "A brief nuclear exchange would be MAD, which means Mutual Assured Destruction.

"General Daniels, and members of the Cabinet,"

186

Morrison continued, glancing into the camera, "I'm afraid there are, indeed, some glaring deficiencies in our whole defense scenario. These deficiencies make our hot line telephone to the Soviet Chairman the very best defense tool we've got right now. It's a defense tool I'm going to use in just a few moments, but first, I'm concerned about some serious shortcomings in our present military thinking.

"Consider, for example, that if we were to have a nuclear warhead exchange with the Soviets, thousands of nuclear explosions would be created all over the world. These thousands of explosions would fill the world's atmosphere with poisoned earth, radioactive fallout, and death. There could be no radio communications in such an atmosphere of radioactive interferences. Without radio communications, all our systems would break down. There could be no air flights in such a contaminated atmosphere, either, since it's a fact that jet engines can't operate reliably in debris-cluttered air. Do you remember way back in 1980, when Mt. St. Helens erupted? Commericial jet flights had to be rerouted to cleaner atmosphere areas.

"Consider also, General, your EC-135 Looking Glass flights are monitored by radar screens everywhere. It's no big challenge for a Soviet intelligence agent with a computer and memory bank to determine which flights are noncommercial, military flights. By a process of elimination, the agent could quickly determine where your EC-135's are and have them destroyed. But if we have a nuclear warhead missile exchange first, which is most likely, your Looking Glass EC-135's wouldn't even be able to fly anyway. A heavily polluted, debris-cluttered atmosphere would foul up their engines. Even if by some unlikely miracle your EC-135's could fly, they'd be useless, since they rely entirely on radio transmissions which would be distorted or obliterated by heavy, radioactive interferences. To me, Looking Glass EC-135's seem worthless.

"Finally, if we were to have the nuclear exchange everybody dreads, how could it be ended? Ever think of that? Assuming all our leaders and their command posts are destroyed, and Soviet leaders and their command posts are destroyed, too, who would there be left to negotiate a settlement? Also, how could such a settlement negotiation take place, if radio communications are blanked out by radioactive interferences? The truth is, our war-centered thinking has created the prospect of a war without end. What have we done to wage peace?"

President Morrison raised a few more questions, insisting that the U. S. couldn't continue to have a war centered defense policy, since it's unable to stop a war after it's started. At present, Morrison could see no way to stop a nuclear war. How could it be stopped? Who would be left in the Soviet Union that the U. S. could talk to and negotiate with? Even if there were someone, how could anyone talk through unusable communication lines? Nobody even mentioned any kind of mechanism or ability the U. S. would have for communicating with Soviet military and political leaders to arrange a "Cease Fire."

On the other hand, Morrison pointed out, if the whole world were destroyed by an all-out nuclear warhead exchange, there wouldn't be any need to negotiate, since just about everybody would be dead anyway. So the entire arms race has been insane. Billions upon billions of dollars have been spent to wage a suicidal and stupid war, and nothing has been spent to prevent it, end it, or even control it. Such an omission is not only incredibly stupid and outrageous, it's downright criminal. The President insisted the U. S. couldn't continue on such a course and expect to survive. Therefore, it had to pursue every possible alternative to war, since war was no longer thinkable, but an obsolete remnant of an ignorant past.

In conclusion, the President said he intended to follow the 2,000-year-old advice of Aristotle, The Thinker, who urged the use of all the available means of persuasion in a particular situation. The U. S. hadn't even begun to do this, so, speaking into his intercom, the President asked his secretary to send in Harry Brown.

"Maybe Brown has something," the President said. "Anything! I'll look at anything! Then as soon as I can get through to Chairman Golgolev on the hot-line phone, I'll settle the matter peacefully with him."

18

RECONCILIATION INITIATIVES

In one of the few times since its installation, the red, hot line phone on Chairman Golgolev's desk rang out in ominous emergency. Acting quickly, he pressed a button at the base of the phone and placed the handset on an amplifier and speaker attachment. "Vasil Golgolev here!" he answered.

"Chairman Golgolev, this is U. S. President John Morrison. I had to phone you and express our deepest sympathy and concern over the unfortunate loss of your freighter Krasnodar and crew of 40. I assure you, Mr. Chairman, the United States had nothing whatsoever to do with your loss. We now believe we know some facts about what happened. Are you able to spare a few moments to hear what they are?"

After hearing a translation of Morrison's statements, Golgolev replied that he was willing to hear what the President had to say, but advised him that the situation in Moscow was quite agitated. Soviet demands for damages were extremely urgent. He was having a tough time keeping control. The military people and Politburo officials wanted to take the whole Krasnodar matter into their own hands and end, once and for all, America's many exploitations and treacheries.

"I appreciate your situation, Chairman Golgolev." Morrison responded. "I want you to know we feel many similar pressures here, too. H. B. Exports, for example, must be paid for the wheat delivered to your ship. The vessel agent's fee and other expenses must be paid in full, also. Please be assured, Chairman Golgolev, our United States Coast Guard and other agencies will assist your own investigative people in verifying the facts and arriving at the truth, so all our monetary claims against each other can be peacefully settled."

President Morrison reviewed his knowledge of the facts with Chairman Golgolev. A sudden, severe storm on Lake Superior, coupled with other unfortunate developments, caused the Krasnodar to sink. Specifically, the Krasnodar's radioman said "hatch hydraulics gone," so it was believed that the huge storm waves he reported had flooded through the ship's open hatches and into its heavily loaded holds, causing it to sink. Also, the entire cargo of 25,000 tons of water-soaked wheat rapidly swelled and broke up the ship as it was sinking. The radioman shouted "Breaking up! We're breaking up!" Although it was very difficult to hear everything the radioman said, because of all the background noise, Morrison felt that what had been heard didn't suggest any foul play. Besides, there were a number of important witnesses who heard the Krasnodar's Captain disclose in Duluth that the malfunctioning, hatch-closing hydraulic system was scheduled for overhaul in Odessa.

Chairman Golgolev acknowledged the importance of what President Morrison had said, and had dared to hope for the President's hot line call amid the persistent and compelling demands of Soviet citizens for vengeance. Yet, Golgolev was concerned about a report that an American may have sabotaged the Krasnodar, so an appropriate U. S. reply to Soviet compensation demands was needed, and Swiss Ambassador Clayborn had been sent by Golgolev to get such a reply.

191

"You know, President Morrison," Golgolev remarked through a translator in Morrison's office, "the whole world is very nervous about this Krasnodar affair. It fears the awesome destructiveness of our nuclear missiles. Everyone is anxious for us to settle this matter peacefully."

"Chairman Golgolev, I have met with Swiss Ambassador Clayborn and discussed the Krasnodar affair with him and others who are in my office with me at this very moment. We unanimously agree that there's a way we can accomplish a peaceful settlement. If we can just get this entire dispute out of our hands, we'll avoid the total destruction the world so dreadfully fears. One of your officials and one of our citizens may have a way to do this. Here's what I learned.

"Your Exportkhleb Director, Nikolai Novikov, and our own citizen, Mr. Harry Brown, a Minnesota grain broker, entered into a wheat contract together. Both signed the contract, and their signatures were witnessed by your people and ours. I've just had some conversation with Mr. Brown on this matter. He's here in my office right now. He tells me your Director, Nikolai Novikov, and he are old friends from student days. He said in the interest of improving peaceful relations they agreed to settle all their disputes by a scientific process of problem solving Reconciliation.

"Let me read you the Reconciliation Clause from their contract, Chairman Golgolev. It states that 'any dispute relating to this contract is to be settled in an amicable and mutually satisfactory manner under the guidance of Reconciliation Alliance International.' This is something new to the world, Chairman Golgolev. Do you understand it?"

Golgolev replied through Morrison's translator that Comrade Nikolai Novikov had come to the office on urgent business, but hadn't had an opportunity to discuss it yet, because of Morrison's hot-line call.

Perhaps now was a good time for Novikov to express his views. Novikov agreed, confirming that his urgent business was about the Reconciliation Clause in the Soviet wheat contract with Mr. Brown.

"The Krasnodar affair is a contract related dispute," Novikov pointed out. "Our Krasnodar was in Lake Superior transporting the first wheat shipment under our contract with Harry Brown's corporation. The Krasnodar dispute between our two countries, therefore, should be settled in a mutually satisfactory manner, under the guidance of Reconciliation Alliance International. This is what Harry Brown and I have to say. This is what I came to tell you, Comrade Chairman, and what Mr. Brown came to tell President Morrison. This is what we agreed to in our contract.

"For your further information, Comrade Chairman and Mr. President, Reconciliation is defined as a problem solving process of peacemaking, whereby individuals or groups cooperate amicably to reach a mutually satisfactory settlement of their disputes. As Mr. Brown can tell you, we agreed to the idea and we're working together now to establish it.

"War is no longer practical, if it ever was. We believe our process of Reconciliation is now the process the world should adopt to settle its disputes. Courts and arbitration methods are adversarial. They don't make friends of enemies or foster peace and friendship. They only increase animosities and hostilities, because of their win-or-lose decisions. If the Reconciliation process isn't adopted soon, we'll eventually destroy ourselves."

Chairman Golgolev approvingly responded to President Morrison that it seemed they had a valid contract to resolve their conflict by means of a unique new concept. However, he still didn't know how the concept would work, where it would get done, or even who would do it. President Morrison agreed with Golgolev on those questions and suggested Mr. Brown inform them of the answers. That arrangement was acceptable to Golgolev, so Morrison invited Brown to talk into the speaker phone hot-line hookup.

"Mr. President, Chairman Golgolev," Brown began, "what I suggest is that Swiss Ambassador Clayborn, Mr. Novikov, and I select a mutually acceptable panel of Reconciliation facilitators. The United Nations Secretary General can act as panel chairman. We'll meet with the Reconciliation panel as soon as possible in Geneva, and, using scientific problem solving techniques as needed and appropriate, we'll develop a mutually acceptable dispute settlement."

"I'm pleased, Harry," Morrison happily acknowledged. "Those arrangements sound fine to me. How about you, Chairman Golgolev, any suggestions?"

"President Morrison, I'll respect the provision of the contract on this. Do you have anything to add, Nikolai?" Golgolev asked.

"Comrade Chairman, Mr. President," Nikolai responded, "I'm confident Harry and I can satisfactorily work out the details for you. We'll get the job done. I firmly believe that if representatives of nations can meet in a spirit of cooperation and good will, they'll eventually resolve their disputes and be able to live in peace and friendship."

Golgolev complimented Novikov and suggested to President Morrison that maybe they can make wars disappear forever. Morrison agreed and observed that there was no progress in warfare. War was unthinkable. War today would be doomsday for the earth. It must never be allowed to happen. They must make it impossible for war to happen. Morrison said he'd cooperate with Golgolev, with Novikov, with Brown, and with anyone else, to not only secure a lasting peace and prosperity for the USA and USSR, but for the rest of the world as well.

"When we're through with this hot-line phone

call," President Morrison resolved, "I'll immediately order our military to a nonalert status. Then I'll commission Harry Brown as Special Ambassador to represent our nation in implementing the new Reconciliation process at Geneva. I very much appreciate your support of this effort, Chairman Golgolev."

"And I yours, Mr. President," Golgolev affirmed. "I sense this is a great moment in history for our two nations and the world. Perhaps we can create peace in our time for all time.

"I'll commission Nikolai Novikov as Special Ambassador to represent our peace-loving Union of Soviet Socialist Republics in this new Reconciliation process. Also, after this phone call, I'll order our military to a nonalert status."

Golgolev concluded by admitting that President Morrison's hot-line phone call was most welcome, and he looked to the day when they could meet each other face to face, perhaps at Geneva.

President Morrison thanked Chairman Golgolev for his good will, and looked forward to meeting him, too. In conclusion, Morrison again extended his sympathy and the heartfelt wishes of the entire U. S. at the tragic loss of the Soviet Krasnodar and crew.

Chairman Golgolev acknowledged Morrison's expression of sympathy and promised to relay them to the Soviet people. Then, hanging up his hot-line phone, he turned to Marshal Plekhanov and ordered him to implement, without delay, a nonalert status for all Soviet military and civil defense units.

Marshal Plekhanov replied that he'd execute the Chairman's order right away, and after exchanging farewell's with Golgolev, the Marshal left.

Next, Chairman Golgolev turned to Novikov and congratulated him for his remarkable initiative in the Krasnodar affair. The Chairman officially commissioned Novikov a Special Ambassador to represent the USSR at the Reconciliation session in Geneva, and Tatyana Borshak was asked to arrange proper certification papers for Novikov and his two assistants. Also, Golgolev promised Novikov any additional support he'd need in his new assignment.

For example, Golgolev said he was assigning Marshal Plekhanov and his General Staff to help Novikov in his efforts to resolve the Krasnodar affair and get full compensation for Soviet damages. Specifically, Novikov was to use the Marshal's fast plane to fly to Geneva or any other place he needed to go. He was to also use the Marshal's staff people to help him bring the Reconciliation panel together.

"Make the Marshal's staff pay the hotel bills, too," Golgolev added. "Maybe we can teach these military officers how to spend money carefully, if we make them pay the bills. I for one am fed up with their thousand ruble hammers and five-hundred ruble nails. They've been spending our hardworking people back into serfdom. It must stop. Military spending and the arms race have prevented proper progress towards the realization of our ultimate socialist goals. But that's another subject, Nikolai. You have your work to do right now.

"Our people will be very proud of you, as I'll be, too, if you and Harry Brown can achieve the results you seem to believe you can achieve. Good luck to you!"

"I'm honored, Comrade Chairman, to represent our nation," Nikolai replied as Golgolev shook his hand and hugged him. "The overriding goal of our socialist revolution is to benefit the future of mankind."

19

BROWN'S COMMISSION

After President John Morrison's hot–line phone contact with Soviet Chairman Vasil Golgolev was ended, he congratulated Harry Brown for his unprecedented peacemaking initiative, and commissioned Brown a Special Ambassador of the United States. Brown's assignment was to work with Ambassadors Novikov of the USSR and Clayborn of Switzerland to satisfactorily settle the Krasnodar affair. Whatever additional support Harry needed, the President ordered General Daniels and his Joint Chiefs to provide it. The U. S. military had the resources, and Morrison wanted Harry to have them.

"Believe me," Morrison added, "it'll make my heart happy to see military men, so efficient at destruction, turning their minds to a peacemaking and friendship promoting alternative. Think of it: U. S. and Soviet military leaders, bitter enemies, working together for peace and friendship!"

Picking up a booklet on his desk, the President smiled and spoke again.

"I'll ask the Secretary of Defense to rewrite this *Defense Against Ballistic Missiles* booklet, and highlight what may prove to be the best practical defense we have, the new, peacemaking, Reconciliation process. If we can get generals from opposite sides of a conflict conversing and cooperating with each other, we won't need the burden and threat of outrageously expensive nuclear weapons. The USA and USSR can at last disarm themselves and dedicate their future efforts to achieving world peace, friendship, and prosperity, rather than continue to build deadlier and more expensive weapons of destruction."

The President again commended Brown for his outstanding achievement and added that the hopes of the U. S., as well as the President's own hopes, were with Ambassadors Brown, Clayborn, and Novikov. The President concluded by shaking hands with both Brown and Clayborn.

"I'm honored, Mr. President," Brown replied. "My two business associates and I will work quickly with Ambassadors Clayborn and Novikov to get the job done.

"Ambassador Clayborn, can we assist you with anything right now?" Brown asked. "I'm sure General Daniels can put one of his fast jets at your disposal."

Ambassador Clayborn responded that some fast air transportation would be most helpful, since they both needed to get back home, attend to their personal responsibilities, and quickly proceed to the logical next step, the selection of a panel of Reconciliation facilitators.

President Morrison approved, and expressed his desire that they get moving fast on their new assignments.

Turning to General Daniels, the President, as Commander in Chief, ordered him to get the U. S. military into a nonalert status as soon as possible, and to discontinue the impractical and costly EC-135 Looking Glass flights. Also, Daniels was asked to have Ambassador Harry Brown flown to Taylorsville, Minnesota, and, at the same time, have a military engineer install a videoscreen and satellite hookup between Harry's office, Mr. Clayborn's office in

Switzerland, and Novikov's office in Moscow. This hookup would save the Ambassadors long air flights and precious time in getting a Reconciliation panel together.

"General," President Morrison continued, "I want you to know in advance I appreciate your cooperation in these efforts. I also want you and the others to know that my criticism of our military situation was in no way intended to reflect adversely on you. You have your job to do, and you're most highly qualified and respected by me. My earlier remarks were merely intended to reflect my intense dissatisfaction with our whole system of defense, including its objectives of more and more nuclear warheads, rather than development of a nonadversarial, nonviolent, nondestructive system for worldwide peace. I know from our previous discussions on this subject that you yourself have shared similar thoughts. I wasn't being critical of you at any time. I value your service highly."

"Thank you, Mr. President," Daniels answered. "I've taken all your remarks in that spirit. I never felt you were being critical of me. I agree with your statements about our military situation. Your criticisms are valid. I, too, realize our EC-135 Looking Glass operation may be futile. The only reason I let that operation continue, however, was because I thought it had good training values. It gave our personnel opportunities to practice their assignments in realistic settings. However, we'll discontinue these flights as part of our return to a nonalert status. We'll look for other, less costly ways of training personnel. Also, we'll pursue a program of conversing and cooperating with the Soviet military, so we can, as you say, wage peace instead of war."

The President complimented General Daniels for his positive response, and urged everyone to get going and get their important duties done. He said the whole world was angry with the Americans and the Soviets for

199

developing such deadly mechanisms for waging war, and that it was time they both developed a reliable mechanism for keeping the peace.

PART III.

RECONCILIATION

20

SELECTION OF FACILITATORS

Back in Taylorsville the next day, Harry Brown rushed into his office at H. B. Exports, Inc. He could hardly wait to tell his partners the news of his assignment as Special U. S. Ambassador. He was also anxious to tell Maxie and Bert about their new roles as his Special Ambassadorial Assistants.

After Maxie and Bert heard the news, they congratulated Harry, and Harry acknowledged the debt of gratitude he owed them. The three marveled at the events of the past week and wondered whether some unearthly power was propelling them to some higher destiny on earth, far beyond the mere selling of grain or processing of export documents. It was exciting for them to contemplate the role they might be playing in history. They were absolutely convinced they'd hatched the right idea at precisely the right time in history. A Reconciliation Clause in their wheat contract with the Soviet Union had been an inspiration for them that surpassed all ordinary expectations, and now seemed a stroke of good fortune for the USA and USSR. It offered these two quarrelsome nations a chance to temporarily free themselves from a militarily, politically, and socially disastrous confrontation. It even had the potential of creating world peace and disarmament.

Meanwhile, the Min-Dak Farmer's Co-op was anxious about getting paid for its 25,000 tons of wheat, because co-op officials had heard the news that the USSR refused to pay for it. They were also aware of the USSR's various demands for damages. What could Harry Brown do now? His business was without funds, except for the small amount Maxie and Bert had loaned it to keep the three of them going a little while longer. There was simply no way H. B. Exports, Inc. could pay the co-op at that time.

Nevertheless, Brown dispatched Bert Jackson to the Min-Dak Co-op, and instructed him to remind the officials that their contract payment terms allowed a full 30 days to pay. There were still nearly three weeks left to come up with the money.

"Also, Bert," Harry added, "we'll need to prepare a presentation for the Reconciliation session in Geneva. I'd appreciate it if you could begin by getting all our documents together, including a copy of our contract with Nikolai. Phone Duluth Vessel Agent Hjalmar Haggarson and have him prepare his testimony, too. Tell him to meet us in Geneva, and that we'll provide him an airplane. Finally, contact the U. S. Coast Guard, the Corps of Engineers, and any others you think useful, so we can get their inputs, too.

"Data on previous Lake Superior storms and sinkings would be helpful. I'm thinking specifically of the circumstances surrounding the sinking of the Edmund Fitzgerald. Maybe you can also find some Ojibway tribal historian or somebody else who's a Great Lakes expert and can contribute additional information about Lake Superior."

Bert assured Harry he'd find out all he could, and Harry wished him success. As Bert left, Harry turned to Maxie and asked her to assist him in contacting

Ambassadors Nikolai Novikov and Manfred Clayborn about the selection of Reconciliation facilitators. Nikolai and Manfred had agreed to be in their offices that day, and Harry wanted to try reaching them on the new satellite communications system the U. S. military had just put in place. He was quite anxious to use this powerful tool as he and Maxie walked to a corner of the outer office, where a videoscreen and other equipment had been installed. Since Maxie was briefed earlier on the operation of the system, Harry asked her to make the necessary contacts.

Maxie agreed, then activated the equipment and began punching in some entry codes she read from an operating manual. She asked Harry to stand in a video transmitting area taped off on the floor, where the system's camera and microphone could pick him up. Also, she asked him to watch the videoscreen in front of him, so a good image could be transmitted.

After Maxie activated a few switches and manipulated several controls, a weak image of Ambassador Manfred Clayborn appeared on one-half of the large videoscreen in front of Harry Brown. Maxie continued adjusting various knobs on the control panel, so that the videoscreen image of Clayborn could be made clearer. When Clayborn's image was completely tuned in, and he and Brown were able to hear each other clearly, Maxie repeated the contact process to bring in Nikolai Novikov's image on the other half of the videoscreen. When the three were able to converse with one another as though they were sitting at a single conference table, the meeting began.

"How wonderful we can communicate like this from three different locations on opposite sides of the earth," Brown observed. "How fortunate we are to have this satellite communications equipment!" The others expressed their enthusiasm, also, then Brown stated that the reason for their meeting was to make their

Reconciliation session arrangements. First, they needed to select a panel of facilitators.

"Are you ready with your recommendations, Manfred?" Brown asked.

"Yes!" Clayborn replied. "I've already contacted Dr. Jawarlal Raman, Secretary General of the United Nations, and he has agreed to help us. Dr. Raman was educated at Punjab University in India, where he received B. S. and M. S. degrees. He then earned a Ph.D. at Cambridge University in England. Prior to his election as United Nations Secretary General, Dr. Raman served as India's Ambassador to the U. N. Earlier, he was a professor who lectured on dispute settlement. His lectures became so popular, he has now given them in the USA, USSR, Canada, Switzerland, United Kingdom, Japan, and other countries. At the present time, he's so much in demand, he can't possibly accept all the lecture requests he gets. We're fortunate Dr. Raman is willing to act as Chairman of our panel of facilitators. Are you gentlemen in agreement on the participation of Dr. Raman?"

"I'm not sure," Novikov reacted. "Secretary General Raman is a respected world leader, but I'm concerned about his strict religious views, and whether they would affect his performance. I'll accept him only if you can assure me he'll be impartial in guiding our efforts to a satisfactory conclusion. What's your thinking, Harry?"

"He's fine with me," Harry indicated. "Nikolai, I don't think you'll have any worries about Dr. Raman, I've heard he's fair-minded. Manfred, what's your thinking on the matter?"

"He'll be very good," Clayborn affirmed. "I can assure you, Dr. Raman will be most impartial. He's very well regarded throughout the entire world. You'll have no worries with Dr. Raman."

"Based on your assurances, Manfred, and yours, too, Harry," Novikov responded, "I'll accept Dr. Raman.

Who else are you recommending for the panel, Manfred?"

"I have six other individuals to propose to you. I'll call up their images on the screen, one at a time, and describe the qualifications of each. I ask you to please withhold your reactions until I've finished presenting all six candidates. Then, at that time, I'll answer your questions.

"The first individual, and these names are presented in alphabetical order, is Senator Perez Cordierat, who is in the Spanish Senate. He previously occupied various diplomatic posts to which he was appointed after a successful teaching career. He graduated from the Universities of Salamanca and Valladolid. Senator Cordierat has succeeded in peacefully settling many bitter disputes. For his outstanding achievements, he has been awarded the Grand Cross: Order of Civil Merit.

"The second individual is Dr. Angelica Fabriano. Dr. Fabriano is a Professor at the University of Rome. She currently lectures on 'The Importance of Research, Creativity, and Logic in Problem-Solving.' Dr. Fabriano attended the Universities of Turin and Rome, earning her Ph.D. at Rome. She received the Nobel Peace Prize for her study of *Successful International Dispute Settlements and War Avoidance.*

"The third individual is Abdul Khaldun, Director of Economic Affairs for Sudan. Mr. Khaldun attended the University of Khartoum, where he majored in psychology and received B. Sc. and M. A. degrees. For his achievements in peacefully resolving disputes among groups and tribes of his countrymen, he was awarded The Order of the Two Niles and a Medal of Merit, First Class.

"The fourth individual is Japan's Ambassador to the USA, Togawa Noguchi. Ambassador Noguchi graduated from Tokyo Imperial University. He has written many articles on peaceful, nonadversarial, dispute resolution. For his contribution to the progress of humanity, Ambassador Noguchi received the First Order of Sacred Treasure and many other decorations.

"The fifth individual is Dr. Suvrana Sharma. Dr. Sharma is active in promoting the Doctrine of Nonviolence. She has won numerous awards, including a Nobel Peace Prize for her book, *The Mechanics of Developing Nonviolent Solutions to National and International Conflicts.* Dr. Sharma is a graduate of the Universities of Calcutta, Vikraim, and Udaipur. She received a Ph.D. at Udaipur for her studies of the reasons why political systems come into conflict, and the various methods by which conflicts can be peacefully settled.

"The sixth individual is Chou Wang-Tzu, a native of China. Mr. Wang-Tzu is head of a large publishing firm in Beijing. He attended South West Associate University in Kumming, China, graduating with honors. Recently he was honored by the World Peace Movement for his *Study of Dispute-Settlement Advice Given by the Worlds Great Philosophers.*

"There you have my recommendations, gentlemen. I now invite your responses. Do you have any comments or objections regarding any of the six facilitators I just described?"

Novikov commented first, expressing some objections to two of the six individuals, because of their possible anticommunist sentiments. Brown advised him not to worry, however, since Novikov's concerns about anticommunist sentiments were canceled out by Brown's own worries of anticapitalist attitudes, so there was no sense worrying about any of them. Besides, Ambassador Clayborn emphasized the point that the individuals were each dedicated to the peaceful settlement of disputes. They wouldn't let their personal views of communism, or capitalism, or any other "ism" interfere with their neutrality as facilitators. Also, they wouldn't enforce any kind of settlement on anyone. It would be up to Brown and Novikov to decide that. The facilitators assist in developing the settlement. They stimulate cooperative and creative thinking, and help design mutually acceptable solutions. However, they don't force any kind of solution on anyone, since Brown and Novikov must both agree to the settlement.

After some further discussion of the candidates, Brown and Novikov yielded to Ambassador Clayborn's representations and assurances, if for no other reason than to give Reconciliation a chance to prove itself, and as a positive step towards world peace. Novikov concluded the discussion of candidates by asking Clayborn what he suggested for the specific Reconciliation session arrangements.

"My suggestion is that we meet whenever we can get our facilitators together," Clayborn answered. "I propose we meet in Geneva at the Palace of Nations, which, as you may already know, is the European Headquarters of the United Nations. You'll both like it there very much. I'll be your host and make sure you enjoy your stay. If we can get our panel together immediately, we'll schedule our session for next Thursday. I'll arrange a breakfast for us at 8:30. Is this satisfactory to you two?"

"The timing seems somewhat tight, Manfred," Novikov remarked, "but settlement of the Krasnodar affair has our highest priority, so we must get it done without delay. There shouldn't be any delays whatsoever. I mean no offense to anyone, Harry, but I'm worried that some berzerk commander in either your nation or ours might accidently push a button and fire the doomsday missiles that will devastate all of us. The rest of the world is worried about this, too. Anything can happen on either side of these internationally tense situations that our world keeps getting into more frequently. Something has to be done now to end disputes quickly and peacefully before they get out of control and destroy the whole world. I hope the Reconciliation process is the answer, and I certainly intend to give it my best effort."

Novikov concluded by thanking Brown and Clayborn and assuring them he'd meet them at 8:30 a.m. Thursday. He also said he'd bring Naddy and Helga along as his assistants, noting that Naddy was quite anxious to see Bert Jackson again, and that perhaps the two were becoming quite fond of one another.

Brown said he was all for Bert and Naddy's romance, and that the world needed all the good love stories it could get. He also said he'd bring Bert and Maxie with him, since they were his official ambassadorial assistants.

"Well, gentlemen, looks like we're making some progress," Clayborn concluded. "I'll see you both for 8:30 breakfast on Thursday in Geneva. To prevent any confusion about our arrangements, in approximately three hours I'll send each of you a confirming wire and news release. You, in turn, can give copies of this release to your news media people and get the pressure off yourselves by referring them to my office. In the future, this news media task seems an appropriate duty for the chairman of a Reconciliation panel. I'm happy to help out with it right now, however, at least until the chairman of our session is able to do it."

Brown and Novikov both found Clayborn's approach acceptable and agreed to wait for his newswire before contacting representatives of their own news media. After that, the three said their farewells and signed off the system. When the video images of Clayborn and Novikov faded from the screen, Harry asked Maxie to turn off the communications equipment. He told her he had to get home, get his family packed, and get going to Geneva.

"I certainly hope Bert gets back soon, so he can get

ready, too," Brown commented. "How about you, Maxie, you set to go?"

"I travel light, Harry," Maxie replied. "I can be ready in a few moments."

"Good! Let's plan to meet at the airport before sunset, say 8:00 p.m., so we can be airborne by dark. Then we....Well, I'll be....It's Jamie Baston and Julius Fiske!" Brown expressed surprise as Baston and Fiske entered the office area.

"Hello, Mr. Brown, Maxie," Baston politely greeted. "Meet Big Julie Fiske, my boss."

"Please to meet you!" Fiske exclaimed. Then, in a subdued tone he said, "Ambassador Brown, I won't take much of your time. I just want to apologize for my bad behavior and make amends."

"Your apology is accepted, Big Julie," Brown graciously replied. "You must care quite a bit about it to come up here to Taylorsville, all the way from Texas. It's good you came, but I must admit I'm shocked. Frankly, Big Julie, I've been amazed at you for a long time. It seems you've been trying to destroy our small business almost since we started. I could never understand why, either, because we'd never think of hurting you. How could you have wanted to hurt us?

"Your company is so big; ours so small. We should be helping one another. We can refer customers to you when you have what they need, and you can do the same for us. It's such a simple courtesy. The good of our customers should be our primary concern. My belief is that we're all here on this earth to help one another.

"Don't get me wrong, Big Julie. Whatever bitterness we've had in the past, I want you to know I appreciate your coming to me now. However, I'm amazed to see you."

"I'm here to make amends, Ambassador Brown," Big Julie replied. "I've read the papers, and know about the Krasnodar tragedy. It could have happened to me,

210

instead of you. You must be in a real financial jam with all that wheat gone and the Soviets refusing to pay for it. I'm sure you'll work something out eventually, you always seem to be able to do that, but I want to help you now, all I can. Besides, I owe you a real favor for not turning Jamie Baston over to the Duluth police and getting my company in trouble. You're a real gentleman for acting so nobly. I very much want to help you.

"Ambassador Brown, I calculated that you must need at least $3-1/2 million to pay for the wheat you bought from the farmers. I know your bushel cost is none of my business, so I won't ask you about it. What I'm going to do instead is simply give you a check in the amount of four million dollars." Big Julie handed Brown the check. "I've written on it that it's a six-month, no-interest loan, but you can pay me back whenever the Krasnodar affair gets settled with the Soviets. I hope we can be friends now and help each other howsoever we can, though we be competitors."

Brown held Big Julie's check in his hands for a few moments. He looked at it with some satisfaction, but he also gazed at it skeptically. He wondered whether some ulterior motive had driven Big Julie to perform such an unprecedented act of philanthrophy. Leopards don't change their spots. A greedy Big Julie isn't suddenly transformed into a charitable, financially generous person, especially with competitors he keeps trying to destroy.

No, Brown thought to himself, Big Julie was scared out of his wits by something or somebody. Fear forced him here to Taylorsville, perhaps fear about his exposed meddling with the wheat shipment in Duluth. Big Julie may be afraid Baston's red-flagging of hopper cars was fanning Soviet suspicions about Big Julie himself. Maybe some Soviets and Americans suspect Big Julie of sabotaging the Krasnodar. That's it, Brown reflected. Big Julie was worried the Soviets would eventually accuse

211

him of destroying the Krasnodar, and he had too much at stake. He didn't want to destroy his billion dollar grain deal with the Soviets and wind up paying $65 million in damages besides.

It wasn't true, of course, that Big Julie Fiske or James Baston sabotaged the Krasnodar, Brown continued thinking to himself. Security around the ship was so tight, nobody could have boarded her unnoticed. Nevertheless, Big Julie seemed traumatized by the danger he was in. Maybe he was worried about the possibility of a guilt by association witch hunt. He was probably imagining some kind of international lynch mob effort to punish him. Good! Brown concluded. I'll accommodate Big Julie by nurturing his fears in the hope he'll reform for good.

"Big Julie, you're really helping me," Brown at last acknowledged. "I'll accept your check as a token of friendship, but I want you to know I won't cash it unless I absolutely have to. If that time should ever come, I'll notify you first, then pay you back as quickly as I can. I don't like being in debt to anyone for any length of time.

"Now, then, I'm trying to get ready for the Reconciliation session in Geneva, Switzerland. It's Thursday at the Palace of Nations, 10:00 a.m. If all goes well, this unfortunate Krasnodar affair between the Soviets and us will be settled in a peaceful, mutually satisfactory way.

"However, there's a serious problem you'll have to help us with, Big Julie. The Soviets think you and Jamie sabotaged the hatch hydraulics on their Krasnodar. As you already know, a number of persons, including some Soviet citizens, witnessed Jamie's illegal red-flagging of our hopper cars in Duluth. That's why you two should both come to Geneva this Thursday. It's important you tell the truth to the Reconciliation panel, that red-flagging our hopper cars was all you did, and that you never touched or even came near the Krasnodar."

212

"Ambassador Brown is right, Big Julie." Baston insisted. "I say we go!"

"That's fine with me," Fiske agreed. "We'll be there, Mr. Brown, at 10:00 a.m., Thursday, in the Palace of Nations."

Brown smiled, saying he was glad they'd both be there, and that he looked forward to being on good terms with them in the future. He even assured them of a military jet to get them to Geneva on time.

Fiske was happy Brown was happy, and began smiling, too. He enthusiastically shook Brown's hand, and said his goodbyes to both Maxie and Brown.

Baston, however, pleaded with Maxie for a few words in private, asking Big Julie to wait outside in the car. Fiske agreed, and he and Brown left the office together, since Brown was going home to pack for his flight to Geneva.

As soon as Brown and Fiske left, Maxie turned to Baston, frowned, and began talking in a stern tone. She wanted to know what kind of lies Baston would tell her this time.

"Maxie, I'm so sorry about the foolishness I attempted in Duluth. I'm especially sorry for hurting you. I'm really very fond of you. Is it still possible we could be friends?"

"I don't know, Jamie," Maxie wondered. "You lied to me once, how do I know you aren't lying again?"

"When I told you at the hotel coffee shop my word is my bond, I meant it," Baston assured. "The only questionable thing I told you was the news reporter stuff, but even that wasn't entirely false; I do perform a kind of reporter function in the Fiske company. Also, do you remember your Harry Brown saying in Duluth I was honest about my attempted tampering with your shipment?"

"But why would you do such a thing in the first

place, Jamie?" Maxie asked. "There must be a major defect in your character."

"Maxie, please forgive me," Baston pleaded. "Big Julie ordered me to do it. I didn't really want to do it, but I was weak willed and obeyed him. I know now it was completely wrong of me, but at the time I was under pressure and afraid of what Big Julie might do. Today my relationship with Big Julie is drastically changed.

"After getting back to Galveston from Duluth, I resigned my job and gave Big Julie a sharp tongue-lashing, telling him how wrong he was. I also told him I'd become very fond of you, and said what wonderful persons you, Harry, Bert, and the others are. I regretted betraying the trust you had each placed in me, and I warned Big Julie he had to change his ways, too, and become a gentleman.

"Wealth requires responsible behavior, but Big Julie became more irresponsible the wealthier he got. I wanted no part of it. I told Big Julie the best thing for him to do was get up here in person and apologize to you folks, then start looking for ways to use his wealth constructively. When I finished, Big Julie was so startled he couldn't talk, so I walked out on him.

"The very next day, the newspapers ran headlines about the Krasnodar sinking, the Soviet alert, and you know the rest. Suddenly Big Julie showed up at my place in his chauffered limousine. He said I'd changed his life, and that he wouldn't let me quit. Then he mumbled something about my being his conscience. That's why we came here today. Big Julie said he wanted to take my advice and come see you in person to clear his conscience.

"Maxie, I want you to know I'm happier now than ever, because I was honest in admitting my guilt in Duluth. I'm happy, too, because I could get up here and apologize to you again, in person. Now that I've done it, I feel much better. Please forgive me."

"That's quite a story, Jamie," Maxie approvingly remarked. Then, softening her voice somewhat, she said, "We're all human, Jamie. We make mistakes. Like Harry, I'm glad you admitted your mistake. If it wasn't for your honesty and intervention with Big Julie, ·we wouldn't have his four million dollar check to cover our wheat costs."

After a thoughtful pause, Maxie looked intently at Jamie, broke into a smile, and graciously said, "I guess I can forgive you."

"You won't be sorry, Maxie!" Baston assured. "I'll arrange to meet you in Duluth properly, just as soon as your next wheat shipment goes out. We'll start all over again with each other, too, and I'll show you the best time ever. Maybe if I can get away from Big Julie for awhile in Geneva, we'll even get a chance to go out together there."

Suddenly a loud honking sound interrupted the conversation. It was Big Julie in the car outside, getting impatient.

"Let him wait, Maxie," Baston chided, taking her in his arms and kissing her.

"Oh, Jamie!" Maxie emotionally sputtered, "I feel so good about you again." Then she reached up, put her arms around Baston's neck, and kissed him back as hard as she could.

Afterwards, the two said their goodbyes and parted. On his way out the door, Baston yelled back that he looked forward to seeing Maxie in Switzerland. Maxie shouted she was glad he'd be there, too. Meanwhile, Big Julie ended all further conversation by repeatedly honking the car horn.

21

GENEVA SESSION

"Ladies and gentlemen," Ambassador Clayborn began, "on behalf of Switzerland, welcome to this Palace of Nations, the European Headquarters of the United Nations."

Clayborn glanced around the large, crowded, brightly lit assembly hall. He had a good view from the raised platform where he stood. In front of him was a heavy, well-polished, mahogony speaker's stand with the United Nations symbol emblazoned in brass on the outside panel. As he looked over the top of the stand into the audience, he recognized many individuals. Harry Brown and Nikolai Novikov were seated in the front row with their assistants, Bert Jackson, Nadezhda Konya, Helga Baranovna, and Maxine Gadsden. Clayborn had met with them for breakfast that morning.

Behind Brown and Novikov and their assistants sat the various Reconciliation facilitators. Still further back were various other guests, some of whom Clayborn knew, and some he hadn't yet met, including Julius Fiske, James Baston, and Hjalmar Haggarson. However, Clayborn smiled at everybody.

"We're gathered here this sunny Thursday morning to begin the first International Peacemaking

Reconciliation Session." Clayborn continued. "This session brings together two of the world's most powerful nations, the USA and USSR. It's particularly appropriate on this occasion, therefore, that we meet here in tiny Switzerland, which has been described as an 'Island of Peace.' The reason for this description is that for hundreds of years, since the 1500's, Switzerland hasn't taken sides in any armed conflicts. A strict neutrality policy has been maintained by the Swiss throughout the major wars of this century. Switzerland is hopeful, as is every nation, that the new process of Reconciliation will be successful, and that all wars will be avoided forever.

"A frightening new era cast its deathly shadows over the world in 1945, with the explosions of the first atomic bombs. The unleashing at that time of incredibly destructive and radioactive forces was frightening enough. What has happened in recent times, however, over forty years later, surpasses all credibility of human endeavor.

"I'm referring to the fact that as of this very moment, life on our planet is cursed with the threat of instant and total annihilation. Not only is one out of every five nations in the world engaged in war right now, but, sad to say, fifty thousand nuclear warhead missiles are ready and waiting to be unleashed on everyone. How can we comprehend the destructive power of so many missiles? What does this nuclear missile talk mean?

"Looking at the problem another way, the combined power of all the allied bombs dropped in World War II totaled three megatons of TNT, which is three million tons. Today's stockpile of nuclear warheads totals 20,000 megatons of TNT, which is 20 billion tons, or the equivalent of 6,667 World War II's. At the current rate of the international arms race buildup, we'll soon be threatened with 7,000 World War II's, all unleashable in the same instant.

217

"The 'Little Boy' atomic bomb dropped on Hiroshima in 1945 had the destructive force of some 12-1/2 kilotons of TNT, which is 12,500 tons. This is a minuscule amount, compared to the ravaging power of just one of the hundreds of submarines patroling our oceans today. Consider that one of today's subs carries enough nuclear warhead missiles to equal the firepower of more than six World War II's. Six World War II's from only one modern submarine! Such firepower, multiplied by hundreds of submarines, thousands of bombers, and tens of thousands of multiple warhead Intercontinental Ballistic Missiles, totals a firepower able to destroy the entire world's surface at least a hundred times over. In the face of such an unprecedented, overwhelming, and alarming devastation potential, our world's nations must quickly find a reliable peacemaking alternative to war. I'm sure our meeting here today will be a productive step in that direction.

"At this time, therefore, before beginning our session, let's bow our heads and call upon our Maker in prayer:

Almighty God, our Creator, we humbly ask you to inspire this Reconciliation proceeding. Make of it a good example among people everywhere, that lasting peace may be achieved in our time, and warfare abolished forever.

Almighty God, our Creator, bestow your Eternal Spirit upon us to guide, enlighten, and protect our lives, that we may avoid injustice, violence, and rash judgments in all our dealings. Help us as individuals, organizations, and nations to develop peaceful methods for settling disputes, that we may make friends of enemies and create a world of happiness

218

and prosperity for everyone, everywhere.
Amen.

"Now, ladies and gentlemen, to begin our session, it's a privilege to introduce a leader of the highest rank, former Ambassador to the U. N. from India and now United Nations Secretary General, Dr. Jawarlal Raman."

While the audience applauded, Ambassador Clayborn withdrew to a seat near the rear edge of the raised platform, and Dr. Raman approached the speaker's stand. Dr. Raman had a towering, authoritative appearance. Perhaps it was an impression created by the combination of his sharply ascetic, dark-skinned, thin lipped facial features, combined with his piercing dark eyes, narrow nose, small mouth, heavy eyebrows, and thick, black, gray-streaked hair. He stood nearly six feet tall, had a slender build, and wore a white shirt, pinstriped charcoal suit, and matching black tie with narrow red stripes. There was an attractive, energetic, and captivating look about him that inspired everyone to be attentive when he spoke.

"Ladies and gentlemen, it's a pleasure to welcome you on behalf of the United Nations. Ambassador Clayborn's success in bringing this unique group together, a group of such outstanding talents, is an achievement worthy of the deepest acknowledgment. We thank you, Ambassador Clayborn, and your country, for extending to us this beautiful, 'Island of peace' setting on the shores of Lake Geneva.

"Permit me to depart from my brief remarks for a moment to tell you a story. There were two guards on duty walking their posts. One said to the other, 'What do you think of our regime?' The other said, 'I don't know, same as you, I suppose.' The first guard replied, 'Then it's my painful duty to arrest you.'

"Ladies and gentlemen, it's my painful duty to inform you that all's not well with the United Nations

219

regime. I hope you'll not arrest me for saying so. Let's consider the facts and realities with which we're confronted. Let's begin by looking first at the United Nations Charter.

"On June 26, 1945, the U. N. Charter was signed in San Francisco, California. On October 24, 1945, the U. N. came into being with 51 member nations. Today, there are over 150.

"The first article of the Charter specifies that the purpose of the U. N. is 'to maintain international peace and security.' The preamble of the Charter pledges nations 'to save succeeding generations from the scourge of war, which twice in our lifetime has brought untold sorrow to mankind.' Also, membership in the United Nations is restricted to 'peace-loving' nations.

"Forty years later, by 1985, the world had suffered more than 100 agonizing wars. Today, as Ambassador Clayborn mentioned a few moments ago, one of every five nations in the world is at war. Perhaps the major reason for so many wars is the adversarial manner in which nations are allowed to conduct themselves during proceedings of the General Assembly.

"The U. N. General Assembly is divided up into opposing groups, much like a congress or parliament is divided into bitterly opposed parties or factions. For example, there are various blocs of nations, such as the Western Nations Bloc, the Afro-Asian and Third World Nations Bloc, the Soviet Nations Bloc, and so on. This splintering of nations into adversarial blocs or factions promotes angry arguing and hostility, which prevents the U. N. from fulfilling its peacemaking role.

"Needless to say, the constant quarreling in the U.N. is a shameful and intolerable activity for an organization dedicated to preserving world peace. We should all be ashamed of ourselves. Bitter arguing makes enemies, not friends. It doesn't encourage peace.

"There's no scientific process of problem solving

220

and peacemaking in an atmosphere of bitter arguing and quarreling. There's no scientific process of problem solving and peacemaking in an environment of legalistic, adversarial systems and procedures. Hatreds are intensified. Conflicts are globalized. Wars are increased. To eliminate this deplorable circumstance, the U. N. must purge itself of politics.

"It's time that a scientific process of problem solving and peacemaking be installed throughout the U. N. organization, so that it can become a good example for all nations and all people, and a model for the world of how disputes can and should be settled. Let the General Assembly turn its conduct from arguing and bickering to creating mutually satisfactory settlements of disputes. Let it reconcile warring nations, rather than push them into larger and more destructive wars.

"Ladies and gentlemen, in all our dealings with each other, let's look for alternatives to hostility and warfare. That's not to say peacekeeping weapons or law enforcement will no longer be necessary. To stop the naked, relentless aggression and terrorism of some nations, there may need to be some collective, non-nuclear armed action authorized by the U. N. Security Council. However, for settling most disputes, it's essential we place an emphasis on nonviolent alternatives. The Reconciliation process has the potential of becoming that alternative.

"Before continuing further, let's take a moment here to define what is meant by Reconciliation. The word, reconciliation, means bringing back into unity, balance, harmony, or good standing, and that's what we aim to accomplish today, between the USA and USSR. However, spelled with a capital R, the word refers to a specific process.

"Both Ambassadors Harry Brown of the USA and Nikolai Novikov of the USSR pioneered a Reconciliation Clause in their wheat sale contract. This clause requires that any disputes relating to their contract be settled in a mutually satisfactory manner by a process of peacemaking Reconciliation. Such a contract clause is fortunate for the world, in view of the Krasnodar crisis, and it's the reason we're all here. Would that every contract had such a clause. For the purpose of developing a worldwide understanding of Reconciliation, both Ambassadors Brown and Novikov agreed to a definition. Here is what they say: *'Reconciliation is a scientific, problem solving process of peacemaking, whereby individuals or groups cooperate amicably to achieve a mutually satisfactory settlement of their disputes.'*

"Ladies and gentlemen, let's work quickly at our task today of creating a mutually satisfactory settlement between the USA and USSR, so both countries become good friends again. Let's use our time efficiently and make 4 p.m. our completion deadline for a settlement of the unfortunate Krasnodar affair.

"At this time, I call upon our facilitators to carefully search their keen minds and share with us any bits and pieces of sound advice, wise counsel, and peacemaking instruction, which will make our Reconciliation tasks easier, more orderly, and better informed. Each will have the opportunity to speak, and each will be introduced briefly, in alphabetical order. Immediately afterwards, we'll have a brief recess, then begin the problem solving segment of our session.

"The first facilitator to speak is Senator Perez Cordierat of the Spanish Senate. You may already have seen his outstanding credentials listed in the program booklet. Among his many honors, the Senator was awarded the Grand Cross: Order of Civil Merit for his outstanding achievement in the peaceful settlement of several bitter political disputes. It's an honor to present to you, Senator Cordierat."

Dr. Raman withdrew to his seat at the rear of the platform as Senator Cordierat approached the speaker's

222

stand. Cordierat was almost completely bald, except for some neatly arranged strands of gray hair at the sides of his head. His skin was darkly tanned. His eyes were dark; eyebrows thick, bushy, and gray. His nose was large and slightly hooked; his mouth somewhat thick-lipped. He stood five and a half feet high, had a plump build, and wore a light-gray suit that matched what little hair he had. His tie was deep blue, accented by the crisp white shirt he wore. He was very determined and had no trouble getting the audience's attention after the applause died down.

"Dr. Raman, honorable guests, and distinguished associates in this session, I'll begin with the prayer of Moses: 'Hear, O Israel, the Lord our God, the Lord is One.' So are we all one people, of the same first parents, and brothers and sisters in the same human family. Why is it, then, we don't get along?

"Notice I used the word 'don't,' rather than 'can't.' There's a reason for this. The word 'don't' implies we *choose* not to get along, while the word 'can't' implies it's *impossible* for us to get along. I believe it's possible to live in peace with each other. For some foolish reason, however, we choose not to. Whether Atheist, Buddhist, Christian, Communist, Confucian, Hindu, Jew, Moslem, Taoist or some other belief, we can, if we choose, learn to live with each other in peace and friendship, rather than persist in making war.

"The essential purpose of all human government should be to promote the common good, which is the peace and prosperity of all its citizens. Unfortunately, few governments have been able to do this on a lasting basis. Why have governments failed at peacemaking and waged wars with one another down through the ages? The reason is because they really didn't want peace or weren't willing to work hard enough to achieve it. Instead, they've squandered their limited resources on armaments, and sacrificed their lives in warfare.

223

"The creature, man or woman, throughout millions of years, from the very beginning, has never been completely happy and at peace. That poses another question. How can we expect to be at peace with others, if we cannot be at peace with ourselves? We must develop inner peace, if we're to achieve peace in the world outside ourselves. To develop inner peace, we must overcome our pride, vanity, greed, lust, envy, gluttony, and other imperfections.

"A favorite story illustrating the point of man's pride and vanity, is the Story of Hadrian:

> The Emperor Hadrian came back from his mighty conquest of the world. He said to his subjects, 'You must now regard me as God.'
>
> Hearing this, one said, 'You'll be happy, then, Excellency, to help me in this moment of need.'
>
> 'How can I help you?' asked Hadrian.
>
> The subject said, 'My ship is stranded in a calm, everything I own is on it.'
>
> 'All right,' Hadrian said, 'I'll send my fleet to rescue it.'
>
> 'Don't go to that trouble, sir,' the subject said. 'Just send a small breath of wind.'
>
> 'Where am I going to get some wind?' Hadrian asked.
>
> The subject answered, 'If you don't know that, how can you be God who created the wind?'

After this experience, Hadrian was a humbled man.

"In approaching our difficult tasks today, we need to be humble about our own acheivements. We should be ready and willing to learn from others, and cooperate with them in developing the best settlement possible. Our task as facilitators is to help make peace by bringing others together in a spirit of cooperation and friendship. We need to act with a sense of urgency, too, since it could be a matter of life and death for us all, as well as the preservation of the earth.

"In the earlier centuries of human existence, it was often said that whoever saved an individual life saved the entire world. Now, in this era of nuclear warhead weaponry, we must save the entire world in order to make it safe for an individual life. I look forward to working for the peaceful settlement of the Krasnodar affair, and I look forward also to the peaceful settlement of all disputes, and the cooperative, scientific solution of the world's many problems."

At that conclusion, the audience vigorously applauded, and Senator Cordierat returned to his seat, while Dr. Raman came to the speaker's stand. Dr. Raman expressed his gratitude to the Senator and everyone else, for coming to Geneva on such short notice. Then he introduced the second Reconciliation panel facilitator, Dr. Angelica Fabriano.

Dr. Fabriano was a professor who taught problem solving at the University of Rome. She received the Nobel Peace Prize for her study of *Successful International Dispute Settlements and War Avoidance.* As she approached the speaker's stand, the audience applauded, and Dr. Raman smiled at her and welcomed her before returning to his seat. Angelica also smiled at Dr. Raman as she passed him.

Dr. Angelica Fabriano was an elegant, fashionable, distinctive-looking woman dressed in a black business suit that was accented with a white lace blouse, and black, medium-heeled shoes. Her long, sleek, charcoal black hair was pulled back from her olive-skinned, delicate featured face and dark brown eyes. A well-proportioned, medium-height figure added to her attractiveness, which was exceptional. As the applause began fading, Dr. Fabriano spoke confidently, without hesitation, and with firmness of purpose.

"Dr. Raman, honored guests and associates, rather than get academic at this time and lecture on the techniques of creative problem solving, I'm going to use a different approach, one that draws from the rich cultural heritage of the Christian faith and reviews some treasured stories. The first of these is the New Testament Story of the Good Samaritan. Jesus of Nazareth taught his followers 2,000 years ago that the greatest law of all is to love your neighbor as yourself. A lawyer, however, asked Jesus, 'Who is my neighbor?' Answering, Jesus said:

> A certain man went from Jerusalem to Jericho and fell among thieves who stripped him of his clothing and other belongings, and wounded him, and left, leaving him half dead. Then, by chance, there came by a priest who, when he saw the injured victim, quickly passed him by on the other side of the road. Likewise, a Levite passed quickly by on the other side of the road. But a Samaritan had kindness for the victim and went to him, and bound up his wounds, pouring in oil and wine. He then set the injured man on a horse, and brought him to an inn and took care of him. The next day when the Samaritan departed, he took out some money and gave it to the host saying, 'Take good care of him, and whatever you spend additionally, I'll repay you when I come by this way again.'
>
> Which of these three was neighbor to him who fell among the thieves?

The lawyer answered that the Samaritan who was kind to the victim was the neighbor. Then Jesus told the lawyer to go and do likewise.

"What a wonderful lesson that age-old parable is for all of us! Instead of nations passing each other by 'on the other side of the road,' let them pursue friendship and neighborliness like the Good Samaritan who was neighbor to the injured and dying robbery victim.

"In a scientific approach to problem solving, it's necessary to always have a friendly, neighborly manner. We want to avoid lawsuits. Jesus warned us about them when he urged those with disputes to 'make friends quickly with your opponent....' Also, he said 'love your enemies, and pray for those who persecute you,' and, 'whoever shall force you to go one mile, go with him two.' Likewise, the Apostle Paul says 'it is already a defeat for you, that you have lawsuits with one another.'

"The alternative is that we cooperate peacefully with one another. To do this, we must get accurate and relevant facts, so we'll be able to develop a mutually acceptable dispute settlement. We can get accurate and relevent facts by using what I refer to as the ASK concept formulated 2,000 years ago by Jesus of Nazareth, who also added the Golden Rule to the concept. Jesus said:

Ask and it shall be given to you; Seek and you shall find; Knock and it shall be opened unto you. For everyone who asks, receives; and he who seeks, finds; and to him who knocks, it shall be opened. Or who is there of you, when if your son asks for bread, will you give him a stone? Or if he asks for a fish, would you give him a snake? Therefore, all things whatsoever you would that others should do to you, do

you even so to them: for this is the law of
the prophets.

This message of inquiry, research, and respectful
treatment of others is not only good advice for
Reconciliation, it's good advice for both individuals and
nations in their day-to-day dealings. We need to use this
advice in researching and solving problems. In terms of
the A-S-K formula, we should *Ask* questions of the right
people; *Seek* alternative, peaceful solutions to our
problems, rather than violent ones; and *Knock* at the
door of the other person in the dispute, our neighbor, so
that there can be open communications about the
problem, rather than armed warfare. Finally, we should
follow the Golden Rule by treating others the way we
wish to be treated ourselves.

"Another favorite story told by Jesus is the Story of
the Sower. It teaches us what different effects our ideas
will have on others. Jesus said:

> Behold a sower went forth to sow; and
> when he sowed, some seeds fell by the
> wayside, and birds came and ate them up.
> Some fell upon stoney ground, where they
> didn't have much earth. These began to
> grow, but because they had no deepness of
> earth, the sun scorched them, and because
> they had no roots, they withered away.
> Some fell among thorns, and the thorns
> grew and choked them. Still others fell on
> good ground and brought forth fruit, some
> a hundredfold, some sixtyfold,, some
> thirtyfold. He who has ears to hear let him
> hear.

When we brainstorm ideas to solve a problem and
develop a settlement, many ideas will be discarded, some

will be partially developed, and only a few will succeed. We mustn't be discouraged, however, because our successful ideas will bring forth fruit thirty, sixty, even a hundredfold. Also, since we're trying to locate the most potentially successful idea, anything anyone contributes to this process is welcome.

"The concept of a scientific process for problem solving and peacemaking is in its infancy. For this reason, we need to pioneer ways to improve it for those who'll come after us. The challenge is exciting, especially when you realize the desperate condition of our world, and that one of every five nations is at war.

"The Apostle Paul, an early persecutor of Christians who later became a major Christian leader and teacher, gave us a prophetic view of the difficulties we'll all face during the last days of the earth. Many believe the Apostle Paul was talking about our world today when he said:

> ...in the last days, critical times hard to deal with will be here. For men and women will be lovers of themselves, lovers of money, self-assuming, haughty, blasphemers, disobedient to parents, unthankful, disloyal, having no natural affection, not open to any agreement, slanderers, without self-control, fierce, without love of goodness.

What a frightening prospect! Even though it can be argued that Paul was talking about our world today, I'm enough of an optimist to look on the bright side. I say the very fact of our assembly here in this large room gives us hope for tomorrow, especially as we change ourselves and the world's nations from peacebreakers into peacemakers.

"Let's develop humility in our attitudes and

behavior by recalling that past and present wars are evidence of past and present failures. Pride and arrogance caused these wars. Pride and arrogance were responsible for the failures. We must get rid of our pride and arrogance. The Book of Proverbs tells us, 'He that is arrogant in soul stirs up contention.' Therefore, we must avoid all pride and acquire humility, if we're to succeed at bloodless, nonviolent peacemaking.

"In conclusion, I quote again from the teachings of Jesus of Nazareth who said, 'Blessed are the peacemakers, for they shall be called the children of God.' I'm grateful for the opportunity today to share in the future of our world, a future of peacemaking."

After Dr. Fabriano concluded her remarks, the audience applauded and she returned to her seat. When Dr. Raman rose to speak, he expressed his gratitude to Dr. Fabriano for sharing so many good ideas. Then he introduced the third Reconciliation panel facilitator, Mr. Abdul Khaldun of Sudan, whose achievements in settling disputes made him the recipient of a Sudanese Medal of Merit, First Class, and The Order of the Two Niles.

Abdul Khaldun wore a green, cotton twill suit with a white shirt and green-flowered white tie. He was a portly, tan-skinned, medium-height man with a large, gray-haired, balding head. His face was partially covered with a short gray beard, and he had a large, well-sculpted nose undercut by thick lips that were formed into a broad smile. His soft dark eyes seemed to sparkle as he looked intently at the audience. When the welcoming applause ended, he began speaking.

"Ladies and gentlemen, the question before us is, 'How can we arrange peace?' Some ask should we even try? I say that to try when there's little hope is to risk failure. Not to try at all is to guarantee it. Our world must have peace, since without peace, it will die.

"Another question is, 'How many are for peace?'

"One billion Christians and Jews say, 'Thou shalt not kill.' They are for peace.

"One-half billion Moslems teach 'peace through submission to God,' which is the meaning of the word 'Islam.' They are for peace.

"One-half billion Hindus teach reverence for all life, since all beings have souls. They are for peace.

"One-third billion followers of Confucius preach peace from good moral character and following their version of the Golden Rule, 'What you do not wish for yourself, do not do to others.' They are for peace.

"One-third billion Buddhists strive for Nirvana, which is complete peace and love. They are for peace.

"One-third billion Taoists teach peace through kindness to all persons and things. They are for peace.

"The rest of the world's population seeks peace through similar religious, moral, and humanitarian goals. They are for peace.

"In brief it can be said that the whole world seeks peace, especially when we consider that over 150 nations on this earth are members of the United Nations, which is an organization chartered to achieve world peace.

"Unfortunately, world peace has not been achieved. As you already heard, one in every five nations today is at war. Talk is cheap. Time is short. Deeds are essential. Our nonviolent, problem solving methods of peacemaking must be swift and effective. It's a testimony to humanity's helplessness that there could be so many armed conflicts which are not yet settled. This continuing warfare in the world desperately proves our need to reach out and help each other. Also, the enormous threat of nuclear war demands that a nonviolent peacemaking mechanism be immediately created, especially if worldwide nuclear disarmament is to be achieved. In answer to the question, 'How can we arrange peace?', why don't we simply mandate it in all our dealings?

"One quick way is to get the whole world to adopt a nonviolent, peacemaking approach to settling disputes by including a Reconciliation Clause in all the world's agreements, contracts, and treaties, just as Ambassadors Brown and Novikov did in their wheat contract. The Holy *Koran*, the great book of Islam, says, 'Be not averse to writing down, whether it be small or great, with the term thereof...and have witnesses...and let no harm be done to writer or witness.'

"Getting in writing the requirement for peacefully settling disputes assures us a beginning to the end of all wars. It also eliminates any arguing or slipperiness about how disputes are to be settled. Failure to specify a nonviolent, peacemaking process in writing, may result in the violent warfare that none of us wants.

"All existing agreements, contracts, and treaties should be amended to require a problem solving, peacemaking process, — and the process should be made effective on a retroactive basis. This can easily and quickly be done by transacting a single document among all the nations of the world, specifying that the peacemaking process is mandatory for settling all disputes. It should also include a specific statement forbidding warfare and other forms of armed conflict or violent, life threatening, property destroying behavior.

"Some additional remarks I have at this time relate to our lack of spiritual health. I believe that one reason we have no peace in the world today is because we're spiritually sick within ourselves. Our major problems are that we have no physical self-control, no self-denial, no self-improvement. We're killing each other and ourselves in our efforts to get more physical pleasures and treasures. At the same time, we're ignoring our spiritual destinies of self and social perfection. Armed warfare and other forms of mutual destruction are tragic denials of our spiritual destiny. They serve to destroy us spiritually as well as physically.

232

"Our spiritual responsibility to the physical realm is to leave it in a better condition than we found it. Our failure to do this is leading to the very serious consequence of our physical world's rapid destruction.

"Why can't we improve ourselves spiritually, just as through various professions and sciences we're able to improve ourselves physically? Modern medical scientists, for example, seek to understand and improve man's physical body. Ecologists seek to understand and improve man's physical environment. Nearly all the world's scientists seek to understand and improve man's physical life. Isn't it time, therefore, that each of us try to understand and improve ourselves spiritually, so we'll be better able to settle our disputes peacefully?

"Unfortunately, there are too many who destroy, rather than create; who tear down, rather than build up; who kill and maim, rather than heal and save. On a larger scale, companies, organizations, and governments, as well as individuals, should be evaluated on the basis of whether they improve, create, enhance, or make better the common good; or whether they destroy, tear apart, break down, reduce, or corrupt it.

"Families, tribes, companies, organizations, governments, and nations are made up of people, so it's people who must get the job done. If people everywhere can be converted into nonviolent peacemakers, then the organizations they belong to can become peacemakers, too.

"We live in a world of systems. Financial, political, and social systems are made up of people. In a system, somebody does something to someone with some kind of result. That result can be good or bad, so systems are good and bad, or constructive and destructive. People in families, organizations, and nations need to work together to change systems for the better. Some things we can do are:

(1) Turn injuries and offenses by another into an opportunity for peace and friendship, rather than increased hostility.

(2) Admit our own bitterness about something, try to understand it, and work to overcome it.

(3) Determine the specific flaws of those who injured or offended us, see whether we have the same flaws, then remove them from ourselves and forgive them in those who harmed us.

(4) Strive for peacemaking in all our activities, using problem solving Reconciliation instead of reckless retaliation.

(5) Finally, before supporting politicians, we should find out their method of settling disputes. If they're warmongers, abandon them; don't let them hold public office. If they're peacemakers, cherish them; don't let them leave public office.

"These are my beliefs, ladies and gentlemen. These are my suggestions."

The audience applauded enthusiastically for Mr. Khaldun, who slowly left the speaker's stand and returned to his seat. At the same time, Dr. Raman got up, walked to the stand, and, after the applause ended, complimented Mr. Khaldun and thanked him for his excellent advice. Then Dr. Raman introduced the fourth facilitator, Mr. Togawa Noguchi, Ambassador to the United Nations from Japan.

Ambassador Noguchi was a world expert on settling disputes, and was a recipient of the Japanese First Order of Sacred Treasure and other decorations. He had a short, slender physique, and was wearing a dark-brown suit with a white shirt and dark-brown tie. His head was shaved, giving him the look of a tan-skinned Buddhist monk in modern clothes. Also, he wore amber-framed eyeglasses that rested on his small nose. With his dark shiny eyes he looked amusingly at the audience until the applause faded. Then he began moving his thin lips to speak.

"Dr. Raman, associates, and guests. We don't have many lawyers in Japan. The reason for this happy fact is that we don't have many lawsuits. Without lawsuits, we don't need lawyers. Confucius, an ancient Chinese philosopher, said 'We should make it our aim that there be no lawsuits at all.' That's why Japanese hate going to court. We try to settle disputes peacefully among ourselves, so we can continue our good relationships. Courts and lawsuits extend conflicts and offend our nature. They don't bring parties together in harmony and peace. We have a law establishing a formal Reconciliation service. The preamble to that law states that 'The main object of Reconciliation lies in reaching a solution to a case based upon good morals and with a warm heart.' Our Reconciliation service employs a presider and two experienced lay people. No lawyers are needed.

"It's socially unacceptable for someone to start a lawsuit in Japan. There's a story told by our Buddhist citizens that illustrates the problem of lawyers and their lawsuits. The story is based on the question, 'What is an elephant?' Here's how it goes:

Men arguing and disputing are like blind men quarreling about what an elephant looks like. Once a governor ordered that all men born blind be brought to one place and be divided into groups.

235

Each group was asked to identify an elephant. The first group of blind men was given the elephant's head to touch, the next touched one ear, another touched the tusk, another touched the trunk, another the foot, another the main body, another the tail, another the tail tuft, and so on. After each group of blind men had felt the part that was shown, the governor asked the first group, 'What sort of a thing is an elephant?'

The first group, having touched the head, answered that an elephant is very much like a large pot. Those who felt the ear said an elephant is like a shallow basket. Those touching the tusk said it was like a plowshare, those who felt the trunk were convinced that an elephant is like a huge snake. The group who touched the foot thought an elephant to be like a large pillar. The group who felt the main body thought the elephant to be like a grain storage building. The tail group thought an elephant to be like a rope. The tail tuft group was sure the elephant was very much like a broom.

Soon they all began quarreling, shouting, 'Yes, it is!' or 'No, it's not!' 'An elephant is not that!' or 'Yes, it's like that!' and on and on until they began hitting one another. The governor was happy about this event, though he stopped it. He declared to his subjects that hermits and scholars who hold different views, but who argue and dispute with one another, are like the group of blind men describing the elephant. They don't know what it is and what it is not. In their ignorance, they quarrel over nothing, wasting their lives and setting a bad example for others.

"When we assist others in settling disputes, we must avoid useless arguing, fighting, and quarreling. Rather, we should cooperate in a scientific manner, using relevant and verifiable data to achieve realistic and lasting settlements. Lawyers with their lawsuits are like the blind men arguing and quarreling when describing an elephant. That's why we avoid lawyers and lawsuits in Japan, and why it's socially unacceptable to use lawyers and lawsuits for settling disputes.

"The lesson of the elephant serves also to warn us about jumping to conclusions in identifying a problem, or developing a settlement solution. We must first help each other grasp the entirety of a situation before attempting to define or describe it.

"To resolve the dangerous, present-day threat of nuclear warfare, we must urge the nations of the world to stop arguing and quarreling with each other, and start using a nonviolent, scientific approach to settling their fights. We don't have much time to change, so change must come swiftly. After Hiroshima and Nagasaki, we Japanese know the importance of timing in making changes. When the USA and USSR have warheads equal to 1,600,000 Hiroshima atomic bombs, we had better not wait too long to change."

At that dramatic conclusion, the audience applauded loudly while Ambassador Noguchi sat down. Then Dr. Raman got up and agreed with Ambassador Noguchi, especially with the urgency of his concerns. "If the world could swiftly settle its existing conflicts," Dr. Raman noted, "complete nuclear disarmament could become a reality."

The fifth speaker Dr. Raman introduced was Dr. Suvrana Sharma, who was active worldwide in

237

promoting the Doctrine of Nonviolence. She was a Nobel Peace Prize winner, too, because of her teaching of the mechanics for developing nonviolent solutions, and her valued assistance in settling national and international conflicts. Dr. Raman stood at the speaker's stand waiting for Dr. Sharma, as the audience began a round of welcoming applause. When she approached, he stepped back, and, clasping his hands, bowed his head slightly in a form of acknowledgment characteristic of his Hindu religion, which was the same religion of Dr. Sharma. Dr. Sharma clasped her hands also, bowed to Dr. Raman, and proceeded to the speaker's stand as Dr. Raman returned to his seat.

Dr. Suvrana Sharma looked quite colorful in her long, red silk sari with gold-threaded trim. In the tradition of her province, she wore the loose end of her sari over her head as a kind of shawl. She was a short, round faced, amply built woman. Only a few strands of her shiny black hair were visible from under the golden edge of the sari hood she wore. She had dark eyes, narrow eyebrows, a delicate nose, and an attractive mouth with a smiling, friendly expression.

In the lower center of her forehead, just above the bridge of her nose, Dr. Sharma wore a 'kumkum,' or round dot of powder. The kumkum is often regarded as a mark of beauty, but its placement on the forehead at the center spot has a religious significance. The wearer is supposed to concentrate on the dot to focus attention on spiritual themes. Sometimes the kumkum dot is made with red powder, sometimes black. Dr. Sharma wore red.

When the applause ended, Dr. Sharma suddenly bowed her head towards the audience, raised her clasped hands as if in a gesture of prayer, then began her speech.

"Honored guests, I'm here today because I had the good fortune to be invited. What I have to say is offered in good faith, because I have much to learn about scientific problem solving techniques. There is, however, an area of understanding where I may be of help. It's the matter of religious and spiritual beliefs, which, unfortunately, seem to be at the root of so many world conflicts.

"Fanatical intolerance of other beliefs has resulted in hundreds of millions of deaths in World Wars I and II, and wars in Afghanistan, Egypt, Iran, Iraq, Israel, Korea, Nicaragua, Vietnam, Lebanon, and many other countries. Added to the destructiveness of these wars are the tragedies of millions of homeless and starving refugees. Fanatical religious fundamentalism and intolerance is promoting much of this misery. Fanatical religious fundamentalism and intolerance are the curse of our world's history and present era. I also include Atheism in this fundamentalism category, because Atheism, or the belief in no God, is the religion of no religion.

"Whether we're scientists working in research laboratories to learn truth from carefully controlled experiments, or whether we work with soil to grow huge plants from tiny seeds, we live by belief and faith, faith that our experiments will tell us something, and faith that tiny seeds, if properly nurtured, will grow into great plants.

"Even Atheism, which is the belief in no belief, requires enormous faith. The Atheist believes there's no God. It takes enormous faith to believe that, because more knowledge is needed to deny the existence of something than to accept it. For example, Atheism suggests that nowhere in our entire universe, or in other universes beyond ours, is there to be found that Something, that Being, that Creator we call 'God.' Such belief requires considerable knowledge of our universe and of other universes, and of all creation, since it asserts with confidence that there's no Supreme Being. In solving problems, we must be careful about denying the existence of something. We have to have an abundance of very good, very reliable information to be able to do that.

"Consider that we see many stars in the *night* sky, but cannot see them when the sun is shining. If you cannot see stars when the sun is shining, can you say there are no stars in the *daylight* sky? We say stars are there because of belief and faith. Not seeing them doesn't mean they're not there. Saying you don't believe in a Supreme Being called 'God,' doesn't mean there's no God.

"Reason tells us God exists, just as several thousand years ago, the Greek Leucippus of Miletus and his pupil Democritus of Abdera, reasoned there was such a thing as an atom. They never saw an atom, nor did anyone else back then ever see one. The survivors of Hiroshima, however, can assure you there are such things as atoms. The word 'a-tom' comes from the Greek. It means 'incapable of being cut' or split, because several thousand years ago, it was regarded as the smallest particle of matter. In 1945, however, we succeeded in splitting the atom and releasing its incredible nuclear power. That power, used for destructive purposes, is a power we're now trying desperately to control and prevent from destroying us. One way we can prevent the atom from destroying us is by becoming tolerant of our differences.

"Most wars throughout history were fought because of religious and racial intolerance. Why do nations insist on the superiority of their religion, or race, or political system? It's so foolish and vain and intolerant. Everyone should realize we live in a world of diversity.

"Consider water, the essential of life. Water is called by many different names. English say 'water.' Russians say 'voda.' Latins say 'aqua.' French say 'eau,' others say 'pani,' and the list goes on and on for all the languages of humanity. So it is with 'God,' 'Allah,' 'Jehova,' 'Hari,' 'Brahman,' and so on. There are as many different names for God, the Supreme Being or Great

240

Spirit, as there are languages. We must be tolerant of these differences, and stop insisting on the righteousness of our own way.

"There are many different ways and means of approaching and worshipping God. Every religion and human belief system shows a way, just as you can climb to the roof of a house by using a ladder, staircase, rope, vine, or other means. Who can say one is better, if they all get you there? The one that's best is the one you have at hand and use. Don't force your neighbor to use it, however, and don't insist that your neighbor worship God as you do.

"From time to time, when humanity grows away from religion, God sends an Avatara, Savior, or Messenger, all one and the same, to show us a way or ladder to climb to perfection, or heaven, or everlasting life. Whether the Avatara whom God sends is called Rama, Krishna, Buddha, Christ, Mohammed, or some other name, it's the same Messenger who keeps coming back to this world to make major changes and cause major revolutions. That's another reason to follow one's own religion, if that religion is a ladder to God. A Christian should follow the teachings of Jesus Christ. A Mohammedan should follow the teachings of Mohammed. A Buddhist should follow the teachings of Buddha, and so on, for all the world's sacred religions.

"People wall off their lands by means of boundary markers, fences, shrubs, or other means, but who can wall off the vast sky or Great Spirit that serves everybody? Both the indivisible sky and Great Spirit surround us all, and include us all. Yet man, in ignorance, says, 'My religion is best!' It's like the blind men arguing they each hold the true answer to the question Mr. Togawa Noguchi just posed for you, 'What is an elephant?'

"When man is inspired by the truth, he knows there's one, eternal, all-knowing God, just as the Greek

Leucippus and his pupil Democritus reasoned there was an atom. Call God the 'Uncaused Cause,' 'Prime Mover,' 'Supreme Judge,' 'Master Intellect,' 'Architect of the Universe,' these names all describe one and the same almighty, all-knowing, all-present Being. All the brutal terrorism, bloody riots, and bitter wars, wars of intolerance and hatred among men of differing beliefs, cannot change the nature of God any more than they can change the several thousand years old hypothesis of an atom formulated by Leucippus and Democritus.

"For that reason, our revered teacher Shri Ramakrishna warned us a hundred years ago to stop our useless arguing and fighting. We're one large family. We should work at getting along with one another. As you stand firm on your own faith and opinion, please, I beg you, allow others the freedom to stand firm on their faiths and opinions.

"Arguing and fighting are unacceptable in convincing others of what you assume is their error. The real error may be yours, or, in reality, there could be no error by anyone. By the grace and inspiration of God, I pray we'll understand our own mistakes, and not cast stones at others. Or, in the absence of mistakes, I pray we'll not cast stones for any reason.

"When a bee is outside the fresh flower, it noisily buzzes around, but once inside the flower, it quietly drinks the nectar. So long as men and women noisily quarrel and bitterly fight about doctrines and dogmas, they haven't tasted the nectar of truth. When they do taste it, they'll become quiet and nonviolent like the bee in nectar, full of peace and happiness as they partake.

"My brothers and sisters, let's work together noiselessly, like bees in nectar. Let's all become nonviolent. If for no other reason, let's be nonviolent as a good example for our children. If we choose not to set a good example, then we choose to deprive ourselves and our children of a peaceful life and a secure future.

However, I'm an optimist. I believe we'll have a future as bright as our growing conviction that our only practical approach for settling disputes is one that's nonviolent, nonadversarial, and noncompetitive. We want cooperation, not competition; friendship, not friction; peace, not provocation. It seems we may have all three of these in the Reconciliation process."

Dr. Sharma concluded her remarks to heavy applause and walked slowly to her seat as Dr. Raman returned to speak. He praised Dr. Sharma's suggestions, and remarked how enriching it was to receive so much wise instruction from so many speakers that morning. Then he introduced the sixth and final Reconciliation facilitator, Mr. Chou Wang-Tzu of The People's Republic of China.

Mr. Wang-Tzu was recently honored by the World Peace Movement, and awarded the World Peace Medal for his book, *Study of Dispute Settlement Advice Given by the World's Great Philosophers*. Though slightly taller and somewhat younger than Togawa Noguchi, Mr. Chou Wang-Tzu was, nevertheless, equally stately and slender. He wore a high-collared dark blue suit in the manner of his countrymen. His gray-streaked black hair was well trimmed. His sharp, gaunt features were made to appear more severe by his somewhat pale complexion. Although he had a disciplined, ascetic look, he nevertheless smiled graciously, radiating a happy, friendly attitude while he waited to speak. When the applause ended, he began.

"Distinguished Reconciliation panel members and honorable guests, it's a privilege to be with you this morning. How fortunate to have so many outstanding thoughts come together at one place and one time. But our time is quickly passing, and we have much to do to accomplish Dr. Raman's highly ambitious, 4 p.m. objective of a mutually satisfactory settlement of the

243

Krasnodar affair. Therefore, I'll discuss only a few thoughts.

"Approximately 3,000 years ago, Tzu-Kung asked his wise teacher and master, Confucius, 'Is there any saying one can act upon all day every day?' The Master said, 'Yes, it's the saying never do to others what you would not like them to do to you.' This is what Mr. Khaldun quoted earlier, and is another version, of course, of what Dr. Fabriano told us about the teaching of Jesus of Nazareth, who said, 'Whatsoever you would that men should do to you, do you even so to them....' Jesus says what to do, Confucius says what not to do. Side by side these two wise rules cover all human relationships in terms of what to do; what not to do. It would be good if nations could adopt these rules in their dealings towards one another. They're helpful guides, too, for the peaceful settlement of conflicts.

"Confucius, the Master, also said, 'He who won't worry about what is far off, will have something worse than worry close at hand....' This is good advice for us now, for the United Nations Organization, and all the world's nations. If we won't concern ourselves with the future consequences of our present adversarial dealings with one another, we'll soon have something worse than worry close at hand. If we don't stop our arguing, bickering, conflicting, and warring ways, we'll soon have worldwide nuclear destruction and the end of all life on this planet.

"Toward the end of his long career our illustrious Chairman Mao Zedung wrote:

> The only way to settle questions of an ideological nature or controversial issues among the people, is by the democratic method, the method of discussion, of criticism, of persuasion and education, and

244

not by the method of coercion or repression.

Chairman Mao wrote that in a 1957 book entitled, *On the Correct Handling of Contradictions Among the People.* In this same book, Chairman Mao also wrote:

> As for the imperialist countries, we should unite with their peoples and strive to coexist peacefully with those countries, do business with them, and prevent any possible war....

Nobody with any sanity really wants war. Everybody, it seems, is in favor of peace. However, we need to plan the future we want. If we really want peace, we must plan it, then work our plan so we can achieve it.

"In addition to the teaching that we must concern ourselves with far off events, Confucius observed that 'One who will study for three years without thought of reward is hard to find.' In other words, it's hard to find dedicated individuals who will patiently apply themselves to learn what's needed, then plan what's proper, all without expectation of reward. Where can such people be found today?

"Our world is too concerned with creature comforts, selfish pursuits, instant successes for immediate gain. Consider what's being written. There are over a hundred thousand new books published each year, over 50,000 new titles in just the USA. How many of these books are about how to make peace, how to solve problems, how to reconcile warring nations? Do you know of a single one?

"There are few such peacemaking books I can name. Yet, peacemaking books are desperately needed right now, more so than any other kind of book. The reason is that study of peacemaking is a matter of our world's self-preservation. Instead, our world is obsessed with the

245

stockpiling of nuclear warheads. We're on the brink of our self-made, suicidal extinction. Nobody seems to know how to think peace, make peace, or keep peace. Apparently, dedicated individuals who will study peacemaking for three years without thought of reward are nowhere to be found. Spending three years thinking about, studying, and planning peace is a task that, without thought of reward, doesn't appeal to anybody. So who is there to do it? At this late hour for the world, where is the person who has done it? Who is even making any effort to find such a person? Confucius understood human nature very well nearly 3,000 years ago, when he said that such a person 'is hard to find.'

"Hopefully, my brothers and sisters, our session today will focus the world's attention on our need for peacemaking studies. Our session may even encourage a few individuals to dedicate themselves to study peacemaking for three years without any thought of reward.

"I have but two closing remarks to share with you. They also come from ancient Chinese thought. One is advice about government; the other is a formula for peace. First is the remark about government. When Tzu-Hsin was Warden of Chu-fu, he sought advice about government. Confucius, the Master, said, 'Don't try to hurry things, your personality won't come into play. If you let yourself be distracted by minor considerations, nothing important will ever get finished.'

"Some say today we can't see the forest, because we're too busy squabbling over trees. We're too distracted by minor considerations, so that nothing important ever gets finished. To use Ambassador Noguchi's illustration of 'What is an elephant,' we tend to argue and fight over a trunk, while remaining ignorant of the other parts, thus failing to correctly answer the initial question or grasp the larger view. We should take time to consider the larger view, the major

246

issues, the differences that alienate us, and do what's important. In terms of settling the world's disputes, we need to establish our chief priority, which is to encourage individuals, groups, and nations to focus on settling their major differences and scientifically solving their serious problems. In conclusion, please consider an ancient Chinese formula for peace:

> If there's right in the soul,
> There will be beauty in the person;
> If there's beauty in the person,
> There will be harmony in the home;
> If there's harmony in the home,
> There will be order in the nation;
> If there's order in the nation,
> There will be peace in the world."

The audience applauded, Chou Wang-Tzu sat down, and Dr. Raman came to the microphone and spoke. He said that Mr. Chou Wang-Tzu had honored them with his refreshing insights and ancient advice on peacemaking. After thanking him and all the speakers, Dr. Raman announced that they had now completed the preliminary remarks portion of the session, and, ever conscious of making the most efficient use of the brief time they had allowed themselves, he had three requests.

First of all, when breaking for lunch, Dr. Raman asked the panel of facilitators and representatives of the USA and USSR to reconvene in a smaller meeting room next door to the assembly hall. This would enable the session efforts to get started quickly. Also, in the interest of saving time, lunch would be served to the session participants in the next door meeting room, so they could start the next session while they ate.

The second request Dr. Raman made was that later on that afternoon, when the USA and USSR had reached a mutually satisfactory settlement, the panelists should select one of its members to report the settlement to the various guests and news media representatives in the large assembly hall.

Dr. Raman's third request was directed at those who were going to be called upon by the panelists to present reports or other inputs. They were asked to return to the assembly hall right after their lunch, so they could be available when needed. For those who weren't eating lunch in the next-door room, Dr. Raman announced that lunch would be available in the downstairs cafeteria. Finally, there being no other business at that moment, Dr. Raman temporarily adjourned the session.

22

RECONCILIATION SETTLEMENT

Various individuals were sitting, standing, or strolling around the large assembly hall in the Geneva Palace of Nations. Some were alone, some were scattered about in pairs, and some were gathered into small groups. All were waiting for the outcome of the first international Reconciliation session. Various news media representatives from all over the world were anxious to rush their stories to waiting newswires, presses, and radio or television news centers. Others present included ambassadorial officials and dignitaries from every nation, plus key resource persons like Vessel Agent Hjalmar Haggarson, and James Baston and Julius Fiske, as well as representatives of the U. S. Coast Guard, and others whose inputs were examined by the Reconciliation panel.

At exactly 4 p. m., session Chairman Dr. Raman entered the hall, followed by the panel of facilitators, and Ambassadors Harry Brown of the USA and Nikolai Novikov of the USSR. When Dr. Raman reached the speaker's stand, there was an anxious and noisy scurrying about for seats by those who were standing, moving around, or conversing in groups. Photo flashes exploded everywhere, and blinding video camera lights came on, as an expectant crowd started quieting down.

"Ladies and gentlemen," Dr. Raman began, "we have good news for you this afternoon. Not only have we concluded our session by the targeted time of 4 p. m., we've also achieved a mutually satisfactory settlement of the Krasnodar dispute without waging any kind of suicidal warfare. Our world is still here, thanks to the good will of our new breed of peacemakers, the Reconciliators.

"To inform you about the particulars of today's settlement, our session panel was unanimous in electing Ambassador Togawa Noguchi of Japan, I present to you Ambassador Noguchi."

The audience approvingly applauded Dr. Raman's brief introduction, and after the applause subsided, Ambassador Noguchi began.

"Honorable ladies and gentlemen, I think the panel chose me as spokesman, because there are so few lawsuits and lawyers in Japan. The panel thinks we Japanese know something the rest of the world doesn't know. The truth is, the teachings of Confucius, Buddha, Jesus of Nazareth, Mohammed, or any of various revered ancients and moderns are no great secret. Their teachings on peacemaking are available to everyone. All we need do is study them and be better listeners and doers.

"One source of good advice in modern times is the Dalai Lama, the revered leader of Tibetan Buddhists. To avoid a worldwide nuclear holocaust, the Dalai Lama has said:

> Concerned people — the leaders — must have willpower. That willpower does not exist. There's only suspicion, and that must be cleared through human contact. The leaders of the United States

250

and the Soviet Union must meet without all the complicated agendas. Let them meet and talk on a basis of human understanding. Then they can discuss important issues.

"Honorable ladies and gentlemen, what the Dalai Lama says is what our panel today also says. The leaders of the USA and USSR should meet here in Geneva 'and talk on a basis of human understanding.' Furthermore, the panel requests President John Morrison of the USA and Chairman Vasil Golgolev of the USSR to do two things when they meet here: (1) Ratify today's settlement; and (2) Formalize peacemaking Reconciliation as the process for settling all disputes between their two nations, or any other nation."

The audience interrupted with enthusiastic applause at this announcement by Noguchi. When the applause ended, Noguchi continued.

"Looking at the facts of the dispute settled today, it was determined that:

(1)   The USSR contracted to purchase 1-1/2 million tons of wheat from H. B. Exports, Inc., of Taylorsville, Minnesota, USA.

(2)   In Duluth, Minnesota, the USSR's ocean bulk freighter, the Krasnodar, was loaded with 25,000 tons of wheat, which was the first shipment under the contract.

(3)   The heavily loaded Krasnodar sailed out of Duluth Harbor.

(4)   A violent storm suddenly unleashed its fury on Lake Superior and, unfortunately, on the Krasnodar, which was in the middle of the huge lake at the time.

(5)   The Krasnodar broke up and suddenly sank; there were no survivors.

(6)   Just before the disaster, there was a brief, barely audible message from the Krasnodar radioman. He

251

spoke of fifty-foot waves, failed hatch cover hydraulics, and the ship's breaking up and sinking.

(7) Unfortunately, as news of the disaster was relayed around the world, it was understood by the USSR that the Krasnodar had been either attacked or sabotaged, and that the USA had started a war.

(8) Consequently, the USSR refused to pay H. B.Exports, Inc., for the 25,000 tons of wheat accepted by the USSR and loaded on the Krasnodar.

(9) Instead, the USSR demanded $65 million as compensation from the USA for its lost ship and crew. Meanwhile, the USSR prepared for all-out nuclear war.

(10) The USA denied all Soviet claims, then it, too, prepared for all-out war to defend itself against the USSR.

(11) Subsequently, leaders of both the USA and USSR learned that Messrs. Harry Brown and Nikolai Novikov had placed a tiny Reconciliation Clause in their wheat sale contract. This clause specifies a scientific, problem solving process of peacemaking, whereby individuals or groups cooperate amicably to reach a mutually satisfactory settlement of their disputes. Both USA and USSR leaders agreed to honor this Reconciliation clause.

(12) It was also determined that a foolish attempt to delay the first wheat shipment had been made in Duluth by an H. B. Exports competitor, before the wheat could be loaded on the USSR's Krasnodar. However, this attempt at delaying the shipment was discovered before any harm had been done.

(13) The USSR claimed that the hatch cover hydraulic system failure could have been the result of sabotage. There's no evidence to suggest this was the case, but neither is there any evidence to say it wasn't. On the other hand, it was established by various witnesses that the Krasnodar's hatch hydraulic system had been malfunctioning on the way to the Duluth Port. Also, there was verification that the malfunctioning

system had been scheduled for overhaul and repair in the Port of Odessa.

(14)   The USSR, nevertheless, continues to demand economic satisfaction for its lost crew and ship. Although there's insufficient evidence to say the USSR is entitled to satisfaction,there are few direct reasons to say it's not.   Such facts as the heavy load of wheat, the malfunctioning hatch hydraulic system,the radioman's distress message, and the severe storm, were determined to constitute sufficient evidence that the Krasnodar disaster was not due to sabotage by the USA, and that the USA owes no damage payments.

(15)   The USA, on behalf of H. B. Exports, Inc., continues to demand payment for 25,000 tons of wheat, which payment is required by contract, since the Soviets accepted the wheat when it was loaded on their Krasnodar in Duluth.

"After a review of the various facts, all the many questions were reduced to one: What's the quickest, best, most mutually acceptable settlement for this unfortunate Krasnodar affair, a settlement that will reconcile the parties so they can live in peace and friendship?

"There was much creative thinking and frank discussion before a workable settlement was pioneered. Hopefully, the Krasnodar settlement will become a mechanism for settling other international disputes having a similarly difficult basis for determining damage payment liability.

"Though it's true session participants found no evidence to support the liability of either party in the Krasnodar tragedy, it's also true both parties suffered economic damages, which, as they firmly insist, require satisfaction. Therefore, in the interest of world peace and the quick settlement of disputes, it was agreed that a No-fault, International Dispute Settlement Fund (IDSF) be established through the U. N., and that USA and USSR damage claims be paid out of this fund. Dr.

Raman has agreed to render this effort his special attention and assistance. Here's how the International Dispute Settlement Fund will work. Initially, each U. N. member nation will loan the dispute settlement fund an amount equal to a mere one twentieth of one percent of its military budget.

"Surely the world's nations can loan a mere one twentieth of a percent of their armaments spending, so that peaceful, no-fault, international dispute settlements can be achieved. This one twentieth of one percent amount is referred to as a loan, since it's anticipated that future no-fault settlements will be paid out of the interest earned by the fund. Unused or excess interest after settlement payments, will be applied to loan repayment.

"Eventually, nations who loaned money to establish the fund will be paid back the entire amount of the loan they originally made. Then, when all loans are repaid, the fund will begin distributing earned interest as dividends. In other words, the international, no-fault fund is a cost free investment in peace, which will eventually pay annual monetary dividends after expenses. Simply put, the fund will make a profit while it promotes world peace. As a result, peacemaking is transformed into a profitable business venture benefitting all nations.

"The first no-fault settlement achieved today is an exception, of course, since there's no International Dispute Settlement Fund as yet, nor any accrued interest to apply to the settlement. However, the $69 million total needed for this first settlement is so very small relative to the fund's initial size, no payment difficulty is anticipated when the fund is established.

"It's estimated that with world armaments expenditures currently exceeding a billion dollars a day, or $365 billions per year, 1/20 of 1% of that amount for an International Dispute Settlement Fund totals $182,500,000. Annual interest on such a vast amount at just seven percent, for example, is $12,775,000. Payment of $69 million total damages for the Krasnodar settlement would leave nearly $126,275,000 from the first year's total, which could be used to help settle other disputes.

"When all the world's disputes have been peacefully settled, armaments spending will no longer be necessary, and savings to nations will be enormous. Humanity will prosper as never before in the history of civilization. Nations will turn away from developing terror weapons, and concentrate on developing improvements in human health and living standards. Freed at last from their wasteful expenditures on military armaments, nations will discover that pursuits of a peaceful nature, such as the solution of environmental problems, will finally be affordable.

"In addition to the No-fault International Dispute Settlement Fund, today's Reconciliation session participants recommended establishment of an organization called Reconciliation Alliance International. This organization, which was originally contemplated by Ambassadors Brown and Novikov, is to be established with the assistance of the United Nations organization. It will be made up of representatives elected by national Reconciliation organizations in various nations of the world. Representatives will be elected on the basis of their wisdom, problem solving ability, cooperation, and other desirable qualifications.

"The specific charter objective of Reconciliation Alliance International is to assure the amicable, mutually satisfactory settlement of disputes between individual nations or groups of nations, especially disputes which threaten local, regional, or worldwide peace. National, regional, and local Reconciliation organizations will have corresponding peacemaking objectives in their respective charters. The idea is to assure peace and friendship among all individuals and nations.

"It should be stressed here that Reconciliation is *not*

an arbitration or courtroom action in any shape or form. For example, unlike arbitration or courtroom actions which require 'plaintiffs' and 'defendants' to pay costs, Reconciliation session costs are *not* to be paid for by those being reconciled. Also, Reconciliation isn't adversarial like arbitration or courtroom actions. Reconciliation doesn't permit competition of lawyers for high stakes, win-or-lose awards. Unlike arbitration and courtroom actions, Reconciliation doesn't enforce inequitable judgments. Also, there are no poorly trained or incompetent arbitrators, referees, or judges.

"Those chosen to be Reconciliation facilitators will be some of the best educated, most competent, and wisest representatives of the human race. Their task isn't to pronounce judgments or dictate results. Rather, they assist individuals being reconciled in achieving mutually satisfactory settlements. Thus, bitterness can be ended, and a basis for friendship established. Also, Reconciliation facilitators aren't paid as judges, lawyers, arbitrators, and referees are paid. Rather, the facilitators are reimbursed for their expenses only, including loss of income, if any. This reimbursement will come out of interest earned by the International Dispute Settlement Fund.

"Two more announcements before concluding: (1) It's recommended that both Ambassadors Harry Brown and Nikolai Novikov be honored for their peacemaking initiatives. Not only did they conceive the idea of a Reconciliation process in the first place, but they made the process possible. They're indeed rare, hard to find persons who, without thought of reward, gave the world a wonderful gift: the Reconciliation Clause in their wheat contract. Soon such a clause will be in all contracts, so that the adversarial system of justice will die quickly and quietly, and pass into the bitter history of the millions and millions of deplorable human conflicts it created.

"(2)   The second and final announcement I have today is that our session participants intend to work closely with Dr. Raman and the U. N. to see to it that the Brown and Novikov Reconciliation Clause gets adopted by all the world's nations, and inserted in all the world's agreements, contracts, and treaties, so there will be no more war.   Following this contractual assurance of no more war, will be the swift, complete, and verifiable achievement of worldwide nuclear weapons disarmament.   Such disarmament is a matter of human self-preservation and survival.   Such disarmament is a worldwide necessity."

After speaking his concluding words, Ambassador Noguchi politely bowed to the audience and stepped down from the speaker's platform.   Dr. Raman, smiling, bowed graciously to Ambassador Noguchi when the two passed by each other.   After Ambassador Noguchi was seated and the applause for him began to fade, Dr. Raman made some concluding remarks.

On behalf of the U. N., Dr. Raman expressed his gratitude to Ambassador Noguchi and the other session participants for their outstanding contributions to settling the Krasnodar affair and establishing a mechanism for settling future disputes.   Also, he acknowledged everyone's debt to Ambassadors Harry Brown of the USA, Nikolai Novikov of the USSR, and Manfred Clayborn of Switzerland, since they each played key roles in making the first Reconciliation session possible.

Before formally adjourning, Dr. Raman assured the session participants and other audience members that he'd complete the important tasks remaining, which were mentioned by Ambassador Noguchi. Specifically, Dr. Raman agreed to:

(1) Obtain United Nations approval of a worldwide Reconciliation agreement.   This agreement would require that disputes among nations be settled in an amicable and mutually satisfactory manner under the

guidance of Reconciliation Alliance International. Also, it would prohibit armed conflicts or warfare of any kind for any reason whatsoever.

(2) Get the International Reconciliation Agreement finalized in document form, then properly signed by each and every nation, and appropriately witnessed.

(3) Require that if there's any change in the government of any nation, the new government will renew its International Reconciliation Agreement and provide an authorized signature for the renewal, together with the signatures of appropriate witnesses.

(4) Require that each nation: (a) Ratify its Reconciliation agreement in its respective lawmaking assembly; (b) Make its necessary loan appropriation to establish the International Dispute Settlement Fund, and (c) Take appropriate steps to form a National Reconciliation Alliance organization that will affiliate with Reconciliation Alliance International.

(5) Arrange to have the U. N. transact a worldwide nuclear disarmament agreement based on the international agreement of nations to use Reconciliation in resolving future disputes.

Although it was pointed out previously that Reconciliation Alliance International would be formed through the U. N., Dr. Raman advised that as soon as it becomes established and able to function, it will operate independently. Also, the various National Reconciliation Alliance organizations should operate independently, too.

The audience gave a standing ovation for U. N. Secretary General Dr. Jawarlal Raman, who politely bowed and expressed his thanks. His final announcement was that to achieve formal acceptance of the Krasnodar settlement, the session would reconvene again soon, in Geneva, with President Morrison of the USA and Chairman Golgolev of the USSR. At that time, a multi-point summit agreement would be concluded, documenting the various Reconciliation and disarmament initiatives previously discussed.

Meanwhile, other nations will sign the International Reconciliation and Disarmament Agreement, after which it will be presented to the USA and USSR at the summit meeting, so the signatures of those two nations can be added also. The audience expressed its approval with a concluding round of applause, and the session was ended.

As the audience was leaving the assembly hall, Bert Jackson and Nadezhda Konya quickly joined each other. They walked together down the center aisle towards the rear exit. Bert smiled at Naddy, reached for her hand, and asked her to meet with him for a few minutes outside the building.

Naddy agreed, but cautioned that she'd have to leave soon to meet Novikov and the other Soviet representatives back at the embassy.

Bert replied that he was grateful for even a few minutes with her, then suggested they walk to the garden and find a private place where they could be alone to talk.

Naddy smiled approvingly, squeezed Bert's hand, then asked him what he thought of the session.

Bert expressed his relief to Naddy that the unfortunate Krasnodar affair was finally settled, so the USA and USSR could be friendly with each other always. Most of all, though, Bert was happy he and Naddy could be together.

When the two found themselves outside the building, away from the crowd, Bert put his arm around Naddy and gave her a gentle, cheek-to-cheek hug as they walked towards the garden.

"What are your thoughts about the session?" Bert asked Naddy the same question she had asked of him.

"I like the idea of Reconciliation, Bert," Naddy replied. "Life is too precious to be foolishly destroyed. Nations can't continue their warfare. They have to settle

259

their disputes peacefully and completely disarm themselves, so the world can stop worrying about nuclear destruction and start solving some of its other problems. What about poverty, starvation, disease, and environmental pollution of all kinds, including toxic chemical waste contamination of drinking water, acid rain, and hundreds of other problems? I recently read a magazine article about how acid rain, for example, has ruined lakes, killed fish, even destroyed forests and wildlife. It's shameful how careless we've become with our world. Since our two nations are now able to work together to reconcile their differences, maybe they can work together at solving some of the world's serious social, economic, and environmental problems as well."

Bert concurred, and held out the hope that the USA and USSR would agree to worldwide disarmament. He was convinced there was no good reason why they shouldn't. Citizens of both nations are fed up with the endless spending on war machines, while there never seems to be enough money left over for improving the environment and quality of life. Rather than spending billions to destroy the world, Bert reflected, nations should seek ways of improving it.

Bert and Naddy came to the center of a quiet garden area where they sat down on a wrought iron bench. They were surrounded by golden sunshine, stately trees, and fresh-blooming flowers of every color and kind. Since it was late in the afternoon, approaching the supper hour, they were entirely alone. Bert looked longingly into Naddy's dark eyes. He stroked her cheeks and hair gently, with the backs of his fingers. Then he tenderly kissed her.

"I love you, Naddy," Bert whispered in her ear.

"I love you, too, Bert," Naddy reflected back. Unhurriedly, they both embraced and kissed. The intense love that had burned inside them during the difficult past weeks had finally found a means of physical expression. The sheer joy of their reunion transcended mere words.

Bert and Naddy responded to each other's touch the way most young lovers respond. From their first meeting together in the Taylorsville Park, they knew theirs would be a true and lasting love. The language of their love, so international and universal, crossed all borders, tore down barricades, and flowed from one to the other by means of their tender embracing and kissing.

"Naddy," Bert broke the spell, "I have to ask you something." Then taking her left hand, he kissed it, held it with both his hands, and looked into her eyes. "I have to ask you an important question. Please don't laugh. Will you marry me?"

At this Naddy smiled and closed her eyes in a happy reverie, tilting her head slightly upwards to savor the excitement of Bert's proposal and her love for him. The perfumed scent of the many flowers around her added to the magic of the moment, so that her happiness was complete.

When she opened her eyes again, she glanced lovingly at Bert, put her arms around his neck, and joyfully kissed him. Finally, looking into his eyes, she said, "Yes, I'll marry you, Bert, because I love you with all my heart!"

"My love, my dear love," Bert said, getting up from the bench and gently lifting Naddy's hand and helping her up also. Then they came together in a close embrace and tenderly kissed, clinging to each other for a long time. Finally, they released their embrace and, hand in hand, began walking slowly around the garden. Bert ended the silence by speaking to Naddy again in a soft, loving, gentle manner.

"I'll love you and comfort you as long as I live, Naddy," Bert promised.

Pausing momentarily, Bert reached into his lower right suitcoat pocket and pulled out a suede-covered ring box. Opening it carefully, he showed Naddy a diamond engagement ring that sparkled in the afternoon sunlight. It had a large center diamond that was bordered on each side by a cluster of smaller diamonds, all of which were mounted in a magnificent, bright gold setting.

Bert lifted the ring out of its attractive holder and slipped it on Naddy's finger as Naddy excitedly exclaimed, "Oh, Bert, it's absolutely beautiful!"

"What kind of wedding would you like, Naddy?" Bert asked. "Where should it be? Your parents are both gone, mine, too, so we're quite alone, unfortunately."

Naddy kissed Bert when he said that, then thoughtfully looked about. Suddenly, eyes opening wide, she said, "Let's have our wedding right here in Geneva. It's so appropriate! The USA and USSR will be coming here for their summit agreement, so why shouldn't we come here, too? How symbolic! We'll represent the future of the world, the coming together of different nations and cultures. Geneva is an important meeting place for the world. Let's get married in Geneva!"

"Fine!" Bert agreed, kissing her again. "Geneva is an excellent choice; I like it." Then, looking puzzled, he asked, "But where in Geneva will we get married? You're Communist; you wouldn't want a church wedding."

"Oh, Bert," Naddy smiled, "you make it all seem so complicated. I think we should simply get married right here, outdoors, in this beautiful garden. This is where you proposed to me. Also, we can have our wedding when we come back here for the summit meeting. Your President Morrison and my Chairman Golgolev can attend the ceremony, and since my father isn't living, Chairman Golgolev can present me. How do you like that?" Naddy asked, enthusiastically.

Bert, smiling, gave her a quick kiss, then laughingly replied, "What an ambitiously big thinker and optimist you are! It'll be a miracle if Ambassador Clayborn and Dr.

Raman are able to get our President and your Chairman to come to Geneva for the summit meeting. How can we expect them to attend our wedding when they don't even know us? Besides, they'll be too busy with other matters."

Naddy, looking confident, said, "Chairman Golgolev knows me. I met him recently. Also, my boss Nikolai and Chairman Golgolev are on good terms. Nikolai could arrange it, or, if he can't, at least he'd be happy to present me himself, and Dr. Raman could officiate. I'm sure your Harry Brown would come, too, if you asked him. Let's invite them all: Nikolai, Helga, Maxie, Harry and Josie and their kids, Chairman Golgolev, Hjalmar Haggarson, your General Daniels, our Marshal Plekhanov, Golgolev's assistant, Tatyana, Ambassador Clayborn, and all the Reconciliation panel members, even James Baston and his newly reformed boss, Big Julie. What a happy wedding it will be!"

"I can see how it could become an international event," Bert reflected. "I always did like large, old-fashioned weddings with lots of guests. I just never thought you or I could ever have one. But seriously, Naddy, who will officiate? I don't think it's fair to ask Dr. Raman to do it. As U. N. Secretary General, I'm sure he's much too busy. Besides, officiating at weddings could create a bad precedent for him, taking him away from his other, more important duties. Imagine hundreds of thousands of couples all over the world begging the U. N. Secretary General to officiate at their wedding, after we give them the idea to do it by getting Dr. Raman to officiate at ours. We really need to think about this problem carefully, Naddy. What do you suggest?"

"I see what you mean," Naddy acknowledged. "There seems to be some kind of problem with everyone. If our wedding becomes an international event, we need to be very careful how we plan it. What if the whole world were to see our wedding on television? We

263

wouldn't want to show partiality towards either nation, since, when we're married, we'll represent them both.

"If, as would make me very happy, we had Chairman Golgolev officiate, we could create a precedence problem for him and an additional problem for ourselves. Since he's head of the Communist Party in our country, his officiating at our wedding might cause feelings of rejection and resentment among non-Communists. If, as would make you very happy, we have a Catholic priest or other Christian clergyman preside, the world's billions of non-Christians might feel excluded.

"I think if our wedding is to really become an international event symbolic of the unity of people with different political, economic, and religious views, we shouldn't show any kind of partiality. We want the world to know that unity is possible, and that it's as old as man and woman.

"What should we do? I don't know. How do you think we should solve this problem, Bert?"

"Why, Naddy," Bert chided, "I'm surprised at you. A moment ago you were a genius at solving the problems of where to have our wedding and who we should invite, yet now you get stumped on selecting someone to officiate. Keep thinking, I'm sure you'll come up with a brilliant answer."

Naddy tapped her chin thoughtfully, then remarked, "Perhaps we should simply eliminate the problem by not having anyone officiate. We can officiate ourselves, and all our friends can be witnesses. What do you think of that?"

Bert was enthusiastic about Naddy's idea, so the two decided they'd simply recite their vows to each other in front of witnesses, then exchange rings. They made other plans, too, but the time was getting late, and Naddy had to get back to the embassy for her meeting with Novikov and the others. Bert volunteered to drive her back in his

264

rental car, and the two agreed to announce their wedding plans right away. Naddy said she'd tell Nikolai and the others, and Bert said he'd break the news to Harry and Maxie.

Both Bert and Naddy soon began preparing for their wedding. Naddy asked Bert for a list of the people he wanted to invite, then said she'd mail them invitations as soon as a date was set for the Geneva summit.

Their wedding plans decided at last, Bert embraced Naddy again, and the two kissed. Afterwards, they walked slowly out of the garden, side by side, embracing and kissing each other frequently as they left. They were excited at the prospect of their future life together, especially now, since the world seemed a better place for everyone.

23

SUMMIT CONFERENCE

Nearly three months had passed since the Reconciliation session in Geneva. During that time, Bert and Naddy completed their wedding preparations, a summit meeting was arranged, and now participants were gathered together in the Geneva Palace of Nations assembly hall. Their meeting was about to reconvene, after a lengthy morning session and luncheon break.

The air was filled with noisy sounds of excitement and expectation. News reporters from all over the world, who were being admitted to the afternoon session, were rushing and stumbling into the packed hall in a race to get the biggest story of their lives. Hundreds of news cameras flashed their unearthly lights; security forces were strained; pandemonium was everywhere. Finally, U. N. Secretary General Dr. Jawarlal Raman, who was patiently trying to bring the meeting to order, began speaking in a soft voice that quieted the crowd so everyone could hear what was being said.

"Your attention, please! Ladies and gentlemen, our Summit Conference is now in session!" Dr. Raman made the announcement at exactly 2:00 p. m., striking his gavel several times against the hardwood top of the speaker's stand. "We've had our introductions. We've worked hard for many long hours. Now let's begin the important document-signing segment of our conference. Afterwards, while the sun is still high, we can enjoy a brief international wedding ceremony in the outdoor garden of this splendid Palace of Nations.

"Chairman Golgolev, President Morrison, distinguished ambassadors and other honored guests, you have before you a copy of your newly concluded summit agreement. Let's briefly review it."

Dr. Raman smiled and looked towards the center of the assembly hall. There he could see the major representatives of the USA and USSR. They were seated around a large circular table in an alternating manner, with Chairman Golgolev sitting in one seat, President Morrison sitting next to him on the right, Ambassador Brown on the left, Ambassador Novikov on Morrison's right, and in like manner for the others, so that no representatives from the same country were seated together. As soon as everyone's attention was focused on Dr. Raman, he spoke again. Later, when he began referring to the Summit Agreement, the audience members looked at their own copy of the document, which was distributed to them prior to the meeting.

"The first section states that both the USA and USSR are satisfied with the Reconciliation settlement their representatives transacted several months ago, regarding the tragic Krasnodar affair," Dr. Raman commented.

"The second section states that the Reconciliation process is to be used for settling future disputes between the USA and USSR, or between the USA or USSR and any other nation. We've already transacted a similar agreement with the other nations. They've each agreed to use Reconciliation for settling their existing and future disputes, provided the USA and USSR transact such an agreement, also.

"In the third section, the USA and USSR agree to

fully support the U. N. organization, assure appropriate representation in Reconciliation Alliance International, and allocate their fair share of the necessary start-up loan funding for the No-fault International Dispute Settlement Fund. In the larger context of our community of nations, this third section of the agreement means that the USA and USSR will cooperate with each other, and act together with China, Japan, India, the United Kingdom, the Organization of American States, or any other nation or group of nations, to assure that all nations fulfill their peacemaking Reconciliation commitments to each other and the rest of the world.

"Section four is the agreement of the USA and USSR to cooperate with each other and with other nations culturally, economically, socially, politically, and in any other way appropriate to assure permanent world peace and friendship.

"The fifth section is an agreement to fully support and assist U. N. efforts to achieve worldwide biological, chemical, and nuclear weapons disarmament.

"Section six is the specific agreement of the USA and USSR to destroy their own biological, chemical, and nuclear weapons at the same time other nations destroy theirs.

"Section seven is an agreement for establishing a worldwide system of disarmament verification. This system has already been approved by various member nation representatives to the U. N., on condition the USA and USSR approve it also. It provides that:

(a) All nuclear weapons shall be brought to the geographically closest verification point where they'll be carefully disassembled and destroyed.
(b) Demolition experts appointed and authorized by the U. N. will destroy weapon systems that can't be converted to peaceful use.
(c) Weapons convertible to peaceful use, such as aircraft

268

and shipping, will be processed by U. N.-appointed and authorized converters, who will resell converted items back to original owners or others at conversion cost or less. (This is what we refer to as the 'Swords into Plowshares' provision.)

(d) All salvageable materials, such as scrap metal, reusable structural steel, or other nonmilitary, nonthreatening components, will be sold by U. N. appointed and authorized salvagers to any organizations having peaceful uses for them. Proceeds of such sales, after deduction of costs, will be donated to various international charities and disaster relief efforts approved by a two thirds majority vote of the U. N. General Assembly.

(e) Inspection teams appointed and authorized by the U. N., will evaluate all national military units for worldwide service in a U. N. police force. Any units determined to be unnecessary for U. N. service or standby will be disbanded. This disbanding does *not* apply to nonmilitary, purely domestic police units. However, such police units must be approved for service by a U. N. inspection team, and periodically reevaluated for continued service.

"Section eight is the agreement to permanently establish a system of disarmament inspection teams made up of knowledgeable representatives from Reconciliation Alliance International, the U. N., and other appropriate organizations. On a continuing basis, these teams will supervise, witness, and verify worldwide biological, chemical, and nuclear weapons disarmament, as well as the permanent disbanding of military units. From their respective location assignments, the teams will also report disarmament progress, so the world can know when it has been satisfactorily achieved.

"Section nine is the agreement authorizing the

disarmament inspection teams to maintain surveillance of all remaining weapon systems and individuals using them. These teams will make certain that nations retain a minimal number of nonnuclear weapons and an adequate internal police force for protection against criminal elements and for enforcement of laws.

"Finally, Section ten is a general agreement that the USA and USSR will assist the U. N. in developing other mechanisms and methods for maintaining worldwide disarmament on a permanent basis. This effort is needed because our disarmament program can't eliminate the knowledge of how to rebuild the various weapons we've destroyed. Therefore, it's essential we have a reliable means of preventing the rebuilding or stockpiling of weapons we've forbidden.

"At the end of the agreement document are appropriate signature spaces for USA and USSR heads of state to sign their formal acceptance. Also, there are additional signature spaces for various witnesses. For example, I've been authorized by the U. N. to be a witness. Other U. N.–recommended witnesses are the heads of state of a random sampling of 60 U. N. member nations, plus the six facilitators who served in the First International Reconciliation Session. Swiss Ambassador Clayborn will sign also, but as a strictly neutral nation witness.

"That's it, clear and simple, hopefully. Any unanticipated agreement needs beyond what we have here can be handled through the U. N., which, by the way, has now changed itself to eliminate all adversarial behavior and disruptive political factions and groups. From now on, the U. N. has resolved to stick to its primary goal of peacemaking, and it's amending its Charter to make sure it does what it's supposed to do. Now, then, if Chairman Vasil Golgolev of the USSR and President John Morrison of the USA will please come forward, we can complete the signing of the Summit Agreement."

Applause affirmed the audience's approval of Dr. Raman's remarks. Both Chairman Golgolev and President Morrison proceeded to the signing. Chairman Golgolev was chosen by lot to be first, followed by President Morrison and the various witnesses. Then Chairman Golgolev walked to the speaker's stand and addressed the assembly.

"President Morrison and distinguished guests, throughout the difficult years of our recent history, citizens of the Soviet Union have struggled for a better life. We dedicated ourselves long ago to building a new society, one that will provide a peaceful, prosperous future for our children and the children of other nations. However, the dreadful array of nuclear weapons stockpiled in the world today suggests a different set of consequences, including the reality that there may never be a future society, nor any children, nor any kind of life whatsoever. Therefore, it has become exceedingly clear to everyone, that all nations must eliminate their nuclear weapons, discontinue their adversarial relationships, and end their armed warfare now and forever.

"The repugnant, worldwide arms race was bred by an ever–increasing distrust and tension among us, and has become economically, politically, and socially disastrous. The world can no longer tolerate it, and the USA and USSR can no longer financially sustain it. It's appropriate, therefore, that we have ended it here and now, once and for all, with the signing of a Summit Agreement."

The audience interrupted Golgolev at this point with a prolonged, standing ovation. When everyone finally sat down, Golgolev continued.

"The USSR lost over 20 million citizens in World War II. It became a nation of widows and bereaved families. In the aftermath of this shocking loss of life, we

271

Soviets determined to make ourselves so powerful, that never again would so many of us have to suffer so much. Now, nearly a half century later, the world is drastically changed.

"The awesome destructiveness of nuclear weapons, the excessive stockpiling of these weapons, and the reality of Mutual Assured Destruction, or MAD, if such weapons are ever used, have made any kind of nuclear warfare completely suicidal and irrational. A key question, therefore, is, 'If nuclear weapons are so disastrous to the world's future, why do we have them?' Since the availability and abundance of such weapons contributes to the likelihood of their accidental use, and since any use whatsoever threatens the future of us all, it's absolutely essential we eliminate these weapons as quickly as possible and forever. It's also appropriate to a peaceful future that any kind of international armed conflict be banned as quickly as possible and forever. Let the scientific process of problem solving Reconciliation replace all adversarial and destructive ways of settling disputes.

"We citizens of the Soviet Union are happy to unite in peace and friendship with our World War II ally, the USA. By signing this historic Summit Agreement, we combine the actions of the USSR and USA to assure the world of a peaceful and bright future. Henceforth, let all nations reject any provocative verbal exchanges, adversarial acts, and armed warfare. In the future, let all nations meet in a spirit of sincere cooperation, generous good will, and amicable Reconciliation, so they can settle their disputes peacefully and establish a perpetual friendship."

Again the audience gave Golgolev a standing ovation, during which he smiled and politely nodded. Then President Morrison walked to the speaker's stand and enthusiastically shook Golgolev's hand. As the applause ended, Golgolev returned to his seat and President Morrison spoke.

"Chairman Golgolev, ladies and gentlemen, on behalf of all the citizens of the USA, I want to thank Chairman Golgolev and the citizens of the USSR. Also, I want to express my personal thanks. Chairman Vasil Golgolev's words will live on in history, together with the record of this historic event. Chairman Golgolev, we agree with your every word.

"There's both a remarkable irony in history, as well as a startling reality. At the time of the American Revolution, when our nation gained its freedom and independence from an oppressive monarchy, there were only 600 million people on the earth. Today, a little over two centuries later, there are five billion people on the earth, or 8-1/2 times as many as in 1776. With a mere 600 million people two centuries ago, however, plus the wide open spaces, and horse and buggy travel, the world seemed incredibly large. Today, with 8-1/2 times as many people, plus numerous crowded cities, and ultrafast spaceship travel, our world has become very small indeed. There's the remarkable irony! More people, bigger cities, smaller world.

"The startling reality is that our world cannot survive nuclear warfare. Nuclear weapons have made warfare obsolete, as Chairman Golgolev already pointed out. In the past, armed warfare was the world's familiar method of settling its disputes, and today's adversarial legal systems are an archaic remnant of the brutal, war filled past. Today's adversarial legal systems are a last ditch effort to maintain the spirit of warfare the world had when war was king and made by kings, or declared by dictators and forced on the masses. War has always been a curse to the masses, because warmongers force the masses to provide countless sacrifices of human life, money, and production.

"People throughout history bore the enormous

273

economic burdens of paying for armies and armaments, in addition to enduring the deaths of loved ones, the disfigurement of minds and bodies, and the destruction of homes, buildings, and lands. Wars throughout history have always been paid for over and over again by the blood, sweat, suffering, and deaths of people whose children and children's children were made to bleed more, sweat harder, suffer more severe hardships, and die in ever greater numbers. There are no winners, nor is there any progress in war. With wars, man stagnates, moves backwards, eventually extinguishes himself. His world ends when radioactive fallout begins and nuclear winter descends.

"War is now completely exposed as the symptom of sick minds, since nobody with a healthy mind would wage it. We should regard war as a terminal sickness and dread disease, then exert every effort to get rid of it, stamp it out, end it once and for all, as though it were smallpox, tuberculosis, cancer, or any other threat to our health.

"If we allow our differences to divide us so much that the sickness of war spreads and threatens to consume everyone, then it's time we got rid of war and learned a new approach. It's time we turned to peacemaking Reconciliation. It's time we created constructive and innovative ways of either living with our differences, or reducing or eliminating them. At no time do we want to destroy each other over them, or obliterate the whole world in a final nuclear missile holocaust or doomsday.

"Today is doomsday minus one and holding. We're not a moment too soon in concluding an International Reconciliation and Disarmament Agreement. It's indeed fortunate we acted in time to prevent that frenzy of nuclear flashes which will signify our world's death. Truly, all present and future humanity will be grateful for our historic efforts today at saving the world.

"A long time ago, the Father of our Country, George

Washington, made the statement that 'To be prepared for war is one of the most effective means of preserving peace.' Today, with the development of over 50,000 nuclear warheads, the whole world has so completely changed that the opposite of what George Washington said is true. Today's wisdom says that 'to be prepared for peace, to have a workable, dispute-settling Reconciliation mechanism for assuring peace, is the most effective means of preventing war.'

"Chairman Golgolev, both your country and mine share the shameful distinction of having led the world in nuclear weapons development and destruction technology. How wonderful we've at last reversed our direction! In peace and friendship we can now lead the world towards the development of a new peacemaking technology: Reconciliation.

"I salute you, Chairman Golgolev, and persons of good will everywhere. This is the dawning of a new era in the evolution of interpersonal, intercommunity, and international relationships. Rather than expend for war, we'll promote peace and friendship everywhere. We'll explore outer space and use it for our expanding populations; create an improved economic system to provide a better distribution of wealth and higher living standards for the world's poor; revolutionize farming and improve food technology to make sure everyone has enough to eat; clean up the environment and find ways to use our shrinking resources wisely; and achieve improvements of other kinds, so that our children and future generations will enjoy this world and improve it even more.

"With the agreement we signed today, we changed our world's priorities from self-destruction to self-improvement. What an easy decision it was to make! We only needed to choose the right alternative, the alternative of life, rather than death. Chairman Golgolev and I, our two mighty nations, and the United

Nations, have joined together in choosing a practical process for settling disputes: Reconciliation. It's our pathway to peace, friendship, and life. We made the right choice."

After President Morrison's conclusion, the audience reacted with a lengthy and standing applause, while Chairman Golgolev walked up to President Morrison and embraced him. The two remained standing on the platform as Ambassador Clayborn came to the speaker's stand. Raising his right hand high, he gestured to the audience for permission to speak. When the room grew quiet, he began.

"On the occasion of this joyous and unprecedented world event, I've been asked to make an important announcement. Ambassadors Harry Brown of the USA and Nikolai Novikov of the USSR will be awarded the Nobel Peace Prize. It's not surprising. These two outstanding individuals are most deserving of the award, because of their timely and desperately needed initiative. They gave the world the opportunity of their peacemaking Reconciliation process. Their scientific, problem solving approach to settling disputes and building friendships is the right approach, at the right time, in the right place., As a result, they changed the course of history.

"As a point of information for those of you who may not know about it, the Nobel Peace Prize was established by Alfred Bernhard Nobel, the Swedish chemist who invented dynamite in 1867 and later became one of the world's wealthiest persons. Ironically, Alfred Nobel was educated in St. Petersburg, now Leningrad, USSR, and studied engineering in the USA, so it's intriguing that he was trained by the two countries who later became the world's major military powers. However, when dynamite was used for military purposes, rather than peace, Alfred Nobel was bitterly disappointed. To help correct this tragic misuse of his invention, he used his huge fortune to establish monetary prizes for those who make the greatest contributions for the good of humanity and the cause of international peace. The shared prize in this case will be approximately $100,000 for each of the two recipients.

"Ambassadors Harry Brown and Nikolai Novikov, please come up here to the platform and receive these official Nobel Peace Prize notifications. The award ceremony will take place in Oslo two weeks from today. Norway's Prime Minister will make the award presentation."

The audience vigorously applauded while Brown and Novikov walked to the platform to receive their Nobel Prize notifications. Ambassador Clayborn and President Morrison enthusiastically greeted them and shook their hands. Smiling broadly, Chairman Golgolev stepped between them and embraced them both at the same time. Then Dr. Raman came to the speaker's stand. Imitating Clayborn's earlier gesture, Dr. Raman humorously raised his right hand to ask the audience permission to speak. As the audience quieted down, he began.

"Ladies and gentlemen, on behalf of the United Nations organization, it gives me great pleasure to honor these two remarkable persons, Ambassadors Harry Brown and Nikolai Novikov, by presenting them the U.N. Man of Peace Award."

The audience applauded while Dr. Raman congratulated Brown and Novikov, and gave each of them a bronze, U. N., "We Believe" emblem, mounted on a walnut plaque. President Morrison also congratulated them, and said he had an announcement to make, too.

"Ladies and gentlemen, now that we've arrived at the end of our meeting, Dr. Raman, Chairman Golgolev, and I have just reached another agreement. Harry Brown and Nikolai Novikov will retain their special

Ambassadorial rank and be assigned to assist the U. N. in organizing and establishing Reconciliation Alliance International. Also, next Fourth of July at the White House, I plan to award a gold Presidential Medal of Freedom to both Ambassadors Harry Brown and Nikolai Novikov for their meritorious contributions to world peace."

After allowing the audience a few moments to applaud President Morrison's announcement, Chairman Golgolev stepped to the speaker's stand for an announcement.

"I, too, will present awards to Ambassadors Harry Brown and Nikolai Novikov. This will be done at the Kremlin in Moscow. On behalf of the Presidium of the Supreme Soviet of the USSR, I announce that the International Lenin Peace Prize Gold Medal, historic diploma, and monetary prize of 25,000 rubles will be presented to each of them with my congratulations!"

Brown and Novikov were completely stunned by all the awards. Novikov, who was standing nearest to the microphone, replied first.

"Ladies and gentlemen, both Ambassador Brown and I are deeply honored by these various, prestigious awards. You should know, however, that Ambassador Brown is the deserving one, since he introduced the idea of a Reconciliation Clause in our wheat contract. I merely agreed with him and supported his idea. I'm truly fortunate, therefore, to share in so many honors. Ladies and gentlemen, permit me now to present the man who is really deserving, a man I'm privileged to have as a friend, Ambassador Harry Brown."

Brown couldn't speak for a full fifteen minutes, because of the thunderous and standing ovation he received. For several minutes he attempted to speak, but the enthusiastic audience kept clapping, and cameras of the press kept flashing. Finally, when the applause began subsiding, Harry started to speak.

278

"Thank you, everyone, for your generous acknowledgments. However, I must inform you that I'm really indebted to my longtime friend, Ambassador Nikolai Novikov, who was so modest and noble just now. If Nikolai hadn't been so receptive, encouraging, and helpful, no Reconciliation Clause would have been possible, and the Geneva Reconciliation session would never have taken place. Perhaps we might not have even survived to see this day. Therefore, I'm deeply indebted to Ambassador Novikov, not only for helping make today possible, but for giving us the prospect of a better tomorrow as well."

Brown concluded his brief remarks by thanking Chairman Vasil Golgolev and President John Morrison, pointing out that without their good will and cooperation, none of the successful efforts could have been accomplished. Brown also thanked Swiss Ambassador Manfred Clayborn, U. N. Secretary General Dr. Jawarlal Raman, members of the Reconciliation Panel, U. N. representatives, and other persons of good will who dedicated their lives to achieving world peace and are continuing to work for it.

The audience gave Brown and Novikov another prolonged and standing ovation. Afterwards, Dr. Raman adjourned the session with a final statement.

"Ladies and gentlemen, there's still a large measure left of this splendid Geneva afternoon, and I'm pleased to inform you we're at the end of our session. At this time, you're all invited to assemble outside in the palace garden where we'll witness an international wedding ceremony and enjoy some good music and refreshments. Ambassador Harry Brown's General Manager, Bertram Jackson, and Nikolai Novikov's Deputy Director, Nadezhda Konya, are the two getting married. Even though some of you didn't receive a formal invitation, please understand at this time that all are welcome.

"So that we can all move outside for the wedding, this meeting is hereby adjourned."

24

CONCLUSION

Sweet melodic strains from the strings and woodwinds of an orchestral ensemble could be heard through the floral scented air. Familiar compositions of Franz Schubert and Amadeus Mozart provided exceptionally pleasing sounds, as a gracious gathering of wedding guests were positioning themselves in the Palace of Nations garden. Flowers everywhere were in full bloom, showing their best colors in the bright sun, and yielding their finest fragrances. Such an enticing setting put the crowd in a festive mood.

Suddenly, the orchestra struck up the 'Wedding March' by Alexander Guilmant and the procession began. The orchestra was located off to one side, towards the rear of the assemblage. A special platform had been constructed for it, and served as a kind of rallying point for the guests, who had been milling about in growing numbers, but who now focused their attention on the ceremony that was just starting.

Soon bridal attendants could be seen processing down a grassy aisle, the borders of which were roped off by thick white cords supported by movable chromed posts and pedestals. The aisle led to a circular center area, which was also bordered by white cord and chromed strands. In the middle of the area was a small, white canopied platform.

Leading the procession were Brown's two youngest children, Jeanie on the left side of the aisle, and Johnny on the right. Jeanie, age four, wore a blue satin gown with white lace trim. She was carrying a tiny bouquet of red, white, and blue flowers in her left hand, while holding her brother Johnny's arm with her right. Johnny, age seven, wore a tuxedo over a starched white shirt with wing collar, and red, white, and blue striped silk ascot. A fresh red carnation was in the left lapel of his oxford gray cutaway. His gray and black striped trousers were accented by his shiny black shoes.

Following Brown's two younger children were 11-year-old Sara Gadsden, then Brown's two older children, Suzie, 14, and Jack, 17. Sara, Suzie, and the other female attendants, like Jeanie, each carried a red, white, and blue bouquet, and were identically dressed. Also, Jack was dressed identically to his younger brother and the other male attendants.

Behind the children came Maxine Gadsden and James Baston. Next, Helga Baranovna was accompanied by Manfred Clayborn. Then came Josie and Harry Brown, followed by Anna and Nikolai Novikov. At the end of the procession, USSR Chairman Vasil Golgolev escorted the bride, Nadezhda Konya, on his left arm.

Nadezhda was dressed in a magnificent, long sleeved, white satin gown with a high, lace-fringed collar. Her shoes were of woven white silk, and on her head she wore a white lace veil. At the peak of her veil, just above her forehead, she wore a tiny red star, not too large to be distracting, nor too small to be seen. It was a star of an appropriate size to honor the flag of her country. In her right hand she carried a splendid rosette bouquet of bright red, matching the red star she wore.

Both U. S. President John Morrison, acting as best man, and Bertram Jackson, the groom, were standing at the end of the grassy aisle, which was bordered by white cord. They stood at the right side of the entrance to the area encircled by the white cord, and both were dressed the same as the other male attendants.

When the procession approached the large, white cord circle, the attendant couples separated themselves from each other, females to the left, males to the right, walking around opposite sides of the circle in step to the processional march. When they were approximately halfway around, they stopped and faced the small, white canopied platform that stood in the center of the circle. Behind the rear of the platform, and between the lineup of attendants, there was a flag of the USSR on the right, a flag of the USA on the left, and a flag of the U. N. in the center.

President John Morrison and Bert Jackson stepped towards Nadezhda Konya as she approached, and Chairman Vasil Golgolev presented her to Bert by gently and ceremoniously taking Nadezhda's right hand and placing it in Bert's left hand. Having done that, Golgolev processed with President Morrison to the left of the circle, where they both stopped and faced the center platform. Bert and Nadezhda moved slowly around the right side of the platform to the stairs at the rear. Then, mounting the stairs, they stepped up to the top where they stood under the white canopy and faced their wedding guests.

The music continued for a few more moments until it reached a conclusion, after which there was silence. At that moment, Bert and Nadezhda turned to face each other and Bert spoke these words:

> I, Bertram Jackson, Citizen of the United States of America, on this day, in this place, in front of these witnesses, agree to marry you, Nadezhda Konya, Citizen of the Union of Soviet Socialist Republics. I

take you as my wife, and I pledge to you my lifelong love, livelihood, and loyalty.

Then Nadezhda Konya spoke her acceptance to Bert:

> I, Nadezhda Konya, Citizen of the Union of Soviet Socialist Republics, on this day, in this place, in front of these witnesses, agree to marry you, Bertram Jackson, Citizen of the United States of America. I accept you as my husband, and I pledge to you my lifelong love, livelihood, and loyalty.

At this point, President Morrison moved to the edge of the small platform where he opened a ring box and held it up to Bert, who carefully removed a gold, diamond-studded wedding ring of a design matching the engagement ring Nadezhda was wearing. Placing the ring on the appropriate finger of Nadezhda's left hand, Bert spoke these words to her:

> With this ring, Nadezhda, I confirm our marriage, and as the gold is perfect, so may our love and our lives be perfect also.

After Bert finished speaking, Chairman Golgolev moved to the edge of the platform where Nadezhda stood. When he got there, he took a small container from his suitcoat pocket and, opening it, held it up to her. Nadezhda carefully removed a gold wedding band from the container, and slipped it on Bert's left hand ring finger. Then she spoke these words to him:

> With this ring, Bert, I confirm our marriage, and as the gold is perfect, so may our love and our lives be perfect also.

284

After a loving embrace and gentle kiss, both Bert and Nadezhda turned toward the audience. Maxine Gadsden then came to the edge of the platform and handed an 8 x 10 inch plaque to Bert, who began reading from the plaque, alternating sentences with Nadezhda.

PLEDGE OF PEACE AND FRIENDSHIP

We pledge ourselves to be Ambassadors of Peace and Friendship.
Wherever and whenever we can, we'll replace hostility with kindness, hurt with help, and suspicion with trust.

Instead of quarreling, we'll cooperate.
Instead of complaining, we'll compliment.
Instead of frowning, we'll smile.

We won't demand satisfaction; rather, we'll seek to satisfy.
We won't demand attention; rather, we'll learn to listen.
We won't demand we be loved; rather, we'll learn to love each other.

We'll each find peace by working at forgiving.
We'll each find happiness by developing understanding.
We'll each find friendship by learning to be friendly.

For the sake of our marriage and for the future of the world,
This is our Pledge of Peace and Friendship.

The audience applauded, and the orchestra ensemble struck up a rousing recessional, "Trumpet Voluntary in D" by Purcell. As the couple left the platform and walked down the grassy aisle, they radiated a happiness rivaling the brightness of the maturing sun and promising an even brighter tomorrow.

INDEX

GB (chemical warfare), 185
GB (see Sarin)
genetic aberrations, 171
Geneva (Switzerland), 194, 196,
203, 208-209, 212-213, 215-216,
225, 249, 251, 258, 262-263,
265-266, 279
GI bill, 5
Gleensheen Mansion (Duluth),
107
gluttony, 224
God, 218, 223-224, 231, 239-242
Golden Rule, 227-228, 231, 244
Goldstrike Formula, 15, 18-19, 38,
58
Golgolev, USSR Chairman Vasil,
34, 134-144, 146-148, 154-155,
157-166, 172-173, 186, 189-197,
251, 258, 262-264, 267, 270-273,
275-279, 282-284
grade certificates, 119
grafters, 50
Granada, 66-68, 138
Grand Cross: Order of Civil
Merit (Spain), 206, 222
Grand Ol Opry (Nashville,
Tennessee, USA), 44
Grayback (USA submarine), 185
Great Lakes (Canada & USA),
18, 56, 78-79, 107, 115, 119, 203
Great Lakes Pilotage Staff
(Cleveland, Ohio, USA), 78
Great Spirit (see God)
Greater Western Caucasian
Mountain Region (USSR), 109
Greece, 240-241
greed, 224
Guilmant, Alexander, 281
Gulf Coast (USA), 11, 83-84, 92
H
Hadrian, Emperor (story of), 224
Haggarson, Hjalmar, 109-111,

113-115, 117-121, 123, 127-132,
152-153, 203, 216, 249, 263
Harbor Cruise (Duluth), 105-106
Hari, 240
hatches, deck, 116, 118, 127-128,
130, 145, 152-153, 155, 191, 212,
251-253
haughty, 229
H. B. Exports (Minnesota), 9,
36-39, 81, 83-85, 110, 123,
150-151, 191, 202-203, 251-253
healing, 170
health, 255
herbicides, 11
Hercules, 48
hero medals, 49
heroes, definition of, 45-50
hijackers, 48
Hindu, 223, 231, 238
Hiroshima (Japan), 164, 166-168,
180, 218, 237, 240
Ho Chi Minh (Vietnam), 49
hogs, 20
Holcomb (U.S. Coast Guard
Cutter), 128-129, 131
Homer, 48
Honduras, 66
honesty, 62
hope, 229
hopper cars, 15, 38, 57, 81-82,
88-89, 120-122, 211-212
horse, 63
horseshoe, 63
hospital, 13
Hotel (USSR submarine), 160
hot line telephone (USA-USSR),
186-187, 189-192, 194-195, 197
human organizational and social
behavior, 37
human understanding, 251
humility, 224, 229-230
hurricane wind, 167

291

205, 212, 215-217, 257
Swords into Plowshares, 269
systems, 233

T

Tabun (chemical warfare), 185
tango, 70
Taoist, 223, 231
taxicabs, 13
Taylor, Col. Edward (Minnesota, USA), 31-32, 52
Taylor, Fort (Minnesota, USA), 31
Taylorsville (Minnesota, USA), 2, 10-11, 13, 16, 30-32, 37, 40-41, 44, 50, 92, 110, 150-151, 198, 202, 210-211, 251
Taylorsville Hotel, Restaurant and Dance Lounge, 10-11, 16-17, 20, 23, 25-27, 41, 51, 85, 92, 94, 103, 124, 213
Taylorsville Park, 42-43, 54, 101, 124, 261
television, 47, 131, 249, 263
Ten Commandments, 65
Tennessee Waltz, 42
terrorists, 48, 66-68, 134, 138, 141, 155, 221, 242
Texas (USA), 40, 210
Thailand, 67
Third World Nations Block (U.N.), 220
Tillibee (USA submarine), 184
TNT, 158, 164, 168-169, 217-218, 276
Tokyo Imperial University (Japan), 206
tonnage, 18, 81, 109, 115
Tonto (USA fiction hero), 48
toxic waste, 260
transfusions, blood, 170

transplants, bone marrow, 170
troposphere, 167
Trident (USA missile), 164, 180, 184
Trumpet Voluntary in D, 286
truth, 62-63, 66, 188, 191, 239, 242
tuberculosis, 274
tugboats, 83, 108, 117-119, 123, 125
Turin, University of (Italy), 206
Turkey in the Straw, 21
two man rule (USA), 179
Typhoon (USSR submarine), 160
Tzu-Hsin, 246
Zsu-Kung, 244

U

Udaipur, University of (India), 207
UHF (see radio)
Ulysses, 48
Uncaused Cause (see God)
United Kingdom, 164, 205, 268
United Nations (U.N.), 67, 205, 208, 216, 219-221, 231, 234, 244, 253-255, 257-258, 268-270, 275-277
U.N. Charter, 17, 66-67, 138, 220, 270
U.N. General Assembly, 220-221, 269
U.N. inspection team, 269-270
U.N. Man of Peace Award, 277
U.N. police force, 269
U.N. Secretary General, 194, 205, 219, 258, 263, 266
U.N. Security Council, 221
Upper Great Lakes Pilot Association (Duluth, Minnesota, USA), 78
USA, 11-13, 17, 32-33, 35-36, 38, 41, 46-49, 58, 64-68, 77-78, 81-82, 92, 96, 105, 113, 124, 129, 133-134, 137-146, 148, 152,

301

DID YOU KNOW THAT • • •

1. The United Nations Organization is failing to keep the peace, because one out of every five nations in the world today is presently at war.

2. Confucius, Mohammed, Jesus Christ, and the current Dalai Lama of Tibet have valuable advice about peacemaking.

3. Communist Party leaders Vladimer Ilyich Lenin of the USSR and Mao Zedung of China have stressed the importance of peacemaking and the avoidance of war.

4. The adversarial, cumbersome, and expensive legal systems of the USA and other countries don't make friends out of enemies, but increase hostilities instead.

5. Adversarial legal systems are an archaic remnant of belligerent, violent, and war-crazed societies.

6. Confucius said, "We should make it our aim that there be no lawsuits at all."

7. It's socially unacceptable to start a lawsuit in Japan and, as a result, that country has hardly any lawyers.

8. Jesus Christ warned against lawsuits, urging those having disputes to "make friends with your opponent. . . ." Also, he said, "love your enemies, and pray for those who persecute you," and, "whoever shall force you to go one mile, go with him two."

The Apostle Paul said, ". . .it is already a defeat for you, that you have lawsuits with one another."

10. Most of the lawyers in the world reside in the USA, which has only 5% of the world's population.

11. In Washington, D.C., there's one lawyer for every 23 men, women, and children.

12. Most members of the U.S. Congress are lawyers.

13. When Nicaragua complained to the World Court that the U. S. mined its harbors, the U. S. Government sent a delegation of 18 lawyers to attempt and evasion of World Court jurisdiction. Yet, on August 6, 1946, the U.S. signed an agreement to abide by the World Court in such matters.

14. If the adversarial legal systems continue to be tolerated and expanded, they may lead to the death of the earth.

15. The United Nations Charter states that the U.N. is supposed "to maintain international peace and security," yet it's divided into opposing groups and blocs of nations, and operates in an adversarial manner.

16. There are approximately 50,000 nuclear warhead missiles in the world waiting to be launched at everyone.

17. It's estimated that the combined blast force of USA and USSR stockpiles of nuclear warheads is equivalent to 6,667 World War II's, and that such a

force is sufficient to destroy the world 100 times over.

18. It's estimated that a single U.S. nuclear submarine of the Trident class can launch enough nuclear warheads to destroy 200 big cities, and has the equivalent firepower of eight World War II's.

19. The intense heat from each individual nuclear explosion is said to be hotter than the temperatures in the center of the sun.

20. A stockpile of 2,500 Soviet SS-18 missiles has an equivalent blast force of over 800 World War II's.

21. The total Soviet inventory of nuclear warhead missiles is estimated to have a combined blast force in excess of 5,000 World War II's.

22. The Swedish Royal Academy of Science asked 13 international experts what would happen in a brief exchange of 15,000 nuclear warheads. They all agreed it would destroy mankind and leave the entire world uninhabitable.

23. Billions upon billions have been spent on waging war, but virtually nothing to prevent it.

24. There may be no way to stop a nuclear war once it has started, since communications would be destroyed and nobody would know who to negotiate with to obtain a cease fire or surrender. Also, would there be anybody left to surrender?

25. The American EC-135 airborne battle command operation code named Looking Glass, is supposed to be a last ditch defense when ground based missile

launching commands are destroyed. At any moment of any day, there's an EC-135 aircraft flying somewhere over the U.S. with an on-board general and staff, ready to launch retaliatory missiles at the Soviets. Yet, since the operation assumes Soviet missiles would be launched first, how would any U.S. aircraft be able to fly in the debris clogged air? It's a fact that jet engines can't function in a dirty atmosphere. Also, radioactive interferences and distortions would prevent missile launching radio signals from reaching missile silos.

26. The USA and USSR may not be able to destroy each other's missile launching submarines, because when a sub is targeted and a missile is fired at it, the sub will have moved safely away from the targeted area before the missile arrives.

27. Christians, Jews, Moslems, Hindus, Confucians, Buddhists, Taoists, and persons of other religions are for peace. Also, over 150 nations on earth are members of the United Nations, which is an organization chartered to achieve world peace.

28. Vladimir Ilyich Lenin wrote that war is extremely ridiculous.

29. Mao Zedung wrote that the democratic method should be used to settle disputes, rather than the method of coercion or repression. Also, he wrote that the Communists should unite with the imperialist countries and strive to coexist peacefully with them, do business with them, and prevent any possible war.

30. Since the 1500's, Switzerland, an "Island of Peace," has maintained a strict neutrality, refusing to take sides in any armed conflicts.

ORDER COPIES of *The Krasnodar Affair* for relatives, friends, government officials, politicians, religious leaders, teachers, and students.

Please send _____ book(s) to:

Name _____
Address _____
City/State/Zip _____
(Use additional paper for additional addresses.)

Enclosed find $ _____ for _____ book(s) @ $6.95 each U.S./$7.95 Canada. Please add $1.50 mailing and handling per book. Pay by check or money order only, no cash or C.O.D.'s please. Book price and mailing cost are guaranteed for at least one year from printing date. Send order to:

St. John's Publishing, Inc., 6824 Oaklawn Avenue, Edina, Minnesota 55435

NOTE: Write to St. John's Publishing, 6824 Oaklawn Avenue, Edina, Minnesota 55435, for quantity prices on sales promotions, premiums, fund raising, or groups, such as church and school classes, seminars and workshops.

Surviving Motherhood
Donna Lagorio Montgomery

$6.95 U.S., $7.95 Canada

Donna Montgomery is the mother of eight children. She's a volunteer extraordinary, having served as PTA president, women's club president, church council member, teacher in an art masterpeice program, community newsletter originator, editor and writer, master teacher in a religious education program, coordinator of new school programs, caricaturist and public speaker. Donna has been a guest on talk shows all over the country, appearing on many well known shows such as **Hour Magazine** with Gary Collins. Her straightforward sense of humor and common sense are refreshingly entertaining and useful.

Trade paperback   ISBN 0-938577-00-X   L of C # 86-06103-1

Kids + Modeling = Money
by Donna Lagorio Montgomery

Hardcover with index/ $9.95 U.S., $10.95 Canada

Written by the mother of eight children- four of whom are successful models- KIDS + MODELING = MONEY offers countless tips on ways parents can give their child a head start in the competitive world of modeling. In addition to supplying firsthand insights on finding an agency; locating where the jobs are; building the right wardrobe, auditioning for jobs; working for radio, TV and print; managing pay and expenses; and anticipating and avoiding problems; the book also includes valuable advice from professional agents and photographers. Much more than a how-to book, it demonstrates that a professional modeling career can not only bring money and excitement, but can enhance a child's character, build self-esteem, and instill confidence, laying the foundation for "model" adulthood.

ISBN 0-13-515172-4   L of C # 83-19199

Discounts for quantity orders automatically applied.

Add $1.50 postage per book

St. John's Publishing, Inc.
6824 Oaklawn Avenue
Edina, Minnesota 55435

ORDER COPIES of *Surviving Motherhood* for relatives, friends, religious leaders, teachers, and students.

Please send _____ book(s) to:

Name _____

Address _____

City/State/Zip _____

(Use additional paper for additional addresses.)

Enclosed find $ _____ for _____ book(s) @ $6.95 each U.S./$7.95 Canada. Please add $1.50 mailing and handling per book. Pay by check or money order only, no cash or C.O.D.'s please. Book price and mailing cost are guaranteed for at least one year from printing date. Send order to:

St. John's Publishing, Inc., 6824 Oaklawn Avenue, Edina, Minnesota 55435

ORDER COPIES of *Kids + Modeling = Money* for relatives, friends, teachers, and students.

Please send _____ book(s) to:

Name _____

Address _____

City/State/Zip _____

(Use additional paper for additional addresses.)

Enclosed find $ _____ for _____ book(s) @ $9.95 each U.S./$10.95 Canada. Please add $1.50 mailing and handling per book. Pay by check or money order only, no cash or C.O.D.'s please. Book price and mailing cost are guaranteed for at least one year from printing date. Send order to:

St. John's Publishing, Inc., 6824 Oaklawn Avenue, Edina, Minnesota 55435

WHAT PEOPLE HAVE SAID ABOUT THE AUTHOR

". . .one of the most exciting men with a history of bringing innovative ideas to all areas. . .a family man with an independent spirit and impeccable honesty. . ."
— S. L. McDonald, Founder
Medical Wellness Technologies, Inc.
Published in *The Minneapolis Star*

"It was your motivation that initially inspired me. . . the rest is history."
— Ben Gross, Employment & Training
U.S. Department of Labor

Solving the Pueblo Crisis: *"We have carefully studied your suggestions and feel that certain elements of your approach may be useful."*
— James Leonard
U.S. Department of State,
Washington, D.C.

"No moss grows under this man's feet!"
— *Tech Talk*, Vol. 8, No. 2
Society of Technical Writers and
Publishers

". . .a man of excellent character and personality. He is conscientious, industrious, cooperative and loyal. In addition, he is congenial, friendly, and 'alive'."
— Kenneth Hance, Professor
Michigan State University

". . .he has an abundance of common sense."
— Dallas Williams, Professor
University of Nebraska